D1544014

# FINCH MERLIN AND THE LEGEND OF THE LUMINARY

Harley Merlin 17

BELLA FORREST

# ONE

## Finch

So, the secret of the magical world was about to be not so secret, Davin had won himself a crown and a ticket topside, and all hell appeared to have broken loose in San Diego. But we had a slightly more urgent matter to deal with.

A wall of water was powering toward the shore, its frothing tips rapidly turning to liquid jaws, heading straight for us.

Everyone on the stone beach scrambled to push their Chaos into the magical barriers, their palms facing determinedly outward, to stop us from meeting a violent and watery grave. That would've been the second time today that Melody, Luke, Ryann, Nash, Huntress, and I had faced that sort of thing. And drowning was right at the bottom of my list of preferred ways to shuffle off the mortal coil.

I tried to stand and join the brigade, but my last scrap of energy had been spent trying to bring Ryann back from the brink of death. Rooting my hands against the slippery rock beneath me and leaning into every strained breath, I stared listlessly at the horizon. Air shimmered above the stormy water where Atlantis had popped out like a champagne cork, an eerie anomaly concealing a grim secret. Bitter wind rushed in from the oncoming wave and bit at my damp skin. Bitter dread followed, slithering into the pit of my stomach. The former, I could just about handle. The latter… not so much.

Harley braced for impact, standing over me like the protective sister she was. "We need to give it everything we've got!"

The Muppet Babies, old and new, lined up along the shoreline. Only Melody and Ryann stayed on the ground, as exhausted as I was, while Huntress snuffled between them in the role of support dog. O'Halloran wrangled his security team into position while the radio continued to blare bad news about the SDC. Even if O'Halloran had replied, they likely wouldn't have been able to hear him over the roar of water.

Kneeling there, all I could focus on was that radio and the frightened voice on the other end: "O'Halloran? Director? Are you there?" Over and over. How could the SDC have just… plopped out into the open? There were protocols in place. It shouldn't have been possible. And then there was the Bestiary to consider—the one that, y'know, kept every coven in the world running. If the SDC had fallen, did that mean the Bestiary had been exposed, too? I couldn't stop imagining the SDC in the nonmagical world—spreading out like a big, steaming cow patty of stone and metal. As far as visuals went, it was a tough one to think about in detail.

"Ready!" O'Halloran barked. Diarmuid swung his shillelagh menacingly, as if he could keep the wave away singlehandedly.

The thundering wall inched closer. I stared at it, feeling weirdly detached from my body, like map-making ghost-Finch had come back in force. That wave represented our failures. Davin had fooled everyone, and now he'd managed to bring Atlantis to the surface so he could… Actually, I still didn't quite understand what he wanted from raising Atlantis. But I knew it couldn't be good.

"Fire!" O'Halloran gave the order, and the group jumped into action. Bristling torrents of Chaos surged outward in multicolored streams and formed a veritable tsunami of magic that raced out to meet the encroaching wave. A boom rumbled beneath my knees as the two forces collided, vibrating right up my spine.

The wall of water bent backward, the wave curving away from land

and tumbling back into the ocean that had birthed it. I lifted a hand to block the blinding light of the magic, and I noticed Krieger put his hand over Ryann's eyes to protect her retinas. An oxygen mask covered her mouth, and some color had returned to her cheeks.

*We didn't fail. We're alive. Ryann's alive.* My tired brain gave me a kick in the ass. This was just another challenge, to fix what Davin had started. Determination gripped my chest. Lifting a shaky palm, I added Air and Telekinesis to the flow of magic. The wave continued to climb and fall back on itself, creating a strange waterfall in the middle of the ocean, getting smaller and smaller until the sea lay flat again. Well, mostly. The Antarctic winds turned the water choppy, but at least we didn't have a raging stampede of it heading toward us anymore.

Everyone on shore slowly lowered their palms, a few residual sparks floating in the air. Silence carried across the dilapidated terrain, aside from the howl of wind and the clang of old metal from the rusty remains of the whaling port. And the constant, worrying call of the radio.

"Director O'Halloran? Come in!" the voice shouted desperately. "We need... back here! It's... it's very... bad! The Science Center is dust. People... dead. We need you here! It's urgent!"

"How can the SDC be visible?" I finally managed to form a sentence. My mind couldn't make heads or tails of it. Judging by the mixture of blank and strained expressions on everyone else's faces, they were in the same boat. There was no way the coven could've just revealed itself and destroyed the Fleet Science Center. No, there had to be trickery at work. And it reeked of Davin.

O'Halloran stared at the radio. "I don't know, but I have to go back immediately. I need to find out what happened." He looked toward Jacob. "Can you portal me back to San Diego?"

Jacob nodded, trying to keep a brave face. He raised his palms, and bronze magic streaked out and twisted into the air ahead of him. A moment later, he tore open a gap in space and time—a black void, ready for O'Halloran to step into. The edges of the portal fizzed and crackled, exposing Jacob's nervousness, but O'Halloran wasted no time running into the darkness. The SDC needed its director, and he had no choice but to answer their call. A few of the security magicals followed, while others stayed behind with the radio to maintain contact, if and when O'Halloran got in touch to relay intel.

The portal snapped shut behind them, leaving an unsettling silence. Nobody quite knew what to say. The two "anas"—Tatyana and Santana—stared at the ocean, trying to pinpoint the shimmering invisibility of Atlantis. As for the others, they shuffled awkwardly, waiting for someone to take the lead now that O'Halloran had vacated the shore.

"Did Davin do this?" Harley peered down at me, her face tight and intense. "Did he reveal the SDC?"

I heaved a sigh. "It wouldn't surprise me. Maybe he's trying to send us a message."

"Well, I'd say he's sent it—loud and clear," Wade interjected. "My biggest concern is the Bestiary. Does he want something from it?"

Nash joined the cluster. "I don't see why he would, since he's got one of his own now."

"Pardon?" Harley eyed Nash anxiously.

"Atlantis has its own Bestiary. That's how it managed to stay underwater all this time," I explained.

"But it was failing, remember?" Luke walked over, supporting Melody's stumbling steps. The Librarian never liked to miss a powwow.

Melody nodded wearily. "It may be that the Atlantis Bestiary lacks the necessary power for whatever he has planned, so he has taken measures to gain more power from the surface Bestiary. I wouldn't have thought it possible, but he has impressed me with how much he can get done, even behind bars." She paused. "No... not impressed. Stunned."

"What *does* he have planned?" Harley fidgeted with the thin chains of her Esprit, with its five gemstones. Very Thanos. If only she could click her fingers and make Davin disappear, she would've made my entire year. "Are we dealing with Eris part two?"

"I don't know. He said that wasn't his jam, but I don't believe a single bit of the crap that pours out of his mouth," I replied sourly. "He rambled on about wanting to be a hero, and who the hell knows what that entails."

Our conversation stopped as a splash pierced the air. A soggy, drowned rat of a man burst out of the shallows and proceeded to drag himself—robes and all—to shore. Not the sort of mermaid anyone wanted to find on the beach.

"Ovid?!" I gasped as he flopped to the ground, heaving deep breaths. His silver hair lay flat against his forehead, and his lips were a concerning shade of blue.

"*That's* Ovid?" Harley narrowed her eyes at the bedraggled figure. She looked incredibly unimpressed.

"Not very regal, is he?" Santana remarked.

I gave a wry snort. "That's because he isn't. Not anymore. Davin has the throne now."

Ryann shuddered, but not from the cold. "*King* Davin…"

"Wouldn't he be prince consort?" Melody shivered.

Nash eyed Ovid suspiciously. "This is a coup, not a marriage. At least, not yet. And I doubt Davin would settle for any title other than king. Plus, Kaya will agree with whatever he says he is, in her current condition."

"Exactly." I glanced at my sister. "Help me up." She bent and hauled me to my feet, the two of us walking toward Ovid. He was in full pathetic mode now, coughing up water and sobbing like a toddler whose candy was stolen.

"What are you doing here?" I didn't have time for small talk.

He retched, spewing water about an inch from my shoes. "They… expelled me. My own… daughter!"

"Even if she wasn't under a love spell, can you blame her?" Nash asked, coming to my side. "You tried to stab her in the back, and you would've succeeded if you hadn't landed yourself in a pit of equally traitorous vipers."

I eyed the old man warily. He might have been a weeping mass of damp misery, but he was still Atlantean. And that kind of power couldn't be allowed to wander around willy-nilly.

"What do we do with this punk?" Dylan edged closer, the rest of the old Muppet Babies a step behind him.

Melody raised a shaky hand. "We could always move into the old Antarctic Coven. It should have a secure place where we can keep Ovid, and it'll get us out of the cold. If we stay here, exposed to the elements, we won't last long."

"There's an Antarctic Coven?" Luke looked at her in surprise.

"Really?" I added my own surprise. Who in their right mind would want to be stuck out here? Beautiful, sure, but with periods of eternal night or eternal daylight, *and* the freezing weather, it seemed like the perfect place to go nuts.

Melody nodded. "There was, a long time ago, but it got shut down due to the lack of volunteers who wanted to live way out here. There were also several… incidents, which prompted the global commission to close it and separate it from the Bestiary."

"Incidents?" I prompted, my mind immediately jumping to a scenario like in *The Thing*. Kurt Russell not included.

She cleared her throat nervously, eyeing Ovid's slumped figure. "It's probably best I don't tell you about them, but I don't think we'll have the same problems if we're only staying there temporarily. I should be able to get us inside. I just need a minute to search my mind palace and figure out where the entrance is."

"I have never had the pleasure of meeting a Librarian before." Kadar popped up, tingeing Raffe's skin with red. "All that knowledge. I bet her brain is delicious."

Melody's eyes widened in alarm. Kadar had that effect on people, but his bark was worse than his bite, so to speak.

"Kadar!" Raffe snapped, seizing control of the reins. He looked apologetically at Melody. "I'm sorry about him. As far as I know, he's never actually eaten anyone; he just likes to amuse himself by scaring people."

She nodded uncertainly. "That's, uh… comforting."

"Krieger can give you something if you're still feeling weak. You've clearly been through an ordeal," Tatyana interjected. "I'm used to the cold, but I think it would be best for everyone to get away from this shore for a while. Especially now that *this* individual has arrived."

Ovid scowled up at her. "I am a king! I should be in my kingdom! If you think you can capture me and I will go quietly, you have another thing—"

Melody slapped him with one of her transformation spells, rainbow magic spilling out of her hands and winding around his face. A moment later, he had a patch of skin where his mouth should've been. That little firecracker could do some very not chipmunk-like things when she wanted, and I guessed she'd had enough of Ovid, same as the rest of us. Still, only some kind of prison would keep him from escaping into the wider world, and I wasn't about to let him out of my sight.

"Can I assist you?" Krieger offered.

"I think that would be useful," Melody conceded, swaying slightly in Luke's arms from the exertion of using her magic.

I fixed Ovid with a hard glare. "In the meantime, this snake needs to be under watch. Since we've got the brains covered, we could use some brawn. Luke, Dylan, Nash, Huntress, Raffe—well, Kadar, really—you keep an eye on him until Melody can get us into the Antarctic Coven."

"Now that's a task I'm only too happy to do." Dylan smirked and took up a position near the silenced king. The others encircled our captive, Huntress getting right up in his creepy, mouthless face.

"You left me out on purpose, didn't you?" Wade sighed, ever the drama queen.

"Hey, Santana has more fire in her little finger than you do in your whole body, and I didn't include her, either." I forced a chuckle, my lungs hurting. "I figured you'd want to be part of the brain unit, since that's where Harley will be, and we know you two are joined at the hip."

Wade cracked a wry smile. "And I'd just been starting to miss you."

"Aww, I knew you liked me." I flashed him a more genuine grin.

The radio crackled, disturbing our banter. O'Halloran had reached the danger zone, and he had news for us.

"This is Director O'Halloran. Come in."

"We hear you, over." Harley went into secret agent mode, all "over" and "roger" and "yes, sir, no, sir, three bags full, sir."

"I've begun an evacuation of the coven civilians," O'Halloran replied. "They've been sent back to their own homes, or motels, or to local Neutrals. Some will have to go to other covens temporarily, until something else can be arranged."

"Aye, 'tis an almighty state out here! Ach, ye should see the mess. Bodies crushed flat as pancakes! Insides as outsides, the whole shebang!" Diarmuid's voice cut through. A bit of muttering suggested that they were having a private conversation about the interruptions, before Harley stopped them.

"Director, how bad is it? Tell it to us straight."

Diarmuid jumped in again. "It ain't good, I'll tell ye that!"

"It's grim," O'Halloran agreed. "I've kept the preceptors, security magicals, and some of the agents here to help seal the place off, but it's swarming with police and emergency services. This isn't just a magical problem."

"Aye, and they've seen more than they ought te," Diarmuid muttered.

"Like what?" I pressed.

O'Halloran sighed. "It's difficult to say at present, but non-magicals were some of the first on scene, trying to rescue those who weren't crushed." He paused. "There's talk of getting a military presence involved. On the one hand, that helps us, since the police are cordoning everything off and hiding it from the public. On the other hand, once the army gets involved, word is going to spread up the chain of command that there are... odd things inside this random building that's just come out of nowhere."

*Yeah, if that's not odd enough for them...* I thought about all the magical artifacts and books and Grimoires tucked away in the SDC, and panic began to set in. This was bad, however you spun it, but if the army got their hands on the SDC's magical goodies, it'd all end up in a bunker in Area 51, and we'd probably follow suit.

"But that's not all," O'Halloran continued, as we gathered around the radio. Everyone who wasn't watching Ovid, that is. "The Bestiary is on lockdown."

My optimism perked up. "That's good news, right?"

"Not exactly." O'Halloran took a moment, then explained. "*We* didn't put it on lockdown. Tobe did. And we can't access the Bestiary to activate the moving protocols, because the Beast Master has gone into defense mode."

"But if you can't access the Bestiary, presumably the army won't be able to either," I said, trying to understand. "I still don't see the problem."

Diarmuid made it simple. "He's gone crackers, lad! Traps and tricks and spells that'll singe yer eyebrows off, if not worse! No one can get in te get the Bestiary someplace safer, 'cause they're terrified they're goin' te turn into beast food!"

"Has someone put a spell on Tobe?" Harley asked, her gaze turning to the horizon. The invisible bubble surrounding Atlantis shimmered faintly, and I knew what she was thinking. *Did Davin do this, too?*

"Tobe did it to himself," O'Halloran explained. "He crafted a defensive spell in his own mind, after the mess with Katherine, in case anyone ever threatened the Bestiary again. I doubt he ever thought he'd have to use it. His mind has flipped, and so has he. The Bestiary does still seem to be fueling the other covens , but that's not going to work in the long-term."

Nash nodded sagely from his position by Ovid. "And if the army finds a super powerful Purge beast running wild and crazed, they're going to bring the biggest guns they have."

"Precisely," O'Halloran replied quietly, his tone troubled.

"This doesn't make any sense. Why would Davin hit the SDC? Revenge on us is one thing, but he's risking a hell of a lot by exposing the magical world." I looked to Ovid. "Did Davin say anything after Kaya booted us out? Did he mention any of his plans?"

Ovid sat back on his haunches, his brow creased in confusion. He raised a hand to speak, and Melody removed the transformation spell that had covered his mouth. "He spoke of his desire to be the hero of his story, and the hero of the world. The hero that was promised in the legend of the Luminary."

Ovid's frankness concerned me. We had to get him locked up, pronto. I'd seen enough backstabbing from Ovid and Davin to not completely discount the idea that they were still working together. Unlikely, given recent events, but "impossible" wasn't a word in Davin's vocabulary.

"Finch!" Krieger's panicked cry shattered the tense atmosphere.

My head whipped around to find Melody convulsing on the ground. A second ago, she'd been fine. Now... not so much. Luke broke ranks from guard duty and sprinted for his girlfriend, scooping her into his arms and restraining her so she didn't hurt herself. Her eyes rolled back into her head as Luke stared down at her in abject horror. Melody was in serious trouble.

## TWO

## Finch

"Melody? Melody, can you hear me?" Luke pleaded, shaking her gently.

Dylan, Nash, Huntress, and Kadar remained with Ovid, but the rest of us gathered around the Librarian.

"What's wrong with her?" Saskia frowned, tugging the furry collar of her coat tighter around her face.

"I don't know. I don't know!" Luke shook his head helplessly. Even Krieger seemed to be at a loss, rifling nervously through his box of magic medical tricks for something that might help her.

"One moment, she was fine," the doc said, echoing my previous thoughts, his lips settling into a grim line. "The next… she wasn't."

I glanced over my shoulder toward the spot where I knew Atlantis was lurking. Try as I might, I couldn't get a full grasp on the problems we were facing, or which parts Davin was responsible for. He couldn't have done this to Melody, in addition to everything else… could he? This certainly didn't fit with the whole, "I want to be a hero, adored by all" thing. You had to be one cruel devil to hurt Melody Winchester, but Davin had always been a wolf in sheep's clothing. We just had to figure out which pieces were connected, and *how* they slotted together in Davin's grand plan. But this had me stumped.

Melody suddenly stopped convulsing, going limp in Luke's arms. "Melody?" he said urgently. "Can you hear me? Are you okay?"

Her eyes slowly blinked open. "I… just got an information dump. A big one." She swallowed loudly, as though her throat were dry. "I now have access to the knowledge of Atlantis."

Those of us who'd actually been down there gasped in shock. Luke helped her to sit up in his lap. "How is that possible? I thought it was hidden from you."

She leaned into him. "It all just… opened up to me." I watched the cogs whirring in her incredible mind. "It must have happened because the city ascended. The knowledge stayed hidden for as long as Atlantis did. Now that it has opened itself up to the surface world and the Chaos here once more, it has opened itself up to me, too. I can feel it all: history, stories, spells, the works."

"Did you find anything we can use right now?" I prompted. We were sitting ducks out here, with this Antarctic Coven no closer to being found and Davin continuing to wreak havoc from the safety of his new kingdom.

"I don't know if it's usable, per se, but I did find something valuable." Melody fidgeted uncomfortably.

"Tell us," Harley said, her tone gentle. Empath to Empath bonding.

Melody gazed down at her hands, like they didn't belong to her. "I saw what happened. I don't know why, but Chaos wanted me to see, and it showed me everything through its own eyes."

Tatyana crouched to Melody's level. "What did you see?"

"I understand why the SDC was revealed. I know what Davin is up to." She managed to hold Tatyana's gaze for a few seconds before looking out over the stormy ocean. "While Atlantis was rising, Davin performed a powerful, dangerous, and utterly forbidden spell, with Kaya acting as his Witness. Capital 'W.'"

I tilted my head curiously. "What's the difference?"

"A magical Witness is different from an ordinary one. It's more like an accomplice—they take the role of energy source to fuel this kind of spell. That is why it's prohibited, as it would certainly end in death were a non-Atlantean to participate in that kind of thing. As powerful as she is, it has only weakened her temporarily—I saw it for myself." Melody mustered a shaky sigh. "In addition to the energy source, it requires rare ingredients, which Davin stashed away before he was imprisoned: the ivory of a golden narwhal, powdered diamond, the blood of Leviathan, the heart of a selkie matriarch, and the powdered beak of a kraken, among other things."

I noticed Harley stiffen at the mention of Leviathan. That slimy sucker had caused her nothing but trouble, and she still had a deal to uphold with him. Although I doubted children were in the cards for her anytime soon, the knowledge that she'd have to let him name her firstborn weighed heavy on her. Names had power. And I doubted Leviathan had good intentions for Harley's firstborn.

*But how did they get their hands on his blood?* I doubted I'd get an answer. Maybe Ganymede had ferreted some away, centuries ago, when Purge beasts roamed free and before she submerged Atlantis. A standby ingredient for any powerful spells she might have in mind. And definitely before Leviathan ended up in his icebox.

"But what did it do?" Jacob leaned forward eagerly.

Melody lifted her gaze to me. "It remotely hijacked the Bestiary and took over its energy resources—the Purge beasts. Davin can draw as much power from it as he likes, directly to himself."

"That doesn't make any sense." I balled my hands into fists. "Why would he go through all that, just to kick the SDC out of its interdimensional pocket and keep the other covens afloat? What's his game?"

Melody sank further into Luke's arms, and he tightened his embrace. "With that spell came an unexpected issue. The SDC, being the coven in possession of the Bestiary, was disconnected from the network because Davin is, for all intents and purposes, now the possessor of the Bestiary. There can be only one at a time, and because it wasn't moved with the correct protocols and spells, the SDC suffered a violent eviction from its former role."

Santana gave a wry snort. "Wait, are you suggesting that Davin 'Slimeball' Doncaster didn't intend to expose the SDC? Even though he hates our guts, especially Finch's?"

Melody shrugged. "Yes. Not that it matters. The crux of all this is, Davin has access to the Bestiary's power. He can expel other covens if he wants to, now that he knows what will happen if he disconnects one of them. That's a formidable threat to hold over our heads, if we don't give him the worship he's after."

"But how does outing the magical world help him fulfill this hero complex that's biting us all in the ass?" I wondered aloud. The pieces still weren't fitting right.

"Chaos isn't sure about that, so neither am I," she answered quietly. "All we can be sure of is that he has a plan, and he's acting on it. But all's not lost."

Saskia folded her arms across her chest. "Really? Because it sounds like it is."

"What else did you find out?" I interjected, in case Saskia's frostiness caused our beloved chipmunk to clam up.

"I know how to fix this." Melody pressed a palm to Luke's chest, and he covered it with his hand. "I know how to take back the Bestiary's power and restore it to a coven. I doubt it can be the SDC, as the damage will take a long time to repair, *if* it can be, but I can make sure the Bestiary finds a safe haven once more."

I nearly dragged her out of Luke's arms and spun her around. "You absolute genius! How do we do it?"

"The same spell has to be performed in reverse, including the incantation." Melody lowered her head. "And we also need Kaya as a Witness. Every part of the spell has to be the same."

*Why is there always small print?* The universe knew exactly how to kill my buzz, though at least we were a step ahead of where we'd been two minutes ago. Davin's plans might've been a mystery to me, but if we had a way to fix this mayhem, then we still had a fire under us to keep going. And I wouldn't stop until I had Davin in twenty boxes, each one shipped to a different distant part of the globe. His precious amulet wouldn't do him any good then.

"So we're screwed?" Saskia entered as the voice of perpetual teenage pessimism.

Tatyana nudged her lightly in the ribs. "We just have some thinking to do. If Davin performed the spell, then so can we."

"But how do we get into Atlantis if we can't even see it?" Santana added her dubious input. "Even if we could, if these folks are as intense as you say, then I'm guessing they've got an arsenal of hexes on that place to stop anyone from getting in. As long as this Kaya chick is in there, then Saskia's right—we're screwed. Royally."

Wade huffed a sigh. "They have a point. You can bet every cent you have that Davin isn't going to let Kaya out of his sight, on the off chance that we figure out how to undo what he's done."

"Melody?" Ryann spoke up from her makeshift hospital bed on the hard ground. "Did Chaos show you a way into Atlantis?"

The Librarian's shoulders sagged. "No."

"Come on, guys! You all look like you've been slapped with a wet fish, when we should be riding this wave of hope." I scrutinized the group with determined eyes. "This is a wallow-free zone, so snap out of it. Thinking caps on, self-pity hats off."

Harley gave a faint laugh. "I couldn't have said it better myself." She looked off into the distance, clearly donning said thinking cap. "Do you think Erebus might be able to get us in?"

"I don't think we can rely on him anymore. Not that we ever could... for the most part." The new Muppet Babies and I would be floating in the depths of the ocean, about to become food for the fishy creatures that lived down there, if it hadn't been for the Prince of Darkness. But he'd given up his mortal body, and I had no idea where he'd gone. Tartarus didn't belong to him anymore, so he couldn't have gone there. Maybe his daddy-o had reabsorbed him into the Chaos stream, like he'd threatened. But the stark fact remained: wherever he was, he couldn't help us.

Just then, a portal ripped open, drawing everyone's attention. Everyone readied their Chaos in case it was an attack. But a second later, our palms lowered, as Remington stepped out in a fluster.

"I came as quickly as I could," he said, breathless. "The California Mage Council is on its way, and they want answers about what's just happened in San Diego. They're fuming, and they don't plan on negotiating with Davin, so brace yourselves for trouble."

*More trouble?*

Nash eyed the newcomer. "They won't get a chance to negotiate with him. They won't be able to get near him, and I doubt he'll come out to speak to some councilors. The president, maybe, but he won't speak to any monkeys—only the organ grinder." Remington had run for president of the free magical world, but he'd been beat out by the people's favorite: a no-nonsense firecracker of epic proportions, if her reputation was to be believed, by the name of Evelyn Gutierrez. Deep down, I suspected Remington had been relieved not to have that responsibility on his shoulders, though I could've been wrong. He'd been a good loser about it, either way.

"We'll have to talk them down." I let my thoughts spill out like a shipwrecked oil tanker.

Harley nodded. "If they think they're dealing with the old Davin, they're in for a nasty shock. An all-out war with Davin means an all-out war with Atlantis, now that he's their king." She visibly shuddered, no doubt picturing him peacocking around with a crown on his head, finally in the kind of position he'd always dreamed of.

"Yup, and these are Primus Anglicus descendants we're talking about." I gestured toward the ocean. "None of your run-of-the-mill Mediocres. Their weakest link has more power in his right butt cheek than everyone here who isn't me or Harley, with Melody as a possible exception."

Melody herself rallied a little. "Then we need to get into Atlantis before these councilors arrive, figure out what Davin is up to, and talk to him before he can unleash more havoc than he already has. If we under-stand the problem, then we'll have a greater chance of reaching a viable solution. That said, we'll have to approach with caution now that he has a Bestiary's worth of power at his fingertips."

"Two, if you count Atlantis's Bestiary," Ryann corrected.

"I thought we didn't have a way into Atlantis?" Santana countered.

I peered at Ovid. "Maybe Chaos sent us a little assistance."

I'd barely been looking at him for a second when another twist of fate hit. Out of the water behind Ovid, a second figure emerged, stumbling through the turbulent ocean with a petrified expression. My jaw hit the deck. When we'd parted ways, he'd been on a one-way ticket to a prison cell.

"*Hector?*" I managed.

Of all the people in the world, I'd never expected to see him again. Perhaps Chaos really had sent us some help. And I'd been looking at the wrong Atlantean.

# THREE

## Harley

"**I**s this someone we should be concerned about?" I whispered to Finch as another soaked, staggering Atlantean waded out of the icy water. They were easy to pick out in a lineup, with their silver hair and blindingly pale skin, as though they'd never seen sunlight. Which I guessed they hadn't, being stuck in an underwater bubble for centuries.

Nash shook his head and went to the newcomer, helping him out of the water. "This is Hector. He's a friend."

Finch gave a gasp of understanding. "So *this* is the badass who got you out of a few pickles down below. In Atlantis, I mean." He flashed a cheeky grin at me that prompted an eye-roll.

Honestly, though, it never failed to amaze me how he could keep his sense of humor, even when the world around him threatened to crush his spirit into dust. It'd kept me going a few times, during our darkest shared days, and the same went for the rest of our friends. When he'd vanished off the face of the earth, after we parted ways on our separate missions—him dealing with Erebus and Ryann and his new unit, and us old-timers trying to find the djinn who'd crafted Davin's amulet—none of us had given up hope of locating him. Even his occasional frenemy Santana had pulled all-nighters and ransacked the SDC's libraries to try and figure out where he'd gone. And the amulet mission had proven to be a bust, anyway. Wherever that djinn was, Davin had hidden him well—almost as well as the amulet itself. So, we'd poured all our energy into bringing back the prodigal brother. And, though I couldn't even begin to grasp the full extent of what he'd gone through while he'd been missing, I was beyond relieved that he was back with us where he belonged.

*It's a shame I can't say the same for everything else...*

The SDC was in the worst trouble in history, with Tobe having gone haywire and Davin sitting at the helm of it all, playing a dangerous game with the magical world. All for the sake of... what? Regaining lost glory? Becoming some kind of hero?

The new Atlantean broke my train of thought.

"I did what I could to help Nash and his acquaintances, nothing more," Hector said humbly, his strength slowly returning. "Although, I must say, it is pleasing to finally meet the person that inspired such loyalty in Nash and his friends."

Finch waved a hand. "Whatever you've heard, it's all true. Unless it was bad. Then it's definitely not." He gestured to me. "Hector, you saved my pals, so you're very welcome here. This is my sister, Harley. And the members of this motley crew are Raffe, Dylan, Tatyana, Santana, Garrett, Astrid, Saskia, Jacob, and Krieger. I think that's everyone." Finch made the introductions, but this Hector guy wasn't paying attention anymore. His focus lay firmly on the former king, who appeared to be cycling through every emotion available to the mortal mind.

"What is *he* doing here?" Hector gave the king a wide berth, at once nervous and intrigued. After what Finch had told us about Ovid, it didn't surprise me that his people lacked trust in him.

Finch shrugged. "Kaya kicked him out. I guess she figured the shiny new Atlantis, under her united rule with Davin, would be better off without bad memories hanging around like a rancid smell."

"Ah... so you know about Davin. I heard you'd been expelled, but I wasn't sure which developments you learned of before that. To be honest, I wasn't even sure you'd made it out alive. I just headed for shore and spotted people, then I saw Nash. Truly a sight for sore eyes." Hector drew Finch off to the side, and I followed. "I'm glad you made it out."

I frowned. "How did *you* get out?"

Hector bowed his head to me, finally acknowledging everyone else. "I realize my appearance must've come as something of a shock. It is a pleasure to meet you all."

"I'll say it was a shock. I thought you'd be starting a lifetime stint in jail," Nash replied, clearly pleased to see the man.

Hector made a nervous sound. "So did I, but you know I have a few tricks up my sleeve. An opportunity presented itself, and I took it, if only to try and get help from the surface magicals to fix this mess. Seeing you here was somewhat serendipitous. However, my daughter is still in that bubble, and I don't intend to abandon her. I did this for *her*, in the hopes of giving information that might aid your people in stopping Davin."

"What tricks?" Finch raised his eyebrows in interest, and even I leaned a little closer, curious about this strange man.

Nash lifted a wise finger. "A better question would be, what information?"

"They are one and the same, as it happens," Hector continued. "When Kaya raised Atlantis, there was not enough energy in the Bestiary generator, and there definitely wasn't enough for the protective shield that Davin placed over the city. As such, the concealment bubble suffered a great deal of damage. As we speak, Thebian, Apollo, and countless others are working hard to repair it."

"What kind of damage are we talking about?" I asked.

Hector glanced back at the shimmering horizon. "There are cracks in the fabric of the protective shield. I escaped through one such crack, and it may also be a way for your people to get in, provided we work quickly. Davin has every spare hand working on the repairs."

"Why in the name of everything sane would the Atlanteans follow Davin's orders?" I asked. "Forgive me if I've gotten my wires crossed, since I've heard everything secondhand, but have they all forgotten that he tried to kill Kaya? Is he threatening them, or something?" That was one thing I couldn't wrap my head around, though I supposed I didn't have the same detailed knowledge that Finch and his evacuees had, when it came to love spells and the Atlantean hierarchy.

Hector swept a hand through his wet hair, slicking it back. "On the contrary. Kaya has come up with a story about the assassination being a misunderstanding and has exonerated him of all wrongdoing. Meanwhile, Davin is doing everything in his power to prove that he's a benevolent presence. Killing with kindness, if you will."

"He's killing people?" Luke gasped.

"No. I phrased that poorly." Hector pointed at the turbulent ocean. "He has made a decree to the Atlantean people that he will bring back their dead in exchange for their loyalty. He has already resurrected a few loved ones as proof of his goodwill, and… I hate to say it, but it is having an effect. Who can argue with that sort of display? And who can turn away from having a dearly missed soul brought back to life?"

"You have," Nash murmured. Hector had evidently lost someone, and he hadn't taken the same bait as the other Atlanteans. A noble gesture that must've stung like nobody's business. After all, we were guilty of having loved ones resurrected, even though it was frowned upon—Astrid, Garrett, Isadora, my mom and dad, though those last three hadn't been permanent. Truthfully, even now, I'd have given anything to have all three of them alive again. It was a desire that never went away, regardless of how much time had passed.

"But I have been tempted." Hector turned away, his voice thick with emotion. "That is the problem with what Davin is offering—the overwhelming temptation of it. Not everyone is strong enough to fight against that, and I do not blame them."

I sighed in frustration. "So, Davin is winning them over with Necromancy?" I turned to look at Melody. "But how is he even managing that kind of feat? I've seen the exertion it takes to bring back a long-dead soul from the afterlife. It almost killed a Necromancer friend of ours—Alton. And that was for just two souls!"

"It's likely related to the Bestiary at the SDC," Melody answered.

"Right now, he has practically unlimited power at his fingertips. Bringing souls back from the afterlife would be far, far easier than before."

"Ah!" Hector said. "Davin is determined to have the adoration he so desperately desires, and I fully believe that he will drain every energy source dry in order to make it happen."

"And Kaya's okay with this?" I found that hard to believe. Finch hadn't painted her as a monster, merely a misguided queen who'd been in way over her head. Ironic, considering the Atlanteans had been submerged for so long.

Hector frowned, as though he didn't quite understand the question. "Kaya has no say in this whatsoever, due to the love spell that Davin has clearly manipulated her with."

"Yep, he did pour that stuff down her throat," Finch confirmed. "But it was different than the potion that this weeping sack of misery gave me." He jabbed a finger at Ovid. "It worked way quicker. Literally within seconds she was goo-goo eyed over him, calling him 'my love' and other sappy crap."

"I feared as much." Hector sighed heavily. "Regardless, my point stands. She has no say while she is under the love spell's influence."

"Well, she sure as hell wouldn't have wanted dead folks popping up all over the place. She believed in moving on to the afterlife as part of the natural order." Finch shook his head, irritated. He cast an angry look at the disgraced Atlantean king. "I hope you realize, Ovid, that this is all your fault. If you'd just snuffed it like you were supposed to, none of this would've happened. You'd be floating in a haze of peace and harmony instead of retching up seawater after being exiled from your own kingdom."

Ovid slumped forward on the rocks, splayed out in a pretty embarrassing way, scraping up algae and dirt with his fingernails and sobbing into the stone. By the looks of him, he was a minute away from throwing a toddler-style tantrum. Whatever he'd once been, he'd been reduced to a pitiful, bumbling mess. "There's another reason we need to act fast." I focused on something more proactive than mudslinging and kicking a weaselly king while he was down. "The California Mage Council is on its way, and we need to be out of here with a plan of action before it shows up. Melody, if you can get everyone into the Antarctic Coven, will the Mage Council be able to find us there?"

Melody hesitated. "I don't think so. It's been cut off for so long, they may not even know it exists. Either way, the residual interdimensional bubble should keep us hidden."

"Then that's your job—to get everyone somewhere safe, and to get Ovid here in some kind of cell."

She nodded. "Hopefully it won't take too long. It's just a case of finding the entrance, and then the security magicals that your director left can guard him."

"Excellent." I gave her an approving smile. "The Rag Team will head back to the SDC through a portal and provide assistance to O'Halloran. If Tobe has really gone nuts, then O'Halloran's going to need all the help he can get to secure the Bestiary. Once we've dealt with Tobe, we should be able to set the protocols in motion to transfer the Bestiary to a better location. I'll leave that up to O'Halloran, but I think dividing and conquering is our best bet."

Finch added his voice to the Merlin siblings' war room. "Then the new Muppet Babies and I will get to work on Atlantis, and gaining an audience with His Royal Slyness, King Davin."

"Muppet Babies?" Nash cast Finch a faintly amused look.

"It's easier than rattling your names off one by one." Finch stared down at his shoes and shifted awkwardly. I got the feeling his group had had no idea that he called them that. "Anyway, Hector can lead us back into Atlantis through one of those cracks. Melody, you can stay in the Antarctic Coven with Ryann. I won't have him getting his paws on the Librarian or nabbing my girlfriend." Finch looked softly at Ryann. "He'd probably pour a love spell down your throat to get back at me."

Ryann opened her mouth to protest, but Finch cut her off.

"You almost died today, and you're still recovering. Krieger can stay with you, too, until you're feeling better." He stared at her with imploring eyes. "Please, Ryann. I know you want to help, but I need to know you're safe, and Atlantis is the polar opposite of that right now."

"But Nash isn't magical anymore, and he nearly drowned, too. Why is he going?" Ryann refused to take this lying down.

"He's got a military mind that we're going to need to sneak through the city. And Davin might still think he can use Nash's blood, which could keep us alive—a bargaining chip of sorts, if we get caught," Finch explained.

I offered my adoptive sister a sympathetic look. "I know it sucks, but he's right."

"Huntress, you should probably stay behind, too." Nash knelt and ruffled her fur. "It won't be easy to hide you in Atlantis, and if anyone spots you, the jig will be up."

Huntress whined in the back of her throat. I didn't know those two very well, but the warmth between them was impossible to overlook. It rippled out and touched the hearts of anyone who looked at them. I'd always been curious about magicals and Familiars, ever since I'd met Micah and his beloved cat Fluffers, and these two were all the more intriguing now that Nash wasn't technically a magical anymore. I dwelled upon Micah for a moment. He was out there somewhere, not even realizing the danger that potentially loomed over us all. And if that wasn't a reason to clean up this mess, I didn't know what was. We weren't just doing this for the world; we were doing this for all worlds and lives to come. The future that Davin would monopolize if we didn't stop him.

"So, Luke, Nash, and I will head back to Atlantis with Hector and find a way to speak to Davin. We need to hear what game he's playing, straight from the Kelpie's mouth," Finch went on, gazing apologetically at a miffed Ryann. I understood where both of them were coming from, but I was secretly glad that Finch had benched her. I didn't want her getting hurt any more than she already had. She might have been a huge part of my magical world, but she was still a human, and her affection for Finch made her vulnerable. Lux had already made use of it. Davin wouldn't hesitate to do the same.

Hector nodded in agreement. "I will see you safely back to Atlantis. I only hope that I will be able to get you out again."

"This is about buying as much time as possible, until we can forge a concrete plan to pry Davin off the throne permanently." Finch tore his eyes away from Ryann. "And if we can get to Apollo and Thebian, we might have a chance of keeping one of those cracks open long enough to make the return journey. If we promise to break the spell on Kaya, they'll swallow their pride and help us."

Ryann cleared her throat. "You might not have time to do that in Atlantis itself. You weren't conscious for much of it, but the reversal for breaking the love spell isn't a walk in the park. It takes immense power and rare ingredients. I mean, it took two Children of Chaos to break yours, Finch."

*What have you been through, Finch?* To look at him, you'd never know that he'd endured something like that. My heart broke, knowing that I hadn't been there when he'd needed me most. Sure, he could handle himself, and he was standing here on this shore to prove the point. But I couldn't help wanting to protect him the way he'd protected me in Elysium. I supposed I'd always feel that I owed him a debt I'd never be able to repay.

Melody jittered with anxious excitement, drawing everyone's attention. "I can give you the instructions for a potent spell to knock Kaya out. After that, all you have to do is bring her back here and put her in a holding cell in the Antarctic Coven so that we can figure out a less cosmic way of breaking the love spell. It'll be in this vault of Atlantean knowledge somewhere." She tapped her temple. "But it will take me a while to find it, and you need to get going before those cracks close."

"A knockout spell?" Finch rubbed his chin. "Yes… that could work. You give me the details, and I'll make it happen."

"I'll write it down for you now!" She crouched down and patted her pockets, only to produce a few lumps of white mulch that might once have been paper. "Um… does anyone have a pen and paper?"

Krieger hurried over with a small notepad and pen. "A doctor should never be without a pen."

"Perfect!" Melody set to work scribbling the details, while I turned back to my brother.

"If we're going our separate ways again, you should take these." I produced a little box of earpieces from my puffer jacket pocket, which Astrid had given to me, and pressed it into Finch's hands. "Let's hope they work in Atlantis, now that it's not under an entire ocean."

He peered up at me with sad, slightly hopeful eyes. "I'm guessing they work both ways?"

"You send word if you need help, and we'll do the same." I didn't mean to be all business with him, but if I started getting emotional now then I'd probably end up on the ground beside Ovid. I didn't want to separate again. But what choice did I have? Truthfully, when I'd said that the Rag Team was going to go back to the SDC to help O'Halloran, I'd been including Finch in that. But he had his own team, and we really did need to divide and conquer to make any headway with this mayhem.

"And if you could keep yourself alive, that'd be greatly appreciated," Wade cut in, no doubt sensing my reluctance to part from my brother. "I know you like to be dramatic, and you're a connoisseur of inappropriate timing, but if you ruin our wedding by dying, Harley will never forgive you."

"You think I'm going to waste the special dress I bought by keeling over?" Finch shot back. "Forget it. I've got plans to upstage the bride, and I don't intend to miss the looks on all your faces. You might even decide you picked the wrong Merlin once you see my lacy number."

Wade looked horrified, and a ripple of laughter drifted around the shoreline. "Thanks for the nightmares."

"A pleasure, as always." Finch grinned, but it didn't reach his eyes. He was being brave again, putting on that humorous mask of his so he wouldn't reveal his true feelings. I couldn't sense them, either, with him being a Shapeshifter. But I didn't have to. He was scared, and he was worried, and he had the weight of the world on his shoulders. We all did.

With Jacob's help, Ryann made the slow walk to where Finch stood. I stepped back to give them a bit of space, still trying to get used to the sight of them together. I loved that they'd finally figured things out, but after all the "will they, won't they" business, I kept expecting them to have another awkward hug and just leave it at that, like in the old days. But they'd moved on from that.

Ryann looped her arms around Finch's neck and let him take her weight. In front of everyone, she kissed him. The kind of kiss that made poets put pen to paper, and made this sister feel like she shouldn't be watching. I was happy for them—so very happy—but that didn't mean I'd gotten used to seeing my brother kiss my adoptive sister. This was a therapy session waiting to happen.

"You be careful," Ryann murmured, pulling away. "We've only just made it back to each other, and I'm not about to lose you again. Don't do anything stupid when you're back in that city. Get in, get what you need, and get out. Come back to me in one piece."

He dipped his head and kissed her again. "Wild Kelpies couldn't keep me away."

"Watch out for those anyway." She smiled up at him. "And I'll stay here with Melody and Huntress and Remington until you come back. I may not be a magical, but I'm going to do the one thing I can do: I'm not going to let Ovid out of my sight."

"I love you." Finch held her a moment longer.

"Not as much as I love you," she replied, chuckling.

"Hmm... once again, we're going to have to agree to disagree."

My heart swelled. Not only had they figured things out, but they were in love. I could feel it radiating out of Ryann like a beacon. Despite the kissing, I wouldn't have missed this for the world. Not that they noticed. They'd fallen into an interdimensional bubble of their own, crafted entirely out of their love for one another.

Looking back at the churning ocean, I sent up a silent prayer. *Chaos, if you're listening, keep him safe. Please... let him have his happy ending.* If anyone had earned it, it was him.

# FOUR

## Harley

---

After the too-brief farewell to my brother, we made to exit the frosty extremes of South Georgia Island for slightly warmer, though no less perilous, climate. Jacob had been eager to send us all through a portal to San Diego, but I'd vetoed it in favor of a chalk door. We needed subtlety for the task ahead of us, especially with non-magical uniforms prowling around. Police were easy to put on the wrong scent— a fact I'd discovered during my misspent youth—but soldiers were another matter entirely.

*Plus, we don't exactly blend in.* I observed the group waiting anxiously behind me, then crouched low to the ground and sketched out a doorway. There were nine of us in total: me, Wade, Dylan, Tatyana, Raffe, Santana, Garrett, Astrid, and Jacob. That sort of number wasn't going to go unnoticed unless we were very, very careful.

"I still don't see why you wouldn't let me portal us there." Jacob pouted. I knew he liked to feel useful, and he'd really come into his powers this past year. No more mishaps like in the old days, when he'd almost done the same thing Davin had—spilled the SDC out into the real world.

I turned to look at him. "A chalk door doesn't have the drama of a portal, with all the fizzling and crackling, and you best believe the army will catch on that there's something supernatural happening if a great big tear in time and space suddenly rips through the atmosphere."

Jacob shrugged. "Like they don't already know."

"At least they're letting you go," Saskia said, adding another disgruntled teen attitude to the party.

"Don't start," Tatyana warned. "It's going to be dangerous in San Diego, and we need people here to watch Ovid. That's an important role in and of itself."

"Then why don't you stay, and I'll go?" Saskia offered up a sarcastic smile. "Ah, that's right, because you're trying to keep me in bubble wrap again."

Tatyana groaned. "Saskia…"

"Taty…" she countered. Fortunately, at that moment, Finch came in with one of his better-timed comments.

"Ha! You're like the Fellowship of the Ring!" Finch chuckled, pointing at Wade and me. "I guess that makes you Frodo and Sam—the greatest love story ever told."

I almost detached my retinas from rolling them. "Then what does that make you? An orc? Treebeard?"

"It warms my heart to hear you use those words. I knew you were only pretending to be asleep." He gave me a smile that made *my* heart go all warm and fuzzy. I had my brother back, in all his glory.

"You're distracting me." I turned to the sketch on the ground and whispered the *Aperi Si Ostium* spell. The edges fizzed, forming the doorway that'd take us to the literal fallout of Davin's meddling. He was definitely the Saruman of this picture.

Shaking off the encroaching geekery, I gripped the handle of the doorway, ready to swing it open. But not without one last goodbye… just in case. "You better come back, do you hear me? I'm not losing anyone to Davin or Atlantis. Stay safe, stay smart, and get out of there as quickly as you can."

"I love you too, sis." Finch smiled wryly, a glint of sadness in his eyes.

With that, I pushed open the doorway to reveal nothing but the concrete of a darkened alleyway—one a short distance from the Fleet Science Center, so we'd be able to approach the scene of destruction instead of just dropping out of the sky and into the army's lap. I went first, landing with a light thud on the hard ground. The others followed one by one, like tumblers executing their dismounts.

Once the last person was through, the chalk door swung back on itself and vanished into thin air. I caught one last glimpse of Finch's worried face before it closed. I hoped he hadn't seen that same anxiety reflected on my face.

"Let's keep it cool," I instructed. "Pretend we're just curious guards until we can gauge the extent of the damage and how we're going to get inside whatever's left."

"Without a coven, aren't we *really* just civilians?" Astrid said quietly. Her words jarred in my heart. Through the radio yelps for aid, O'Halloran's measured panic, and the treacherous tales of Davin, I hadn't considered one very real possibility—if the SDC was out in the open, separated from the Bestiary's power and suffering untold damage, did that mean it could never be put back together again? A magical rebuild of that magnitude would take months... if not years. What if we couldn't get our coven back? What would that mean for the people who'd called it a home, a school, a sanctuary?

"Let's assess the situation before we jump to conclusions." Wade put his hand on the small of my back for reassurance. "It might not be as bad as it sounds. Maybe the worst of the damage was to the Fleet Science Center."

"And that makes it okay? People still died—the guy on the radio said so," Jacob interjected with a surprisingly mature sentiment.

Wade sighed. "I'm just trying to make sure we don't start with rock-bottom thinking, because we'll have nowhere to go from there."

"Let's move." I headed down the alley before this ethics debate could escalate fruitlessly. Wade had only been trying to ease my nerves about what we were going to see. But I sensed his emotions, and they were anything but optimistic.

As we exited the alleyway, it took every scrap of willpower I had not to skid to a halt there and then. The air left my lungs, and I had to force my feet to keep walking down the rubble-strewn sidewalk. The devastation was center stage on the spot where the Fleet Science Center used to stand.

"*Dios mio!*" Santana hissed behind me.

"Holy crap!" Dylan echoed her sentiments.

O'Halloran's aide had spoken of the urgency of the situation, but I'd assumed that had to do with the nature of what had happened. Now, I realized there'd been another reason for swift action. The non-magicals had responded to the blowout with alarming speed. They swarmed the site of this cataclysmic event, dressed in black uniforms and heavy Kevlar, wielding hefty guns that were undoubtedly locked and loaded to keep out unwanted civilians—a sure sign that these folks really meant business. And they'd made quick work of cordoning off the entire perimeter of the Fleet Science Center, which the coven had squashed flat. Along the cordon, armored vehicles with bulletproof glass and ambulances with silently flashing lights squatted in wait.

Gigantic black tarps were strung to hastily constructed metal fences—the kind you saw at concerts and festivals—with heavy weights holding the barriers in place. It likely had the two-pronged purpose of holding back nosy civilians and keeping the secret of what lay behind the curtains.

"Are they putting bodies in that ambulance?" Jacob froze, his eyes wide and alarmed. I looked to one of the ambulances, where a stretcher with a zipped-up body bag was being placed into the back.

"And they're looking for more." Wade stared at a K-9 unit of soldiers and tough-looking German Shepherds who were wandering around the edges of this horror show. The dogs had their noses to the ground inside the fenced-off perimeter, sniffing around the edges of the black tarps for lost souls. A bark rang out, and the dog disappeared under the tarp. The handler lifted the edge to follow, fading into the shadows beneath. I could only imagine what they might find, and it sickened me to my core. Was this the cost of Davin's bid for adoration? Honestly, seeing the devastation he'd caused, up close and personal, I understood his motivations even less. People had already died. How many more did he intend to use as collateral?

Mercifully, I could barely hear myself think with the roar of chopper blades overhead. Military aircraft battled with news helicopters that were eager for the exclusive scoop.

A loudspeaker bellowed through the air. "You are in a no-fly zone. Turn around, or we'll be forced to fire."

*Do you see what you've done, Davin?* I didn't doubt that the soldiers in that army chopper meant it. Just how far would they go to protect this secret? How much force would they use to defend it, without even knowing what they were defending?

"This is going to turn nasty. How tantalizing." Kadar appeared for a second, his eyes flashing red. "I can smell the tragedy in the air—can't you? Human beings have never learned to keep away from danger. You fools forever run toward it."

"Shut it!" Raffe came back up, pushing the djinn down before he could draw any attention to us.

"What's going on here? We've got a right to know!" A civilian pushed against the barricade, only to be shoved back by soldiers in riot gear.

One of the soldiers put up a hand as though it were its own kind of barrier. "This is a contaminated hazard zone. Do not attempt to come any closer, for your own sake. A gas pipe has ruptured, and we have to secure the area before more buildings are affected by the leak. Stand back."

Fired up, a few more crowd members pushed against the fences. "A gas pipe? Are you for real?" one shouted. "A building came out of nowhere and crushed the Science Center flat. You can't pull the wool over our eyes!"

"Stand back!" The soldier raised a riot shield, and his colleagues joined him, creating a human wall between the civilians and the rubble. Kadar was right—this was going to turn nasty. And I had no clue how to get these people out of here. I didn't even know if it was my place to intervene. We were here for one reason, and one reason only: to help O'Halloran secure the Bestiary and get it to safer ground. Then at least the army wouldn't be able to seize the magical world's most valuable power source and ship it off to Area 51 for intense study.

*Finch has a lot to answer for.* He'd made me watch one too many reruns of *The X-Files*, and now I was letting my mind wander into the world of conspiracy theories. Still, theory or reality, I couldn't risk the Bestiary falling into the wrong hands. Up ahead, an undeterred woman at the edge of the crowd lifted a cellphone, only to shriek in protest as she had it swiped out of her hand by a gun-toting soldier.

"You can't do that! That's theft!" she yelled. "I know my rights!"

The soldier whirled around. "And you'll get to know the inside of a police van if you try to take pictures. This is a matter of national security."

*Bullcrap! You just don't want them to see what's under there.* I had to admit, I felt a touch relieved. I didn't like the way this guy was going about it, but at least they were doing a stellar job of keeping civilians at bay.

"Is that... the Aquarium?" Raffe drew level with me as we continued walking closer.

I followed his eyeline to a thin gap in the patchwork of tarps, to find a glint of bronze and glass. A stream of water flowed right under the barrier and down the street, making my stomach lurch. I desperately hoped that the expulsion into the real world had knocked over a hot water urn. Otherwise, the sea creatures in the Aquarium were suffering a slow death. That place held a special place in my heart, since it was the room in which Wade had proposed. If that had been destroyed... it felt like a part of my history would be destroyed with it. Really, that went for the entirety of the SDC. Any cracks would be mirrored by a wound on my soul.

"That's definitely one of the bronze dragons." Garrett gestured to a strange shape protruding from the mountain of lumpy, concealed rubble. Even with a tarp covering it, I could still see a distinctly dragon-like shape. Wings and all.

*This is real... it's actually happened. The SDC is really out.* A naïve part of me had still hoped that all this was a misunderstanding, or that it wouldn't be quite as bad as we thought, as Wade had said. But now... I couldn't pretend to be hopeful anymore. This was as worst-case as a worst-case scenario could get.

With my mouth hanging open, a peculiar magnetism drew me ever closer to the remains of our coven and the Fleet Science Center that had been its façade. I weaved through the crowd that had gathered, heading for the barricade. There, I gripped the metal bar and struggled for breath. Up close, it transformed into a literal nightmare.

"How do we get in?" Santana stepped up beside me, her tone hushed.

Words failed me.

Astrid slipped in next to Santana. "Well, we can't portal inside, that's for sure."

"Why not?" Jacob asked, flexing his palms.

"Because, given the SDC's current condition, the building lacks the physical integrity for that kind of action. Look." She gestured to the center of the tarp mass, which rose higher than the rest. "The center is still standing. O'Halloran and the others will be holding it up, using their own magic as a temporary bubble to prevent it from crashing down on them. Any interference with that, specifically from magic that augments space in a physical way, may cause it to collapse."

Jacob nodded in half-understanding.

"Wait." My eyes bulged in disbelief. "Do you mean—?" The breeze drifted across the tarps, and the fabric tautened momentarily against something dead center, right where Astrid had gestured. An egg shape, like the top of a dome. There was only one place in the SDC with a dome that large.

Astrid cast me a sorrowful glance. "That's the Bestiary, yes."

"Then we need to get in there. Now." The longer we waited out here, the more effort it would take everyone inside to keep up the temporary bubble around the Bestiary. And if that fell… well, that would start a war unlike any this world had ever seen.

## FIVE

## Harley

"This way." Astrid beckoned for us to follow her back through the tempestuous crowd of bodies crushing forward to get a closer look at the wreckage of the Fleet Science Center. A flock of vultures feeding on the macabre.

Dust filled the air and my lungs, making my throat scratchy and dry. I coughed, using my palm like a mask, and hurried after Astrid. I had no clue where she was taking us, but I knew better than to argue with her. If she had a plan, then she was a step ahead of the rest of us.

"Where are we going?" Santana reached for Astrid's shoulder. "We need to get in, not run farther away. Slinky is in there!"

*Oh, no...* in my shock, I'd forgotten about the feathered serpent. Santana had left the creature behind when we went to find Finch. The snake had coiled himself around her, not wanting to be separated, but she'd forced him to stay put in her room until she came back. The guilt in her voice rang like a death knell. If Slinky had still been in her room when the SDC emerged... well, you only had to look at the vast expanse of rubble to know that wasn't good.

"Can't you get through to him?" I asked hopefully.

Santana shook her head miserably. "I thought it was because I was too far away, being in freaking Antarctica and all. I was sure he'd come out when we got closer to the SDC, but I keep calling, and he's not coming!" Panic rippled through her words.

"I'll get us in, don't worry." Astrid lifted her trusty tablet. She was more attached to Smartie than to Garrett, sometimes, much to his chagrin. She tapped the screen. "I was waiting to hear back from some-one, and they've come through for us."

"Who?" Garrett eyed the tablet with his usual suspicion.

Astrid smiled. "Kenzie."

"Kenzie?" My eyebrows raised in surprise. "You've been in touch with her?"

She nodded. "I didn't want to say anything in case she couldn't help us, but as it turns out, though she gave up her less-than-legal undertakings, she's still got contacts in all the right places."

Kenzie had been not-so-subtly avoiding us after we tried to wrangle her into joining the SDC, so we'd taken the hint and let her be. I'd hoped she'd come around of her own accord, but I'd let thoughts of her slide to the backburner. No doubt Astrid had used Finch as some kind of lure to get her to give us a hand. When it came to my brother, Kenzie always stepped up to the plate. A true friend who'd known him through his dark days and brighter ones and still stuck around.

"Where is she meeting us?" Wade cut to the chase. We'd reached the edge of the crowd and were able to breathe a little easier, aside from the dust. It settled in a strange haze that distorted the sunset, making the whole landscape look like it was on fire. The word "hellish" came to mind.

"Up the street, close to the eastern entrance of Waterfront Park." Astrid was walking briskly toward our destination. I noticed Santana look back over her shoulder at the grim, tarped mass, her eyes glinting with unspilled tears. She was worried for Slinky, and rightly so. If he wasn't coming when she called... I tried not to consider why that might be.

A hasty march later, we arrived outside the concealed magical entrance to Waterfront Park—San Diego's premium shopping and recreation hub for magicals. Fortunately, it hadn't plopped out into the world like the SDC. None of the other covens or magical sites had. The SDC was the sole victim, because Davin had taken the place of our coven. Like Melody had theorized, he'd become the Bestiary's possessor, so we'd been kicked out. Literally.

I scoured the area for any sign of the wayward Morph, but she was nowhere to be seen.

"There you are! I thought you'd gone and stood me up." A figure drifted out of the alley beside us, and the scent of trash wafted into the street—sickly sweet, tinged with decay.

"Sorry," Astrid replied as Kenzie stopped in front of us, pushing her hands into the pocket of her neon yellow hoodie. As discreet clothing went, she'd missed the mark. "We had to fight our way through the crowd of civilians."

She nodded in understanding. "It's no better in there." She tilted her head toward the entrance of Waterfront Park. "Everyone and their mom is hiding out in the shops and bars until they know what they're supposed to do next. They're pretty freaked out. Who wouldn't be?"

*I know I am...* I didn't say it out loud. I had to try and keep it together for me and my friends.

"How come you aren't at home?" Wade's tone carried a hint of paternal concern that made me smile, despite the dire circumstances.

She shrugged. "I came to see what the fuss was about. That's when I got that text from Astrid. I've been digging up the goods ever since." She disappeared back into the alleyway and reemerged with a big, worn canvas bag, which she proceeded to dump unceremoniously on the ground at our feet.

"Dare I ask what's in the bag?" I eyed the packed item, the zipper straining to burst open, and tried very hard to ignore the US Army emblem emblazoned on the side.

Kenzie laughed. "Your coven just exploded into the real world, and you're worried about a little petty theft? I didn't do the stealing, anyway. I still don't do that kind of thing. An old pal of mine did it. You might remember him: big guy, biceps the size of a toddler's skull, tat on his face. He owed me for getting him out of some trouble. Now we're square, though I could've used that debt for later." She waved a hand. "Ah well, at least I know you'll make better use of it than I would've. I'd have just cashed it in for babysitting duties or something."

"Isn't stealing from the US Army getting your friend *back* into trouble?" Raffe asked sagely.

Kadar popped up. "You've got no imagination, Raffe. I thought you'd have learned by now that you don't always have to play by the rules."

Kenzie stared at the transformation. "Whoa… weird."

"You get used to it," I cut in. "What's in the bag?"

Astrid bent and unzipped the duffel. Black fabric showed within, and I spotted the familiar shape of Kevlar. "I asked Kenzie to acquire some emergency soldier packs for all of you, but I assumed she would acquire them from a dress shop, or perhaps the police station in a pinch. I didn't think she would take them directly from the army." She sounded concerned.

Kenzie grinned. "You want to look the part, you need the real deal. Those army folks would see right through you if you walked up in dress gear, and they're not letting the local police near the site. This is your only chance of getting inside."

Dylan gave a low whistle. "You can't argue with her logic."

"No, you can't." Kenzie gestured to the duffel bag. "Either you want this stuff, or you don't; it's no skin off my nose. I can get Crossbones to take them right back from wherever he nabbed them."

"No." I steeled my resolve. "We want them."

Wade nudged me gently in the ribs. "Are you sure about this?"

"If we want to get inside, we have to use whatever means necessary." Wade still had issues with disobeying the status quo, even after over a year at my side, picking up a few of my bad habits. But we had to bend some rules if we were going to meet up with O'Halloran and get Tobe under control.

He sighed. "Okay. I don't like it, but you've got a point."

Wasting no more time, our group slunk into the dumpster alley, where Astrid and I proceeded to hand out the pilfered uniforms, complete with Kevlar vests and all the correct insignia. At the bottom of the bag, I found some pretty realistic-looking guns that made me stop in my tracks.

"Are these real?" I took one out and looked down the sight, pretending I knew what I was doing.

Kenzie shook her head, with a ghost of a smirk. "As if I'd trust you all with human weapons." She picked one up and pointed it at the wall, pulling the trigger. For a split second, my heart lurched, thinking she was about to unleash an ear-splitting shot. It clicked, but nothing happened, allowing me to breathe a sigh of relief.

"These don't have any ammo," she went on. "One of you would probably be stupid enough to look down the barrel, and it'd wind up going off in your face. Just use magic if you get into a tight spot. Less chance of you killing some poor sap on accident."

"Fair enough. Everyone, get dressed and take one of these." I gave the order, slipping into command mode. I'd been working as an agent for so long that it was like second nature now.

The others nodded uncertainly and took a uniform and an empty assault rifle apiece. Soon enough, we were all gussied up and ready to go. I had to say, we made a formidable bunch, all clad in bulletproof black. Even Astrid, with her specs perched on the edge of her nose, looked like she meant business. Or maybe it was the unexpected skill with which she held her rifle, as though she'd done it before.

I nodded down at the bag. "There's one left, Kenzie, if you want to come with us."

She arched an amused eyebrow. "Even with the SDC in bits, you're still trying to get me to join?"

"I'm nothing if not persistent." I flashed her a hopeful smile, but it faded as she shook her head.

"Nah, I need to get back to Mom and Inez. I said I wouldn't be gone long, and they'll start to worry soon." She took the bag and lobbed it behind one of the dumpsters. "Just put everything back when you're done, so Crossbones can pick it up and hopefully get it back before they notice it's gone."

"You sure?" I gave it one last shot.

Kenzie hit me with a stern look. "It just ain't for me, Harley. No offense, but I've got my family to think about. If I run off into that disaster with you, I'm putting myself in danger. And I'm not going to put my family through any more suffering. Sorry."

I relented. "I get it, and I respect it. Thanks for getting this stuff for us, and please give our love to your mom and sister." I paused. "And if you change your mind, you know where to find us."

She rolled her eyes. "Thanks."

Suited and booted for the occasion, I led the way out of the alley, and we headed back to the chaotic scene. The riot atmosphere seemed to have calmed slightly, and the crowd fell into a fidgety silence as we weaved through it, wielding our fake weapons. Like Kenzie had said, if we wanted to look the part, we had to act like the real deal. Judging by the faces of the civilians around us, we had that covered.

*Okay, time to do this the old-fashioned way.* Since there was no more Kid City and no more interdimensional bubble, we had to get through the barricades and that wall of tarp to reach the SDC. The trouble was, we had no idea how many soldiers were already inside the coven. It was time to get creative with the role play.

"Evening." I strode casually up to the barricade, where the sentries were thinnest. Only two of them guarded a gap in the perimeter. "Reporting for duty."

"You took your sweet time." The left-hand guard eyed us from head to toe, while the second barely glanced at us.

I let out an irritated sigh. "The chopper was late. But we're here now, and the colonel wants to see us ASAP." Truthfully, I didn't even know if they *had* a colonel here. I'd just taken a guess and hoped for the best.

"The higher-ups have been diverting them to pick up FBI agents," the second guard chipped in. "But you're here, and we can use all the help we can get. The colonel is inside, though I couldn't say exactly where. It's a mess in there."

"We'll find him," I replied assertively. "But if we stay out here twiddling our thumbs, he's going to have our heads on a chopping block."

The first guard readjusted his gun. "He's barking at everyone, so your heads are probably already on the chopping block."

"Then we should hurry this up before he drops the axe." I held the guy's gaze unwaveringly.

The more reasonable soldier stepped forward and detached the link between the fences, opening the barricade to let us pass. "Better you than me."

"Don't I know it." I realized I was speaking in soundbites, but they appeared to be buying the ruse, and I was grateful they hadn't asked to check our IDs, since we didn't have any. I slipped through the gap first, the others following behind. I didn't stop until we were underneath the tarps.

Industrial spotlights illuminated the darkened world beneath the sheets of waxy fabric, casting a tragic glow upon the destruction that I hadn't wanted to believe in. I came to a brief halt, observing the catastrophe. My heart hurt, as if it had been sucker-punched. The archways and ceilings and walls of the SDC stood in various states of demolition, with glass shards spilling out across the rubble like drops of crystal water. Bronze dragon statues were missing heads, limbs, wings. One was just scaly feet, nothing more. Priceless vases, doorways, and ancient magical artifacts lay in jigsaw pieces that could never be put back together again. And here and there, a different, more modern kind of stone and artifact blended with the familiar masonry of the coven—magical and non-magical colliding in the most heartbreaking way. I saw fragments of signs about telescopes and the carapace of a huge vinyl beetle that used to be in the natural wing of the Fleet Science Center. The science center had been absolutely decimated, with barely a sign of it remaining, aside from those sparse objects and torn-up exhibition pieces.

Wade came up beside me, his eyes fixed dead ahead. "Is that what I think it is?"

In the middle of the ruins, standing proud and untouched, the Bestiary protruded upward. An egg-shaped anomaly, the atrium sparked and fizzled behind a forcefield of violet lightning that shimmered across its entirety. Soldiers gathered in front of it, unable to look away from the ferocious flashes. It was impossible to miss, as fascinating as it was terrifying. The violet defenses hadn't been there before. Evidently, this was another protection protocol that'd activated when the SDC fell out into the open.

"How do we play this?" he whispered.

"Like non-magicals." I took a deep breath and set off toward the Bestiary, picking my way across the broken husk of our former home. We'd only gotten past stage one. It wasn't going to be so easy to get inside the Bestiary's forcefield.

Reaching the spot where soldiers had gathered, I stopped and took a moment to gauge the situation.

"What do you think it is?" I heard a soldier say.

"Looks like some kind of nuclear energy to me," another replied.

"Could be alien," added a third.

The second snorted. "It's not alien, Milton. There's no such thing."

"Does it look human to you?" The third cradled his gun, like it could protect him from any little gray men that might come out.

"Sure it does," the second answered defiantly. "Check out those sparks and stuff—it's electrical, not extraterrestrial."

"If it was human, why would General Whittaker be here?" The first soldier nodded discreetly at an imposing individual who stood off to the left, speaking with another authoritative-looking guy. The general towered over his underlings, with broad shoulders, a sleek crop of graying hair, and intelligent eyes that kept glancing toward the Bestiary. I could hear the rumble of his deep voice from where I stood, though I couldn't make out the words over the fizz and crack of the lightning.

"You there!" A voice drew my attention away from the general, to find another man heading right for us. According to the insignia on his uniform, he was a colonel. And he wore an embroidered name strip across his bulletproof vest: Morris.

I lifted a hand in salute and stood to attention, everyone else copying me with varying degrees of success. "Colonel."

"Who let you in here? What unit are you from?" The colonel readjusted his Kevlar vest, his sharp blue eyes scrutinizing our motley crew. Maybe he'd seen through the façade. I hoped not.

"We're from the Third Brigade, 82$^{nd}$ Airborne Division." I pulled the words out of some half-remembered news story, praying he wouldn't check the details.

His brow furrowed, and he eyed my nametag. "Paras? Why are they sending paras?"

"I don't know, sir. We just came when we were told. It took some time to get a chopper out here, with them being diverted to pick up the FBI." I lied through my teeth, using what the outside guards had said to our advantage. "What happened, anyway? We got the call, our CO dispatched us, and we wound up here. But they didn't tell us anything about what we were walking into." I smoothly directed him down a different path of discussion, in the hopes it would stop him from checking on our credentials.

The colonel sighed, his shoulders relaxing slightly. "Your guess is as good as mine, Captain Vermeer." My insignia made me a captain, which I'd already spotted on my uniform. A role both cool and distinctly unnerving. I didn't know what being a captain entailed. As for the last name, I had to go with whatever had been slapped on my nametag. "All we know is, we've got some of the nation's best scientists examining this thing and going over what happened, but no one can explain it. A building came out of the damn sky, crushed the Fleet Science Center, and this glowing egg is the only thing that seems completely untouched."

"How many dead, sir?" Wade spoke up. His uniform marked him as a lieutenant.

The colonel pointed to a row of black body bags that lay in a cleared area. "Twelve so far, though they're taking their damned time getting these poor souls into the ambulances. Christ knows how many more are under all this." He waved a hand toward the mountain of debris.

"Does anyone know what that building was?" I played up the uninformed non-magical aspect.

"Not a clue." The colonel surveyed the wreckage. "We've got units digging out whatever they can find, but so far there only seems to be a load of books and scrolls and weird objects. It's like a bizarre museum, or something."

Panic jolted my heart. I scoured the debris for these soldiers and spied a couple of them dumping ancient tomes in a big pile, as though preparing a bonfire. I noticed glints of gold and bronze in the pile—a drained Ephemera, a broken blade from the Armory, and something that looked like Krieger's magical detector prototype. I spotted the torn-up pages of a comic book and a battered, screwed-up lump that I recognized as one of my leather jackets. If the former was one of Finch's prized first appearance comics, he was going to lose his mind. Though I supposed not, considering the rest of the devastation.

"But *that* has us all stumped." The colonel jabbed a finger at the Bestiary.

"Any ideas so far?" I prompted.

Colonel Morris shrugged, though the sweat on his brow gave away his true fear. "The best speculation we've got at the moment is that it's some kind of nuclear reactor. But that's just a guess. We've got scouts led by Lieutenant Wilson searching the parts of the building that are more stable, but we lost comms with that team about half an hour ago. I have complete faith in her, but... they've gone silent, so I need to find faith elsewhere and make sure nothing's gone awry."

*This is our shot to find O'Halloran!* I seized it.

"We can go and find Lieutenant Wilson and her team," I offered. "It beats getting under your feet out here."

Colonel Morris hesitated. "Not sure I like the idea of losing more people, but this is an emergency, so I suppose risks will have to be taken.

The thing is, we sent drones in to try and locate the lieutenant, but they all went down, too. Some of the scientists think it's that glowing egg messing with the electronics, but I really couldn't say."

"We're better than technology," I insisted. "And if that thing *is* messing with the electronics, it's not going to mess with us."

The colonel rubbed his chin in thought for a moment before answering. "Fine, but I'm going to give you radios, anyway. And I'm not thrilled about the idea of sending in more troops to find two missing teams."

"Noted." I held out a hand for a radio, which a different soldier immediately handed over, set to the right frequency. He handed more out to the others, who duly clipped the devices to their vests.

"And you'd better be quick," the colonel added. "We've got cranes coming in within the hour so we can start removing surface debris to search for any other bodies. We'll tear this place apart if we have to. Frankly, I reckon it's the best thing we could do."

*No...* I fought to keep my true feelings off my face. What right did they have to come in and raze what was left of our home to the ground? They may not have known it was our home, but still. Hearing that made rational thought difficult.

"We'll find them and report back to you, sir," I assured him.

He nodded reluctantly. "Godspeed."

I led the Rag Team away from the violent defenses of the Bestiary and headed for one of the makeshift tunnels that gaped from the pile of ruins. It worried me that I hadn't seen O'Halloran or any other magicals yet, but I supposed they could've been keeping out of the army's way to avoid winding up in handcuffs. I would've radioed him, but I didn't want to risk anyone else picking up our frequency.

Behind me, Santana sniffled quietly. "Slinky isn't coming out. What if he's trapped under the rubble? What if he's..." She couldn't finish the sentence.

"He's smart, Santana," Raffe said comfortingly. "When the coven started to emerge, I bet he went straight to the Bestiary. He's probably in there right now, but he can't get out because of whatever Tobe has done."

Santana lifted her head. "Do you think so?"

"I know so. Slinky is like a Familiar to you. You'd know if he was gone, and I don't think he is." Raffe put his arm around her in the relative seclusion of the tunnel. A string of lights hung from the passage walls, illuminating our way.

"I think I ought to stay here." Astrid brought me to a temporary stop. "I'm not good with enclosed spaces, and you'll need someone out here to send for help if things go awry."

Garrett put his hand on her shoulder. "I'll stay with you."

I sympathized. Walking into an unstable building wasn't a great time in anyone's book, but we had no choice. Still, I wasn't going to make anyone come with me if they didn't want to. And Astrid had good reason to fear the dark, and to fear the prospect of everything tumbling down on top of her. "Just stay hidden, okay?"

"We will," Garrett replied.

Turning around, I pressed on through the tunnel, with the others at my back. The dust was thicker here, and metal groaned somewhere in the distance, beneath the crunch of glass and stone. O'Halloran and his security team were in here somewhere. And even if it took all night, I was going to find him, and we were going to crack that Bestiary egg open.

## SIX

## Finch

I stood in the entrance of the Antarctic Coven, which Melody had found around the back of one of the dilapidated shelters that'd once been a refuge for old-timey whalers manning their harpoons and scouring the seven seas for any sign of Moby Dick. It was crazy to think that whale oil was once normal. Though, I doubted you'd want to fry your breakfast in the blubber of a baleen. Not unless you were Atlantean or had a penchant for the fishier things in life.

It didn't have the magnitude of other covens I'd seen, but it probably hadn't needed to fit too many people inside. Who would volunteer to live out here, unless they were running away from something? Crazy folks, that's who. Although, I supposed they'd all abandoned ship in the end.

"The décor is… interesting." Ryann stared up at a whalebone chandelier, which had pride of place above the rest of the coven's main room.

It reminded me of a Viking longhouse or some kind of ski chalet, with a timber ceiling and big fireplaces everywhere to keep out the Antarctic chill. All of them had burst into life the moment we'd stepped inside, taking the edge off the total numbness that my body was experiencing. *Extremities? What extremities?* I couldn't feel them anymore. Furry rugs covered the floor, one of which looked alarmingly like a polar bear. Crowded around the fireplace in the central room were enormous armchairs—the kind that made me think some old dude was about to tell me a tale.

And literally everything that could've been made out of whalebone *was* made out of whalebone: lamps, tables, chairs, light fixtures, and even some ornamental monstrosities that would have made any artist question the craft. But it was here, and it was safe, and it had some fairly extreme prison facilities that I hadn't anticipated. Specifically, in the form of a row of six padded cells in the cellar of the small coven. Huntress had sniffed them out, and we'd followed her down into the gloom only to get the fright of our lives when we found One-Eyed Willy himself sitting at a cobwebbed table, his skeleton teeth set in a permanent grin like he had a secret that he wasn't going to share.

Upon further inspection, and swift removal of said skeleton by Nash, we discovered that five of the six cells were... well, they weren't pretty. But one had been clean enough to shove Ovid inside. Melody, Krieger, and Huntress were down there now with the security magicals, taking the first watch. Krieger wanted to run some magical medical tests to find out more about the distinction between Atlanteans and ordinary magicals. As for Melody, I suspected she'd volunteered for the first watch so she wouldn't have to answer my relentless questions about what the hell had happened here. I wanted the whole grisly tale. Call it morbid curiosity. Still, with time running out, it looked like I wasn't going to get any answers soon.

"Are we ready to go?" Luke had said his goodbyes to his lady love, but his reluctance to leave her was palpable.

I nodded. "I think so. Remington, you've got everything covered here, right?" I glanced from him to Ryann in an overt fashion, so he'd understand the subtext.

Remington smiled. "I promise I'll take care of everything."

"Ryann?" I prompted. She was staring off into space, distracted.

"Hmm?" she replied absentmindedly.

"Everything okay?" I had a creeping fear that there was evil in this place. Stephen King stuff—an invisible virus that'd driven the last inhabitants nuts.

She snapped out of it. "What? Oh... yes, all good here. Well, not really, in the grand scheme of things. I'm just worried and scared and confused. But I'll be okay."

"Are you sure?" I knew we had to leave ASAP, but it appeared Luke and I were in the same boat—reluctant to leave our girlfriends.

"Positive. Now go, before the Mage Council shows up. If you cross paths on your way to the water, this entire plan will go up in smoke." She crossed to where I stood and rose on tiptoe to give me another farewell kiss.

I kissed back, savoring the moment while I could. "Stay safe, okay?"

"Same goes for you," she murmured. "I love you."

"I love you, too." I dipped in for one last peck before heading to the exit. Nash, Luke, and Hector joined me, our manly quartet striding out into the biting cold of South Georgia Island. Picking our way across the rocks, we made for the water's edge. I really wasn't looking forward to submerging myself again, but there was only one way to reach Atlantis.

"Brace yourselves." Nash shuddered, closing his eyes as he waded into the bitter water. Hector was already up to his waist, showing no signs of discomfort whatsoever.

Taking a deep breath, I forced one foot in front of the other. A few less-than-heroic gasps escaped my throat as I pressed on, uttering a definite squeal as the water hit the crown jewels. Luke tried his best to act unbothered, but his white-knuckled fists and clenched jaw gave him away.

Soon enough, we were all up to our chins. And any hope I'd had of ever being warm again had vanished.

"What now?" I looked at Hector.

"We go under." He inhaled loudly before plunging beneath the surface.

"Anyone else regretting this plan?" Nash grumbled, before following suit.

With only Luke and me left, I didn't want to be the last one under. Call me childish, but that was the truth. I pinched my nose and ducked down, only to find myself in some kind of... bubble. The cold wasn't nearly as bad inside this thing, and though I'd gotten soaked from wading into that hellish water, the bubble didn't let in so much as a trickle. Hector sat cross-legged on the floor of whatever this structure was, his hands pressed to the transparent curve ahead of him. Nash sat at the back, looking awkward with his knees pulled up to his chest. Confused, I sat down where I was, and Luke slotted in beside me.

"We're traveling by bubble?" It sounded as ridiculous as it felt.

Hector looked back at me with a half-smile. "You'd prefer to swim?"

"Nope, nope, you do your thing, bubble maestro. Anything not to have to go into that water again." I peered through the tensile floor, glancing down at the seabed below us. There were people the world over who'd pay a helluva lot for this, though they'd probably have done it somewhere sensible, like Hawaii.

Hector waved his hand, and the bubble took off. It powered through the water like a submarine, with Hector skillfully maneuvering it with subtle movements of his fingers. I wondered if I'd accidentally been sucked into a virtual reality game. It would've explained a lot about the past year or so. Perhaps this was all a simulation, and soon I'd take off the goggles and be safe and sound in my room at the SDC. Or perhaps that was wishful thinking.

"I've got a suggestion." Nash braced himself against the wall of the bubble. We were being thrown this way and that by sharp jolts as the vehicle changed direction. "Seatbelts."

Hector chuckled. "Apologies. It is a somewhat bumpy ride, but it is the quickest path to the crack in Atlantis that I escaped from. Unfortunately, it is in the base of the city, which is still underwater. Even more unfortunately, this journey is the easy part. Getting back inside the city will be difficult, and that is putting it mildly."

"You got out easy enough. Surely it's the same to get back in, just in reverse." I tried to stay optimistic.

Hector shook his head. "There was nothing easy about getting out."

*Right, of course...* He'd appeared on the shore, and I'd made assumptions. After all, getting into somewhere dangerous and magical was never as simple as, you know, just opening a door.

I tried not to tumble into Luke as the bubble rocketed on, all of us tossed about like a salad. And all around us, the dark ocean closed in, the seabed giving way to the abyss below—so deep that it turned to shadow. A thalassophobe's nightmare. Good vocabulary word: an intense fear of deep bodies of water. Thanks to my time spent in Atlantis, I was turning into one myself.

"How are we going to find Davin once we're inside Atlantis?" Luke's voice went up an octave as he jolted forward, almost cracking his head on my knee.

"If I know Davin, he'll be parading around the throne room in a crown, singing 'God Save the King.' And if he's not, we'll just have to partake in some snooping." I stared down at the unnerving blackness beneath us, imagining a megalodon bursting upward to devour us whole. *Ugh.* "Where Atlantis is concerned right now, I'm pretty sure all roads lead to Doncaster."

The bubble plunged deeper into the darkness at a twist of Hector's fingertips. My gaze lifted upward, spotting a faint fissure of light above. If it hadn't been for that thin fork of illumination, like a permanent lightning bolt, I'd never have known that Atlantis sat above it. Through the gap, I saw a hint of civilization—the metalwork of pipes and machinery, and a speck of light shining through what looked like a sewer grate. Above it was the faintest hint of greenery, suggesting a garden. I didn't recognize it specifically, but at least we had a fixed point in the city.

*The prison cells have to be around here somewhere, then.* Atlantis's penitentiary kept its high-risk prisoners below the city in a curved demi-sphere. That's where the new Muppet Babies and I had broken loose, thanks to the juice that Gaia had souped me up with. I had no actual confirmation that it was due to her, and not the Sanguine influx, but I liked to think that the only benevolent Child I'd ever encountered had given me a pick-me-up to help me on my way.

I guessed that the prison had to be in the center somewhere, but since I couldn't pinpoint where that garden or those pipelines were, I had no idea which way the center might be. I also didn't fancy spending another second in that prison, so I was glad the crack in the protective shell hadn't appeared there. It would've been just my luck to have to enter that place again.

"Stay very still." Hector's sudden warning sent a spike of dread through my gut.

"The last time I heard someone say that, a T-Rex crashed through an electrical fence." I gave in to nervous humor.

Hector stared at me in alarm. "There are dinosaurs in the surface world?"

"No, I was just... never mind." Damn Atlanteans and their ignorance of pop culture. But I did as I was told and didn't move a muscle. Save for my mouth. "Why do we have to be still?"

Nash gasped and tilted his head up ever so subtly. "Because of *that*."

A shadow twisted beneath the fissure of light, scales catching the glow for a split second before the shape receded back into the darkness of the ocean. My heart jumped into my throat.

*What in the name of Steve Irwin—God rest his awesome soul—was that?!* I didn't dare speak, in case the creature heard me.

A moment later, something bumped right into the bubble, knocking it a short distance away from the crack we needed to get to. In vivid, zoomed-in proximity, those shiny scales slithered past the wall of our underwater vehicle. I resisted every instinct to reel away from the creature.

*Channel Alan Grant. Channel Alan Grant. Don't move a muscle.* I repeated the *Jurassic Park* mantra as the scales continued to slither by in a seemingly endless stream. Whatever this beast was, it was looooong. And where I came from, that tended to mean lots of teeth and a bad attitude.

The whip of a tail sent us spinning back toward our original position.

Hector hit the proverbial brakes, clenching his hands into fists to stop us from flying right off into the gloom. I watched the water, waiting for the beast to reappear. It flashed overhead, and this time I caught sight of its face: dragon-like, with a blunt snout crisscrossed with silvered scars across cobalt-blue scales, a painfully deep scar running diagonally across a milky white, unseeing eye. Light glinted off the fangs that protruded from its mouth, like jagged chunks of metal had been rammed into its gums.

"What *is* that?" Luke whispered, voice shaking.

"An ancient sea beast that hails from Caledonia," Hector whispered back.

Nash's eyes bugged. "You mean Scotland?"

"Perhaps. The creature was captured many moons ago by hunters investigating a lake there."

"No way..." Realization dawned on me. If I hadn't been too petrified to even twitch, I'd have howled with laughter. "Are you telling us that's the Loch Ness Monster?"

Hector shrugged. "You would have to ask Iso about the creature's history. I should warn you, we are in grave danger. This beast was not here when I escaped. Kaya must have released it in order to protect Atlantis from outsiders."

"So... us?" Nash shook his head, and a nervous muscle twitched in his jaw. With his magical abilities now in my hands, he was vulnerable out here. Sure, he had military experience by the bucketload, which was why we'd brought him along in the first place—he knew how to be sneaky, and he knew how to fight, but he didn't know how to breathe without air. If this bubble popped, he wouldn't have anything to defend himself from these serpents, aside from a few rusty-ass knives that he'd nabbed from the walls of the Antarctic Coven. Whalebone handles, naturally.

"Be alert. Chances are, this is not the only one that has been released to protect Atlantis," Hector warned, staring out into the gloom.

"Wait, there's more than one Loch Ness Monster?" Luke turned as white as a sheet.

I made the mistake of looking down. Yellow eyes flashed and dark scales shone in the murk as they—in the fabled words of Tenacious D— whip-cracked with their whoopy tails, cutting through the water at breakneck speed. Teeth glinted and jaws opened wide as the slithering beasts gunned straight for us.

## SEVEN

## Finch

"How safe is this—" One of the serpents answered Luke's question for him. It headbutted the bubble, sending us careening off like a misdirected soccer ball. Hector acted quickly, balling his fists and bringing us to a screeching halt. But that was the least of our problems.

Nash lifted his boot, and droplets tumbled off it. "I'd put a firm bet on *not* safe. Water's coming in." Without hesitating, he whipped a pack of gum from his pocket and started chewing. Once he'd softened it up a little, he slapped it on the biggest cracks like window putty. "Never leave home without gum. Duct tape would be better, but you've got to work with what you have."

"Screw this!" I moved into a crouched position. "Hector, how do I get out?"

Hector frowned in confusion. "Why would you want to get out?"

"To stop these Nessies from getting in and gnashing us to death. That's gnash with a 'G.'" I flashed a look at the man in plaid. "I need to get out there so I can deal with these suckers."

Hector hesitated. "You just push through. The tensile surface should bounce back to stop us from drowning while you're... doing whatever it is you plan to do." He hit me with a dubious glance. "You know what you're doing, right? You understand that there are about six of these animals swimming around us, and they want to eat our flesh?"

I narrowed my eyes, determined. "I know what I'm about, sonny."

"You speak strangely." Hector made a little sound of bemusement. "But if you have a death wish, by all means, try and contend with these creatures."

"I have the opposite wish, actually." I faced the bubble wall and did as Hector had instructed. I pushed with my palms until the weird substance gave against my hands. They edged out into the agonizing cold of the ocean. Man, I'd never get used to that. It was like taking a hundred ice baths simultaneously. And I was the sort of guy who'd always preferred to be hot rather than cold.

Gritting my teeth, I pushed the rest of my body through the transparent substance until I found myself floating with a bunch of sea monsters as they swam circles around the bubble. In seconds, they'd come for me. But I was ready.

*Dinnertime, beasts!* I warbled into the water before clamping a palm over my mouth and feeding myself a tendril of sweet, sweet Air. After our earlier brush with drowning, I'd gotten the hang of playing magical scuba tank.

I swam upward, aiming for Big Nessie first. Its marginally smaller buddies would get their turn next. Who knew, maybe this was a cut-off-the-head-and-the-rest-will-crumble situation. I doubted it, but a guy could hope.

The creature whirled around, its one good eye staring right into my friggin' soul. I swore I saw it smile, spreading its mouth to show the full set of sharp teeth. Threading more Air into my lungs, I swam closer and came to a stop at the serpent's level. Bobbing in the current, I closed my palms and concentrated with every fiber of my being. My blood hummed in my veins, freshly invigorated by the Sanguine ability. I could literally hear it rushing through me, whispering a powerful tune.

It had been a while since I'd had to call on my Vader side—the inner Darkness. I had a balance of affinities that kept things ticking smoothly, but my Darkness had always been a tad heavier. I used it now, finding the shadowy edge of it within me and urging it into my palms to supercharge the fury I was about to unleash.

Big Nessie, with that blunt nose and yellow eye, lunged for me as Telekinesis erupted out of my hands, tinged with faint black specks that were barely noticeable in the murk of the ocean. But the beast didn't slow, rushing in my direction at lightning speed. Switching tactics, I turned one palm inward and pushed a burst of Air into my chest. It knocked me out of the way just in time to avoid a watery mauling.

*Oh no, you don't, you big Scottish dope.* I diverted my Telekinesis to the muscled coils of the serpent's body and latched on. I shot forward, dragged by the powerful creature. All part of my flying-by-the-seat-of-my-pants plan. Using the Telekinesis like a rope, I pulled myself closer to the beast as it bucked and writhed. Once I reached its slippery form, I clamped my thighs around its bulk. My undercarriage would never be the same. I strained over the vast width of Big Nessie. I was pretty much doing the splits, and I definitely hadn't warmed up.

*Ouch, ouch, ouch, ouch...* I wrapped the strand of Telekinesis tighter around the serpent and pulled it like a rein. Nessie didn't like that one bit. All I could do was hold on while this aquatic bucking bronco threw me this way and that. I waited until it had to turn and launched a violent blast of Fire at the back of its head. Being underwater, I wasn't entirely sure how this would play out.

The Darkness shivered through my Fire as it surged out of my free hand, pulsing through the water in a liquid inferno of molten rage. The water had no effect on it whatsoever. *That's what I'm talking about!* But it didn't have much of an effect on Big Ness either. After a shake of its head, it went right back to bucking and thrashing, trying to throw me.

This called for creativity. I had an idea, but I had no clue if it'd work. Then again, I'd already ventured into experimental territory. Picking my moment, I pushed off the serpent's back and torpedoed through the water on a flow of Air. I twisted back around to face the creature once more. Below, the Ness family was gathering for a bite.

I closed my eyes and dipped into that pool of Darkness. I let it infuse my Mimicry. I opened my eyes again and focused on the serpent, feeling the familiar rush of transformation skim across my skin. My eyes blurred over from the icy water, but one look at my body let me know that my last-minute improv had worked. I had scales where my skin had been, a massive extension of my real body stretching out into the ocean. I moved my mouth and heard the snap of jaws.

I grinned with my terrible fangs. *Monster Mimicry 101!* I'd Shifted into an exact replica of Big Nessie, and the confused creature pulled up just shy of crunching my head off. But it didn't last for long. It coiled up again like a slinky and sprang at me. This time, I was ready for it. Feeling along the length of my new snaky body, I copied the beast and coiled up, launching forward at the same time. We raced toward each other like exploding streamers. Its mouth opened wide at the critical moment and I ducked downward. Using the tail end of my momentum, I darted upward again as its jaw skimmed over my skull. My new jaws opened wide and clamped down on the beast's throat.

I shook my head savagely, the way crocodiles did with their prey. An angry cry emerged from the beast's throat, strangled by my fangs. With one last, fierce tearing motion, the serpent's throat came away in my jaws. Its final roar echoed through the ocean as it floated lifelessly in the water for a moment. Its head bent forward as a black, oily substance flowed from its throat. The rest of it followed, solid flesh transforming to shadowy wisps of liquid until there was nothing left of the serpent but flecks of darkness that sank down into the abyss.

I watched the mess with my monster eyes, feeling like I could take on the world. I could see clearly again, everything detailed and sharp. And that included the faces of the other Nessies lying in wait. I hoped they might turn tail and flee, but it didn't look like that was about to happen. I'd killed their leader, sure, but they weren't going to crumble. No, they were... preparing to take their revenge.

*Crap...*

All at once, the five remaining serpents blasted through the freezing water. I contemplated staying in my monster form but thought better of it. Now that I'd found myself on a roll, I wanted to try something new. Keeping the monster eyes and nothing else, I switched rapidly back to my original form and pushed a dose of Air into my straining lungs.

To my surprise, another figure burst out into the ocean. Nash, dagger in his teeth, swam straight for one of the serpents. He snatched the blade out of his mouth and plunged it into the beastie as it streamed past. The serpent reeled back in alarm, and a weird rodeo ensued. Nash clung on, diverting the attention of all five creatures. A distraction to buy me time.

*Huh... maybe you don't need magic to be a badass, after all.* And my friend definitely knew how to hold his breath. But the creatures were still moving in my direction. I had seconds before Nash and his entourage reached me, the serpent whipping its head around to try and get a bite of the Plaid Wonder. The other four darted at him for the same reason. He whipped out another dagger and planted it into the eye of one, while avoiding the teeth of another. I had to make each of those seconds count to stop Nash from becoming chunks of snake chow. Quick as a flash, I whipped out my Esprit and transformed it into a switchblade. Dragging the blade across my forearm, a red plume puffed up into the water. I wasted no time delving deeper into my well of Darkness and drove the shadows into my palms. There, they twisted out into the ocean and combined with my rapidly dispersing blood.

*I need to be the monster in order to fight monsters.* The strange thought crept into my noggin as I watched the oncoming serpent squad. As I pushed my hands forward, a veritable artillery of bizarre black blades solidified out of my spilled blood. With a second gesture, they whizzed toward the approaching beasts... and sliced right through them. Nash jumped free of the fray, swimming back to the bubble. Meanwhile, the heads of the creatures kept coming, like they hadn't quite figured out that their bodies were now in pieces. Scaly chunks drifted off in every direction, the dark smoke setting in.

Finally, their yellow eyes realized what had happened. And the light went out in each and every one. The heads floated, suspended in the water, until the dark oil dragged them back to the Chaos. We'd gone from being surrounded to me swimming alone in the gloom.

*Take that, Chaos!* I owed it a lot, but I also had plenty of reasons to be pissed off with it. And this felt like a true victory—a swipe at Davin's reign. He thought he could manipulate Kaya into doing everything he wanted, but he hadn't banked on us being that little bit cleverer than him. And perhaps a touch more powerful.

I scanned the darkness for the bubble Nash had just gunned for and spotted a faint shimmer in the water. I swam for it and pushed through the tensile exterior, plopping into a realm of stunned silence. Luke stared at me, aghast. Hector had gone paler than I thought possible, even for an Atlantean. And Nash wore a worried frown, his mouth set in a grim line. Not quite the celebratory welcome I'd expected, after clearing a path for us.

"Did I miss something?" I broke the strange silence.

Nash cleared his throat, shaking the water from his hair. "That was a lot of rage, Finch. I guess I didn't know you had that in you."

"Says you, getting all stabby. Anyway, don't we all, when something's in our way?" I countered.

"Maybe, but you didn't have to turn them into sashimi." Luke shook his head in disbelief.

"What else was I supposed to do? It's not like we could've tied them up in a neat bow and taken them back to the Bestiary. Hey, I might be wrong, but I think Atlanteans would notice if a quartet of dudes snuck through the city dragging a bunch of Loch Ness Monsters behind them." I gave an awkward laugh, uncomfortable with the vibe in the bubble.

Hector gave a faint whistle. "I do not think any of us expected you to dice the sea serpents as casually as preparing dinner."

I shrugged, pretending I wasn't miffed by their reaction. "The easiest way to fight monsters is to turn into one."

"I'm not sure that's the right way to think about it," Nash replied, his tone concerned. "You use logic, and force where necessary, but you should always keep your humanity. That's what separates us from beasts in the first place."

"Well, it's done now, and we've got a direct route to the city. So I'm going to count that as a win." I kept acting like it was no big deal, but deep down, I felt something new bubbling to the surface. A pressure gathering in my chest. Not the same coronary pain I'd experienced from the love spell. This was something different: a heavy, tight sensation that squeezed my ribs like an accordion.

It could've been an aftereffect of the cold water or pushing Air into my lungs. I wasn't sure. Whatever this feeling was, it didn't matter right now. We needed to keep going. Davin definitely wasn't slowing down, so neither could we. Like I'd said, if you wanted to fight a monster, you had to turn into one. And I needed to start thinking like him if I wanted to end his reign for good.

# EIGHT

## Finch

---

The awkwardness prevailed as Hector maneuvered our bubble car upward until we leveled with the jagged crack in the protective shield. There, we pushed back out into the gut-wrenchingly cold water and swam the short distance to the fissure. Hector went first, forcing his fingers into the gap and pulling himself up. It seemed to work similarly to the bubble car's exterior. One moment, he was in the water. The next, he knelt on the edge of the fissure, looking down at us.

"It will feel as though you're on fire, but all you have to do is pull your body through," he instructed. At least, that's what I thought he said. The sound was fairly distorted.

Nash went next, sending out a flurry of bubbles as he strained against the magic of Atlantis. His fingers curled around the edges of the crack, and he forced his head into the light. He struggled for a second or two, before the gap birthed him into the underbelly of the city above. Hector took him by the arm and hauled him up the rest of the way, until both of them were staring down at us.

Luke followed, and I went last. Hector was right: it burned like you wouldn't believe. The moment my fingertips touched the crack, sparks of white-hot pain blistered them and coursed up through my arms. I grimaced and fought to keep going, thrusting until I was in past my shoulders. The other three grabbed me and hauled me up, the magic stinging like a thousand thorny vines had wrapped around my body. It raked along my skin as I burst through completely, leaving me with an unpleasant tingle. I collapsed to the ground.

"Ow," I grumbled, staring up at a network of pipes.

"I did say that it would be difficult." Hector offered his hand to help me into a sitting position.

"You didn't say painful," I protested, trying to shake off the buzzing sensation in my over-sensitized veins.

Hector gave an apologetic smile. "I might have been a little sparse with the details."

"At least we're inside." Luke glanced around at our surroundings.

"Speaking of which, where are we?" Nash trailed his fingertips across a hefty disc above our heads, which resembled a run-of-the-mill sewer grate.

Hector gestured to the clustered pipes and stone walls that made up the tunnel where we sat. "We are in the foundations of Atlantis—the inner workings that ensure everyone has fresh running water, light, warmth, and a lack of… mortal waste."

"I thought it smelled funny." I wrinkled my nose. It was definitely foul down here.

"Where do we go from here?" Luke ignored me, keeping it business.

I glanced at Hector. "Can you get us to the palace?"

"I can and I will. Although, we have to stay down here as long as possible to prevent detection." Hector rose from his crouched position. He had to stoop to keep his head from smacking the pipes overhead, which clanked and groaned like any good plumbing ought to.

"Hopefully we'll all go nose blind soon, and I won't keep wondering what smells came out of which Atlanteans." I pulled a face.

Nash offered the olive branch of a chuckle to dissipate the awkwardness. "Nose-blind?"

I smirked. "Like when you've eaten garlic and you kiss someone who's eaten it, too. Cancels out. No ruined dates."

"I've always been a mint man, myself," he said, surprising me. I wasn't naïve enough to think that Nash had always been a hermit who preferred the company of his dog to human beings. But the thought of him on a date, freshening his breath for a smooch, proved difficult to wrap my head around.

"Shall we?" Without waiting for a reply, Hector set off down the sweltering tunnel. The heat was welcome after the bone-chilling cold of the ocean.

The three of us surface dwellers trailed after Hector, taking his lead as he hurried through the labyrinth of the Atlantean sewage system. There wasn't much to see, aside from stone walls and pipes and a few discarded bottles—a sign that people came down here to escape the prim and proper world above. To each their own.

"This is where we should exit." Hector drew us to a halt about half an hour later. All of us dripped sweat, and my clothes stuck to me in all the wrong places, but I'd been right about one thing: we had finally gone nose blind. Either that, or the aromas had gotten sweeter the closer we got to the main hub of Atlantis.

"Is the palace up there?" I pointed to the grate overhead.

"It should lead to the gardens outside the palace, yes," he replied. "But we'll have to apply force."

I flexed my hands with a crack of bones. "Allow me."

Sending up two thin strands of Telekinesis, I fed the slivers into the hairline gap around the edge of the grate. I tugged back on the strands, making sure I had a decent grasp. Satisfied, I flung my hands upward and launched the grate right out of its hole. It hovered for a second. Quickly, I moved it to the side, where it landed with a metallic scraping sound. Dust and dirt tumbled down into the tunnel, showering us with coffee-like granules of muck. I shook them off like a dog and stared through the now-open hole. Earth's blue sky stretched above, and the scent of pungent flowers had cascaded down with the dust and dirt. I'd have known that sickly-sweet smell anywhere. These were the palace gardens.

"Give me a leg up," I said to Luke.

"To get over yourself?" He chuckled and interlaced his fingers for me to use as a step. "Sorry, I couldn't resist."

I flashed him a withering look. "Hilarious."

Bracing my hands against his shoulders, I was hoisted through the hole. I grasped the sides and hauled myself the rest of the way, staying low in case anyone spotted me. I appeared to be in a secluded glade in one of the rose gardens, but I could hear the chatter of people nearby.

"Hurry!" I hissed to the others.

Like a dime-store circus act, Nash and Hector used Luke's strength to join me topside. The three of us returned the favor, lying flat on our bellies and reaching down to pull Luke up into the rose garden. Then, like the good citizen I was, I heaved the grate back into place.

"Wait. We can't just waltz into the palace looking like ourselves." I dipped into my Darkness again, drawn by the temptation of how much simpler it made everything. Sending out a short wave of Mimicry, I turned my teammates and myself into ordinary Atlantean soldiers. I figured it was the easiest disguise, and it wasn't my first time wearing an Atlantean face.

"I don't think I'll ever get used to this." Hector lifted up his hands and stared at them, looking deeply disturbed. "We don't have many Shapeshifters down here, and I've never seen anyone use Shapeshifting as easily as you do."

I flashed a winning smile. "Years of practice and one hell of a Suppressor break, my friend."

"A Suppressor break?" He tilted his head curiously.

I waved a hand at him. "Long story—one we don't have time for right now. If we make it out, I'll tell you the whole messed-up tale." I fixed on a gap in the rose garden walls. "Now, if memory serves, this is the way to the palace."

"It is," Hector confirmed.

Falling into a suitably soldierly step, we pressed on. A few Atlanteans gasped in fright as we emerged from the rose garden, but their fear quickly evaporated once they saw we were Atlantean soldiers. And, frankly, I couldn't quite understand why there were so many people wandering about the gardens in the first place. I'd never seen this many folks in all my time down here. Although, I supposed it wasn't down anywhere anymore.

I eyed a few of the small groups as we passed through, trying to figure out if there was some official event going on. Some bizarre dynamics were at play here. In one foursome, for example, three of them were practically bouncing off the walls with excitement, while the fourth stared blankly at the landscape.

"Do you remember how much you loved it here, Grandmother?" a young woman asked, weaving her arm through the older woman's.

The latter didn't reply. She just kept staring into space, a glitter of tears welling in her eyes. Her arm lay limp, as though she wasn't even registering her granddaughter's presence.

"No..." Hector—at least, I thought it was Hector—whispered in shock.

"What?" That sounded like Nash.

"Over there." Hector nodded subtly at a larger group up ahead, who were sitting on the grass and enjoying a picnic. "Do you see the man with the scar across his cheek?"

I did. This guy seemed a lot chirpier than the grandma, laughing and eating to his heart's content. And the people around him couldn't stop beaming. Seriously, I needed a pair of shades to block out the intense light shining off their perfect teeth. But there was something off about his face, like it was on a minor delay; his mouth moving a millisecond before his voice came out.

"He was a friend of mine. A Purge beast hunter like my wife. And those people are his family—I know them well." Hector's voice hitched. "He died during a mission, about a decade before my wife. I was at his Death Day. I watched them jettison his body into the ocean."

"It might not be his body." I resisted a shudder. My guess was, Davin had been borrowing bodies to bring back those who'd died a long time ago. Criminals, maybe—vessels that wouldn't rock the boat.

*You son of a blobfish...* I only had to look at that family, reunited with their loved one, to realize that Davin's tactic was already working. They were thrilled. And who wouldn't be, in their situation? Hector had already run the temptation gauntlet—the chance to have his wife resurrected. And I knew that painful conflict all too well. On Eris Island, Katherine had tried to entice me with the promise of bringing Adley back if I agreed to join her again. I'd refused, but it hadn't been easy.

"They look happy," Luke said quietly.

"And that's going to be one of our biggest problems." I sighed, finally understanding the enormity of what we were up against. Davin was offering the impossible on a silver platter. There weren't many people in this world who could refuse that, regardless of ethics and the effect it might have on those who came back. Astrid was a testament to the fact that not everyone returned the same as when they'd left. It'd taken Gaia's intervention to give her back the missing part of her soul, and I doubted Davin had that kind of clout, even with two Bestiaries at his disposal.

Nash tilted his head toward a different group. "I wouldn't be so sure. That woman over there doesn't look happy at all."

I followed the direction of his head. A trio sat on a bench—a mother and father, by the looks of it, with their daughter in the center. The young woman cried uncontrollably, her hands covering her face, while the parents looked on in despair and confusion.

"I was at peace," she wept. "I was… weightless. I didn't hurt anymore. All the dark thoughts went away, and everything was quiet and calm and beautiful. Why? Why did you bring me back?"

The parents stared into their laps, tears falling.

"We missed you," the mother murmured.

"You'd have seen me again." The daughter shook her head miserably. "All you had to do was wait, then you'd have been at peace, too."

Hector frowned. "I guess there are some mixed feelings about these resurrections."

"That's to be expected," Nash replied, his tone hushed. "There are people in this world who are ready for death when it comes. Can you imagine preparing yourself and finding comfort in the afterlife, only to be dragged back without your input? Some might be grateful, but others are bound to find it overwhelming." He cast a pointed look at me. I'd done something similar to him, after he'd put that poisoning curse on himself. I'd coaxed him away from the brink of death and made him live again. He'd found peace with that, and I hoped he put himself in the grateful category, but he probably knew more about what it took to face death fearlessly than I did.

Unnerved, we carried on through the gardens until we reached the palace proper. There, another familiar sight caught my attention. Thebian, Apollo, and a handful of other royal advisors sat on the steps by one of the service entrances. They looked as exhausted as I felt, hunched over and weary. Apollo's ring Esprit sparked on the grass below him. It appeared to be short-circuiting or something, likely due to all the magic they'd been doing. I glanced at the rest of the group and noticed a few more Esprits spluttering from overuse.

*It's all about who you know.* Not that they'd know it was us initially, given our disguises. But we had wanted to find these two, and fortune had gone and landed them right in our lap. Now if I could just coax them away from the rest of their group, perhaps I could get them to help us out.

Seizing the opportunity, I sauntered to the steps, keeping it super casual and leaning against the nearby wall. "Everything well over here? I could not help but notice that your Esprit appears to be misbehaving."

Apollo glanced up at me with bloodshot eyes. "They are drained, and so are we."

One of the other advisors shushed him harshly, as though he thought there might be spies listening in.

"Do not censor me. It is true! I cannot be punished for speaking the truth, can I?" Apollo let out a strained sigh. A flicker of doubt crossed his features. Perhaps he realized that Davin could, and likely would, punish him for speaking any kind of inconvenient truth.

"Might I have a word with the two of you?" I nodded at Thebian.

Apollo's eyes narrowed in suspicion, visibly wondering if we were Davin's spies. "About what?"

"A matter of grave importance, regarding a group of miscreants who wreaked havoc upon our fair city." I flashed him a discreet wink, and his eyebrows shot up in surprise.

"Of course! I would be only too happy to speak with you on the subject." Apollo rose to his feet. Thebian had missed the hint, but he got up regardless.

The three of us, with Nash, Luke, and Hector alongside, walked casually away from the rest of the exhausted advisors and rounded the corner. We continued a few yards more, slipping into the shadowed seclusion of a copse of willows. The perfect spot for a cloak-and-dagger conversation.

"What in Ganymede's name are you doing here?" Apollo demanded, his tone half relieved, half dumbfounded. "And how on earth did you manage to survive that expulsion?"

"No thanks to you, that's for sure." I hadn't forgotten their betrayal, bending the knee to Kaya and Davin.

Apollo had the decency to look sheepish. "You must understand, my loyalty is with Kaya. I could not refuse when she demanded fealty. She is still in there, somewhere, and I intend to remain close to her until she is able to regain her mind."

"Finch?!" Thebian finally caught up.

"Only took you a few years." I rolled my eyes.

"You are alive?" Thebian gaped at me in disbelief. "I must say, it is a relief to find you well. We... did worry about your welfare after you were expelled from the city without any breathing apparatus or transport."

I hit him with a cold stare. "I'm touched. It didn't make you stand up for what was right, though, did it?"

"Your frustration is not misplaced. However, my sentiments echo Apollo's. We are here to protect Kaya. We could not abandon her to Davin's manipulation, even if we do not care for that wretched man." Thebian lowered his gaze, chastened.

"He destroyed my coven." I hadn't wanted to make this personal, but the words spilled out before I could stop them.

Apollo nodded slowly. "I am deeply sorry. I overheard a conversation between Kaya and Davin, who said that a coven had suffered as a result of the spell that he performed to seize power from the surface Bestiary. I did not know that it was your coven." He paused. "Please be assured that we abhor Davin as much as you do. We only remain for Kaya's sake. She would not want this, were she in her right mind. She has her shortcomings, but *this*… this would appall her."

"She is watching her queendom transform into a throng of adoring fanatics who look solely to Davin with their devotion," Thebian added, his tone bitter.

Nash folded his arms across his chest. "Meanwhile, the outside world is inching closer to all-out war with Atlantis."

Apollo lowered his gaze. "We do not desire conflict. Given present circumstances, if this were to result in warfare, I imagine many of Davin's resurrections would be undone. Atlanteans would suffer. And we do not want that. Kaya would not want that."

Desolation settled over our group. However, at least I could take comfort in the fact that we were all on the same page. Nobody wanted a war. And everyone hated Davin. Sure, they'd disappointed us before, but they were the only allies we had right now. And I had to use that.

"At least you've got some of your morality still intact." I took a deep breath. "Anyway, we've got bigger fish to fry. First and foremost, what's going on with security around the city? We managed to get in through a crack in the underbelly of Atlantis, so if you could leave that open a while longer, it might make up for the fact that you bent your knee and watched while we got jettisoned into the ocean."

Apollo fidgeted with his frazzled Esprit. "Under Davin's instruction, we are putting all of our Chaos into maintaining the protective shield. However, something is woefully amiss. Whatever power Davin stole from your Bestiary, it appears to be affecting his spells. Specifically, it is slowly eroding the shield."

"Hmm… that's a start. If the shield fails, that could work in our favor. Either that, or act as the spark to light the fuse of war." I paused for a moment before diving in with the good stuff. "What if I told you we could fix all this?"

"I would wonder if you were taunting me," Apollo replied dubiously.

"I never taunt." I winked at him. "If you can help us defeat Davin, I'll make sure that Atlantis gets a permanent connection to the surface Bestiary. It'll stay an independent nation. Above water. And you'll never have to deal with eroding shields or running out of juice, ever again."

Naturally, I had zero authority to make this promise. And I was fairly certain I'd have a hell of a time trying to convince the higher-ups of the magical world that it was the right thing to do. But I had to make Beavis and Butthead an offer they couldn't refuse, or they'd never agree to help us out.

"Defeating Davin is impossible while he is connected to the stolen energy of your Bestiary." Apollo gave a defeated sigh. "It is tempting, but it is a fantasy. It cannot be done."

I brought out the big guns. "I don't work in fantasies. And we've got a way to reverse the spell that Davin used to hook himself up to our Bestiary. All we need is access to Kaya and we can undo all of this, without a single drop of blood spilled."

Thebian looked away, unable to meet my eyes. "Another nice idea, Finch, but we have already told you—we will not put Kaya at risk. We are her protectors, and that sounds like the opposite of protection."

I stared at him in disbelief. "Are you kidding me? I'm offering you a way to fix all this, with minimal effort on your part, and you're saying no? What the hell is wrong with you two? This is about all of Atlantis. Are you so narrow-minded that you can literally only think about your queen? I mean, what do you think she'd do if she were in her right mind? Don't you think she'd prioritize her queendom instead of herself? And, anyway, we're offering to *help* her, not hurt her!" The rant came pouring out of me, rapid-fire.

"I am sorry, Finch." Thebian kept his voice infuriatingly calm. "If we were caught aiding Davin's enemy, there would be severe retribution. If that happened, then we would not be able to defend Kaya *or* Atlantis. Our priority at present is solely the queen. Your priority, however... is your prerogative."

*Ah, that old chestnut.* They were passing the buck, wanting me to do all the hard work to get rid of Davin without getting their own hands dirty. I had to take a deep breath to stop myself from cracking their heads together. Every time I thought we were making progress with these punks, they turned around and went right back to being the groveling sidekicks they were when we first met them.

Nash put a hand on my shoulder. "Easy there."

"How can you expect me to be calm when they're refusing to lift a finger for the sake of *their* friggin' city?" I snapped. "They're expecting *us* to do the heavy lifting instead!"

Apollo cleared his throat. "I can at least show you where to find Davin." It was a weak consolation prize, but at least it was something. I mean, we had come here with the intention to find Davin, but it would've been so much simpler if they'd taken us to Kaya first.

"Wouldn't that put you in the line of fire?" I said coolly.

"In a way, but there is little direct risk to Kaya. However..." Apollo frowned, and I could've sworn I saw the seed of doubt bury itself in his mind.

"However?" Luke prompted, leaning in.

Apollo twisted his ring around his finger. "I will say this—if I come to the conclusion that granting you access to Kaya would be in her best interests, then I will do what I can to get you to her. I cannot say that I will come to that conclusion, but I will consider it at great length."

"Then there's one other thing you should hear." I laid my last card on the table. "We've got the means to break the love spell."

Apollo's mouth opened in surprise. "You do?"

"Did you think we'd come here empty-handed?" I retorted. "I might not have a pretty history with your queen, but she's the best ruler you've got. We can help her, but only if you help us."

It was only half a lie. We had the list of ingredients and a spell that would knock Kaya out so we could get her out of the city until we found a way to break the spell. It was a stalling tactic more than anything. After all, breaking the spell last time had required major cosmic intervention. And it just so happened that the Children of Chaos —who'd been a colossal pain in my ass this entire year—had chosen to vanish from the face of the earth. *Typical.* But Apollo and Thebian didn't need to know that. I had to tantalize them enough so they'd take the bait—a grimy leaf out of the Katherine playbook. But hey, desperate times, desperate measures, and all that jazz. Plus, if I'd been honest, they'd have shut me down in an instant. They wouldn't let Kaya leave this city, even if it meant having a better shot at getting that love spell off her.

"I will consider it," Apollo repeated. I heard the conflict in his voice, his features a mess of battling emotions. If that seed of doubt took root, maybe we'd find ourselves with an ally again. "For now, I can only show you Davin's location."

I huffed an exasperated sigh. "Then I guess we'll take what we can get and hope you come around."

"Very well. Follow me." Apollo looked to Thebian. "Return to the others and conjure some story as to why I have not come back. I do not want to arouse suspicion. This is already a grave risk."

Thebian dipped his head. "Be discreet. Be cautious."

"As ever," Apollo replied.

Thebian walked away and disappeared around the corner, leaving our quartet of misfits to trail Apollo to wherever Davin was hiding. He led us through a concealed entrance in the side of the palace, down into the silent cavern of a wine cellar. The scent of dust, an earthy, cork-like tang, and vinegary spillages filled my nostrils. I'd never been much of a sommelier, but this place had more bottles of hooch than I'd ever seen in my life. Racks and racks and racks of the stuff, gathering dust.

"We're not here to party," I joked halfheartedly.

"Neither am I." Apollo hurried up to an enormous barrel and fumbled around. A moment later, he pulled open a door embedded in the wooden planks.

*Well, well, well. Aren't we full of surprises?* Apollo seemed to be craftier than I'd given him credit for. Then again, he'd lived in this palace since he was a kid. Of course he knew all the secret ways in and out.

"This way." Apollo ushered us through the barrel door and into a stuffy, cramped passageway. Flickering torches illuminated the claustrophobic space as Apollo squeezed past us and led the group forward. I removed the Mimicry to conserve energy, figuring no one would see us down here. The stone walls deadened every sound until our own footsteps sounded like they were coming from somewhere else. An unnerving echo, but one I could deal with in order to get a one-on-one with Captain Sleazeball.

"Is this a bad time to tell you that I'm not fond of enclosed spaces?" Hector mumbled, clenching and unclenching his hands.

Luke coughed awkwardly. "Yeah, I'm not the biggest fan, either."

"But water bubbles are okay?" I gave them a pointed look.

Hector shrugged. "You can see out of a bubble."

"It is not much farther," Apollo assured us. Then again, he'd said that twenty minutes ago. He took a left down another passageway, and the stone walls opened out slightly to give us more breathing room. Honestly, we could've been halfway to the Arctic and I wouldn't have known. This labyrinth of narrow corridors gave away nothing about what rested above... or below, for that matter. But Apollo seemed to know where he was going.

*How come he didn't show us this network before?* Using these tunnels would've been far easier than the whole stealing-a-cart-and-pretending-to-be-Atlanteans scheme that we'd used last time. Maybe he'd rediscovered his old haunts after Davin's reign had begun. Or perhaps the entrance had been magically hexed, and he'd had some time to unpick it without sounding any alarms. Either way, I wanted to give him the benefit of the doubt, since he was putting himself in danger by helping us.

"Here." Apollo paused beside a small door in the side of the tunnel.

Black-tinged magic twisted out of him, without him having to lift a hand: that Sentient thing that all these Atlanteans had. Yet another reason for us not to start a war. It flowed into the lock, and a faint *click* followed.

He turned the handle and went in, guiding us down another tunnel. Wider this time, with the distant sound of music floating through the passageway. At the very end, he opened another door and showed us into a very familiar room. The thrones were a dead giveaway. But this wasn't exactly the discreet entrance that I'd been hoping to make. We were literally out in the open, in blatant view of the man himself—Davin, sitting atop his shiny new throne, with his zombified queen at his side. I whipped around in confusion to find Apollo locking the door behind us.

He strode forward until he drew level with me, and guards swarmed to seize us. "Your Majesties, I found these rebels wandering the palace grounds. I present them to you as a gift."

"You backstabbing, cowardly worm!" I shouted in his face.

He grabbed my arm roughly and leaned into my ear. "That wretched man has eyes and ears everywhere. I could not risk being branded a traitor."

"Well, congratulations—you are one!" I hissed, as a different guard hauled me away from Apollo and pretty much hurled me to the floor in front of Davin and Kaya, up on their royal dais.

Davin's applause ricocheted through the throne room as the others were manhandled before this smug audience. "Oh, Finch. You just can't stay away from me, can you?"

"Bite me!" I was too furious to muster a smarter comeback. Apollo had served us up on a silver platter. And, worst of all, I hadn't seen it coming. I should've smelled a rat when he used those tunnels. I *had* smelled a rat; I'd just ignored the stench.

"I knew you'd come back. The moment my beloved expelled you, I was already waiting for our reunion. I have been counting down the hours. Part of me wondered if you'd be sensible enough to give up, but you have never been one to slink silently into the background, have you?"

Davin smirked, loving every second. "You are just so woefully predictable."

*And you're woefully in over your head.* Davin was so used to being a few steps ahead that he hadn't noticed me catching up. I had what I wanted: an audience with him. It might not have played out the way I'd had in mind, but I was a born improviser. And this was my chance to tip the scales back in my favor.

## NINE

## Harley

All around, the ruins grumbled and groaned. We walked through the veins and capillaries that'd once connected the SDC's living, pulsing organs—the studies and libraries and bedrooms that we'd called ours. Masonry and metalwork, shredded paintings and broken ornaments, machinery and ordinary remnants of our lives were scattered across the crumbling corridors. And stone and dust kept drifting down on our heads—a sure sign that O'Halloran's attempts to hold up our coven's broken body were beginning to falter.

"Another one." Jacob covered his mouth with his hand.

Sticking out of a pile of brickwork lay the pale flesh of a limp arm, the rest of that poor soul buried beneath the fallen debris. It wasn't the first we'd seen during our progress through the unsteady hallways, and I doubted it would be the last. We had no way of knowing if they were magicals who'd been in the wrong place at the wrong time, or non-magicals who'd been minding their own business when our coven came crashing down on top of them. When all was said and done, we were the same. Death didn't differentiate.

"Don't look, Jacob." Wade maneuvered our youngest member away from the buried corpse and urged him on down the corridor. No one passed the deceased without a slight nod of respect.

"What if Lieutenant Wilson and her crew have been... uh... harmed?" Raffe whispered anxiously. "There's no way a couple of beasts didn't escape the Bestiary before Tobe went into berserker mode. What if that's why the colonel hasn't heard from them?"

I gulped quietly. "We've got to hope that's not the case." I didn't know this lieutenant or her people, but I didn't need to. If I had my way, no one else would die because of Davin's idiotic, self-centered, despicable actions.

"What's that?" Tatyana's eyes narrowed, her head tilting slightly.

"What?" I replied.

"Don't you hear that?" She closed her eyes, as if it would help her hear better.

I did the same, trying to drown out the sound of the building straining. A different sound shivered through, so subtle that I would've missed it if Tatyana hadn't pointed it out. It was the distinctive moan of someone in pain. A louder sound exploded through the corridor then, as if Raffe had summoned it—a blood-chilling growl.

"Looks like you were right, my friend." Kadar popped up for a moment. "It appears we have some free-range Purge beasts roaming the place. Another delightful hurdle for you all to scramble over in your customary ungainly fashion."

"Fire, dammit!" A barked order rattled through the gloom, coming from all directions, the sound distorted by the broken corridors. A burst of gunfire went off, deafening and terrifying, since we had no idea where it was coming from.

More shouts filled the air, and I managed to hear the faint scratch of an incoming radio transmission in a gap of eerie silence that didn't bode well: "Lieutenant Wilson, please respond! Lieutenant Wilson!" Nobody answered, the transmission fading into a nondescript hiss.

"Where are they?" Santana whirled, visibly trying to pinpoint the mayhem. "I can hear them like they're right next to me, but there's nothing ahead except more darkness. You'd think we'd be able to see the flashes from the guns if they were nearby."

I edged along the corridor and stopped. The hallway branched into three separate passageways. Not so strange, perhaps, but none of this looked familiar to me. And I knew the SDC like the back of my hand. I'd never seen this, though maybe we were in some part that I hadn't ventured into before.

"Does this look weird to anyone else?" I called.

The Rag Team gathered around me, observing the different corridors.

"It doesn't even look like the SDC," Tatyana said, confirming my worries. "I don't remember there being an intersection like this, all cramped together."

Kadar chuckled darkly. "You do understand that the coven is a magical construction, yes?"

"If you've got a point, make it!" I snapped.

His red eyes flashed in annoyance. "If you can't see it for yourself, then perhaps you are not as clever as you claim to be. I already knew that, of course." He puffed his chest. "The interdimensional bubble gave the coven order. It held the designed layout together as its architect intended. Take away the bubble… and you take away the order."

"So, things aren't where they're meant to be anymore?" Dylan furrowed his brow.

Kadar clapped slowly. "The meathead gets it! You know, you should all give him more credit. He's got this incredible way of turning the complex into something very simple."

Dylan scowled at the djinn. "Just because I play sports doesn't mean I haven't got a decent head on my shoulders."

"It's more about the brain inside that pretty head." Kadar grinned. "How many knocks can you take before you lose too many brain cells? I'd say you crossed that threshold long ago. If I were to scoop out what's in there, it would look like pudding. Smooth and undoubtedly delicious. Although, well done for comprehending my explanation, despite my use of some rather large words."

"Kadar, pack it in! Stop being an ass, or you'll get a time-out in the back of Raffe's mind until you learn to behave," Santana cut in.

Kadar pouted. "Spoilsport."

"Are you saying that the laws of magical physics got all skewed during the expulsion of the SDC?" I wanted it pure and simple.

Kadar eyed Santana as though expecting another telling-off. Instead, she gave him a nod, prompting him to continue. "Essentially, the entire structure crumpled and then expanded back out, thrown on top of the Fleet Science Center. Think of it like balling up a piece of paper and then smoothing it out again. It cannot be the same. Once-straight lines are now crooked and cracked, diverting where they did not before."

An idea leapt into my head. "Then that means there might be another way into the Bestiary that wasn't there before. Does it work like that?"

Kadar shrugged. "I don't see why not. However, you might as well have your eyes gouged out for all the good they will do you. You are blind down here. You no longer know the layout, because the map has been redrawn. You could follow one of these pathways for hours and not come any closer to your chosen destination."

"Unless we had some helpful *compas* who can drift through walls." Santana smiled, her eyes twinkling with excitement. "My Orishas can guide us and see if there's a new route to the Bestiary."

"Yes! Perfect!" I shared her enthusiasm. It was our only option, unless we wanted to traipse through this labyrinth for hours.

She dove right in, closing her eyes and calling upon the spirits that defined the history and culture of her people—practitioners of Santeria. Blue wisps shot out of her, spinning around in an excitable vortex. A thrum whistled down the corridor like wind squeezing through the gap of a window. Her eyes opened, and a silent message appeared to flit between her and the wisps, as they stopped twirling and hovered at attention. A moment later, they took off down each of the three paths with a high-pitched whoosh and disappeared through the stone walls, obeying Santana's instructions.

"How long do you think it'll take them to—" Jacob hadn't even finished his sentence before the Orishas whizzed back and bobbed in front of Santana.

A smile crept across her lips. "We have to take the right-hand corridor. They can get us in, but it's not going to be a walk in the park. We're talking soldiers, landslides, all kinds of nasty surprises."

"Honestly, I'd think I was having a mental breakdown if something was simple," I replied wryly, earning a rumble of agreement from the rest of the Rag Team.

We took the Orishas' lead and headed down the right-hand corridor. They fluttered in the air just ahead of Santana. Their bluish glow cast unsettling shapes on the corridor walls, making my heart jolt as it tricked my eyes into thinking ghosts were floating out of the masonry.

"Are you okay? You look a bit… frazzled," Wade whispered, placing a comforting hand on my back.

"I feel a bit frazzled." I gave a faint chuckle. "But it's nothing I can't handle." And it didn't help that more poor souls littered our journey, their lifeless forms jabbing at my heart. Magical or non-magical, they didn't deserve this.

Coming to another fork in the path, the Orishas chose the left-hand passage and soundly disappeared with a barely audible *poof*. At first, I didn't understand what was going on. And then it hit me. Literally. A soldier barreled out of the gloom and careened directly into my shoulder, knocking me into Wade's arms. He caught me, stopping me from toppling over, but the impact pushed him off balance, too. Dylan caught him, joining a panicked game of human dominoes.

"Run!" the soldier howled, pushing past us and disappearing into the corridor.

*What?* My head whipped back around as two more soldiers sprinted out of the gloom, guns poised and rattling off bullets into a hulking great shadow that thumped along behind them. Its feet slapped the stone—a sound I would've known anywhere. The incendiary flashes that peppered the darkness with each gunshot illuminated the beast intermittently, revealing the forever-ugly face of a gargoyle. Its fangs glinted wetly, slick with dark goop, while its black tongue slavered hungrily.

"Fire at it!" one of the soldiers screamed at us, as they sent more futile bullets into the beast. Normal artillery had zero effect on these things, which was part of why they were Katherine's favorites. Finch's too, albeit reluctantly. I thought of Murray and shuddered. Where was that oversized, leathery puppy, anyway? Part of me hoped, despite our love-hate relationship, that he was safely inside the Bestiary.

"What are you waiting for?!" The soldier glanced wild-eyed at us before hitting the gargoyle with more rounds. A moment later, his gun clicked hopelessly. He patted himself down for spare magazines, only to come up empty. The poor guy didn't realize that it could've been so much worse. Gargoyles were pack beasts, and they were only facing a solitary creature who must've escaped from the Bestiary when the SDC flopped out, just as Raffe had theorized. But for them, one was enough. A vision of true terror.

"Captain! Fire!" the first soldier pleaded, her face as white as a sheet.

I realized she was talking to me. Playing the part, I raised my gun, even though it would do no good. I knew what would, though. Beneath the pretense of being the captain, I started to draw my beast-controlling abilities into my chest, preparing to call out to the gargoyle with that resonance that caught them in my spell.

The gargoyle, however, chose that moment to lunge and sink its jaws into the soldier's arm. It shook its head violently, reminding me of an alligator trying to take down its prey.

"Obey me!" I focused my energies, delving into my affinities to add power to my beast control. "Obey me! Let that woman go!" My voice took on that peculiar tone, booming down the corridor. The gargoyle hesitated, its big eyes blinking in confusion as I slithered into its mind. "Let go!" I said, my chest squeezing and my throat scratching from the effort.

The gargoyle dropped the soldier and retreated a few paces, sitting obediently while it adjusted its leathery wings. I'd taken a risk, revealing that ability in front of two soldiers. But the woman who'd been chomped on had passed out, and the other couldn't do anything but stare at the gargoyle. So perhaps I'd gotten away with it.

A figure flew out of the darkness and landed on the gargoyle's back, tackling it to the ground with such ease that she might as well have been knocking down a twig. The woman must've been over six feet tall, with cropped black hair and a furious set of pale blue eyes. I was so overwhelmed by the sheer strength of this newcomer that I forgot to keep a hold of the connection between me and the gargoyle. With the bond severed, it jumped to its own defense. Its fangs snapped in the woman's face, while she struggled to pull an arm around its neck, trying to get it into a stranglehold.

*Who the heck* are *you?* She wore an all-black uniform, same as the other two, but that strength was anything but ordinary. If anything, I'd say it had a touch of the Herculean about it.

"You think you can have a chunk of me, you creep?" The woman grappled with the beast, but the gargoyle managed to get the upper hand. With a stomp of its foot that should've crushed her chest, it pinned her to the ground. Only, she writhed and thrashed as though it hadn't even hurt her. Another sign that we had some Chaos on our hands.

"Stand back!" I bellowed to the beast, now firmly in the rhythm of my beast control. "Come here, and don't move!"

The gargoyle blinked again, licking its lips and unleashing an irritated trill. Reluctantly, it stepped away from its potential dinner and padded over to where I stood. The other conscious soldier scrambled away from it, backing into the wall as though he could escape through it.

"You behave, and stick by my side—do you hear?" I commanded, patting the beast awkwardly on its slimy head. It trilled again, softer this time.

Immediately, the petrified soldier and the warrior on the ground trained their weapons on us. I guessed we did look a bit abnormal, with a gargoyle acting like a tamed dog beside me and the Orishas reemerging from Santana.

"What are you?" The woman got up, panting hard. The business end of her rifle winked at us. "And why are you wearing army uniforms? Are you the ones who did this?" She waggled the end of her gun at the ruins of the SDC.

"Wade? Can you do the honors?" We didn't have time for this nonsense, and Wade had a knack for mind-wiping. It was technically reserved for special circumstances these days, but I figured this fell under that umbrella. Even Ryann probably would've agreed with us on this one.

"Absolutely. The less they remember, the better." He lifted his palms in readiness, only for me to put a hand on his forearm, reconsidering.

"Maybe you could leave her." I nodded toward the woman. "I think there might be more there than meets the eye."

He made a sound of agreement and proceeded to mind-wipe the two other soldiers. Silvered magic threaded out of his hands and winged its way toward the unconscious bite victim on the ground and the terrified man who seemed as if he wanted to sink right into the stone and stay there for good. The tendrils sank into their skulls, unraveling the memories of what they'd seen.

"What the hell are you?!" the warrior woman shouted, her tone going up an octave. "What are you doing to them? Stop it now, or I'll shoot!"

"Everything is going to be all right," I replied calmly. I sensed a torrent of mixed emotions coming out of her: panic, terror, confusion, and the tiniest hint of intrigue. Whoever this woman was, she had no idea what gift she held in her possession. Fortunately, she'd bumped into the right people, even if she hadn't realized it yet.

*Welcome to the magical world...*

## TEN

## Harley

"What are you?" The woman's tone grew more frantic. "Are you Shapeshifters or something? Aliens mimicking us, so you can conquer Earth?"

I raised my hands in a gesture of peace. "How about you put the gun down so we can talk? We're not aliens. We're like you."

"Like me! I just watched you... speak to that thing!" She pointed the end of her gun at the gargoyle.

"And I just watched you tackle that thing to the floor like it was nothing." I kept my voice even, though I was ready to raise a shield if she got trigger happy. Panic could make people do stupid things. "I'm guessing it's not the first time you've done something like that. I bet you can run faster, hit harder, and last longer than your fellow soldiers, and you've always wondered why that is. No ordinary human could take down a gargoyle the way you just did."

"A *what*?" she spluttered.

I patted the creature on its head. "This is a gargoyle. And it's not your biggest fan right now, after you just knocked seven shades of crap out of it. Again, not something an ordinary human can do."

"Why do you keep saying that? What other kind is there?" Her voice trembled, though her grip stayed firm on the gun.

"Our kind. Your kind." I peered at the embroidered nametag on her Kevlar vest and swallowed a gasp of surprise. This was the very woman we were looking for. Lieutenant Wilson, in the flesh. "How about we start afresh, since this is a lot. I get it. I've been in your position, and I was just as freaked out. One day, you think the world is sane and normal, and the next you see gigantic ugly creatures coming out of nowhere and meet folks who can interact with them in ways that seem impossible." I flashed a look at Wade, recalling our first meeting in the parking lot of the casino. I hadn't known what I was then, either. And there'd been a gargoyle there, too, the first guidepost to my journey into Chaos.

He smiled back.

"What's your first name, Lieutenant Wilson?" I continued. "My name is Harley, and these are friends of mine: Wade, Santana, Raffe, Tatyana, Dylan, and Jacob. We'll help you, but you have to lower that gun and listen if you want answers."

The lieutenant glanced at her gun, then at us. "Why should I trust you?"

"Because we are what you are." I placed a hand over my heart. "You're not an ordinary human. Your strength, speed, and stamina aren't ordinary. There's magic in you, just as there's magic in us. I can tell you more, but I'm going to need your name first."

She shook her head defiantly. "There's nothing weird about me. I'm just naturally athletic."

"No, it's more than that, and I think you've always known it." I took a risk, hoping I was right. "Jacob, what can you sense in her?" With a resident Sensate in our midst, we didn't have to go through the rigmarole of a Reading to find out if she was a magical. We had express delivery.

Jacob frowned, scrutinizing her for a second. "It's an unusual vibe. I'd say she's half, at least."

"Half? Half *what*?" the lieutenant demanded.

"Half magical," I said simply.

Tatyana nodded, entering the conversation with her silky, soothing voice. "One of your parents must have secretly been a magical. That is not so strange in our world. Sometimes, it is better to keep the secret, in case of retribution, or persecution, or having someone point a gun in your face because you're different."

The lieutenant blanched, and the muzzle of her rifle dipped, her eyes staring intently into the distance as if memories were haunting her. "My father... He died when I was a kid, but he could... do this thing where he'd put his hands over soil and make a plant grow. I always wondered how he did it. He used to tell me he was a magician, and it was one of his tricks."

"He didn't lie," Tatyana murmured. "He was a magician, just not in the way you thought."

Santana nodded. "It sounds like he had Earth abilities."

"Like this." I figured showing was better than telling. I crouched to the ground and covered a spot with my hand. As I forced Earth into the stone, a stem unfurled, joined by tiny leaves and pale purple petals that spread around a yellow center.

The lieutenant staggered back. "That's it!"

"He was one of us, just as you are one of us." Tatyana had her charm offensive firing on all cylinders, and when she flipped that switch, there weren't many who could resist the welcome of her voice. "Now, how about that name?"

"Cal," she blurted out. "It's short for Calathea."

"That's a plant, right?" Dylan surprised us all with that nugget of wisdom.

She nodded slowly, as if the pieces were coming together. "He loved them. He used to use them for that trick, only he'd make ones with different patterns each time. I always wondered why he named me after that plant. I mean, you get your Roses and your Daisies and your Poppies, but they're for the pretty girls, not the tough ones. My mom said it was a family name, but I was never really convinced. Now I guess it makes a bit more sense, if they were part of my dad's... uh... abilities."

"So, you believe us? You don't think we're aliens anymore?" I gave a half-smile.

"Right now, I'm not sure what to think. But you just made a flower grow out of nothing. And if you can't trust your eyes, what can you trust?" She laughed nervously, and I felt her true emotions rippling off her in powerful waves. She was definitely scared, but there was an undercurrent of relief beneath her nerves, like a longtime mystery had just been solved.

"I understand that this is a lot to take in, but we need to get moving." I started forward, testing Cal. Her gun's muzzle continued to point downward—hopefully a sign that she wasn't going to shoot us all. Satisfied that we were making headway, I carried on down the corridor with her falling into step beside me, though, naturally, on the opposite side of our gargoyle pal.

"You didn't explain what you're doing here," she said as we walked. "You realize that impersonating a military officer is a crime, right? Or are you part of some secret division that I don't know about? I'd believe anything at the moment."

I decided to go with honesty. "This is our home… or, it was. Until it was attacked. Same as non-magicals, there are magicals out there who aren't good people. And the magical brand of evil comes with power that makes them incredibly dangerous. One of those miscreants did this."

"How?" Her eyes widened in horror.

"This place used to be concealed inside a bubble of sorts. Part of the world yet separate from it. A coven where magicals could feel safe and be surrounded by similar people." There was so much to tell her and not much time. This would have to be the abridged intro to the magical world. "This evil magical performed a spell that made the bubble burst and sent it crashing into the Fleet Science Center."

"You've just got spells lying around that can do that? Seems like a bad idea, if you ask me."

I shrugged. "There are spells for pretty much everything, and we don't have a lot of say in what can and can't be done. But there are differing levels of power and ability. The man who did this is extremely powerful."

"Can everyone do that flower trick? I'm not sure what use it would have, unless you were throwing an open house and you'd forgotten to pick up a bouquet, or you wanted to impress your gullible kid. But hey— I'm not judging." A ghost of a smile curved the corners of her lips.

"Each magical has a different set of abilities—usually at least one Elemental, but some have additional, specialized powers. Some can only do one thing, like conjuring a blast of Air or manipulating Water, while others can bring folks back from the dead." I wanted to gauge her reaction.

She gave a low whistle. "If you've got one of those hanging around, we could use them here."

*Ah, if only you knew...*

"What am I, then?" She side-eyed me. "Can you tell just by looking? Do I have a flashing sign over my head that you can all see, or something?"

I laughed softly. "No, but you can tell a lot by what a person displays. Judging by the way you tackled the gargoyle, I'd guess you were a Herculean."

"Like the Greek guy?" Her eyebrow lifted.

"That's where the name comes from, but it's just an umbrella term for magicals who are super strong, super fast, and have superhuman endurance." I glanced at Dylan. "He's one, too."

She grinned, warming up a bit. "Well, I could have told you that just by looking. No one's naturally that stacked. I would've guessed steroids, if you hadn't said this magic stuff existed, but he hasn't got the crazy look in his eyes."

"We tend to leave that to Raffe," Santana chimed in, giving him an affectionate nudge.

"Why, what's he? A maniac?" Cal snorted. When no one else laughed, she suddenly looked awkward.

"I'm... complicated," Raffe replied with a strained expression. I would've bet my life that Kadar was fighting for the spotlight so he could really freak Cal out. But Raffe had gotten better at corralling the djinn when letting him out would've been a disaster.

Cal sighed. "If I had a dime for all the dudes who said that, I'd have... like, a dollar. I don't get out much. But that's the beauty of soldiers—there's no nonsense. Everything's already out on the table, so to speak." She skidded to a halt. "Crap, what about my unit? What'll happen to them? You drew me in with all this magic talk, and now I'm losing my damn mind!"

Wade offered a reassuring smile. "They'll be fine. When they wake up, they'll know to leave, and they won't remember anything about our gargoyle friend here."

"Right, while I'm stuck with the memory of that thing's breath burning the hairs right out of my nostrils." Cal gave the gargoyle a disapproving glare, and it glared right back. "How come it's just walking along with you, like some kind of pet? I doubt it'd win any ribbons at Westminster, unless they add an 'ugly as sin' category."

I was about to answer when my phone rumbled in my pocket. Fishing it out, I saw the name flashing on the screen and felt a flicker of guilt. News would've spread through San Diego by now, even if the media outlets had no idea what they were reporting on. It looked as though the news had reached the Smiths.

"Hold that thought," I whispered to Cal before swiping to answer the call. "Hello?"

"Harley! Thank goodness!" Mrs. Smith shrieked through the receiver. "We heard about the science center on the news, and I tried to call Ryann, but she's not picking up. I'm about to have a heart attack! I called the police, and I called the hospitals, and I called the papers, but every single one put me onto a never-ending hold. Please, tell me you're okay!"

I took a breath. "Everyone is fine, I promise. Ryann is with Finch, and they're... uh... out of town on business, which is probably why you couldn't reach her. I was with them a few hours ago. They were nowhere near the Science Center when it got crushed. The interdimensional bubble failed, and the coven sort of... plopped out. I'm at the SDC now, trying my best to contain this hot mess."

"That's comforting to hear. If you're on the case, then I am certain it's in the best possible hands. Goodness, we were so worried! I had to stop Mr. Smith from marching down to the science center to find out what had happened." She paused. "Did you say the coven is out in the open?"

"I did. It's hard to explain, but I'll swing by to fill you in when I can."

I swore I heard her nod. "That would be great. I have cake samples in the fridge for you to try. And the florist just sent some designs for arrangements, so you could take a look at those and kill two birds with one stone. I can cook some of your favorites, and you can tell me everything over dinner."

She'd segued from catastrophe to cake samples so seamlessly it made my head hurt. Then again, she'd seen me contend with some insane things in the past. Maybe she figured this was nothing I couldn't handle. If only I had shared one iota of the confidence that she had in me.

"Uh... sure, but I don't know when I'll be able to come by. I'll have to keep you posted." I felt a strange tingle on the back of my neck and turned to find the entire Rag Team listening in on my conversation. Their grins made me wish the ground would open up and swallow me whole.

*Don't laugh!* I mouthed to Wade. *Or no cake!*

"I'll start a casserole now. That'll keep," Mrs. Smith said.

I pulled the phone away from my face and looked at the clock. "It's three o'clock in the morning! Go to bed. The casserole can wait." That might have been one of the strangest things I'd ever said, and I couldn't help but smile.

"I won't be able to sleep anyway. And I'll try Ryann and Finch again to see if I can get through." I realized that Mrs. Smith didn't yet know that Finch and Ryann were together in more ways than one, but that little morsel would have to wait. It was their news to share. But I knew she'd be thrilled. Heck, she'd probably start making a whole new batch of wedding cake samples.

"I have to get back to work now." I was eager to end the call before the

Rag Team erupted into hysterics. Besides, I felt silly for talking about casseroles while the coven was literally falling down. "I'll check in again soon. Please try and get some rest."

"You take care of yourself, Harley, and keep me in the loop." She sighed quietly, making me feel suddenly sad. "I always worry about you, even though I know you're more than capable. But what sort of mom would I be if I didn't fret over you a bit?"

I wanted to reach through the phone and hug the flip out of her. "You keep that casserole warm for me, okay?"

"Of course, sweetheart." It was our way of saying we loved each other. Mrs. Smith expressed affection with food and warmth, and I expressed it awkwardly. But I supposed it didn't matter what you said, as long as the feelings were right.

I swiped the button and slipped the phone back into my pocket, feeling totally disoriented. And now I had to face the clowns. I could feel them all preparing a tidal wave of jokes, but they didn't get to utter a single one before a fuzzy voice crackled through the radio attached to my vest.

"Captain Vermeer, come in. Over." The colonel had made good on his promise to check in on us, though it took me a second to remember that *I* was Captain Vermeer, according to my Kevlar vest.

Cal went pale, running an anxious hand through her short hair. "Crap... he's going to want answers." She peered down at me from her lofty height. "What do we tell him? He doesn't know what you... uh, *we* are, does he?"

I shook my head. "He has no clue. He sent us down here when you didn't respond, and since it was on our way, we decided to go with the flow." I reached for the radio button. "Let me handle this."

She nodded.

"This is Captain Vermeer, over." I waited for his reply.

"Any updates on Lieutenant Wilson and her team, over?" the colonel replied almost instantly.

I pushed the button. "That's a negative, over. We're in the belly of the ruins. No sign of them or any of the drones." I eyed a crashed drone at that exact moment, the propellers bent out of shape, the camera lens smashed. "So far, nothing to report. Permission to proceed? Over."

The colonel sighed into the radio. "Affirmative, over."

I let go of the radio and set my sights on the hallway up ahead. As if I needed his permission to carry on. He was on our turf, not the other way around. And we had a Bestiary to break into.

## ELEVEN

# Harley

Continuing down the labyrinth of unfamiliar and disorienting ex-hallways, with the wispy blue glow of the Orishas keeping us on the right path, I felt the weight of this entire disaster grow heavier with each step. It might have been the dust in the air, making every breath feel like inhaling molasses, or the unbearable heat that continued to increase. Or perhaps it was the glimpse of limbs in the rubble, which we had no choice but to ignore.

*Davin told Finch he didn't want to be like Katherine—but this feels a lot like her handiwork.* When death and destruction came knocking on a scale like this, it was hard not to draw parallels. Still, if Davin hadn't intended for this to happen, then what *had* he intended?

"Is anyone else about to melt?" Dylan complained. Because of his muscle mass, he'd gone from brisk stroll to sweaty mess.

"It must be whatever Tobe did to protect the Bestiary." Wade nodded into the darkness ahead. "You all saw that purple lightning—that much energy generates a heck of a lot of heat."

I took as deep a breath as the thick air would allow. "Then that means we're getting closer."

"No offense, but it feels like we're wandering in circles," Cal chimed in. "Maybe you know something I don't, but my unit and I were already lost when you appeared. There's no logical sense to the layout of this place."

I sighed. "There used to be."

Cal eyed me curiously.

"More magical stuff, but I don't want to confuse you right now." I kept right on walking. "I'll explain it once we've secured the Bestiary."

She hurried to catch up to me. "You keep mentioning that word, like I'm supposed to know what it means. What is the Bestiary, exactly?"

"Think of it like a power plant that keeps everything going," Wade explained.

Santana fidgeted with her necklace. "And if it goes down, you're going to see a lot more of these places falling into the real world. I don't need to tell you what a mess that'd make."

"Right." Cal dipped her chin to her chest, her face a mask of consternation. "So, pretty important?"

"About as important to the magical world as air, water, and cell service is." Santana kept scouring the debris for signs of Slinky. They'd developed a powerful bond since she'd purged him, and it wouldn't surprise me if they became Familiar and magical one day. They already had rudimentary telepathy, which usually meant that the feathered serpent came when she called. A stone of dread formed in the pit of my stomach, knowing that he still hadn't answered her.

*He'll be safe in the Bestiary. He has to be.* If he wasn't, the loss would destroy Santana.

Tense silence settled over the group as we continued on through the dilapidated maze. The heat and claustrophobia might have been increasing, but there was no other sign of the Bestiary yet. No purple lightning, no furious roars of a defending Beast Master, and no O'Halloran.

*Where are you?* The temptation to radio him grew more and more pressing, but I still couldn't risk any military folks eavesdropping on our conversation. If they sensed spies in their midst, they might bomb this place to smithereens just to eradicate the threat of something they didn't understand. That was the trouble with humans—fear of the unknown could make them rash, taking action to destroy rather than to learn.

We rounded the next corner, guided by the Orishas and their eerie whispering, when a blast of blinding light exploded about six inches shy of my face. I ducked down and raised my hands, leaping into a defensive mode. A wave of Air emerged from my palms and hurtled down the narrow corridor. I heard the guttural "ugh" of the Air making impact, knocking our attackers to the ground, but it was too dark to see who we were dealing with.

"Stand down!" Wade barked, lighting up a fireball and pushing it out into the hallway. It hovered in the air, casting a bronzed glow.

A handful of figures lay sprawled on the ground, a few of them trying to get back up. I still couldn't see their faces clearly, but they weren't dressed in the same military getup as the rest of us.

"Try that again, and ye'll feel the blunt end o' me shillelagh!" A sharp, familiar voice cut through the shadows. "I can crack a skull with one knock, ye mark me words!"

"Diarmuid! It's us!" I called, terrified at the thought of the tiny leprechaun sprinting through the gloom in our direction.

"Eh? Who's 'us' when they're at home?" Diarmuid replied.

I rolled my eyes. "The Rag Team!"

"Harley?" O'Halloran's voice entered the mix. "Is that you?"

Diarmuid snorted. "Trust a Merlin te knock their director on his arse."

"We came to find you," Wade answered. "It didn't seem like a good idea to radio you, with military crawling all over the place." He cast an apologetic look to Cal. "No offense intended."

"Only partially taken," she replied, peering into the darkness.

"Who's that?" O'Halloran appeared in the glow of the burning fireball. He lifted his brow and observed the new addition. He clocked the gargoyle at the same time, and his frown deepened.

"This is Lieutenant Cal Wilson," I said. "We found her on our way to you, wrestling this gargoyle that escaped the Bestiary. There are probably more creatures out there, but the layout has gone crazy, as I'm sure you're aware."

O'Halloran looked agitated. "Hopefully any loose beasts won't find a way through the perimeter. It's another reason the layout is messed up—to keep anything inside from getting out. A self-preservation protocol, of sorts." He dusted dirt from his pant legs. "We've been holding things together, mostly, but it hasn't been easy."

"Yeah, because explaining the presence of scary-ass creatures is going to be way harder than explaining how a massive building just dropped out of nowhere," Santana muttered sarcastically. "We might as well call it a two-for-one."

O'Halloran glanced between Cal and me. "How come you didn't... you know?"

He wanted to know why we hadn't wiped her mind. Since the Katherine debacle and the Battle of Elysium, mind-wiping had become a bit of a moral gray area. It always had been, honestly, but the ethical argument had hyped up after Katherine involved non-magicals in her ascent to godliness. But it was still our first and last line of defense against non-magical discovery, and we resorted to it a lot more than we let on. I tended to keep that from Ryann, knowing she'd be disappointed, but we had to protect ourselves.

"She's a magical," I said simply. "Well, half. Like I said, we found her beating the living daylights out of this gargoyle and put two and two together. Jacob confirmed it."

O'Halloran's other eyebrow twitched skyward. "And you didn't know, Lieutenant?"

Cal shrugged, acting more nonchalant than she felt. I had my Empathy on high alert, trained on her in case anything concerning popped up. "Nope. I'm a little bummed about it, to be honest. All my life, I thought I won stuff for my talent—races, competitions, military selection. Turns out, it was some kind of wizardry. Kind of feels like cheating, you know?"

"Have you managed to get close to the Bestiary?" Santana cut in, no doubt thinking of Slinky. "My Orishas led us here. I'm guessing you're looking for the same thing?"

O'Halloran nodded. "The back entrance is just up this hallway. We were almost done unpicking a barrier of hexes when you came around the corner and scared the crap out of us." He pointed to our disguises. "Apologies for that, by the way. I saw black uniforms and figured the army had finally reached us."

"Easy mistake to make," I assured him. "Now, how about we get into the Bestiary and try to reduce the collateral damage on this mess?"

O'Halloran unleashed a heavy exhale and turned around. "This way."

We followed him up another wrecked corridor, which branched into four more tunnels. A few security magicals, having recovered from my Air blast, had returned to their work on unpicking the hexes that protected the left-most tunnel. A forcefield shimmered faintly, fading more with every hex they unraveled. Finally, we had a way into the Bestiary.

"Is it done?" O'Halloran addressed his team.

One of the security magicals nodded as the faint glow of the forcefield vanished entirely. "The passageway is clear."

"Then let's not waste any more time." O'Halloran approached the tunnel tentatively, as though expecting a torrent of violent magical retribution to come crashing out of the passage. He took a few steps, and... nothing happened. I watched him breathe a sigh of relief as he beckoned us to follow him.

At the end of the corridor stood a doorway, which O'Halloran opened with the same hesitance as before. The door swung open to reveal a vast room, with that crackling purple lightning skimming over the domed roof of the Bestiary, lighting the place up like an eerie disco. I didn't recognize the room, but closed glass boxes held agitated wisps of black smoke. We were in the right place.

Aside from the deafening snap and fizz of the purple lightning, the Bestiary lay quiet. Much too quiet.

A shape shot out from between two glass boxes, heading straight for

Santana's throat. I almost hurled a fireball at the creature. Only when I saw the jeweled flash of bright feathers did I realize that Slinky had finally answered Santana's call. But something was definitely off. Slinky wrapped around Santana's shoulders and lashed out with his tongue, darting his head forward repeatedly, as if he were trying to tell us something.

"What is it, Slink?" Santana stroked the feathery critter, trying to calm him, but he kept slithering frantically over her skin.

An almighty roar, so loud it briefly drowned out the cacophony of the lightning, split the air. The double doors at the opposite end of the hall burst open, and a hulking Beast Master entered on all fours, wings tucked behind his back while his talons clacked on the marble floor. Tobe barreled straight for us, but he looked nothing like the Tobe I loved. This version had murder in his usually gentle amber eyes. His fangs flashed menacingly as he cleared the distance between us.

My hands went up. "Tobe, stop! It's us!"

He kept coming, with the strength to take down every last one of us if he wanted to. We had to act.

*I'm sorry, Tobe.* I hurled everything I had at him, dipping into my Darkness to fortify the impact. Trying to incapacitate Tobe was like trying to tranquilize a rhino with a cup of hot cocoa, so we needed everything we had. The strands of all four of my Elemental abilities intertwined and hit him with a vortex of sheer force that sent him skittering backward. His talons raked into the marble, gouging the stone with an ear-splitting screech.

All around me, magicals jumped into action. Wade flung a liquid torrent of Fire from his palms, the ten rings of his Esprit glowing green. Raffe had given the reins to Kadar, who was gearing up for a beast-on-beast battle royale. Dylan copied him—the two of them settling in to launch attacks of brute force on the Beast Master. Tatyana burned with fierce white light, calling on the spirit world, while Santana unleashed her Orishas. Cal didn't seem to know what to do. I felt her fear sparking off her in barbs of terror. I imagined all her military training had gone out the window the moment she'd seen a half-lion, half-bird charging us.

"Tobe!" O'Halloran boomed. He lashed out with a barricade of Air, while his other hand twisted rapidly, conjuring a forcefield of some kind. It knitted together right before our eyes, the powerful hexes weaving together like threads on a loom.

From his vantage point on O'Halloran's shoulder, Diarmuid leapt down and led the charge, with Kadar and Dylan sprinting after him. They made a bizarre squad, and Tobe didn't seem the least bit intimidated. Now that he'd regained his balance, the Beast Master let out another unholy roar and started right back up again, his fangs bared as he bore down on the approaching trio of djinn, Herculean, and leprechaun.

"What happened to him?" I shouted, between bursts of combined Elementals and a few lassoes of Telekinesis that Tobe simply swiped through with his talons. Until now, I'd had no idea he could do that. Then again, he was well over a millennium old; he was bound to have some tricks up his sleeve.

"It's that defensive spell I told you about," O'Halloran yelled back, still weaving frantically. "He probably doesn't even know what he's doing. Thanks to the spell, his singular purpose is to protect—he'll go right through all of us to make sure the Bestiary stays safe, unless we can stop him."

That was looking impossible. Dylan, Kadar, and Diarmuid launched themselves at him, bringing him to a temporary pause. Claws slashed and fangs snapped, while Tobe's skull took a battering from Diarmuid's legendary weapon. Kadar went for a slightly different approach, pouncing on Tobe's back like he was about to take on the worst rodeo of his life. Dylan attempted to wrestle Tobe to the ground, narrowly avoiding a bone-crushing bite that would've ended his life. I heard Tatyana scream, but Dylan managed to whip his head back in time. Still, he had the common sense to retreat and regroup before he tried again.

*Oh, Tobe...* If he had any idea what he was trying to do to his friends, he would never forgive himself.

"Diarmuid, Kadar! Get back!" O'Halloran commanded, and the two immediately obeyed.

Tobe saw his opportunity and started running, only to collide face-first with the intricately woven forcefield that O'Halloran had conjured. It spread over him like a net, dragging him to the marble floor and rendering him immobile. It reminded me of the way that we caught other Purge beasts, only there were no Entrapment Stones or Mason jars needed. Just O'Halloran and his desperate desire to save us.

Beneath the glowing net, Tobe thrashed and roared, but it was as though his feet were glued to the floor. He couldn't swipe at the strands, nor could he bite into them with his powerful jaws. I couldn't help feeling awful, seeing him like that—trapped and furious and completely out of his mind. This wasn't his fault. He'd thought he was doing the right thing, implementing a protocol to keep the Bestiary safe. He clearly hadn't realized it would end up like this.

"What do we do now?" Dylan padded back, mopping sweat off his brow.

O'Halloran was about to answer, when a strange pinging sound emerged from the director's pocket. Fumbling, he plucked out a flat silver disc, which flashed slowly.

"What's that?" Santana asked, stroking Slinky's feathers to comfort him. The poor thing had evidently been through a lot, trying to avoid the Beast Master.

O'Halloran waved his hand over the mirrored side, and Remington's face appeared. "An old method of communication, which uses similar tech to the mirrors that used to be in the Assembly Hall. I gave one of these to Remington before we left South Georgia Island, in case our radios were compromised."

*Huh... thanks for spreading the joy.* We could've used one of those to find O'Halloran in the first place, but perhaps there was a reason he hadn't handed out more. If it was like the mirrors in the Assembly Hall, then it only connected to one other mirror. I guessed these were a pair, able to call the other but nothing else.

"O'Halloran? Can you hear me?" Remington's voice came through loud and clear.

"I'm here," O'Halloran replied, visibly irritated by the timing of this interruption.

Remington grimaced on his side of the disc. "We've got a problem. One we were prepared for, but still." He glanced at something over his shoulder. "The Mage Council arrived on the shore about five minutes ago. The others are hidden in the Antarctic Coven, safe and sound, but I waited outside for the council. I'm pretending that I'm the only one still here, and everyone else has gone."

O'Halloran's eyes narrowed. "And what are they saying?"

"They're angry. Furious, in fact, that Harley and Finch went ahead and put plans in motion without running their missions by the Council first." He sounded nervous, his gaze continuously darting over his shoulder, as if he expected the councilors to appear behind him at any moment.

"Mage Council?" Cal whispered, finding her voice.

I sighed, peeved that *they* were peeved with my brother and me. "They're like local government officials. They're all about doing things by the book and love red tape. They'd rather sit on their asses and discuss options than actually do something. But they've got a vested interest to act, this time. I wouldn't be surprised if they declare war on the person who wrecked our coven and exposed the magical world."

Cal shuddered. "I know exactly the kind of people you mean."

"I'm going to have to call you back, Remington," O'Halloran announced. "We've managed to get Tobe under control, but we still have to find a way to break this spell he's put on himself. He's the only one who can move the Bestiary someplace safe, so you can understand the urgency here. After that, we'll have more time to deal with the SDC."

Remington nodded. "Understood. Stopping Davin is the priority here, before the Council decides to start something that we won't be able to prevent. Maybe Tobe will know a way to sever the connection with Davin. If not, at least we can rest assured that the outside world won't get into the Bestiary."

"I hope not, for all our sakes." O'Halloran finished the call and slipped the disc back into his pocket. His brief conversation was a stark reminder of how much we still had left on our plates.

And, once more, all roads led to Davin. He'd started this, and we had to finish it. One way or another. Preferably before anyone else died.

## TWELVE

## Finch

"You're calling *me* predictable? Have you taken a look in the mirror lately?" I snorted in Davin's direction. "But hey, maybe you're right. There's a part of me that can't help wanting to wipe smug, dangerous assholes off the face of the earth. And you've had the top spot ever since I dealt with my mother!"

Davin flinched slightly. I wouldn't have noticed if I hadn't been scrutinizing his every slimy move. "I have said this before, and I will say it again, since you appear to be hard of hearing. I am nothing like your mother. I do not intend to be anything like her, nor do I wish to pick up where she left off. For one, there are too many provisos when you step into godlike territory. Funny you should mention looking in a mirror—I enjoy my features too much to watch them flake away, unable to contain the power inside me."

"Is this going to be a long list?" I sniped, already sick of the sound of his voice. He talked a decent talk—I guessed as a result of his fancy London upbringing—but I called major BS.

His eyes narrowed. "Secondly, there is more than one way to skin a cat. In this day and age, celebrity is more akin to godliness than going to the trouble of becoming a Child of Chaos. Not to mention, it has a higher success rate." I sensed it *was* going to be a long list.

"What, so you're planning on becoming Insta-famous or something? Are you going to start a YouTube channel? Or maybe you're planning to release an album and break the internet?" I wasn't going to let him have the satisfaction of reeling off his diatribe without some choice interruptions.

His eyebrow arched. "I know you think you're amusing, but you're actually rather tiresome. Like a comedian who should've known their career was over a long time ago." He paced the floor, obviously losing his train of thought. Just as I'd hoped.

"I just think you're a little past your prime to win over the masses." I shot him a sour smile. Nash, Luke, and Hector were glaring daggers at me, no doubt wondering what the hell I thought I was doing. Riling Davin up might not have seemed like a good idea, but I knew what made him tick. And he hated being interrupted.

Davin stiffened. "I have a new philosophy now—one of benevolence and turning the other cheek."

"Are we talking in proverbs now? Are you sure being in that cell didn't turn you a little cuckoo?" I met his furious look as it fired my way. "Oh, and stealing power from the Bestiary and causing the SDC to explode into the real world isn't exactly what I'd call benevolent. You've made enemies out of people who were ambivalent before."

He bunched his hands into fists, visibly losing patience. "I did not intend for that to happen. An oversight in the hijacking spell, though at least it had the benefit of hitting you where it hurts the most. An unexpected perk."

"You call accidentally starting a war a *perk*?" I shot back.

"There will be no war," he replied confidently, getting back into his rhythm. "And the outside world will soon see that they have no cause to fear magicals. Indeed, my plan will be an antidote to this current panic and concern. I have ignited the fuse, yes, but I am also the one who will put it out. That is part and parcel of my ascent to victory and admiration."

I tugged against the grip of the guard who held me, but I might as well have tried to squirm my way out of Alcatraz. "See, you say this isn't a Katherine thing, but you're using her vocab. Ascent? Victory? I'm having déjà vu."

Davin grumbled in the back of his throat and stormed down the steps toward me. "I will be a hero, not a villain. Back in London, I was adored and revered as a bridge between this world and the afterlife. People flocked from all around to have me reconnect them with their loved ones, however temporarily."

I shook my head. "Nope, you conned them. You were a charlatan eager for their money, not their comfort. You might as well have had a cheap crystal ball and draped your front room in velvet, burning sage and playing ethereal music, for all the good you did them."

"It did not start out that way. I did find their loved ones, until the toll became too great." He stopped a few feet from where I stood. "Nevertheless, I was lauded in magical and non-magical circles alike. I was welcomed at every soiree and party, never without an invite to some function or another, with friends in the highest of places. Katherine took that from me, because I was foolish enough to believe in her goal. She tarnished my good name. I will seize it back for the benefit of everyone... including myself."

I almost spat at him, but I wasn't *that* crass. "You tarnished your own damn name. You followed power, and it bit you in the ass. Don't blame anyone else, and don't try some feeble sob story on me. I have about as much sympathy for you as a tortoise that keeps chucking itself onto its back."

"You may change your mind." Davin smiled secretively. "If I am the tortoise, that seems quite fitting. Slow and steady wins the race, if I remember correctly."

"That depends how smart the hare is." I held my ground.

He laughed to himself. "Not smart enough to stay away. But there's hope for you yet, if... you'd care to join me in my endeavors. I know you to be resourceful—you've proven that over and over, throughout your time in Atlantis, and even before. I've almost rooted for you a few times, but never outwardly. That would have gone against this little dynamic that we have going."

"As if I need you as a cheerleader," I snarled at him, sick of his stupid face and his endless knack for rising to the top, like pond scum. "I wouldn't join you, even if we were the last two people on earth and you had all the water."

"People change." Davin shrugged. "You may realize that I do have all the water, and when you are thirsty enough, you will swallow your pride and come to my side."

I wrinkled up my nose in disgust. "I'd never be that desperate." My gaze flitted to Kaya, who watched from the dais with a sort of absent interest. Her eyes had this faraway, glazed look. "Kaya, I know you're in there somewhere. You're stronger than this. You knew something was wrong when we had the love spell put on us—you have to know that this is all kinds of messed up!"

She blinked slowly. "How can love be 'messed up'? It is the most wondrous gift a mortal being can receive, and I am blessed to have it."

I rolled my eyes. "Davin tried to kill you! He's using you—you know he is! Somewhere, deep inside that clever head of yours, you have to know that this is wrong."

"No, Finch." Her voice hardened. "*You* are wrong, misjudging Davin so outrageously. He is the promised hero, and he shall bring comfort to the world. You have only to listen to him, and you will understand."

*You're all the way under, aren't you?* I hated seeing her all zombified and stupid like this. She was a *queen*. She was supposed to be leading her people, but Davin had swooped in and stolen the crown for himself, just like he'd stolen power from the Bestiary to fuel his weird hero complex. And I couldn't see a way to get through to her, especially now that Apollo had corralled us right into Davin's hand like a painfully loyal sheepdog. If he'd just had some common friggin' sense, we might've been able to get Kaya out of here and start breaking the spell Davin had put on her. I flashed Apollo a pointed look. *I hope you're pleased with yourself, assclown. You've doomed her, and the rest of us, too.*

Davin smirked. "A noble attempt, but you could try and appeal to her until your tongue fell out, and it would do no good. She is mine, now and forever." He leaned closer, lowering his voice to a whisper. "I fueled this particular love spell with a little something extra, but you already knew that, didn't you?"

"You're a snake."

He shrugged. "Better a snake than a mouse." He resumed his polite distance. "Now, even if you don't intend to aid me voluntarily, I'm not about to waste you as a valuable resource. You are to get the president of the United Covens of America to sign an executive order absolving me of all crimes and granting me full immunity and autonomy within magical society."

I laughed coldly. "Would you like a side of unicorn with that?"

He ignored me. "That immunity and autonomy will encompass Atlantis. I have had a lot of time to think about this, and I have grown fond of this city. The people here already love and admire me for giving them back their loved ones. They understand what I am trying to do, and as such, they have become the cornerstone of my greater plan—an example that the wider world will be able to appreciate."

I recalled the listless faces I'd seen in the palace gardens. He evidently thought resurrection was an infallible gift that everyone could enjoy, but he'd gotten it wrong.

"Bringing the dead back from the afterlife isn't all candy canes and fanfares, Davin." I hit him with a serious look. "The living might be happy about it, but have you stopped to consider how the formerly dead feel? I saw some of them out there, and they looked... vulnerable and sad. The living got back what they lost, sure, but you've also taken something from the people who died. You've taken their peace, their reward, and put back all the pain they might've felt in life. The afterlife isn't a punishment. It's light, and comfort, and total serenity, where loved ones get to reunite once their mortal days are done. You should know that better than anyone. I mean, how many times have you looked beyond the veil, huh?"

Davin shifted awkwardly, a hint of confusion drifting across his face. "It is what they want."

"No, it's what they *think* they want—the living, and some of those who crossed over." I forced him to hold my gaze. "There'll be people who are thrilled to be back, but you can't just stick everyone under the same banner and hope for the best. And you're planning on making this permanent, right? You're going to just keep everyone alive, indefinitely?"

"Yes," he said uncertainly.

"Then you're robbing them of something incredible!" I said. "I don't know who or what made the afterlife, but it was created to be a safe haven for departed souls. We are *supposed* to die, so we can reach that place." I nodded down at my body. "These forms are temporary shells so we can make memories and fall in love and know what a strawberry tastes like and how a winter wind feels on your face and see sunsets and sunrises. We take all those experiences with us to the afterlife. We don't lose anything. But if you keep everyone alive, then we *will* lose, more than you know."

I would've wholeheartedly agreed with the idea that physical existence was superior, had I not seen my father's spirit. He was happy, reunited with Hester in a world beyond our living comprehension. He had regrets, of course, and he wished he'd had longer to spend with me, but all that pain would've vanished again once he returned to the afterlife. And that was worth everything, even the suffering of those left behind, because— when the time came—there'd be understanding. We'd see the people we'd lost, and everything would be all right. To be dragged back from that... I could only imagine the agony.

"You are beginning to sound like the rest of the magical community," Davin spat, evidently taking my words as a personal slight against his Necromancy. "There is nothing unnatural or immoral about what I can do. I have chosen to live, time and time and time again, and I would not exchange that for anything."

"That's *your* decision!" I barked. "There are people who don't want that. Look outside and tell me that everyone you brought back is happy about it. Ask them. I dare you!"

Davin puffed out his chest. "I see joy and relief, and I hear their gratitude. To them, my power is the most precious and beautiful in existence. Everyone will soon see that, including those without magic. I won't discriminate with my gift."

"Davin, for once in your life, listen to me! Get this through that pig head of yours—even if they're happy now, life is exhausting!" My own exasperation took over. "No one can go on and on and on, indefinitely, and they shouldn't. It takes the beauty and urgency out of things. Why learn a language, or the piano, or bother to get out of bed, when there'll be a million tomorrows? And you'd better believe it'll open up the world to some crazy stuff—people will kill people, knowing that it doesn't matter. Violent crime will soar."

"You won't convince me that I'm on the wrong path, Finch, so I suggest you save your breath." His eyes glinted with annoyance, but I was on a roll here. I wouldn't shut up until he forced me to.

"Look, I've had my fair share of loss. It hurts, and it's gut-wrenching, and grief is… brutal. There's no other word for it. But it's part of being human. It's an experience that bonds people and makes people share stories and makes them understand the value of how short our time on this planet really is. *That* is vital!" I kept right on going. "Take death away, and we might be fine for a while, but then people will get tired of slogging through every day. Not to mention the fact that there isn't room for everyone. You'll put a strain on this planet that'll implode the whole damn thing! And I doubt you can bring a planet back from the dead, no matter how much power you steal."

Earth was already struggling. Add back in everyone who'd died, and the damage would be irreversible. We were meant to pass on. What was more, we had somewhere to go. If people knew for certain that there was an afterlife, then they wouldn't be afraid anymore. But I knew Davin wouldn't be interested in that—telling everyone the truth instead of resurrecting the dead. That wouldn't have made him a hero, just a messenger.

"Then what of the lives that were lost when the SDC crushed the Fleet Science Center? It was an accident, after all. Are you content to let them remain dead, while you stand on your moral high ground? Or are there extenuating circumstances for your ethics?" Davin shifted the crown on his head as he spoke to me. "After all, friends of yours were resurrected. I don't see you making any complaints about that."

I gritted my teeth. "They were given a second chance, but Alton didn't grant them eternal life. There's a difference!"

"I don't see one." Davin smiled smugly. "I notice you haven't answered me about those who died at the Fleet Science Center and, indeed, the SDC."

"Their blood is on your hands." I sighed, feeling backed into a morality corner. "I'd rather you hadn't 'accidentally' killed them, but it's not my place to decide who lives and who dies. It's not yours, either."

"Ah, but it is my place. And I'd rather not have blood on my hands. Those days are behind me, so I intend to wash them clean." Davin lifted his hand and snapped his fingers.

A blinding spark of purple light flashed where his fingers met, as if the friction of his skin had ignited it. His eyes lit with that same violet glow as a sheen of energy rippled over his body and pulsed out into the world, detonating from the center of his chest. The swell of it pushed past me on its outward trajectory, the air rushing from my lungs as though I'd taken a plunge back into the freezing ocean beyond the city. All around me— inside me—I sensed an impossible energy oozing off him. The Bestiary's energy. And he'd turned himself into the lightning rod.

"What did you do?" Nash wheezed, clearly feeling the same effect.

Davin held out his arms, grinning manically. "I fixed it. The people who died are alive again. These hands are clean of their blood."

*Oh, you've got to be kidding me!* The world had gained a reverse Thanos. And I didn't even want to think about the army's reaction to a bunch of dead people coming back to life before their very eyes. Wriggling body bags, people emerging from rubble, and screaming… so much screaming. It'd be mayhem. He hadn't fixed anything; he'd just made it worse, and way weirder than it already was.

"If you think this will prevent war, you're wrong." Nash struggled against the guard who held him. "The non-magicals will descend into panic, and that'll make them trigger-happy. They might even turn their guns on the people you think you've helped. Is that what you want? Killing people twice?"

Davin shrugged. "That won't happen, not once they understand the miracle that I'm offering. Perhaps you have less faith in this world than I do." He gestured up to the glass dome ceiling. "I had hoped to make a slower case for myself, with more measured steps, but I'm beginning to like starting off with a bang. Yes… it's better that we're already emerging into the open. I will lead everyone into a brave new world, where magicals and non-magicals live in harmony, uniting them with the one thing everyone can agree on—life prevailing. The whole world will love me for it."

"That's why you stole all that additional energy, isn't it?" Luke made a show of staring in disbelief, even though we'd already discussed the possibility. Likely, he wanted to hear Davin admit it before he'd properly believe it. "So you can snap your fingers and bring people back, without it taking that same toll on you that it did before."

*Someone's been listening to the Librarian.* He'd picked up a thing or two about gaining information, though I doubted Davin would be hesitant to reveal the truth. He liked to crow about his triumphs.

"Bingo!" Davin strolled back to the dais and bent to place a kiss on Kaya's forehead. "I couldn't very well perform mass resurrections with the power I was naturally given. It would kill me, and the amulet would have to keep bringing me back. Even if it didn't kill me, I'd be thrown into a fit of Purges again and again. Nobody wants that."

"You might fool the non-magical world with these tricks, but you won't pull the wool over the magical world's eyes. They know you. They know your name." Nash clenched his jaw, a muscle twitching. "They won't trust you, no matter what."

Davin waved his hand at Nash. "You underestimate the influence of grief and loss, Nash. Soon, they will all see that I am the answer to their prayers. I will be adored again." He ran a finger around the inside of his collar, perhaps feeling more heat than he was letting on. "I have made mistakes, and I wish I could undo them, but they have brought me here. This is my destiny—to be the lynchpin in this pivotal shift in the history of the world. It is my chance to redeem my past transgressions and make the name of Davin Doncaster great once more!"

The sheer magnitude of his delusions formed a rock of dread in the pit of my stomach. He literally couldn't see past the celebrity and adoration that he desperately wanted. And that made him more dangerous than he'd ever been. Terror shivered through me like an electrical current. I couldn't even begin to imagine what this would do to the world. Actually... I could, and that made it all the more horrifying.

"This isn't washing your hands clean or getting redemption. This is you adding a planet's blood to your hands." I couldn't hide my desperation this time. He had to listen to me. He had to. But he wasn't paying attention anymore.

"Finch, you will get the president to sign off on the executive order." He brought his gaze back down, filled with his own pomp and circumstance. "I do not want a war. However, I will march into one if I must. If it should come to that, I have no doubt that the non-magicals and the magicals will kill one another, and I will be there to resurrect them. They will be so grateful for their second chance that they will swear loyalty to me. I will be their savior. No matter how this plays out, I win."

A choice expletive lurked on the tip of my tongue. His delusion and messiah complex would be harder to unravel than whatever he'd done to Kaya.

"The way this proceeds will be entirely up to you, Finch," Davin continued. "If you bring back the president's executive order, then you will prevent war. If you refuse, then so be it."

I didn't know all that much about executive orders. Harley had spoken about them a few times, but I hadn't really been listening. Shame on me, I know, but shop talk got really boring, really fast. And I had the attention span of a gnat. From what I could vaguely recall, executive orders were absolute and irreversible in the magical world. Once one was signed, it acted like a spell, becoming embedded in Chaos so that it couldn't be undone.

*The higher-ups aren't going to like this...* But what choice did I have, with World War III on the table? Davin had wedged me into a doozy of a Catch-22. And I needed more time to wriggle out of it. Agreeing to go to the president might well be the opportunity I needed.

I was about to answer when a strange sensation prickled through me like a thousand miniature hedgehogs racing up my veins—a cosmic vibration. It wasn't the Bestiary energy, but it *did* feel familiar. And there was only one person who had that kind of connection with me.

*Erebus?* I sent the thought out into the ether. We'd never had a telepathic link, but stranger things had happened.

Silence echoed back. Nevertheless, that prickly sensation stayed with me. He was still hanging around somewhere, in his Chaos form, and I was still technically under contract. But with his otherworld out of bounds thanks to the djinn liberation, I had no clue where he actually was. Children of Chaos couldn't just wander around the mortal world as they pleased, which meant he had to be... where? I could've used his help right about now.

"Oh, I should add..." Davin drew my attention back. "If you don't go through with this, or if you attempt to deceive me in any way, I will do to other covens what I have done, albeit unintentionally, to the SDC. Let that be your motivation. I know you enjoy playing your little games at my expense, but don't test me on this."

"You wouldn't do that," Luke interjected. "That'd only freak people out and make them less inclined to trust the magical world."

Davin chuckled. "Wrong. With death no longer an obstacle, I can make amends for anything."

Once more, I believed him. He'd do whatever it took to get what he wanted. However, even with the stolen Bestiary power, he wouldn't be able to achieve the freedom and tranquility he desired. Nobody wanted to follow a leader into war. He had to get the president's blessing, or he'd start off his Atlantis reign on the wrong foot, and his name would continue to be associated with all things bad. He wanted his slate wiped clean. He wanted Necromancy to be valued and protected, not shunned and prohibited. And I was his steppingstone.

I took a shallow breath, already hating the words that were about to slip out of my mouth. "Fine. I'll do it."

"Not so fast." Davin smirked, in his usual style of assholery. "I have one more condition."

*Why am I not surprised?* To be honest, I was shocked he hadn't rolled out a scroll of provisos as long as my arm, just for the dramatic value. He loved a show. Especially when he had the spotlight.

"I want Melody and Jacob to join my service," he said, and Luke looked about ready to blow. "I could use a Librarian and a Portal Opener to help facilitate the great plans that I have for the future of Atlantis." He spoke loudly, so that all the Atlanteans in the room would hear him. Even Kaya mustered a faint, drugged smile, her eyes twinkling but empty.

She'd have been able to help us, but I didn't know how to reach her, being in this predicament that Apollo had forced us into. Apollo had known about our intention to break the love spell on her, yet... he hadn't breathed a word to King Blobfish. I cast him a curious look, which he quickly turned away from. Would he tell the king, or would he keep that little morsel to himself? After all, Apollo's loyalty forever lay with Kaya—not Davin.

"No!" Luke snarled, trying to wrench free of his guard. "You can't have her!"

"Not now," I hissed at him. "Stay quiet."

Luke gaped at me like I'd asked him to put on a dress and do the hula. "Are you serious? Did you hear him?"

"I heard him," I whispered and tried to convey what I was feeling through a look. I had no intention of letting Davin have Melody, but we needed to prioritize—one thing at a time. "Stay quiet. For now."

Luke fell silent, but I could tell it was taking every ounce of willpower he had not to lash out again. Even Nash looked ready to commit extreme violence on Davin, if he'd been able to break free of the guard who held him back.

Davin sneered, turning up his nose like he'd smelled something rancid. His own bullcrap, probably. "You have twenty-four hours to make this happen before I release another coven out into the open." Without another word, he waved his hand, and one of those terrifying white portals—the kind that had already given us a watery brush with death— tore open above our heads.

I held my breath on instinct as the portal dragged Luke, Nash, and me out into the world beyond. My heart sank as I caught sight of Hector, untouched by the portal. Two more guards seized him and clapped him in a neck Cuff. Davin obviously had other plans for our ally. And, as we whizzed out of there, there was nothing we could do to help him.

*One problem at a time...* That was the only way we were going to make a dent in this mountain of trouble.

## THIRTEEN

## Finch

The portal spat us out in the water, irritatingly close to the shore. A few more feet and we'd have landed on dry land. But that wasn't Davin's style. He'd gotten in one last jab, to make sure we were well and truly pissed off. And after we'd only just gotten dry, too.

But at least he hadn't hurled us out where the rocks would've dashed our brains into jelly, so I supposed that was a small mercy. Not that he'd suddenly decided to be altruistic. He needed me in one piece. Still, the ocean current was strong, and the water swarmed around me. It slipped up my nostrils and stung my eyes. Scrabbling wildly, I clawed my way to the surface. I burst through with a splash and gasped a shivering breath, hearing Nash and Luke doing the same nearby.

"He c-couldn't have j-just opened that p-portal on land, c-could he?" Luke stammered, bobbing in the cold.

"Of course not. That'd be doing us a favor," I replied sourly, forcing myself to swim to shore. The other two followed, the faint splash of our movements cutting through the whistle of the Antarctic winds.

Nash hauled himself out first, shaking off like Huntress. "Biggest piece of work I've ever come across, and totally nuts to go with it." He wrung out his plaid shirt, the fabric creasing. "Not that Apollo is exactly in my good graces either. What came over him?" His teeth chattered, but he otherwise made a decent show of being unaffected by the cold.

"I'm wondering that myself." I didn't even bother to try and take the edge off my sopping wet everything. "He said he was worried about Davin having ears everywhere, but then he didn't pipe up about our plans for Kaya. So, either he's lying, or he's being selective with the truth."

"Isn't that the same thing?" Nash cocked his head.

I shrugged. "All I know is, we've got two fewer allies than we had before. If Apollo sold us out to Davin, you can bet your ass Thebian knew about it."

Luke raised a finger. "Three less, if you count Hector. I saw them take him away."

"Yeah, last thing I saw before Davin shot us through that portal," I confirmed grimly.

"Poor guy. He must've known what could happen, but he came with us anyway." Nash seemed particularly disheartened by Hector's absence. He'd known Hector better than the rest of us, and Hector had gotten him out of a couple of scrapes. It was only natural that Nash felt slightly responsible.

Luke shivered violently. "What d-do you think they're g-going to do to him?"

I glanced out at the distant horizon, where Atlantis shimmered faintly. "They're going to take him to that prison, and he won't see the light of day again unless we get him out."

"Then we will," Nash insisted.

"I agree, but that's not the highest priority right now. We've got to get to El Presidente before Davin drops another coven out into the open." I sounded unfeeling, but I did feel bad about getting Hector entangled in this. He'd escaped, found us, and helped us out only to get captured again. But I had to stop dwelling on things I couldn't control, or I'd end up detouring on side quests and never achieve our main goal. No distractions. I had to be colder and more detached to have a hope of fixing the mess Davin was intent on making. I had to be more like Doncaster himself. More like the Finch I used to be.

"You're f-forgetting what he said about M-Melody." Luke wrapped his arms around himself in a vain attempt to keep out the biting cold. Standing out here was an open invitation for pneumonia or hypothermia, and we couldn't risk that on top of everything else.

"I haven't forgotten, but we have to put that on the backburner also. At least until we get this executive order out of the way." I trudged up the rocky shore to the derelict whaling station, not stopping until I reached the abandoned house that doubled as the entrance to the Antarctic Coven.

"Put Melody on the b-backburner?" Luke sounded horrified. "And what if h-he comes for her, huh? What then?"

I sighed, feeling like a top-class jerk. "Then we deal with it. But he's got a lot going on, and hopefully that means Melody is safe for the time being. So we need to keep our eyes on the prize and get to the president before our twenty-four hours run out."

Nash grabbed me by the shoulder. "You're not actually going through with this, are you?"

Meeting his gaze, I saw confusion and caution in his eyes. He was a man of morals, the "never back down" school of thought. I liked to think my own moral compass pointed north more than it pointed anywhere else, but Davin had put us in an impossible situation. War or no war. Obedience or exposure. And that meant behaving in a way that didn't feel remotely good or comfortable. Surely, Nash got that. He was always the first person to say it: if there was another option besides war, then you had to take it.

I stayed calm. "We don't have a choice. I'm hoping it won't get as far as Davin wants, but we need to buy ourselves some time; otherwise, we only have twenty-four hours. If we haven't come up with a different plan by then, then I have to do what I can to stop another coven from suffering the same fate as the SDC. More importantly, we have to make sure that this doesn't turn our world into a battleground."

Ignoring the blaze of Nash and Luke's bemused stares, I whispered the entry spell that Melody had taught us: *Reserare Ianuam,* a variation on the opening spells we were used to, if a bit of a tongue-twister. But it worked. The doorway opened into the hunting-lodge chic coven, and a sight that made my blood run cold.

Ryann lay helplessly on one of the polar bear rugs. Melody, Krieger, Huntress, and Remington stood around her, their heads snapping toward us as we entered. I didn't waste time. If there was one thing I couldn't detach myself from, it was Ryann. I sprinted for her and dropped to my knees at her side, resisting the urge to scoop her into my arms. If she'd had a fall or some other injury, moving her would be bad.

"What's wrong with her?" I looked at Krieger, my throat tight.

He scratched the back of his head awkwardly. "We don't know."

"Melody?" I moved on, desperate for answers.

"Same here. I have zilch," she replied apologetically. "She passed out about half an hour ago."

Krieger nodded. "She has been through a lot in the last twenty-four hours, and we mustn't forget that she is non-magical. I imagine that her body has been under so much strain that she simply couldn't handle it anymore, and her brain is doing its part to try and help her recover."

"Lux possessing her won't have helped," Melody added. "When Lux left her behind, it would've taken an enormous toll on her. This is likely just a protective measure, as Krieger said, so that her body can repair itself."

Luke hurried to Melody's side and wrapped her in a tight hug that left her looking confused. I didn't know if he would tell her what Davin had said, but I had to leave that to him. I had Ryann to worry about.

"What happened in Atlantis?" Remington skimmed right over the fact that my girlfriend was lying unconscious on the floor, dealing with the fallout of having a Child of Chaos take the reins from her.

*I'd be a hypocrite if I called him out on it.* He was doing the same thing as me—prioritizing. It was only then that I remembered the looming threat of the California Mage Council. Had they arrived already?

"Davin spun us around, naturally." I pulled Ryann into my arms and stroked her hair, watching the subtle flicker of her eyes beneath her eyelids. "But not before making some demands. You know how he is."

Remington flashed a concerned look over his shoulder, at a door in the far wall of the main room, just below a rather fetching art installation of—you guessed it—whalebone. "I should warn you. Delegates from the California Mage Council are here. I tried to keep them talking on the shore, but then Melody came running out to tell me about Ryann. I'm sorry, I had to let them in."

"Do they know about Ovid?"

Remington shook his head. "No. I've managed to keep him hidden. He's still downstairs being watched over by Saskia and the security magicals that O'Halloran left us."

"Who are we dealing with?" I kept hold of Ryann, to try and center myself.

"Rasmus Erikson, Jasper Gold, Selena Cortez, and Mairead O'Malley." Remington's expression didn't exactly invite confidence. I didn't know any of those names from my elbow, but I got the feeling they'd know who I was. I didn't mean to sound arrogant, but a lot of people knew my name after the Battle of Elysium, and even if they didn't, I tended to get on people's radars. Not always for the right reasons.

"Then we should face the music. Davin had some interesting things to say, which I'm guessing these folks are going to want to hear." I mustered up some motivation and lay Ryann back on the ground, planting a gentle kiss on her forehead. After bombarding Nash with frantic licks, Huntress immediately padded over and rested her head on Ryann's chest, a gesture that I appreciated. It took everything I had to tear myself away from the woman I loved, but I had to get my ass in gear and my mind focused on the task at hand.

"Tell me you've kept them plied with Antarctic grog or something," I muttered, as Remington and I made our way to the creepy doorway. I took one look back at the rest of the group. Nash sat on the floor beside Huntress and Melody, scratching the perpetual itch between her ears. Luke and Melody spoke in low voices, their foreheads practically touching. And Krieger stood around looking uncomfortable, making a show of sifting through his medical bag to avoid looking like a quack.

Remington gave a tight chuckle. "Tea and coffee seemed more appropriate."

"I don't know, they might not get out the torches and pitchforks if they're three sheets to the wind." I cast him a glance of camaraderie. "They're annoyed with me, right? Give me a number on the Santana Catemaco scale of pissed off so I can brace myself."

Remington put his hand on the door handle. "A solid eight."

"Perfect." I rolled my eyes, mentally preparing for the onslaught.

He swung the door open. At a circular table of polished mahogany, sitting in wingback armchairs of dark-green leather that wouldn't have looked out of place in a fancy boardroom, were the four horsemen of the Apocalypse. Or rather, the horsemen and horsewomen. I immediately spotted Mairead O'Malley. That curly shock of bright ginger hair, and the constellations of freckles on her sun-averse skin, could only belong to someone of Irish heritage. Selena Cortez had to be the woman beside her, with a wavy mane of dark hair and an intense set of hazel eyes. As for the men, both of them had brown hair and wore severe expressions. One had blue eyes, and one had green, and they were both in their thirties, at a guess. In fact, all of them were pretty young, per the direction that the magical authorities had gone after Katherine-gate.

"Councilors." I strode into the room with more swagger than I felt.

Mairead drummed her fingertips on the table. "Ah, the famous Finch Merlin finally decided te show up, did he?"

"As you probably know, I've been otherwise engaged." I sat on one of the ostentatious armchairs, while Remington took the seat beside mine. We were a veritable round table of animosity and wariness. *What a treat.*

"You've been to Atlantis and back in such a short span of time?" one of the dudes said dubiously.

"It's amazing what you can get done when you put your mind to it... and avoid all the red tape." I needed to rein in the sass, or it'd wind up getting me into a whole world of trouble. "Sorry, I don't think I know you."

The man put out his hand, and I shook it limply. "I'm Jasper Gold."

"Which makes you Rasmus Erikson?" I nodded to the other guy, who just nodded back. *The silent type, huh?*

Selena Cortez chimed in, making me squirm in my seat under the glower of her sharp eyes. "As you can imagine, we're less than impressed by your actions, and your sister's. There is a reason for every rule that we have, yet you seem determined to flout them. It might have worked in your favor in the past, but things are different now."

I raised my hands in mock surrender. "No offense, but I'm going to stop you there. If this is supposed to be a tribunal, then you're wasting valuable time. Time that we don't have." Before any of them could protest, I relayed everything that had just happened with Davin. Once I finished, you could've heard a pin drop.

"Well, smack me arse and call me Siobhan—that's a fair tale you've got to tell." Mairead let out a low whistle. "Of course, you told him where he could stick his executive order, aye? That's why you got yerself booted out of there?"

I shook my head, wishing it could've been that simple. "I had to say yes, to buy time. He's threatened to expose more covens if I don't, and that'll mean more casualties, which'll just lead to more of his oh-so-benevolent resurrections. We won't be able to keep it contained." I didn't recognize the voice coming out of my mouth. When had I gotten so matter-of-fact?

"No." Rasmus finally spoke. A sole word that echoed volumes.

Jasper leaned forward, elbows resting on the mahogany. "I agree. It is a flat 'no' from all of us, Finch, which you ought to have anticipated. We have our rules, as Selena said. And we will not negotiate with the likes of

Davin Doncaster. He may threaten as he pleases, but it won't change our stance."

Frankly, I had anticipated this response, which was why I'd hoped to skirt around the Mage Council entirely. I understood their point of view. Hell, I shared it. But this was far from black and white.

"And you'd risk the magical world getting exposed? More than it already has been?" I prompted.

Selena cleared her throat. "From what you've said, it sounds as though Davin already intends to expose the magical world. It would be insanity for us to give him carte blanche to do what he likes with his Necromancy."

"Which we aren't doing, so you know." Mairead sat back in her chair and folded her arms across her chest. "That eejit isn't getting no executive order out of anyone, and that's the end o' that. He's not going to be king neither, so he might as well chuck that crown o' his into the ocean, for all the good it'll do him."

Remington sighed and offered me a sympathetic look. "Davin can't stand up to the entire magical community, Finch, no matter how powerful he thinks he is."

"Exactly." Another contribution from Rasmus.

"We will send our armies to destroy him if that's what it comes down to." Selena eyed me closely. "If I'm not mistaken, you were the one who called us to arms in the first place, through your sister. Everyone's ready to mobilize. They just need the go-ahead. We can't, and we won't, let a terrorist dictate how we live."

Mairead cut in. "Aye, and I'm not sure you understand what an executive order means for the magical world. If it gets issued, it's binding. Davin will be protected from every magical down to the last soldier. He'll be untouchable!"

"Oh, I understand." I splayed my hands on the table, staring at the ridges between my knuckles. "But you need to take a second to listen to what you're saying. I don't want Davin getting any more power than he already has, but I also don't want this world—magical and non-magical alike—getting roped into a war we can't win. You say Davin can't stand up to the entire magical community. I agree, but a million plus descendants of the Primus Anglicus, who Davin has eating out of the palm of his hand, can. A war with Davin means a war with Atlantis."

Selena's intense eyes bugged out of her head. "A million plus?"

"And that's not all. Davin will sit back and watch everybody die. He told me as much himself, and I believe him." I clenched my hands until the knuckles cracked. "And when everyone who fought is gone, he'll pick and choose who to bring back, selecting those who'll serve and adore him. The non-magicals will buy into his hero complex, too—you can stake everything you own on it. If other covens are revealed, it'll ramp up their fear of the unknown. Who do you think they'll side with if that happens? The magicals who want to stay secret and couldn't do anything about the deaths of innocent people, or a charming Necromancer who can bring everyone back *and* is willing to shine a spotlight on magic?"

Rasmus stared intently. "From Chaos comes order. If we surrender to Davin, it will be worse in the long run than a war now. All the Mage Councils are in agreement."

I felt duped. "Wait, so you already knew what you were going to say before you came here, no matter what?"

"We did," Rasmus replied plainly.

"Then why did you bother to come at all?" My hopes of getting through to them were slipping through my fingers like sand. "I've met with Davin. I've heard everything he has to say, and I believe every word. He *will* play the long game if he has to. And if you're willing to watch millions die because of a war you've sanctioned, then all of you need to take a long, hard look at yourselves. However we do this, he wins. That's the crux of it. So we need to play a little fast and loose with the rules in order to stand a chance of stopping him."

Jasper tutted with disapproval. "We don't play fast and loose with rules, Finch."

"Then you're dooming us all to misery and failure, and you'll be bowing to King Doncaster before you know it." I didn't try to hide the irritation in my voice. This was why I hated the establishment. They were so set in their ways that they couldn't see the wood for the trees. We could've sat here for hours, going over the same thing, and it wouldn't have made a difference.

A knock at the door offered a brief reprieve, as Melody poked her head in. "Ryann is awake, Finch. She's asking for you."

I pushed back my chair and gave a sarcastic bow. "If you'll excuse me for a few minutes. We can carry on beating this dead horse when I get back, though I hope you'll give it some thought while I'm gone." I didn't wait for their reply as I exited, heading straight for the woman I loved. I really couldn't detach my mind when it came to her, especially when I was getting absolutely nowhere with the councilors.

She sat up against one of the threadbare sofas, blinking in a daze. Krieger had her hooked up to a breathing contraption, condensation steaming up the mouthpiece. I guessed he'd thought she needed a bit of extra help. Meanwhile, Huntress had her head in Ryann's lap, while Ryann stroked the pupper absently. I figured that was a good sign.

"Hey, you." I knelt at her side and pulled her to me. She gingerly put her arm around my waist and leaned her head against my shoulder. Another good sign that the lights were on and someone *was* home. "What happened to you, huh? How do you feel?"

She lifted a hand to her mouthpiece and pulled it down to her chin. Krieger flashed her a concerned look, but he didn't move to replace it. "Tired," she mumbled.

I held her tighter. "You've had a Child of Chaos camping out inside you for weeks. That's bound to leave you a little fatigued."

She chuckled faintly. "I thought you went to Atlantis."

"Been there, done that. Already got kicked out." I kissed her hair, inhaling the intoxicating, strawberry-vanilla scent I loved so much. That was true wizardry—how she smelled like that, even when she hadn't been within ten feet of anything that bore the scent since before we entered Atlantis.

"Is it bad?" She peered up at me with sad eyes.

I shrugged and buried my nose in her hair. "It's going to get worse."

"Can I do anything?"

I hugged her as close as I dared, careful of the breathing apparatus. "No, you just focus on getting better. That'll make it easier for me, knowing you're here and safe and on the road to recovery." I kissed her hair again, trying to keep my focus on her. But my stupid mind was already wandering.

*They won't let me leave of my own free will, knowing that I disagree with them and the task that Davin gave me.* Lucky for me, they didn't know this coven well. Nobody did. But there had to be another way out. Even if there wasn't a physical doorway that'd get me the heck out of here...

Absentmindedly stroking Ryann's hair, I closed my thoughts off to everything other than Erebus. I needed that son of a nutcracker to hear me. I couldn't have done this before, but I had some new Chaos in my blood now. Perhaps that would be enough to bridge the divide between where I was and wherever Chaos had dumped Erebus.

*I need to get out of this coven, Erebus, and I need you to help me reach the president.* No answer came back, but I kept up my inner monologue, just in case he happened to be listening. *It's the only way to stop a war. I'm not going to let Davin have his pick of who's left so he can create a dominion full of adoring fans. You know him better than I do. I need you now. I need you to help me with this. I can't stop him on my own.*

Maybe, after all this time, I'd finally lost the plot. Or maybe I was just desperate, trying anything and everything to figure out a solution. I hated admitting that I needed Erebus, but I hoped that a bit of flattery might get me somewhere. If he could even hear me. I had to believe that he could, for the sake of my sanity. Otherwise, all of this would've seemed ten times more hopeless.

*Erebus? I know you care what happens to this world. I know your father cares, though he can't intervene directly. But Chaos stepped in when Katherine tried to seize global control. Maybe we were flung together back then for a reason —so we could stop it from happening again. Or am I going crazy?* I sighed wearily. *Is this even reaching you? Ground control to Major Erebus? Honestly,*

*I'm usually the one trying to get you to shut up, and now I'm desperate for you to say something! I know you're out there. Please, Erebus... help us.*

I stilled as a pulse of those spiky hedgehogs prickled through my veins again. Another cosmic vibration.

*Erebus? Is that you?*

## FOURTEEN

# Harley

I approached Tobe with caution, digging into my Darkness to try and feed my influence into his mind.

"Listen to me." My voice resonated painfully in my chest and raked up my throat, as though I'd swallowed barbed wire. I knew the sensation all too well. My beast control was in full force, but that didn't mean it'd work on Tobe. He wasn't a simple gargoyle that could be easily manipulated. "Tobe, we need you to calm—"

He lunged forward beneath the magical net, his fangs flashing as they sliced the glowing threads apart. The spell that O'Halloran had conjured was no match for his Chaos-born might. I staggered back as his golden eyes burned right into my soul, filled with such rage and menace that I could've been staring into the eyes of a ravenous tiger. His talons scraped the marble.

"Harley! Get back!" Santana sent her Orishas to protect me, the wisps spinning around me in a violent fury, creating a vortex. I needed to move, but his eyes held me frozen to the spot. Fight or flight had gone out the window. All I could do was stare at this *creature* who would kill me in a heartbeat. Whatever defense mechanism he'd triggered, it'd reduced him to a mindless monster.

Tobe growled, the vibrations shuddering underfoot. "If you touch the Bestiary, I will tear you to shreds, as I have torn your meager spell to shreds."

*So, he can still speak...* Perhaps that meant he hadn't descended entirely into monster territory. Although, I'd met plenty of monsters who loved the sound of their own voice. Davin, for one. Nevertheless, hearing Tobe's voice, however distorted and gruff, gave me hope that we could get him back.

"Tobe, this isn't you," I pleaded. "This is magic talking."

He roared so loudly that I covered my ears, terrified they would start to bleed. "Leave while you still can!" Suddenly, he wheeled around and sprinted for the doorway he'd burst through, vanishing into the wider Bestiary beyond. But my intact state was another promising sign that, deep down, he remembered who we were and didn't actually want to rip us to pieces.

"This is bad, isn't it?" I stared after Tobe.

O'Halloran sighed. "Worse than I thought."

"Aye, ye don't say?" Diarmuid tapped his foot impatiently on O'Halloran's shoulder, having returned to his usual spot. "You really had him purring like a kit, didn't ye?"

"I was certain that spell would work on him." O'Halloran fidgeted with the buttons of his shirt, looking devastated. The director and the Beast Master had developed a friendship during O'Halloran's tenure. Sometimes I'd find O'Halloran with Tobe in the Bestiary, the two of them shooting the breeze for no reason besides enjoying each other's company.

"Do you have any idea what this defense mode entails? Did he ever mention how he created it?" Wade asked, clearly trying to bring some calm back to the group. My heart still pounded in my chest after facing down one of the world's most powerful Purge beasts. He might've been my sweet and kind friend, but that didn't diminish his ancient strength.

O'Halloran shook his head. "All I know is that it was triggered when the Bestiary got hijacked. I don't even know how to start with getting him back on track." He looked stressed. I didn't need Empathy to feel his nerves.

"The Bestiary is still functional, and no other covens have been exposed." I straightened up, using my agent voice. "We've got to take that as a positive."

Kadar tutted under his breath. "You really need to learn to look beyond the surface of things." He closed his eyes, and black smoke billowed from his scarlet skin. "The Bestiary might seem functional, but it's unstable. You can feel it. It's all wrong. Energies are spiking where they shouldn't be, and it won't be long before the army picks up on that. They'll think this place is nuclear."

"I worried that might be the case." O'Halloran walked up to the nearest glass box, but the creature inside didn't appear. Black wisps continued to whirl within. "Tobe likely believes that the best way to protect the Bestiary, and to deal with the instability, is to keep everyone out. Including us."

"Well, that's not going to cut it. You heard Kadar—the Bestiary isn't safe here, under the scrutiny of the army." I refused to back down or be chided by a djinn. "I don't know if I can use my beast control on Tobe. I tried, but it didn't have enough time to take hold. If I tried again, and could somehow give myself more time, then maybe I can get through to him."

Slinky lashed his tongue against Santana's cheek, prompting her to speak. "He's our *amigo*. He may be a Purge beast, but he's got a conscience."

"And a thousand years of wisdom and countless tricks up his sleeve," Tatyana added quietly. "He's not going to give in without a fight, and we might not have what it takes to control him."

Santana stroked Slinky's scales. "But we'll try, if it means getting you the extra time you need to see if you can work your magic on him. We'll help however we can."

"A worthy adversary, to say the least." Kadar grinned, his eyes glinting.

I kept my chin up. "We'll need him if we're going to move this Bestiary someplace else. And if that means bringing a fight to him and exhausting every possible option we have, then so be it. He's in there; we just need to get him out."

"What if the fight spills outside the Bestiary?" Tatyana sounded troubled. "No offense, Lieutenant, but your people won't hesitate to shoot indiscriminately if things get any stranger."

Cal nodded slowly. "I wish I could disagree with you."

"I can deal with that," O'Halloran cut in. "If I can borrow Santana and Tatyana, then we should be able to build a protective shield around the Bestiary."

"A forcefield around a forcefield." Santana tilted her head in thought. "That might be mad enough to work. If it gives us a chance to avoid the business end of the army, I'll try anything." She made light of it, but I sensed anxiety lurking beneath, like a riptide tugging at her insides.

O'Halloran gave me a nod. "Take the others and do what you can to help Tobe. I know I don't need to say it, but you're going to have to work together." He directed a firm gaze toward Cal. After all, she hadn't shown much enthusiasm about being one of us. But she understood teamwork, and she'd seen a wild Tobe. I prayed that'd be enough for her to work alongside us.

"I'm not giving up until he's back to normal." I meant it.

"You might not have a choice if you can't get him back to normal. Not that there's anything normal about this," Cal muttered under her breath. Sharp terror pulsed from her. She'd seen a heck of a lot in a short time, and now she was entering the dragon's den with us. Of course she was terrified.

With Wade, Raffe, Dylan, and a reluctant Cal following me, I headed for the doorway that Tobe had disappeared through. Pushing it open, I half expected it to be hexed within an inch of its life. The kind of stuff that'd throw us back or vaporize us, or something a little more creative, like turning us into slugs. But nothing happened.

*Odd...*

Cautiously, I stepped through into the next hall with the others flanking me. As the second door closed behind us, a strange sound bristled through the silence beyond. A weird... fizzing. Squinting into the gloom, I noticed a peculiar light winging its way between the glass boxes that littered the space. It moved fast, heading right for us.

"Fireballs!" Wade yelled, diving forward with Fire of his own.

As though he'd unleashed their power, the approaching fireballs picked up speed and rocketed through the air, melding together until we were facing an entire wall of licking flames. Tobe had set booby traps, and this was almost certainly just the first one.

Cal's eyes widened in fear as she ran for the door behind us. She yanked on the handle, but it wouldn't budge. "We're trapped!"

*Crap...* The wall of fire was seconds from incinerating us.

"Take cover!" I grabbed Cal by the arm and hauled her to one of the nearby glass boxes. Like a police officer with an arrestee, I shoved her head down and made sure it didn't go past the top edge of the box before crouching in beside her. The others did the same, seeking refuge behind the beast boxes.

The wall of fire rolled past and slammed into the wall behind us, skimming over our hiding places. But the heat... it felt as though I'd gotten stuck in an incinerator with no way out. Sweat beaded on my forehead, and my lungs struggled with the burning air, but at least we'd escaped the first wave.

I peered around the side of the box to find more of that strange light hovering in the distance. Fiery sentinels, waiting for us to emerge so they could launch another attack.

"Kadar, can you make it through to the far door?" I nodded to another doorway in the distance, which led deeper into the Bestiary. This room was smaller than the last, and I doubted Tobe would be lingering here. I guessed he was letting the booby traps do the hard work, in the hopes of deterring us.

Raffe's skin turned that familiar shade of red. "I am a djinn. What do you take me for? A Sylph?"

"Is that a yes?" I shot back.

He sighed dramatically. "Yes, but the rest of you will be charming piles of ash if you follow."

"When the next wave hits, you get to that far door and wait for us. If there are any hexes on it, unpick them before we get there." I turned my attention to Dylan and Wade. "We need to use our combined Elemental powers, or we won't make it through. Can you blend your Fire and Earth to create a tornado around us?"

Wade nodded. "No problem, but we need to get close together."

"Okay, let's huddle." I reached for Cal, but she shrugged me off.

"I'm fine. You don't need to hold my hand." She got up of her own accord, her bravery shining through.

Wade, Dylan, Cal, and I gathered in the open aisle while Kadar prepared for the sprint of his life. No sooner had we emerged from our hiding places than another glowing light started toward us. Wade and Dylan worked fast, their palms up as they streamed their Chaos together. Wade forged the tornado of Fire first, while Dylan ducked down and pushed his hands against the Bestiary floor. Rocks bubbled up from the ground, getting caught in the vortex and creating a spinning wall of stone and fire to protect us. I did my part next, threading Telekinesis and Air into the cyclone to fortify the elemental walls. I'd have doused the entire fire wall in Water, but there wasn't any around.

"Will this work?" Cal whispered, a sheen of sweat glowing on her forehead. That was the trouble with hiding inside a Fire tornado. The heat was close to unbearable.

"Let's hope so." I tried to spot Kadar outside the spinning walls, but it was too dense to see anything at all. The real reason I'd asked Kadar to go on ahead. "Kadar! Go! And direct us toward you! We're flying blind here!"

"You best hope I'm not in the mood for barbecue!" he shouted back. But Raffe would keep him in check... *right?* Shaking off any doubts, I heard his footsteps thudding on the marble as he ran.

A few moments later, his voice bellowed through the hall. "Go straight forward!"

We moved in unison, all of us keeping our individual threads of magic pouring into the whirlwind. I heard the angry rush of the next fire wall getting closer, and the heat turned up a notch as it passed us by. A few rocks skittered into the center, carried by the momentum of the fire wall. But it didn't breach our barrier.

"You're veering left! I said straight!" Kadar yelled.

Adjusting our position, we kept walking. Dylan, Wade, and I breathed heavily. Fire wall after fire wall collided with the tornado, until it genuinely felt as though we were roasting inside an oven. Cal staggered along with us, staying close to my side.

She dragged her sleeve across her forehead. "I'm never complaining about San Diego summers again."

I smiled. "It can't be much farther now."

"You're almost here!" Kadar shouted.

One last barrage smacked into us, sending a big chunk of rock skimming past Wade's head. He ducked just in time, and our eyes met in a mutual expression of fear.

"That was close," he said with a strained chuckle.

I nodded. "I like your head attached to your body, so let's pick up the pace."

We practically ran the last few yards, guided by Kadar's voice.

"Stop!" he instructed. "The fire is gone."

"Gone?" I barked back.

"Yes. It has simply vanished. You must have made it past whatever sensors that pussycat has implemented," Kadar replied.

Tentatively, I released my Chaos, while Dylan and Wade did the same. Sure enough, the glowing sentinels had gone, leaving nothing but silence and a doorway ahead of us. I looked back into the hall, where the walls now bore black streaks from the scorching they'd endured. The glass boxes weren't much better, all of them stained with a gray frost that obscured anything inside.

"I'm guessing there's going to be more of this." Cal's shoulders sagged.

Wade inhaled deeply, mopping the sweat off his face. "That's probably a safe bet."

"Any hexes?" I looked at Kadar, but the djinn shook his head.

"I couldn't sense any."

Knowing that we had no other choice, I stepped up to the doorway and pushed it open. A larger, wider hall lay beyond. Pushing forward, I tried not to flinch as the door closed behind us. I already knew there was no way back, after Cal had tried to reopen the last door. No... we had to go through.

I took another step into the hall, and the temperature took a nosedive. A chill washed over my skin, turning the sweat icy cold. Breathing nervously, I watched the puffs of condensation expelled by my lips.

"I shouldn't have said anything about the heat," Cal murmured. "I knew I shouldn't have said anything about the heat."

Wade lit up a fireball and held it close to Cal. "This should take the edge off."

I held out my palms to copy him, and the lights went out, plunging us into darkness. A sliver of moonlight glanced in through the dome over-head, along with the eerie purple tinge of the lightning that was keeping this place protected from the army. But it wasn't a whole lot to see by, and we didn't know what might be lurking in the shadows.

I strained my ears, listening for any unusual sounds. I heard the thrum of a helicopter outside. And... something else. A whispering that brought all the baby hairs on the back of my neck to attention. Dark shadows slithered from the passageways between the Bestiary boxes. It was only then that I noticed that something was very wrong with this setup. The whole layout of the Bestiary was different. The glass boxes weren't glass anymore. Their panels had turned into mirrors, reflecting the shadows that emerged, until it looked like there were thousands of them.

Yeah, we were literally playing a game of smoke and mirrors now.

## FIFTEEN

# Harley

"What the heck is that?" Cal grabbed my arm and jabbed a finger at the shadows.

My heart pulsed in my throat. "Our next challenge."

"How do we fight *shadows*?" Dylan gaped at them, his fists up and ready to punch them into submission. Probably not the way to defeat these things. I imagined he'd just end up going twelve rounds with air.

"That's something we have to figure out." Wade looked pale in the moonlight.

"Speaking of figuring things out…" I swallowed my panic, battling for calm. "Which band did you prefer for the reception? I liked that swing band—King Louie, maybe—but I could go for the ceilidh band too, in honor of your Irish heritage. We could have two, if you wanted."

Wade stared at me like I'd lost my mind. "You're talking about wedding bands *now*?"

"If we don't make it out, I want to know that we came to a decision about it. A marriage can succeed or fail based on its choice of band. That's what Mrs. Smith told me, and she seems to know a heck of a lot about it." I tried to ignore the shadows drawing closer. "I could've asked you about flower arrangements, but then you'd probably just ask these things to finish you off."

He laughed in nervous disbelief. "I think a ceilidh could be fun, but I did like the swing band, too. What did Mrs. Smith think?"

"She liked both, so I guess we're going to have to shell out for two bands." The shadows edged nearer, and the Bestiary temperature descended to sub-zero. My teeth chattered as I tried to keep my optimism up.

"Wait, you two are getting hitched?" Cal nodded in approval. "Nice catch, Harley."

I hugged myself for warmth. "Thanks. I like to think so."

Our idle chatter died as the sinister shadows finally started their attack. One swept forward and barreled into Dylan, hurling him full force into one of the mirrored boxes. He slammed into it with a thud, a wheezing gasp escaping his throat as he struggled to his feet. Whatever these things were, they were powerful and angry. I felt their rage bubbling over like a boiling pot. An army of miniature poltergeists, with us in their sights.

My palms shot up, and I sent a torrent of Fire at them, only for it to sail straight through their wispy forms.

Another surged forward and grasped Wade with its shadowy fronds, picking him up like rag doll and lifting him into the air. He fought back, lashing out with fireball after fireball, but it made no difference. After reaching enough height, the shadow dropped him like a stone.

"Wade!" I cried out, sending out a cushion of Air to catch him. I was a second too slow, since I could barely see. The cushion caught most of him, but his head bounced off the floor. As I deflated the bubble, he didn't get up.

I ran for him, ducking and weaving around the shadows. "Wade? Wade, can you hear me?" I put a finger under his nose to check whether he was still breathing. Sweet, sweet air puffed onto my skin. He was alive, just unconscious.

A shadow approached, forcing me to wrap a lasso of Telekinesis around Wade and drag him back to the rest of the group. Dylan had recovered and rejoined the others. But this wasn't going to be easy. And I had no clue where to start with these things. If we couldn't use Elemental magic, then we were pretty much screwed.

"What are they?" Dylan panted.

Kadar shuddered, more smoke billowing from his body. "Djinn wraiths."

"Pardon?" Cal looked like her head might explode, though she hadn't so much as flinched at the sight of Raffe turning into a red demon-looking creature.

"Bottled spirits of former djinn masters. Ancient souls, from the days when djinn were stuffed into lamps and forced into servitude by greedy individuals. This was our revenge." He waved a hand to indicate the encroaching line of shadows. "The djinn trapped their masters' souls and stuffed *them* into bottles instead during one of our more successful rebellions. After that, people rarely dared to turn us into genies."

"But why would Tobe have them?" Dylan asked, echoing my own thoughts.

Kadar shrugged. "Who knows what that kitten has hidden away in this place? They are a useful resource for occasions such as this. As with poltergeists, their rage makes them powerful, and we can't so much as touch them."

"Then how do we fight them?" Dylan was a man of brute force, and if that wasn't going to work, then that put at least two of us out of the running: Cal and Dylan. The Herculean contingent.

Kadar eyed me pointedly. "This is one for the Light."

I understood immediately. "Everyone, charge up your Elemental abilities and hit these bastards where it hurts. I'll do the rest."

"What do you mean?" Cal demanded, clearly freaked out.

"You'll see."

Dylan raised his palms. A moment later, twisting ropes of Telekinesis shot out. Taking a deep breath, I delved into my Light affinity and let strands of it gather in my palms. With a push that made my muscles burn,

I sent the tendrils out toward Dylan's Telekinesis, letting the Light infiltrate the thrumming magic. The ropes shimmered with a warm, golden glow as they spiraled up and attempted to snag the wispy forms around them.

To my relief, one of the ropes managed to ensnare a shadow. The spirit struggled as the ropes went into python mode, wrapping around the wraith until the entire thing burst into a flurry of red sparks that drifted to the ground like sparkly scarlet snow.

"Yes!" Dylan punched the air. "How do you like that?"

Raffe switched places with Kadar and unleashed a wave of Fire. Dylan set to work forging more ropes while I fed their various forces with touches of Light. In between, I launched attacks of my own, using everything in my arsenal: Telekinesis, Fire, Air, and Earth. Each burned with a new brightness, now tinged with Light. Ordinary brute force might not have worked, but magical brute force seemed to be doing the trick.

"How do I help?" Cal asked, her tone strangled. "I'm trained for combat, not this! I don't know how to cast magic!"

"Just hang back." I sensed her getting overwhelmed. A storm of mixed emotions raged inside her, and her eyes had that spooked expression of a horse about to bolt.

I hit another shadow with Light-infused Telekinesis, squeezing the creature until it exploded into a flurry of those red sparks. With my other hand, I fed Light into Raffe and Dylan's magic, watching as more of the shadows disintegrated. In a way, I supposed this was freeing them.

"I just want to go back to the way things were," Cal whispered beside me. She sank to the ground and drew her knees up to her chin. "My life was simple and happy. I was successful as a lieutenant. I don't want this. This is… too much!"

I wanted to help her, but we still had a handful of wraiths to deal with. "Just hang in there, Cal. I know you're overwhelmed, but it gets better."

Another two shadows erupted in a fountain of sparks, leaving three more to contend with. I lashed out with a burst of Fire and some of the ropes that had done the trick for Dylan. Imbued with Light, the Chaos made quick work of them, until only one remained.

"I didn't ask for this." Cal rocked back and forth with her eyes closed, as though she could just imagine all of this away if she focused hard enough. "I need to get out. I need to get back. This isn't real. I got knocked out, and this isn't real. This is a nightmare. It has to be!"

I looked back at her. "Take deep breaths. I swear this will get easier."

Dylan sent up another spiral of Telekinetic ropes, and I pushed one final tendril of Light into it. The fronds seized the last wraith and gripped it tight, wrapping it up and squeezing hard, until the creature finally gave in and turned into red sparks. The moment the final wraith had been defeated, I sank to Cal's level and held her by the shoulders.

"You're okay, Cal," I said softly.

She shook her head. "I'm not, though, am I? I'll never be okay again. Now that I know what I am, I can never have a normal life." Her eyes shot open, and she glared at me, like she held me solely responsible for what was happening. "I didn't ask for this! I don't want this! Why did you have to tell me what I was? Why couldn't you have just done to me what you did to the rest of my unit? Why didn't you just make me forget?" She was on the edge of a full-blown panic attack, and I had to get her back to reality, grounding her before she became a danger to herself.

"I know it feels like your life is over, but it's not. It's just beginning." I sounded like some kind of motivational speaker, giving out soundbites. But I needed to be honest if I was going to get through to her. "I used to be like you. I had no idea what I was, and then Wade came along and revealed the truth. I didn't want it, either. I wanted to be normal. I didn't have much, but I liked my life, and I liked what I'd built. I kept trying to push against it."

Cal blinked in confusion. "Then how did you end up here?"

"The more I thought about it, the more it made sense. I'd been the odd one out my entire life, because I had these abilities that were strange and scary and came out of nowhere. I'd always had to explain them away as coincidences." I spoke quickly, fearing that if I slowed down, I might lose her. "But when Wade told me what I was, it frightened the life out of me, *because* it made so much sense."

"But I wasn't the odd one out. I was doing just fine," she murmured miserably.

"Then you were one of the lucky ones. I know it doesn't feel like it now, but it's a good thing to have answers about yourself." I gripped her shoulder for reassurance. "It's not easy, and you don't have to be part of magical society. I pushed back for a while, too. I was scared, and I knew that my life would never be the same. But continuing to ignore the truth doesn't change what you are. It's better to be around people who can help you understand than to try to muddle through alone."

Cal dipped her chin into the notch between her knees. "But *how* did you end up here? How did Wade convince you?"

"I'm not sure it was him, in the end." I smiled at her. "The magical world has a way of pulling you in. That's how Chaos—or magic, as you'd call it—works. Once you're aware of it, it takes hold. You can't forget it or ignore it, and you start to realize that you can be—"

My words were knocked out of my throat as Tobe lunged from the darkness, smashing us both through a mirror.

## SIXTEEN

## Harley

Pain splintered up my back, and impenetrable darkness shrouded my vision. I had a vague awareness of voices around me—loud ones, crying out in panic. But I couldn't see them. All I felt was agony and searing hot breath on my face.

*Wake up, Harley. Open your eyes!* I struggled with my eyelids, cranking them open millimeter by millimeter as consciousness came back. I almost wished I'd stayed in darkness. Tobe's amber eyes glowered at me, mere inches from my face, his fangs flashing with menace. Behind him, Wade's fists grabbed chunks of Tobe's fur. Cal and Dylan used their Herculean strength to try and haul him off. Even Raffe had switched back to Kadar again, and the djinn wasn't pulling his punches. But Tobe endured as though nothing was happening, his focus fixed on me.

"I told you to stay away!" he snarled, way too close for comfort.

Jagged shards of shattered mirror dug into my back, sending shooting pains through my nerves. "And I told you to listen," I wheezed.

"You dare question me?" Tobe roared. He whirled around with a paw extended, his claws protruding like daggers. With the flat of his padded palm, he swatted the others off him like flies. Wade careened back into one of the mirrored boxes, the front panel shuddering but not cracking.

Cal tumbled to the ground and skidded a short distance, Dylan landed on top of a box, and Kadar performed an impressive slide backward, his black claws digging into the marble floor.

Terror and pain swirled in my winded chest, creating a maelstrom of instinctual force out of nowhere, a catalyst that released my balanced affinities of Light and Dark. Both sides poured into my being, filling up every vein, pumping up my muscles and organs until I felt like I could punch right through one of those mirrored boxes without breaking a sweat. But I didn't need the Light and Dark for brute force, not when I could be subtler.

"You. Will. Listen!" I roared into Tobe's face, matching his monstrous volume. The sound burned my throat, like I'd swallowed acid, and the resonance thudded in my ribcage. My lungs could barely handle the impact, but I didn't let it faze me. I was already in pain—what was a little more?

Tobe flinched. "You are not welcome here. You have made yourself an enemy of the Bestiary that I have sworn to protect!"

"Listen to me! Obey me!" I bellowed, every cell in my body alight with the fuel of my affinities. I let it flow into my beast-controlling ability and pushed the sensation outward. Tobe flinched again, shaking his head as though something were crawling across his face.

"What are you doing?" His eyes flashed with anger.

"OBEY ME!" The mirrored boxes trembled as my voice filled the Bestiary hall, vibrations shivering through the ground and through my bones, until I feared they might shatter. I'd never gone this deep before, and it scared and enthralled me in equal measure.

Tobe lowered his head, the way big dogs did to offer submission. A growl rippled out of his throat, but his head stayed down, and his hackles softened. It took a second for me to realize that I'd done it—I'd brought the Beast Master to heel. Fear and pain were potent motivators, and I'd used both to my advantage.

"What have... you done?" He strained to speak. It made me wonder how long this hypnosis would last. If I kept pouring both affinities into every cell, there was a good chance they'd explode. This was too much power. Still, I had to use it while I had it.

"I'm helping you." I raised a hand and slapped my palm across his cheek so hard that the impact ricocheted through my arm, right up my neck and into my jaw. My teeth juddered and my eyes bulged, my body going into overdrive. As my hand connected, a blinding white light surged from my palm, and the glow undulated across Tobe's face before racing along his furred neck and torso.

The same white light filtered into his eyes, making his feline irises burn brightly for a moment. He blinked and shook his head, but not the same way as before. His lips sank over his fangs, and his muscles rippled beneath his fur as he sat on his haunches, looking more like a housecat than I'd ever seen him. If it hadn't been for the ruffle of his huge wings, that is, which folded around him in a feathered embrace.

"Harley?" He met my gaze, confusion flashing in his eyes as he observed the broken box behind me. "Did I... harm you?"

*I did it...* Tobe was befuddled, but he was back.

"Nothing I can't handle." I tried to force a smile, but it came out as an uncomfortable grimace. With the blend of Light and Dark leaving my body like adrenaline, my souped-up muscles suddenly felt weak, replaced with nothing but sharp, shooting agony.

He edged closer and put his paw on my hand. "I have hurt you. I can see that." His voice was thick with regret and sadness. "Please, accept my sincerest apologies. You know me. I have never sought to harm you, nor do I wish to begin now. I have one sole excuse—that I have not been myself. When the Bestiary was threatened, I descended into a red haze of fury that I would not have been able to vanquish, had you not given me a much-needed slap back to reality."

"You remember what happened?" I struggled to my knees, holding his gigantic paw in both hands. I didn't blame him for what he'd done. Like he'd said, he wasn't himself. He'd done something stupid to defend the Bestiary, but if he hadn't, then we would be up a certain creek without a paddle right now. Thanks to his extreme measures, the army was still being kept at bay, and the secret of the Bestiary had not been revealed. Silver lining and all that jazz.

He nodded slowly, turning to face the others, who were in varying stages of getting back on their feet. "I harmed you all. I am eternally sorry, and I hope that you can find it in your hearts to forgive me. I did not mean to inflict injury upon you, but I could not control my behavior. That does not diminish what I have done. I shall feel sorry for a long while."

I gave his paw a squeeze. "You've got nothing to apologize for. You did what you thought was right and protected the Bestiary, as you promised. And you're back now." I took a breath. "And we need your help to move this place somewhere safer, before the army breaks through."

Wade interjected anxiously. "Umm… we might have a problem there."

"What do you mean?" Tobe addressed him firmly, back to his stoic self.

"Yes, what do you mean?" I repeated, the urgency rising in my throat.

Wade unclipped his radio from his Kevlar vest and pointed to a tiny red lightbulb. It had gone out. "Our radios were off this whole time. That colonel must be going out of his mind right about now." He fiddled with the knob a bit, and the red light flickered back to life.

"Captain, come in. Captain!" Sure enough, the colonel's voice crackled through. "Captain, backup is on its way. Whatever danger you're in, men are on their way. Hang in there, over." I couldn't gauge much from his fuzzy voice, but I sensed he'd gone into full panic mode. Not just for our sake, but as a result of all the weirdness that he'd almost certainly never faced before in his career or life. And our army issue was a lot closer than we thought, getting closer by the moment.

Tobe growled faintly. "All communication devices were disabled upon stepping into the Bestiary. I designed the defensive protocols that way and aligned them with the spell that turned me into that… terrible monster. Now that I am myself again, it appears your radio is working, and we are in something of a predicament."

"You can say that again," Cal muttered.

Tobe eyed her for a moment, as though just realizing there was someone new here. "I apologize for not making a more polite introduction, but we must act swiftly."

The radio crackled again. "If you can hear me, Captain—be alert, over!" He definitely sounded freaked out this time. "The dead... risen! Something has... over!"

"The dead have risen? What's that supposed to mean?" Dylan gave me a blank look.

I gulped, dread forming a lump in my throat. "I think it means exactly what it sounds like."

"Davin..." Raffe hissed.

I nodded. "Who else could it be?"

"Davin? He has done this?" Tobe furrowed his furry brow.

"We think he's performed a spell that stole energy from this Bestiary, but it had the side effect of revealing our coven," I explained rapidly.

Tobe looked aghast. "If that is true, then he would have the might to conjure spells of mass effect."

"Like bringing a whole load of dead people back to life?" Dylan asked the question we were likely all thinking.

"It would be possible, yes," Tobe confirmed.

*But why?* That was the part I still couldn't wrap my head around. What was he hoping to prove? I didn't get much time to dwell on it, as the sound of voices rose beyond the lightning of the egg's forcefield. The soldiers were close. And after undoing the hexes that'd kept the route to the Bestiary on lockdown, we'd left the door wide open.

"We must move the Bestiary immediately." Tobe's ears flicked back and forth, picking up on the sound of the soldiers. "I will implement the emergency measures embedded in the Bestiary's interface. However, I do not wish to leave if there are other magicals remaining nearby. Did anyone else come with you?"

My eyes widened. "A few, yes."

"Then gather them as quickly as you are able. I will begin the protocols to move the Bestiary, but you will not have long," Tobe instructed.

I nodded. "We're on it." Gesturing for the others to follow, I sprinted back through the halls and skidded to a stop by the back entrance where we'd left O'Halloran, Santana, and Tatyana.

I wrenched the door open. "Come inside!"

"Huh?" Santana stood inside a whirlwind of Orishas, her palms raised.

"Get inside! Tobe's back to normal, and the Bestiary is leaving!" I shouted, noting the glowing white figure of Tatyana.

O'Halloran wasted no time scooping Tatyana up and running for the door. Santana followed, dispersing her Orisha vortex and crossing the threshold into the Bestiary without another word as Jacob launched himself forward and skidded past us to safety.

"We need to send word to—" Wade started, only for his mouth to drop as the two people I was certain he'd been about to mention rocketed around the corner: Astrid and Garrett, running for their lives by the looks of it. Both of them were wide-eyed with horror.

"The dead are coming back to life!" Astrid shouted, without missing a step.

Garrett swerved around a pile of rubble that began to move, a dusty head and pallid limbs scrabbling out of the debris. A forlorn face, streaked with dirt, poked out of the rock pile—a young woman, tears streaking her cheeks.

"Where am I?" a thin voice pleaded. "What h-happened to m-me? I w-was in Heaven, and n-now... Did I d-do something wrong? Did they k-kick me out of Heaven?" My heart broke for the poor girl. I wished we could've helped her, but there was no time. Not unless...

I turned to Jacob. "Is she a magical?"

He shook his head. "No... she's not."

"Then we have to leave her." I hated the words as soon as I said them. She looked so confused and upset, stumbling to her feet. A moment ago, she'd been dead. That was a lot for anyone to process. But we couldn't bring her with us if the Bestiary was about to move. At the very least, it'd be more troubling for her.

Wade put his hand on the small of my back. "I'll take care of it." He lifted a hand and sent out a thin strand of bronze light, which slipped effortlessly into her temple. Her eyes flashed as her knees buckled beneath her, and she collapsed to the ground. She wasn't dead again, merely unconscious. Wade had performed a mind-wipe spell, and I prayed that it would take away her obvious pain, even if it was only temporary comfort.

But I still felt bad about leaving her here. Using my Telekinesis, I picked her up and carried her farther up the passageway, away from the rubble. There, I set her down where someone would surely find her. I wished I could've done more, but this would have to do.

"What is going on?" Garrett gasped as he entered the Bestiary. "We've just had to run past about twenty people who were dead and now aren't. The soldiers are freaking out. It's happening all over!"

I hit him with a grim look. "It's Davin. He's doing this remotely with the energy he's stealing from the Bestiary."

Kadar reappeared for a second. "That appears to be the most obvious explanation, though it seems outlandish, even to me. However… it would explain why he felt the need to steal such potent power, if he intended to use it for such extensive means."

"We have to get back to Tobe." I looked at O'Halloran. "And you need to get every other magical who's still here into this Bestiary—pronto!"

O'Halloran immediately took out a radio. "Come in, this is Alpha One. Rendezvous at the zoo, ASAP." He'd used code to hopefully fox any army radios that picked up the communication.

"On our way!" a voice replied, though it wasn't one I recognized.

"I'll stay here and make sure only our people enter." O'Halloran stood in the doorway. "You go check on Tobe and see how things are progressing."

With that, our slightly larger group made the return journey through the Bestiary, but we didn't stop at the hall where we'd left Tobe. He wasn't there anymore, but I had a feeling I knew where we'd find him. Pressing on at breakneck speed, we burst through a towering set of double doors into the main room of the Bestiary. The atrium sparked and crackled, bright energy surging up and down the cables inside. And Tobe stood at the bottom, his demeanor agitated, toying with all sorts of secret levers and buttons on a panel I'd never seen before. It appeared to have come directly out of the atrium itself.

"Is everyone here?" Tobe lifted his head for a second.

"Not yet. They're on their way," I replied, panting.

He returned to his tapping and pulling. "We do not have long. Once I have completed all the protocols, I have only minutes before I must displace the Bestiary. If I wait longer than that, it will reset."

"They're coming," I repeated, worried about what might happen if we left them behind.

"This is insane." Garrett ran a hand through his sweat-drenched hair.

Wade went to his friend. "What happened back there?"

"Well, we were guarding the entrance to that passageway, when a whole flood of troops came in, weapons at the ready. We had to fall back in case they thought we were some of the newly undead." He glanced at Astrid; this was probably a little too close to home for the pair of them, who were also members of the resurrected. "Smarty led us through the new layout, right to you."

Astrid clutched the tablet to her chest. "We bumped into some soldiers on the way, though I don't know if they were undead or not. They were dazed and trying to get out, but we couldn't stop to help." Her voice was thick with emotion. "And then we understood why the troops came. People were rising everywhere, crawling out of the rubble and crying out for answers. It was… devastating. They're all so confused. They're going to have so many questions, and there'll be nobody who can answer them."

Tobe interrupted, talking loudly to himself. "Goodness… where to go? I need a safe destination, but not one that will draw Davin's attention."

An idea popped into my head. "The Antarctic Coven. Nobody knows about it, and it's been isolated from the rest of magical society for ages."

Sure, it meant the magical world's source of energy would be terrifyingly close to the person who'd seized control of its power, but maybe that was the cleverest way to go. If we hid the Bestiary right under

Davin's nose, he might not think to look there. Plus, it'd be hidden by the Antarctic Coven's interdimensional bubble, so no one would spot it, and it was far enough away from non-magical society to at least take the weight of it being properly investigated off our shoulders. As for the rest... well, we could figure that out later.

"Yes... that might work." Tobe started tapping away, inputting the destination.

O'Halloran exploded into the main hall with the preceptors and other magicals in tow.

"Push the button!" he cried. "Everyone is here, and the soldiers are almost at the Bestiary's back entrance. I put up a barrier to hold them back, but it won't last long."

Tobe slammed his paw down on the interface, his gaze drifting across us all. "I suggest you hold on to something."

A blast of searing light shot up from the center of the atrium and spilled out, falling across the entire Bestiary and transforming the purple lightning into a swirling mass of sparkling bronze. A second blast tore through the atrium, and a deafening boom exploded outward. The Bestiary rose over the remains of the SDC, and I could just imagine the headline: "UFO Seen Flying Over San Diego."

The building started to spin, and we spun with it. It was like my least favorite carnival ride. I lunged for the handle of a nearby Bestiary box and clung for dear life as the Bestiary erupted from the ruins of the SDC and the Fleet Science Center, with every last magical and Purge beast safe inside.

*Next stop... Antarctica.*

## SEVENTEEN

## Finch

I held Ryann a while longer, knowing I couldn't delay the inevitable forever. I had to go back to the confederacy of dunces at some point. Honestly, I was surprised they hadn't marched out to keep an eye on me and make sure I didn't run off to get the executive order for Davin.

"Are you sure you're okay?" I kissed her softly.

She leaned into me. "I will be. I'm just worried about you."

"And we'll go on and on in an endless cycle of worrying about each other, until one of us is dead." I meant it as a joke, but the pained look she gave me made me realize it was too close to home.

Krieger sat in a nearby armchair, rearranging bottles and pots from his medicine bag. "I'm sure there is no cause for concern, Finch. She is dazed, but she will be well again once she has rested properly. Surviving possession by a Child of Chaos is no mean feat, but my physician's intuition tells me that the fatigue will wear off."

"I'd say there's cause for concern." Luke shot me a dark glare from where he stood by the roaring fireplace with Melody.

"Luke," Melody said quietly. "You can't blame Finch for Davin's demands."

My eyes widened in surprise. "He told you?" I'd assumed Luke would keep Davin's request to have Melody and Jacob in his service to himself, until circumstances forced it out of him. Even then, I'd thought he would've done absolutely everything in his power not to tell Melody what Davin wanted from her.

"He did." She nodded. "And I wanted to tell you that, while I'm not too pleased about trading my service as a commodity, I'm on board with anything we have to do to give him the impression that he's winning. If that means pretending to be in his service, I'll do it. I know how to handle myself, and though he might have the Bestiary's power at his fingertips, I've got all of Chaos's knowledge at mine. And knowledge beats power, because knowledge *is* power." She tucked a strand of dark hair behind her ear and toyed with the silver earring that dangled there. A subtle hint that she wasn't feeling as brave as she sounded.

"Do you think you can convince Jacob?" I needed to get all my ducks in a row in order to craft a decent plan… one that might actually work.

Melody tilted her head from side to side. "I can try. I don't know him very well, but I've been told that I'm very persuasive when I want to be." She smiled shyly up at Luke. His expression said clearly that *he* wasn't on board with any of this. "Once we explain why, and that it only needs to appear as though we're doing Davin's bidding, I'm sure he'll agree. We just have to hope Davin's head has grown so inflated that he takes the bait and believes we're sincere. That will be the hard part."

"We'll do what we can to help." Nash gave a firm nod, and Huntress barked her agreement.

Luke scowled. "If it doesn't get us killed."

It would be a delicate tightrope to walk. Davin had a keen nose for all things fishy, but he did currently seem blinded by his own clout. For one, he refused to see that he was in too deep, and that not everyone was thrilled to be resurrected. Perhaps that childish refusal to look beyond his own surety would spread into the rest of his perceptions. Perhaps he'd blindly believe that we were obeying because he had so much faith in the threats that loomed over us. Covens popping out like whack-a-moles and a potential war that could devastate the whole world were fairly intense threats, after all.

Remington padded out of the dunce chamber, his head low.

"Well, you look happy," I said sarcastically. "I take it they've had a chat about my suggestion, and they're not going for it?"

He sighed. "They're still unwilling to deal with Davin's demands. They think that, even by giving the illusion that they're letting Davin win, they're actually letting him win. And they don't like that one bit. It'd require them to ignore too many rules, and they do love their rules and regulations."

I groaned in annoyance. "They realize that the magical world no longer has control over the Bestiary, right? I mean, come on! They have to get that Davin is calling the shots here, whether they like it or not. And I'm the only one with even half a solution right now. They need to sit up and friggin' listen, or it's going to be war, war, and more war, until Davin rises to the top anyway."

"I've tried telling them that, on your behalf, but they are... stubborn." Remington grimaced and perched on the armrest of one of the obnoxious chairs.

"I'm going to go back in there and make them understand, until they get so sick of the sound of my voice that they have no choice but to give in. Either that, or I'll just figure out a way to do it without them." I winked at Remington. "Not that I'll tell them that. I'm just going to give them the illusion of free will, same as we're going to give Davin the illusion that we're bowing down to him. And if they don't bite, screw them."

I kissed Ryann once more, settling her back against the sofa. Getting to my feet, I strode halfway across the main room before an almighty rumble tore through the Antarctic Coven. I toppled to the side like a drunken sailor, clutching the back of an armchair. Melody and Luke gripped the mantelpiece, Krieger held tight to a whalebone lamp, and Remington fell backward into an armchair. Nash dove to the ground, and

Huntress put her paws on his back, covering him like a comrade in battle. Shouts of fright went up from the room where the councilors were holding court.

Another shudder ripped through the coven, and I struggled not to fall over. My head whipped around, trying to figure out where the vibrations were coming from. On the far side of the room, close to the doorway of the dunce chamber, a glowing rupture in time and space appeared.

*Jacob?* I waited for the usual pulse of air and the black hole that followed, but it didn't come. Instead, the split grew wider and wider, taking on a familiar shape. A massive set of double doors appeared in the wall. Black and imposing, with handles shaped like lion heads, they dwarfed the rest of the Antarctic Coven. It would've been funny if it hadn't been so terrifying.

"Holy crap!" Remington looked as though his eyes were about to fall out.

I glanced at him, still fighting to hold on to the armchair. "Is that what I think it is?"

The doorway settled into the too-small wall, and the tremors faded. Fortunately, no gigantic subterranean worms burst out, and there was no Kevin Bacon to be seen. A niche reference, but we *were* talking about monsters here. The Antarctic Coven groaned and strained a bit before accepting the Bestiary into its interdimensional bubble, flexing to make it fit.

"Why is it here?" Ryann squeaked, trying to stand. I ran to her and put an arm around her waist.

"O'Halloran must've given the order," Remington replied from across the room. He made a cautious approach to the double doors. His shaky hands reached out for the lion's head knockers. He'd just mustered the courage to pull the doors open, when they burst outward of their own accord. Harley and the old Muppet Babies, along with O'Halloran and a bunch of other magicals, staggered out like the last ones leaving the club.

"Harley!" Ryann broke out of my hold and rushed toward her. I hurried along behind, in case her residual Lux sickness swiped at her again. The two women embraced while more people emerged from the Bestiary: a soldier I didn't recognize and my furry pal Tobe. He bundled me into a hug, and I sank into it, holding him as if he were my very own gigantic teddy bear.

"It is good to see you well, Finch." His low voice soothed my soul. "I have heard much of your plight and did what I could to aid your sister in her pursuit of you, though I did not have the pleasure of hearing that you had survived due to the… unfortunate circumstances that ensued."

Dylan clapped Tobe on the shoulder. "Our Beast Master literally went into full beast mode."

"I am wholly recovered now," Tobe said quickly. If he could've blushed, he'd have done it right now. Clearly, I'd missed some juicy gossip.

"What happened at the SDC?" Krieger shuffled over and asked the question I should have asked.

Harley kept one arm linked through Ryann's as she regaled us with the entire tale. I listened, hooked on every word. But there was one particular part that sucker-punched me right in the gut.

"So, he's started already." I clenched my jaw.

"Started?" Harley frowned my way.

"Davin's messiah complex." I gestured to the others who'd joined me on my Atlantis trip. Hector's absence still resonated. "We got back from Atlantis not long ago, and he's got a big list of demands and ideas for the rest of the world. Starting with resurrecting as many people as possible to show he's this fancy hero who can deliver your deceased loved one to your door by express post."

"What?" O'Halloran pushed to the front of the group. "He said that to you?"

I nodded. "And it looks like he's putting his dead people where his mouth is."

A radio crackled with panicked voices, but since the magicals were all here—at least, the ones we knew about—I guessed those voices belonged to the army. "The shiny orb thing just… vanished! It's gone! The egg thing is gone!" Their description confirmed that they were definitely non-magical. Tobe would've had a few things to say about them calling his Bestiary an "egg thing."

"How are you getting their signal?" I looked to O'Halloran. Either non-magical communication technology had undergone major improvements in the last few years, or…

He patted his radio. "I enhanced it so we'd have a direct line to what the non-magicals were saying."

"What do you mean, it 'vanished'?" Another voice cut through the crackly receiver.

"I mean… it disappeared, right in front of our eyes!" the first soldier replied.

*The cat's head is out of the bag.* Not the whole feline, mind you, but the military clearly knew there was something wonky going on. And the cleanup—*oh, the cleanup*—was going to be an absolute chore. I had a feeling the upper echelons of magical society wouldn't think of scrubbing minds as so much of a gray area when it came to covering up our deepest, darkest secret: our existence.

The California Mage Council finally scurried out of their rat hole, screeching at the top of their lungs and crying out for answers. Except Rasmus. He simply looked around the room, observing quietly.

"What is going on here?" I heard Selena say, striding up to O'Halloran. They blended into the fray of people, everyone chattering a mile a minute in a gaggle of confusion and concern.

*This is my chance…* and I'd be damned if I wasn't going to take it. Slyly, I took Ryann's hand and led her to the periphery of the twittering group. Rasmus had stopped scanning the room and turned his attention to O'Halloran, who was trying to explain.

"And ye didn't think te consult us first? How's that for leadership?" Mairead tore into him, only to get an earful from his Irish assistant.

"Aye, and what would ye have done, ye grumpy auld sow?" Diarmuid's miniature cheeks turned scarlet with fury. "Ye'd have sat on yer arse and let them outsiders find the Bestiary, and then we'd all be in a right auld fettle."

Mairead reeled back in disgust. "How dare ye speak te me like that!"

"I'll speak te ye how I please. Ye ought te respect yer elders!" Diarmuid didn't back down, and I didn't want him to. As long as he held the council's attention, I had a narrow window in which to escape.

"But think of the mayhem you've caused!" Jasper protested. "It will take weeks, if not months, to wipe everyone's minds after they have seen a giant structure disappear in front of their eyes!"

O'Halloran raised his hands in surrender. "I'm not saying the cleanup will be easy, but I had to act. The Bestiary fuels every coven. If that fell into military hands, then Diarmuid is right—we'd be in a much worse scenario. It had to be done."

I beckoned to Harley and Jacob, who gave me a funny look before slinking away from the group. The others didn't even notice, though I saw Wade give his beloved a side-eye that she didn't pick up on. Anyway, he had the common sense to look away and make sure everyone stayed distracted. He'd learned to trust me over the years... well, enough not to go blabbing when I acted surreptitiously.

"What's up?" Harley whispered, as we ducked behind a wall. I couldn't risk the council spying us, but I knew I didn't have long before they noticed I'd vamoosed.

"I need your help." Taking a breath, I reeled off everything that Davin wanted, not only from me, but from Melody and Jacob. I left the executive order until last. "Jacob, can you get me to the president's office?"

Harley grasped my wrist. "Finch, you can't do this. This is insanity!"

"We have to let Davin believe that he's succeeding. That executive order will be all the 'proof' he needs that we're being good little servants to his grand scheme. I don't like it any more than you do, but we have to use whatever tactics we can to get the upper hand. If that means giving him a few of the things he wants, so we can snatch it all away later, then that's what we have to do!" I hissed back. We didn't have time for this.

Jacob nodded. "I agree, and I don't mind playing my part, either. I took a few drama classes at school. I can put on a show."

"Jacob, this is real life, and you being anywhere near Davin is a terrible idea! And Finch getting that order for Davin is an even worse idea!" Harley argued. I hadn't expected so much pushback from her... but perhaps it didn't matter. I had Jacob and Melody, and they were the two people I needed most for this. Bad Finch had come back with a vengeance, and he had no qualms about slipping around folks to make things happen. Still, I wanted Harley to have my back.

I peered around the corner to make sure the council was still otherwise engaged. "Harley, I know it sounds like I've lost my marbles. But I need your help. You've got a voice that people can't help but listen to. I need you to stay here and keep the council from noticing I've gone, or they'll royally screw with my plans. And it's the only plan we have, if we want to stop a war and stop Davin. He needs to think he's firmly on his meteoric rise, or we'll have zero chance of getting ahead of him."

Harley's expression softened. "You've thought this through, huh?"

"I may act like an idiot most of the time, but I wouldn't even suggest this if I hadn't gone through the details with a fine-toothed comb." I gave her my most earnest eyes. "We have to give a little to gain a lot. And he's already started on his mission, so we need to start ours before he gets too far ahead."

"I think he's onto something, Harley." Jacob offered his support. *Ah, from the mouths of babes.*

Harley huffed out a weary sigh. "You really think this is our only shot?"

"I really do. Trick him, the way he's tricked us." I paused. "I'm working on that part, but it'll need everyone's focus. We'll have to sever his connection to the Bestiary, break the spell on Kaya to see if she has any shiny ideas about how to undo what Davin has done, and do all of that while stopping a war that'll only win him more fans in the long run, when he brings everyone back to life. Everyone he thinks will be valuable to him, anyway. And we'll need to be close to him, so we can kick him in the balls at the perfect moment."

She stared at me for a few seconds before giving a slight nod. "Do it. I trust you. I'll stay here and run interference. But if this doesn't work, Finch—"

I swooped in before she could finish her sentence. "Then we're all on a one-way train to Davinsville, where he'll never stop crowing about how good it is to be king."

"I just wanted to make sure we were on the same page." She managed a half-smile, but I could tell she was on the edge of a nervous breakdown.

Jacob lifted his palms. "This isn't going to be subtle, unfortunately. And I can't get you into the office, since I don't know where it is. I can only get you close to the Washington Coven."

"Just get me as close as possible, as quick as you can." I braced to leap through the portal the moment it opened. There was one other thing I hadn't told Harley or Ryann, but that could wait. My sister would never have agreed to what I was about to do.

Jacob didn't hesitate. Bronze energy surged out of his palms and tore a hole in space and time. I waited just long enough for a people-sized gap to appear before yanking Ryann through the portal with me. She let out an alarmed shriek, echoed by Harley. But the portal snapped shut before Harley could do anything about it. I wasn't being a jerk, even though my sister was probably cursing my name right now. There was a method to my madness.

Ryann had endured a Child of Chaos piggybacking on her for weeks, and that meant she might still have a connection to Lux. Faint, maybe, but hopefully still there. And I prayed, with every shred of optimism I had, that we might be able to wrangle the married monstrosities into giving us a hand again. Since I couldn't find Erebus myself, I needed to call on the one person who might be able to locate him.

His wife.

"Finch!" Ryann gaped at me as we stumbled out into a side street. From my cult days, I had a vague idea of where the entry to the Washington Coven could be found: a bar with the not-so-discreet name of All the President's Men. And if Jacob had his coordinates right, we wouldn't be too far away.

"Sorry." I flashed her an apologetic smile. "I didn't want to say anything in case Harley held you back. You said you wanted to help, and honestly, I need you with me. I should've told you, but there wasn't time. If you're not feeling up to it, I can find somewhere safe for you." I did mean that, deep down. I'd never lead her into any situation she didn't want to be involved in. Even though I had just dragged her through a portal against her will.

"I'm going to kill you, Finch Merlin!" Harley's voice thundered through my earpiece. "If Jacob wasn't being so stubborn, I'd be strangling you right now!"

*Oh, Jacob, my buddy, my pal.* He'd saved my bacon, evidently not opening a portal for Harley so she could jump through and hand my ass to me.

Ryann held my hand tighter, no doubt hearing the same threat in her ear. "I won't leave you to do this alone. You're right. I said I wanted to help, and I'm going to. I just might be a little slow."

"Hey, I'm the slow one in this relationship." I lifted her hand to my lips and kissed it gently.

"So… how do we get in to see the president?" She straightened up, ready for business.

I grimaced slightly. "Well, that's hurdle number one."

She smiled, a hint of mischief in her eyes. "Then it's lucky you *did* bring me. During my internship with Miranda Bontemps, I learned a few things about the magical government. And that includes a surefire excuse to get us inside."

"Just when I thought I couldn't love you more." I grinned at her, and she grinned right back. We'd been through so much together, and here we were again, facing one of the biggest challenges we'd ever come across. And it felt good to have her at my side. If anything could get us in to see the president, it was Ryann's incredible mind.

"I don't suppose you're in the mood for a drink, are you?" I waggled my eyebrows at her.

She frowned. "Now? I thought we were on a deadline."

I laughed. "You'll see."

After all, the most obvious way of getting into a place was to try the front door.

## EIGHTEEN

## Harley

F*inch Merlin, I'm going to wring your scrawny little neck!* Running off by himself was one thing, but dragging Ryann along with him? If he didn't have a damn good reason for it, he'd feel my wrath when I saw him again.

"You!" Jasper Gold's eyes bugged out of his head. We'd had a few run-ins during my time as an agent, tracking down rogue cultists who needed to be locked away. And they'd never been particularly warm and fuzzy encounters. He liked to give off the air of an affable cool guy, but he was a rulebook-loving hothead beneath that sleek surface, and it didn't take much to ruffle his feathers.

"You're going to have to be more specific." I held his furious gaze without fear.

He pushed through the group, his council minions flanking him. "Can you tell me why it is that whenever there's a Merlin around, chaos ensues?" He jabbed a finger at me, which I didn't take kindly to. "He was supposed to stay here, where we could keep an eye on him. Now you've let him go, and we know precisely what he intends to do!"

I gave an innocent shrug. "You should've said something. I didn't know you wanted to keep him here, and he didn't say anything about it." Sure, I could've killed Finch for snatching Ryann like that, but he was my brother. Nobody got to speak about him in that tone of voice, except me.

"Ach! He'll have spilled the beans to you the moment you saw each other!" Mairead O'Malley chucked in her two euros. She was usually the lesser of the council's evils and easier to deal with, but Diarmuid had gone and riled her up, and now I seemed to be on the receiving end of her anger. "We told him under no circumstances was he to proceed with getting the executive order. And don't you dare tell us you didn't know about that, else I'll brand you a barefaced liar!"

"He'll be punished for this." Rasmus was a man of few words, and he'd always set my nerves on edge. But I'd had enough of these punks throwing their weight around and trying to lay down the law at every turn, especially when they were small fry in comparison to some of the people I liaised with.

Selena nodded. "There are rules for a reason, and the pair of you seem hellbent on disobeying them whenever possible. Finch will not be permitted to get away with this. I don't care what sort of hero everyone thinks he is, after that Katherine nonsense. It's time he learned that just because he did something good once, it doesn't give him carte blanche to do as he pleases for the rest of his days."

I straightened up and got loud. "Don't you get sick of singing the same freaking song all the time?" The room fell silent, everyone gaping at me. "Had we bowed down to the covens' rules and regulations, none of us would be here today! You mentioned Katherine like she was just some blip in magical history. Well, here's a refresher for you: while you were all twiddling your thumbs and discussing what to do, we were acting on everyone's behalf, preparing to fight her to the death in Elysium. We ended her before you even left your council chamber. Oh, and in case you forgot, a bunch of you joined Katherine's side! How's that for obeying the rules, huh? Finch gave up his freedom for yours. And if you can dismiss all that, then you need to reassess what you're on the council for." I stood there, breathless and furious, trying to ignore the startled stares of the people around me.

Rasmus narrowed his eyes. For a second, I genuinely feared his retribution. Instead, he said something that surprised me. "You think us cowards?"

"I'm not saying that, but I think you all rest on your laurels. You expect results without letting anyone actually go out and get them, and then you get on your high horses when someone *does* do something. You're walking paradoxes!" I was out of breath by the time I finished.

"You're right. We have sat back. Now, it is time to fight." He stormed across the coven's main room and stomped out into the biting cold of the South Georgia Island climate. Another shocker I wasn't expecting.

Curiosity got the better of me and, apparently, everyone else. We hurried after him, only to watch in alarm as he paused on the rocky beach and lifted his palms.

"We need to attack *them* before they attack us!" he shouted. A humongous fireball emerged from between his hands. With one mighty push, he flung the fireball all the way to Atlantis. He likely wanted to see just how impervious the city's shield was.

"Oh dear, oh dear, I wouldn't do that if I were you!" Melody flew past me and raced across the terrain, with Luke in hot pursuit. I didn't understand her sudden panic, but if she was afraid, then we all had to take note. On the near horizon, the fireball hit its mark… and immediately vanished into the faintly shimmering bubble.

A split second later, Melody skidded to a halt a few feet away from Rasmus, who burst into flames. His scream pierced the air, sending icy daggers of terror up my spine. Judging by everyone else's horrified faces, they felt the same way.

"Rasmus!" Jasper cried, hurrying across the rocks to him. Luke managed to tackle him to the ground before he could get too close to his colleague. Rasmus flailed wildly, his entire body going up like a bonfire.

It only got more painful to watch as Rasmus made a mad dash for the ocean. He leapt into the freezing water headfirst and disappeared beneath the surface to try and put out his spontaneous combustion. I scanned the churning water for any sign of him.

"Oh, Chaos, no…" Mairead clamped her hand across her mouth, her eyes focused on a particular spot in the ocean. I followed her line of sight until I saw it—a body, floating. Rasmus had rushed in without thinking, and Atlantis had retaliated. A cautionary tale for us all, not to mess with the integrity of the invisible city. Or its king.

"Someone get him out of the water!" Selena yelped, though I noticed she made no move to follow her own suggestion.

Remington shot me a look, and I gave a nod. Together, we walked to the edge of the shore, past a sobbing Melody. We'd almost reached the water, my ears filled with the sounds of shock and devastation from the gathered magicals, when we received another shock to the system. Remington and I stopped dead in our tracks.

"You've got to be kidding me," Remington whispered.

Rasmus floundered in the water, very much alive. Gasping for air, he made an ungainly swim back to the shore, arms splashing and feet kicking desperately. He dragged himself onto the rocks and crouched there on all fours for a moment, spitting saltwater onto the slick ground. He lifted his head, and I could've sworn I saw a subtle flash of purple in his eyes before it faded away.

"I'm… alive," he rasped. "I'm… alive!"

Jasper pushed Luke away and sprinted the short distance to his friend, helping him up. "Oh, thank Chaos! I thought you were a goner."

Rasmus shook his head, spraying droplets of water onto the rocks. "No, you don't understand. I was dead, and now I'm not." His eyes twinkled, and my Empath senses tingled. That was gratitude, if ever I'd felt it. It rolled off him in powerful waves. "Davin did this. Davin brought me back. I don't know how he knew I had died, but he did. And I am grateful."

*Oh, no…* He'd been caught in Davin's charm offensive—and swallowed the bait hook, line, and sinker. And Davin couldn't have chosen a better candidate to spread the word of his benevolence. Rasmus was a highly respected member of the California Mage Council, with connections to the government. Geez, I only had to look at him to know his entire mindset had shifted. There was nothing like a bit of death to sway people in Davin's favor, especially when personally experienced.

I turned to Selena. "You need to keep an eye on him. I know he's your colleague, but keep him under close observation."

She frowned. "You think he might be in trouble?"

"Davin just resurrected him. Yeah, I'd say he's in trouble." I swallowed my agitation. "With the Bestiary's energy at Davin's fingertips, there's no telling what else he's capable of, aside from these remote resurrections. He wants the world's adoration. Maybe that means he's able to alter people's minds, too, during the resurrection." I was spit-balling, but it made horrifying sense. What if this was how he planned to sway those who opposed him? Off them, bring them back, add in a dose of mind-altering, and the world would be his oyster.

Jasper's voice drew my attention back to the debacle on the beach. "Are you sure you're okay? Are you sure you actually died? What do you remember?"

Rasmus sat up, grinning like a loon. A side of him I'd never seen before. Rasmus Erikson cracking a smile was tantamount to Hell freezing over. "I was standing in a… parlor of some kind, in an old house some-where. Rain pattered against the window, and people walked by on the street outside. I may have seen a red bus pass down the road, but I can't be sure. Anyway, two armchairs rested beside a roaring fire. Davin sat there. He was waiting for me. He… welcomed me and said he had chosen to speak with me specifically. He said he had sensed my passing." He swept a hand through his sodden hair, apparently oblivious to the fact that he'd get hypothermia if he sat out there much longer. "It felt like a dream yet very real. I sat with Davin, and he poured me a drink. Before he handed it to me, he asked me if I would be thankful and if I would think kindly of him if he brought me back."

*He took you to London. He took you to the place where he was happiest—where this all began.* It was so very Davin to make it all about him. And it didn't sound at all like a dream, more like a spiritual transportation to an astral plane that had been designed to Davin's specifications. What worried me more was that Davin had 'chosen' to speak with Rasmus specifically. Did that mean he'd spread his Necromancy net worldwide, after his blanket resurrection, with some kind of alarm to be triggered when someone else died? Or had he pinpointed those in positions of authority, knowing they'd have more sway if he brought them back?

"Are you certain?" Jasper sounded dubious.

Rasmus nodded effusively. "I held out my hands for the drink and said that, yes, I would be thankful. He gave me the drink, and I sipped it, and… here I am." He sighed, turning over his shoulder to gaze lovingly at the distant city, which was invisible to the naked eye. "Davin is genuine. He wants harmony, not war. He has invited everyone he resurrected, magical and non-magical alike, to come to Atlantis. It is his… mecca, for those who have been restored to life, and it will be a mecca for those who wish to bring others back to life, too. They have only to request it, and he will see it done. He wants to bring joy to people and offer them the impossible: a chance to regain what has been lost, breaking down the barrier between this life and what comes after."

I could hardly believe this was the same person, a guy who, in all the time I'd known him, had barely said fifty words. Now he was prattling on like a man possessed.

"Screw the rules." Rasmus beamed, still impervious to the cold. "This is a new world. A new life. A new era brought to us by Davin. It is time to change the status quo and the way we view Necromancy. There is nothing underhanded about it. It is… beautiful! It is peace and poetry in motion!"

I rarely swore, but I really wanted to right then. In the space of one resurrection, Davin had proven how dangerous his power had become. He'd seduced Rasmus to his side with such ease, and I had no doubts that there'd be more like him popping up all over the place: envoys to share his message of love and beauty and hope. It didn't sound so bad, put like that, but this was Davin we were talking about. He twisted love into hate, beauty into ugliness, and hope into despair. And, like Mr. Smith had taught me—if it looked too good to be true, it probably was.

Unless my brother and I found a way to beat Davin at his own game, we'd be fighting a tide of fanatics. And we'd lose against a current that strong. We'd all lose.

## NINETEEN

## Finch

M ulder and Scully, eat your hearts out! If it hadn't been for the seriousness of the situation, I'd have been in my element. Literally living a very particular dream. One I never imagined I'd be able to get Ryann on board with.

"Remind me why he had to buy suits to go for a drink?" Ryann smoothed down her super-sleek lapels, looking absolutely jaw-dropping in her tailored getup. It hugged her in all the right places, bridging the gap between haute couture and special agent. The store owner had said something about cigarette pants being the right fit for her, but I had no idea what that meant. Either way, he'd been right—everything fit her perfectly. And, not to toot my own horn, but I didn't look too shabby, either.

"If we're going undercover, we have to look the part." We'd made a brief pit-stop before heading to All the President's Men—the bar that served as the secret entrance to the Washington Coven. I could've Mimicked us into some snappy outfits, but I wasn't sure how primed the coven's magical defenses would be. And I didn't want us getting caught with our proverbial pants down.

She took a step toward me and pressed her hand to my chest. "Well, you look good. I can't deny that."

I chuckled. "If I hadn't seen this tired, ugly mug in the mirror myself, I might've believed you."

"Don't do that," she said softly, peering up into my eyes.

"Do what?"

"Put yourself down like that. There's a reason why even princesses can't keep their mitts off you, though you'll always have me to slap said mitts away." She rose on tiptoe and kissed me on the lips, drawing a few sly grins from passersby.

I kissed her back, sinking into the moment. "There's no one I'd rather have slapping away all the mitts in the world, even if I don't agree with you." I pulled away and gazed at her. She never ceased to amaze me, just by existing. I knew people called it the honeymoon phase for a reason, and all the things you found intriguing and exciting and wonderful about a person could turn into the things you hated five years down the line. But I had a feeling that wouldn't happen to us. Not for me, anyway. I just had to hope she'd always find my sense of humor endearing. No mean feat, but if anyone could endure me, it was her.

"And you're sure this is the right way to go?" She kept her palms pressed to my chest. "I'm not trying to dampen your enthusiasm. I support this, and I do think you have the right idea, but I need to know you're sure."

I tucked a wayward strand of hair behind her ear, so it wouldn't mess up the slick bun she had going on. "I'm certain. And I'm glad you support me, even if I did drag you here without talking to you first." I paused, Bad Finch disappearing for a minute. "I shouldn't have done that. I worry about you enough when you're not involved in some risky quest, and I've gone and pulled you into this one."

She smiled, and my world exploded into vivid Technicolor. "You're an odd one, Finch Merlin, but that's why I love you." She kissed me again, and I held her close. "As for worrying about me, you don't have to. I'd have come with you, whether you'd asked or not. One way or another, we'll find a way out of this mess."

"That's the kind of pep talk I needed. I love you, too—so much." Guilt gripped my insides. Ryann had been in a heap on the floor about an hour ago, and now she was about to break into the Washington Coven with me. Bad Finch had a lot to answer for, and I'd given him free rein back at the Antarctic Coven. Still, her words steeled my resolve. If she was happy to come along for the ride, then who was I to argue?

"Then should we put these suits to good use?" She flashed me a daring grin. And I had to force back all kinds of Gillian Anderson in *The X-Files* daydreams.

I kissed her once more, savoring it before things took a turn for the crazy again. "It'd be a shame not to."

Still a little tingly, we wandered through a network of rain-soaked streets. Ah, Washington. Non-magicals went about their business, yakking away on their phones. Either they hadn't heard about San Diego, or they were too busy to care. The human condition in all its oblivious glory.

"This way." We slipped down a side alley and emerged onto another seemingly innocuous street.

Halfway down, an old-timey sign swung from its fastenings. It depicted the signing of the Declaration of Independence, with the bar's name written in fading paint around the image. In a way, some people might've thought it a bit anticlimactic to hide the entrance to the Washington Coven in such an ordinary place. But if we'd had to schlep up Capitol Hill and try to edge inside one of the capitol buildings, we'd have had to deal with way more than just magical security.

"This is how we get into the coven?" Ryann side-eyed me.

I nodded and gave my face a quick alteration with a flutter of Mimicry. "Strange, but true." With that done, I ducked into the bar. Ryann was fine the way she was. Nobody knew her around these parts.

Inside, low music played from tinny speakers, and the place was pretty much empty. A few casual drinkers nursed beers at the dusty, sticky tables, and a bored-looking bartender cleaned a single glass behind the bar. Knowing there was more to the bartender than met the eye, I sidled up to him. There, I took the suit receipt out of my pocket and Mimicked it into two visitor's badges, feeling very Doctor Who with the psychic paper.

The bartender scrutinized the "badges" for a few seconds before nodding to a door at the side of the bar. Above the lintel, it said "Smoking Room."

"Thanks." My voice came out higher than usual—the sound of the peppy aide whose face I'd borrowed.

Together, we headed into the supposed Smoking Room. Beyond lay a crisp white space with chairs neatly laid out—a waiting room of sorts, where magicals sat in cross-legged agitation. A few read through notes, evidently awaiting some kind of interview. Others just sat casually, staring into space. On the far side, I noticed another door. A security magical stood guard over it.

A mousy woman with a frazzled mop of gray hair scuttled in behind us and went directly to the far door. She flashed her badge at the guy on duty, and he immediately let her pass. I supposed that made sense. Not everyone would have to wait out here before being allowed in, or it'd kill the efficiency of the coven staff.

"Ready?" I whispered.

Ryann gave me a slight nudge. "When you are."

Straightening my sleeves, I walked toward the guard with an air of purpose and flashed the Mimicked badges at him. I made to step past him, when he put out his arm to block me.

"Not so fast, Mr. Doyle, Miss Christie." The guard squinted at me. "You don't have the authorization to go through." I might have selected those names on purpose, as an homage to my favorite sleuth writers: Agatha Christie and Sir Arthur Conan Doyle. I wondered if I'd made a mistake. Could he see through the façade?

I feigned outrage. "What do you mean? I'm already late for a meeting with the security council about what's happening in San Diego, and if I'm not there soon, then I may as well not bother coming back to work."

The guard shrugged. "Not my problem. If you don't have authorization, I can't let you in, or I'll be in the same boat."

*Oh... touché.*

Ryann stepped in, flashing one of her high-kilowatt smiles. "We spoke to Karen from MR about it last night, and she said we'd be fine to use our old badges until she could get new ones to us. I know they've expired, and you've got to be thorough, but we only realized they were out of date while we were leaving the office late yesterday. We went straight to MR, but Karen had to get home to the kids after the news broke about San Diego, and she kept saying she didn't have time to do it immediately. She promised us it'd be okay, and we really do have to get to this meeting, given the current crisis."

*Ryann Smith, you clever creature!* In the magical world or the non-magical, you could always find a Karen in HR or MR. Sometimes more than one. A haircut of Karens, if I were to pluralize.

The guard hesitated. "Karen *has* been a bit all over the place since the news broke."

*Yes! Nailed it!* I could've hugged Ryann, if it wouldn't have given the entire game away.

"I think everyone is," Ryann replied smoothly, never breaking character. "It's a difficult time, and it's going to be even more difficult if Director Wallis is down two people."

The guard visibly relented. "Fine, but you've got to promise me you'll get those IDs updated before you leave today."

Ryann nodded solemnly. "We promise. After our meeting, we'll go straight to Karen and insist she get this ironed out."

The guard opened the door for us. "I hope your meeting goes well. I've only picked up bits and pieces of what's been happening, but it sounds like we need everyone we can get working on a solution."

"Our thoughts exactly." Ryann stepped past him with me in tow. Neither of us looked back until we heard the door close behind us. The gatekeeper had returned to his post, not realizing that he'd fluffed his job by letting two miscreants like us into the Washington Coven. Still, he shared our sentiments. We also wanted to get things figured out; we were just going about it in a slightly different way.

I gave a low, quiet whistle. "And the Academy Award goes to... Ryann Smith!"

She laughed softly. "It's easy when you actually do know a Karen in Magical Resources. Only through email, mind you, but it pays to have connections. And Miranda Bontemps had them by the bucketload."

"I could totally kiss you right now." I leaned into her and got a playful shove in return.

"We probably shouldn't draw unwanted attention by smooching in the hallways like a pair of teenagers." She tilted her head toward the main thoroughfare of the Washington Coven—a cavern of sandstone pillars, intricately painted ceiling friezes, and a whole bevy of stern mahogany doorways leading to Chaos-knew-where. "Our challenges are just beginning."

I sighed. "We've got to get to the president, convince her to sign an executive order that she's *really* not going to like, and get it back to Atlantis before our twenty-four hours are up."

Ryann gulped. "And just look how many security magicals are patrolling this place."

A veritable army of black-clad security magicals were doing their rounds of the palatial hallways. And we were striding right into the center of it all, with only Mimicry and Ryann's formidable acting skills to see us through to the other side.

## TWENTY

## Finch

---

As covens went, Washington might've been the most regal. Some uniformed tour guide could've told me that nothing had been altered since this place was founded, and I'd have believed it. It felt old, by American standards. And it smelled old, filled with that comforting, musty scent found in museums and libraries and galleries the world over.

"This is incredible." Ryann drank it all in. If she'd been wearing specs, they'd have fogged with geeky excitement.

I smiled at her. "It's not bad."

"Oh, come on. Even you've got to admit this place is amazing."

The white walls were draped with UCA flags—the good old stars and stripes, but instead of stars there were fifty miniature emblems of known abilities. And in the center stripe, a solid bronze circle represented Chaos itself. Pillars and mock Italian architecture took pride of place, with domes aplenty and cloistered walkways that led deeper into the coven. Dim sunlight glanced through the glass panels of the domes overhead, bathing the marble floor and plush white carpet runners below in a cozy glow that made you want to curl up by a fire with a good book.

"It might even be prettier than the non-magical Capitol building," Ryann waxed on. "I wish I could take pictures, but I imagine some of these security magicals would have something to say if I whipped out my phone and started snapping."

I laughed. "You'd have a hard time snapping anything with your phone. If it survived a drowning in the ocean depths, then you need to write the best review of your life."

Her nose crinkled. "Ah, I forgot about that. It's weird, isn't it, how we've all come to rely on those little screens? No one had a phone in Atlantis." She sighed, gazing at the architectural prowess around her. "I do miss having one now, though."

"We should probably find the president's office." I lowered my voice in case anyone happened to be listening.

She nodded, tilting her chin in that defiant way I loved. "I remember Miranda asking me to arrange a meeting between Daggerston and one of the president's aides, to discuss import regulations on what she called 'private investments.'"

I pulled a sour face. "You mean stolen artifacts for Daggerston to sell to the highest bidder?" I hated that guy. The worst kind of social elite.

"Well, yes, I imagine it had a lot to do with that." Her tone carried a bitter edge. "Anyway, when the aide replied, they told Miranda and Daggerston to come to a holding room on the second floor. I'd bet the Opal Office isn't too far away."

Where the non-magical White House had an Oval Office, we had an Opal Office—a mighty feat of geological wizardry, where pretty much everything, down to the desk, had been crafted from pure opal. By all accounts, it was one of the most extraordinary things in the world. I'd never seen it with my own eyes, but Katherine used to have pictures of it secreted away. Part of me wished I'd taken a closer look at her collection of images, knowing that she'd probably had a bunch of notes about back entrances and hidden ways in and out of that room.

*Chaos, I hated you, Mother Dearest. But damn, did you have good resources!* Dark Side Finch would've done anything to get his hands on them. But half my mother's library had been taken away by security teams, and whatever secrets remained had crumbled to dust when we'd gone to

Atlantis through Eris Island. Now, no one would ever know just how far my mother's knowledge had reached.

We walked through the cavernous, Venetian-style hallways of the magical Capitol building. Reaching a marble staircase at the far end of the main hall, we climbed two floors, following Ryann's memory. Nobody gave us so much as a second glance. We looked the same as everyone else, all suited up with an air of purpose about us.

At the top of the second level, we turned the corner to be met with hordes of Secret Service magicals.

"I think it's safe to say we've got the right floor," I murmured.

"You'd think they'd make them look a bit less like..." Ryann trailed off, searching for the right word.

"Henchman?" They might as well not have been wearing their black uniforms. Their straining muscles almost looked fake, as though someone had jammed a bicycle pump into their biceps and pecs and gone to town. And they'd made sure to have their Esprits on show. A warning to anyone who might get any ideas. Every single one was a primed Herculean, by the looks of it.

Ryann chuckled nervously.

"The question is, how do we get past these beefcakes? It's not like they'll just give us directions." I leaned against the fancy golden balustrade and rested my hand on a carved acorn. My attempt at nonchalance.

Ryann hit me with a determined glance. "Can you Mimic my ID into a colonel's?"

My mouth fell open. "What?"

"There's something so satisfying about wrangling a gang of gym bunnies." She didn't seem as if she was going to back down. "And maybe, with the right documents, we *can* just ask for directions."

"Call me a hypocrite, but that seems a bit... risky."

She shrugged. "We need to take risks."

Reluctantly, I put my hand into my pocket and transformed the suit receipt into a bona fide ID, labeling Ryann as an undercover colonel for the Secret Services. I'd seen a few knockoffs on Eris Island during some of Katherine's sneakiest raids, so I knew what they looked like. I palmed it into her pocket in a way that would've made David Blaine proud. I'd need to stay close to her to ensure the Mimicry stayed put. But I didn't plan on leaving her side, so that worked just fine.

"Lead the way, Colonel O'Neill." Another name to satisfy my inner nerd. I couldn't resist.

She frowned. "O'Neill?"

"*Stargate*. Kurt Russell. 'Nuff said."

Her eyes glittered with amusement. "O'Neill it is. And what should I call you? Captain America?"

"I'm flattered, but I went for Captain Russell. 'Captain America' might've rung a few alarm bells." I flashed her an encouraging smile.

Cracking her neck and squaring her shoulders, she marched up to the first duo of Secret Service bodybuilders with all the confidence of a high-powered executive. The first officer opened his mouth to speak, but she shoved the ID in his face before he could get a word in. "Colonel O'Neill and Captain Russell, here to speak with the president regarding the recent upset in San Diego. We're dealing with a missing Bestiary here, boys, so I suggest you take me to her and don't stand here letting flies into your mouths."

I fought not to release the biggest snort of my life as the Secret Service agents stared at her in total bafflement. I had to say, she was so sexy when she was bringing gigantic men down to size.

"Colonel O'Neill?" The officer scrutinized her ID, seemingly satisfied that it was legit.

"Do you want me to tattoo it on my face so you don't have to squint?" she fired back. "We're wasting time. So I'll ask again—take me to President Gutierrez before you wind up on a battlefield instead of loitering here as a glorified bouncer."

The officer visibly gulped. "Of course, ma'am." He glanced at me. "Sir. Follow me."

Drawing a few stares and some stifled snickers from the rest of the Secret Service magicals—who'd just watched their colleague get his ass handed to him—we trailed the unlucky guy through the black-clad throng. He paused beside a plain wall, where a UCA flag hung. There, he pulled the flag aside and waved his hand across a tiny notch in the surface of the wall. A door appeared out of nowhere, and Ryann and I were immediately ushered through.

The officer led us through a long, ominously dark hallway to another door. He waved his hand over a panel on the side of the doorframe, and the second door clicked open.

"Please enter." The officer gestured for us to go in, which we did. He closed the door behind us, leaving us alone in the most incredible room I'd ever seen. It really was all carved from opal, making me feel as though I were inside an enormous gemstone. The pearly sheen glinted in the sunlight that came through silky white drapes. The floor flashed pink, then green, then gold, depending on how the sun hit it. And the desk was a sculpted beauty, so sleek and shiny that I wondered if paper just slid off.

A woman stood by the window on the far side of the room. She held her hand up to shade her eyes, gazing out at Capitol Hill. Evelyn Gutierrez—leader of the free magical world. I didn't know much about her, but after so much upset, people felt safe with her in the top role. She was the salve to public unrest. With a noble profile and her dark hair pinned back in a stylish ponytail, she gave off the vibe of innate confidence and skill. And the sharp, burgundy pantsuit that she wore certainly added to the impression. No flashiness, just well-tailored lines and a few accessories.

She turned slowly. "And what can I do for you?" Her voice came out clear and sophisticated.

I dropped the Mimicry and showed my real face. "We're here to discuss recent events."

"Finch Merlin?" A flicker of shock registered on her poised face. But she quickly recovered. "What are you doing here?"

"Ah, my reputation precedes me." I was one step closer to executing the first stage of my plan. "I know you've got panic buttons hidden all over this office, but please don't press one. We need you to listen. It's a matter of global importance, and you're going to want to hear what I have to say."

She hesitated. "Is this about Atlantis? I received your sister's message to mobilize our military, and I have put measures in place in case we must attack or defend." Her brow furrowed. "Or have there been developments I am unaware of?"

Seizing the opportunity, I rattled off everything she needed to know. She didn't say a word, but her intelligent brown eyes watched me closely. I finished relating my plan about how we could beat Davin at his own game by giving him an inch so he didn't take the whole mile.

"I loathe the guy with every fiber of my being, and I wish I didn't have to ask this, but I think it's the only way to get close enough to stop him," I said. "We need to make sure this doesn't spark a war, because he'll manufacture a planet of loyal followers. He has to believe he can do what he's set out to. It's the only way to prevent mass death, mass resurrection, and those who don't bow down being the only ones who stay dead."

The president said nothing for a while. Finally, she adjusted her simple gold necklace and hit me with a presidential look that made me feel about two feet tall. "You understand what you are asking, don't you?"

"I do," I replied.

"An executive order is the single most powerful piece of paper out there," she continued. "Given that they are binding accords with Chaos, only five have ever been issued. And all of those were implemented in order to settle disputes between warring magical factions. The first prohibited the use of the Cognis ability, for magicals with said power could control the minds of others. The second forbade the theft of another person's abilities, after the Sanguine Brotherhood decided to seek vengeance upon those who hunted them for their blood."

I raised an eyebrow. "The Sanguine Brotherhood?"

"A group of vigilantes who traversed the United States, stripping magicals who had stolen Sanguine blood of all their abilities. I am surprised you have not heard of them, given your unusual education." She gave nothing away in her tone. I supposed that was what made her so good at her job.

"And what about the Sanguines?" Ryann cut in. "Why didn't anyone sign an executive order to protect them and stop their blood from being taken without their consent? Do you know how many Sanguines have died because of hunters?"

The president eyed Ryann curiously. "And who might you be?"

"Ryann Smith, of the SDC's Human Relations department."

"Ah yes, the adoptive sister of Harley Merlin." She knew her stuff, that was for sure. "As for your question—yes, I am aware of the death toll for Sanguines, and I regret that none of my predecessors signed an executive order to protect them while it would have made a difference. To my chagrin, they were more concerned with the theft of ability than of life."

I frowned. "What about Ephemeras? Isn't that technically stealing an ability?"

"Yes, but it does not affect the person it has been stolen from. A loophole of sorts," she explained. This time, I heard a note of curiosity. "Although, I should ask how you know about the existence of Ephemeras, since they are a contraband item."

"Blame my unusual education, as you called it." I suppressed a wink. "I really think this is the only way to save our world and the non-magical world. He wants to be a hero, and he'll stand on a mountain of bodies to get it. Sign this executive order, legitimizing the use of Necromancy and absolving him, and he'll think he's won. And then he'll lower his guard just enough for us to have a chance."

The president shook her head. "That is where I struggle to believe in your plan, Finch. If I sign this executive order, that will be it—no magical will be able to touch Davin. If it were solely regarding the Necromancy, then I would be more willing. But to absolve him would grant him immunity."

*Which is exactly what he asked for...* This endeavor was starting to feel like a colossal failure. He'd been smarter in his request than I'd realized.

I'd thought he wanted immunity against being charged for past crimes—not everything he might do from this day onward.

*I can't give up now. There has to be a way past this, but... I need help.* No sooner had I thought it than my blood did its spiky thing again. It didn't fill me with confidence. I'd felt that sensation before, and nothing had come of it. Wherever Erebus was, he couldn't cross worlds to aid me with Chaos rules laying down the law.

"What on earth!" The president stumbled away from the window. A shadowy figure drifted through the pane, coming in from beyond the interdimensional bubble. My palms went up on instinct, and the president's did the same.

"Erebus?" Ryann cried out.

The smoky shape drifted closer before coming to a stop in front of the opal desk. It hovered there, its wispy edges taking on a vaguely human form.

"Erebus?" I parroted.

A familiar cackle filled the room. "I wondered how long it would take you to finally get here. I have been waiting."

"Waiting?" I barked. "And you didn't think to—oh, I don't know—come to *me*?"

"Why would I, when this was your inevitable destination?" Erebus shrugged his smoky shoulders, the black mist of his being swirling inside the temporary edges.

"Did you just say..." The president gawked at the Child of Chaos. For a moment, I thought she might keel over.

Erebus bowed. "I am Erebus, Child of Chaos. A pleasure to meet you, President Gutierrez."

The president had to lean against the wall to stay upright. "And you are here, inside my office. An actual Child of Chaos."

"A treat for you, I'm sure." Erebus's red eyes flashed with amusement. "I have come to assist my old friend Finch." He turned to me. "Thank you for summoning me, by the way."

I cocked my head. "Summoning you? Don't get me wrong, I'm glad you're here. But I didn't summon you."

He chuckled. "Your plea brought me back from the decrepit, crumbling otherworld I was thrown into. Not my own, for obvious reasons." His words dripped with annoyance at the djinn. "Your cry for help formed something of a loophole, allowing me to reside in this world, in this form, for as long as I am connected to you by our deal. It appears that I have a duty of care toward you, as part of that exchange. Who knew?"

"You... heard me?" I mumbled.

"Every word." He flashed a gaping, toothless grin that made me feel a bit queasy. "Now, speaking of loopholes, I have one for you, President Gutierrez. You might be concerned about the consequences of signing this executive order, as it means no magical will be able to touch Davin. However, semantics will be our friend. An executive order like that needn't make mention of a Child of Chaos."

An involuntary smile spread over my face. I knew there was a reason I'd wanted him here.

Erebus bristled, his smoke swirling violently. "And I am dying to pass my judgment on that wretched specimen so that I may finish what I began when I allowed him to drown and he tricked me by cheating death. He won't be so fortunate the next time we meet."

He'd slotted the missing pieces into the puzzle I'd been struggling to solve. And man, did it feel good to have some cosmic intervention.

## TWENTY-ONE

## Finch

———

**B**ut something smelled off about this. Gratitude and relief were spilling out of me in an emotional hemorrhage, but this didn't feel very... Erebus. He was a Child of Chaos. He didn't have to lift a finger to help me if he didn't want to.

"Did your daddy-o put you up to this?" That didn't seem right. Chaos had pulled him away from South Georgia Island. The father of magic hadn't let him stay put to fulfill some part of our deal that I'd never heard of before.

"Or is this about Kaya?" Ryann cleverly inquired.

*Ah... bingo.* One look at the swirling smoke, and I knew she was right. The wisps began to trickle out of his temporary edges, like he couldn't control them.

"I'll be damned if I will allow Davin to steal Kaya's mind and make her his unwilling slave. And I will not permit him to disrupt the natural order of the planet." Erebus bristled. So, maybe he *had* changed a little. "Nor can Davin be allowed to have the Bestiary's power. That is sacred, forged from the spiritual energy of my father's gifts. We all benefit from my presence here, instead of... where I have been."

Ryann peered at him. "Which is where, exactly?"

"That is none of your concern," he replied sternly.

"No, where have you been?" I insisted. I wanted to know what had kept him.

He groaned, his red eyes flaring. "In an otherworld that once belonged to a Child of Chaos who has since returned to the Chaos stream."

"They got kicked out?" I knew that Chaos had threatened to do just that to Lux and Erebus, but I hadn't really expected their father to go through with something like that.

He shook his head slowly. "No, Moros chose to return to the Chaos stream from whence we came. He no longer wished to be a Child, for several centuries of enduring his particular duties left him... unwilling to continue."

"Moros?" Ryann had gone into education mode. "I don't know that name."

"The Child of Doom." Erebus turned his wispy face away. I wondered how the Children felt when they had to say goodbye to one of their own. I supposed it would be like any other death—painful and wrenching, with only memories left. And they'd have to wait a lot longer before they were reunited.

Ryann nodded, offering him a sympathetic look.

I laughed awkwardly. "Are you sure he's not still around? With everything Katherine and Davin have gotten up to, it seems like there's a lot of doom and gloom going around."

Ryann shot me a look just as Erebus's wispy head whipped back. "It is no matter for jesting, Finch."

"Sorry." I'd never been one for appropriate timing. "You said you were in his otherworld?"

"I was, though it is falling to pieces." Erebus's churning smoke steadied in its whirling. "Since it belonged to Moros, I had no ability to manipulate its design, and it would not listen to my commands. As such, I have been bored enough to listen for you. You should be grateful that I ended up there."

"I am grateful. Really grateful. But you already know that." I fidgeted with my shirt lapels. Frankly, I was disappointed he hadn't mentioned my snappy threads. He'd developed a taste for fashion during his spell as a human. Apparently, that had dissipated with his solid form. "Anyway, we're getting sidetracked. We don't have a lot of time. President Gutierrez, what do you say?"

The president hadn't said a word during this entire exchange. She'd just stood there, gaping at the smoky figure of Erebus. "You're really the Child of Darkness?" she spluttered.

He swept toward her and raked his ghostly fingers across her arm. Her eyes shot wide as she stumbled back into the wall. Her hand flew to her arm, rubbing it as though a biting cold had set in.

"I apologize f-for d-doubting you," she stammered.

Erebus shrugged. "It has been known to happen."

"Ms. President?" I prompted, desperate to get this ball rolling.

She glanced at me and gave a subtle nod before turning back to His Lordship. "If you assure me that you will deal with Davin, Erebus, then I will write the executive order this minute."

"You have my word," Erebus replied. I knew he meant it. Getting his mitts on Davin was a long time coming, and now he had even more reason to toast that weasel. The Necromancer had messed with the wrong queen.

The president walked slowly to her desk, evidently struggling on shaky knees. Meeting a Child of Chaos for the first time had that effect on people. I'd almost forgotten that, for most folks, it was a novelty instead of an irritation.

She sat down and took out a piece of paper. Pausing to draw a few deep breaths, she opened a glass box that sat on the desk. The panes were tinted red. I wondered if that meant it was a special kind of pen, like the famous red telephone you saw in movies. She clutched it tight, and silver light spiraled out of her palm and into the pen. As the nib began to spark with magic, she touched it to the paper and started to write.

"Our priority is to ensure that Davin believes he is the victor. That will allow us to get close to him—closer than he would permit if he suspected you were not obeying." Erebus floated closer to the desk while he spoke, peering over the president's shoulder. She stiffened, her hand trembling as she wrote.

"Come away from there," Ryann said sternly. "You're making her nervous."

Erebus laughed but did as she'd ordered. "This piece of paper should be enough to bring down Davin's defenses."

"Not to mention Melody and Jacob pretending to be in his service," I added. "That was his other request. Not the pretending part, of course."

Erebus nodded. At least, I thought he did—it was hard to tell in his current form. "Then they must also play their parts well. With these ploys converging, Davin will relax into his self-confidence. That will be his second mistake."

"His first being Kaya?" I really needed to learn when to shut my trap.

His eyes flashed. "Among other things." He drifted around the room. "I will lie in wait until his defenses are down. It is easy to hide in this form. I shall bide my time until the opportune moment for me to emerge and break Kaya's love spell." He glared at me, like he expected me to come back with a sassy retort.

I raised my hands in mock surrender. "Hey, no complaints here. Breaking Kaya's love spell happened to be on my to-do list, anyway."

He gave a quiet harrumph before continuing. "After we save her from Davin's control, we will move swiftly to reverse the Bestiary spell. This *will* be the order in which things happen." He waited again, but I still had no complaints. "During that stage, I will fight Davin to keep him distracted, as I will be the only one powerful enough to make an impact. I am no longer limited by a puny mortal body." He'd tried to sound smug, but it came off regretful. I knew why. No mortal body, no mortal wife. *No Kaya.*

"So, we'll be handling the reversal?" I prompted, feeling a bit sorry for him. Just a bit. He had saved us from the ocean, after all. And he'd come here to save our butts again. That earned him at least some sympathy.

The president lifted her head from her work. "And you're sure this is our only avenue to avoid war and Davin's success?" She still didn't sound convinced.

"I am sure," Erebus answered bluntly. How could she refuse, with Darkness telling her how things were going to go down? Rules might have come from Chaos, but Chaos's Child stood right in front of her. And rules were made to be broken.

## TWENTY-TWO

## Harley

A whalebone lamp hit the wall and smashed to pieces, the shards skittering across the floorboards. Mairead shrieked as the cluster of magicals that O'Halloran had brought ducked for cover. Only the Rag Team stayed where they were, their palms raising in perfect unison, ready to back me up if things turned even nastier.

"You need to get a grip!" I sent out a lasso of Telekinesis and grabbed Rasmus around the waist. His condition had gone from bad to worse, this sudden fury ignited by the mere mention of doubting Davin's "noble intentions." Rasmus had gone into a total meltdown.

"You won't touch him!" Rasmus raged back. Fortunately, Nash had had the common sense to clap him in a pair of Atomic Cuffs not long after he'd returned to shore post-resurrection. Rasmus hadn't been happy about that, but he'd have been a lot harder to deal with without them. The Cuffs were courtesy of O'Halloran, who was doing his best to keep everyone calm, leaving us to contend with a loose cannon; Rasmus ran wild in the main room of the Antarctic Coven, prepared to give everything to defend Davin.

"Rasmus, you're a smart guy. Just ease up, so we can have a sensible discussion." I tried a soft approach, since yelling at him hadn't worked.

He hunched over, glaring. "You've made your stance clear. You want to hurt Davin; you don't want to talk. And I won't let you do it!"

Melody snuck over to my side and whispered in a low voice. "We might have to put him downstairs."

I arched an eyebrow at her. "Downstairs?"

"There are cells down there. That's where we're keeping..." She glanced around. "His Majesty. Saskia is watching him, with the security magicals that O'Halloran left behind. We should probably put Rasmus there, for his safety and ours. But it might be best if we keep the other resident a secret for as long as we can. The Mage Council seems... unhinged, and I wouldn't want them doing something rash, like trying to use him as leverage."

"Good idea." I gripped Rasmus tighter about his waist just as O'Halloran entered the room.

"Let go of me!" Rasmus howled. Done with his Davin-induced ranting, I dragged him across the room, following Melody to a doorway. I presumed that it led down to the belly of the Antarctic Coven.

"Where are you taking him?" O'Halloran asked. He looked annoyed and resigned.

I hit him with an equally exasperated look. "There are cells downstairs. He needs to be in one pronto, before he wrecks this place and us in the process."

O'Halloran stepped aside. "Proceed."

I continued to haul Rasmus along, trailing Melody down a perilous set of ancient, creaking steps into a shadowed basement that reeked of rot, despair, and... a faintly metallic scent that turned my stomach. But that was the least of my problems. Rasmus's message was clear as crystal—or rather, the message Davin was sending through the recently resurrected. One way or another, the people of this world would come to love and adore him. They would be loyal to a fault. Case in point, Rasmus going ape at the slightest notion that we weren't convinced of Davin's graciousness. Yes, there were those who didn't want to be back in the land of the living. But for every one of those, there were far more who thought the way Rasmus did. Or perhaps Davin had realized not everyone wanted to be brought back, so he'd started on a little mind influencing to deal with potential dissenters.

*Death has a way of revealing people's true colors.* It took something special to stand in front of the Grim Reaper without fear, and it took something even more remarkable to let the scythe fall without a whimper of protest. Sometimes that bravery was due to a sacrifice made for another person, or the peace of mind that came with old age, or readiness at the end of a lengthy sickness. Sometimes it was knowing that you'd done all you could in this world or reaching a point where you didn't want to fight anymore. Death could set people free, letting them wing their way contentedly to the afterlife. Still, death wasn't always fair, and many people would do anything to avoid it. Rasmus was exhibiting that in raw form, his behavior stemming from the most primordial part of his heart. He wanted to protect Davin because the Necromancer had chased the Reaper away. To Rasmus, attacking Davin was tantamount to attacking life itself.

"Well, aren't you a sight for sore eyes." Saskia glanced up from the blue glare of her phone screen. How she even had cell service out here was beyond me. "If you're worried about the prisoner, he hasn't made a peep."

I tugged Rasmus into the dim light. "I'm worried about this one, currently."

Saskia toyed with a strand of her blonde hair. "Who's he?"

"It's a long story, and I don't have the energy for it right now. He needs to go in a cell. Tatyana can fill you in."

She shot up from her stool. "I'll take a break, then." I didn't have time to reply before she disappeared up the stairs, no doubt to get all the juicy details from big sis.

She pushed past Remington and Cal on her way up as the two came down into the basement level to join us. I suspected our newcomer had come out of sheer curiosity. Their radios hadn't stopped crackling since we'd come back from the SDC, and the sound rattled my nerves. I'd turned mine off.

"Can't you shut those off?" I wrangled Rasmus toward one of the cells while Melody got the door open. The interior was a horror show. Rust-red streaks smeared the walls, and that metallic scent assaulted my nostrils. "Isn't there another one we can use?"

Melody shook her head. "The only clean one is occupied."

"Well, then, this one will have to do. Sorry, Rasmus." I flung him into the cell and slammed the door behind him. He immediately hurtled himself at the small circular window in the door and pressed his face against it, puffing out condensation like a raging bull. His fists pummeled the inside, creating a percussion that made me want to put on head-phones and never take them off. To make it worse, the radio fizzed to life again.

"More trucks are arriving, over," a gruff voice said.

"Send them to the colonel. He'll tell them where to go," another replied.

I grimaced. "Please, for the sake of my sanity, turn those off. There's only so much anxiety a girl can take in one day."

Melody put her hand on my shoulder and squeezed gently. "It's better for us to have an open channel so we can hear what's going on in San Diego. It's a lot to deal with, but burying our heads in the sand isn't going to do us any favors. It's only going to get stickier from here."

I sighed. "I know. But that constant static. It's like bees buzzing in my skull." I looked to Remington. "What's happening there? Why are more trucks arriving?"

The poor guy looked ready to collapse. "The SDC ruins are being investigated by the non-magical military. They're bringing specialists in." He turned the volume down on his radio. "The longer we leave the SDC out there as it is, the more information the government will be able to gather. And the more the magical community is exposed, the harder it's going to be for us to clean this mess up afterwards."

"Rock, meet hard place—right?" I banged a fist against the cell door, in the hopes of getting Rasmus to stop. It didn't. It only made him beat harder.

Remington nodded, and slithered a spell through the door. "Exactly. O'Halloran and the other magicals who were still inside tried to hide as much as they could, but there's still a lot left out there, waiting to be discovered by the wrong people." Rasmus's door battering ceased. I opened the porthole window to find the guy asleep, under the influence of Remington's magic.

"Why are you so sure they're the wrong people?" Cal countered. "Shouldn't everyone be on an even playing field? Doesn't everyone have a right to know that magic exists?"

*Ah, that old argument again.* There were so many points for and against it, but I didn't have the clarity of mind to race through every single one. Nor did I have the energy to hash out an ethical debate. So I kept it simple.

"Imagine we were aliens."

Cal squinted in confusion. "Huh?"

"Imagine we were an alien race, with unusual abilities that immediately made us more powerful than ordinary humanity. What would the military do? Don't think about it, just give me your first answer."

She paled. "They'd bomb you sky-high."

"And that's why, for now, revealing magic to the entire world isn't an option. Especially not with tensions already running so high." I saw that she understood. As a woman in the army, she probably understood better than most what the stakes were. However things played out, someone would lose.

Cal ran a hand through her hair, her forehead furrowed. "I... think I'm starting to get the bigger picture."

"It won't all make sense straight away." Melody offered her a charming smile. "But give it time, and the pieces will slot together. I can't pretend to understand the shock of learning about magic for the first time, but baby steps tend to work out well in most scenarios. Actually, no... I suppose that's not true. Not with this Davin situation, anyway, but... oh goodness, you see what I'm trying to say, don't you?"

Cal chuckled faintly. "I think so."

Jasper and Selena appeared in the stairwell. Two people I was dying to see... *not*. Weirdly, they had their coats on, as if they were going somewhere.

"We... uh... just wanted to pop down to say that we... um... have had second thoughts." Jasper cleared his throat. "The three of us have decided that it might be prudent for us to leave you and your brother to handle Davin. The way you dealt with... uh... Rasmus has shown us that we may have bitten off more than we know how to chew."

Selena buttoned the front of her black trench. "However, we aren't planning to abandon you, before you start slating us as cowards. We are leaving so that we can be of assistance."

The tag team switched between pre-rehearsed words. "We're going to head out now and rally more magical forces, in case things go awry. We must be prepared for every possible scenario."

"What about Rasmus?" I gestured behind me.

"We're going to leave him in your care until a solution can be found," Jasper replied awkwardly. "He is of no use to us in his present state, and there is much we need to do. Apologies, but he is safer here, where he can't harm anyone." He paused. "If he does happen to regain some clarity, please let him know how sorry we are to leave him like this, and that we will come back for him." I looked at the cell door, now blissfully silent.

*Unbelievable...* What were we, a home for strays and unwanted resurrected beings? I thought about protesting but knew it wouldn't do any good. They already had their coats on, for Pete's sake. Plus, they didn't wait for me to answer. By the time I looked back to the stairwell, they'd gone. And I guessed they wouldn't be back anytime soon.

"I guess government officials are the same whether you're magical or not, huh?" Cal muttered sardonically. "Always running from responsibility."

I flashed her a conspiratorial look. "I'd normally agree, but it's probably a good thing they're running away. If they stayed, they'd only get underfoot. And they aren't the only ones with a lot to do."

"Should we head back up, or did you want to stay awhile to watch Rasmus?" Melody toyed with her earring—a nervous tic I'd noticed.

"I think I'll stay down here and—" I didn't get to finish as fresh footsteps pounded down the stairwell. I braced for the Mage Council to hit me with an addendum. Instead, Finch and Ryann sprinted down, taking the stairs two at a time... and they appeared to have found a friend. A faint shadow trailed them down the steps and into the basement. Red eyes sparked in the gloom. I'd have known those eyes anywhere.

"Finch!" Melody yelped excitedly. "You're back! Wait... where did you come from? Jacob is upstairs, so he couldn't have portaled you back in. And who, or what, is that?" She eyed the shadow with rightfully wary eyes.

Finch gasped for air. "The president let us use a mirror. Anyway, that's not important." He brandished a scroll, neatly tied with a scarlet ribbon. "We got it! The executive order: signed, sealed, and soon to be delivered, if it hasn't already taken hold."

As for the shadow—well, he'd never been one to miss an opportunity for drama. "Melody Winchester, I'm surprised at you. Don't you recognize an old friend when you see one?"

She turned as white as the executive order. "Erebus?"

"In all my glory." His red eyes flashed with amusement, but I didn't find any of this funny.

My heart stopped beating for a second. "You got it?" Was I supposed to be happy? Because I definitely didn't feel that way. Seeing that paper made it official. Davin had the immunity he desired, absolved of all wrongdoing, with the ability that had caused this chaos freshly legitimized. Now he could rule his Atlantean kingdom in peace, resurrecting folks until he had the entire world singing his praises.

"This is just a way for us to get close to Davin." My brother had clearly spotted my discomfort. "What's written here won't stop us from beating him. We've got a plan for that. So, when you're ready, the real work to dethrone Davin and get the Bestiary back can begin." He smiled so wide I couldn't help but feed off his enthusiasm, even if I had major doubts about this entire endeavor. But I didn't have a better solution. Finch's idea was all we had.

*I trust you, bro. Please, please be right about this.* I turned my attention to Erebus.

"Is he part of this plan?"

Finch gave a shrug. "He got bored and decided to help us out."

"Are you going to keep telling everyone that?" Erebus retorted sourly.

"Hey, I'm just repeating what you said." Finch smirked in his trademark way. "If you didn't want me telling people the truth, then you should've come up with a better excuse."

I rolled my eyes. They'd been reunited all of two seconds, and they were already sniping at each other like frenemies. "Any sign of your wayward wife, to give us an extra pair of cosmic hands?"

Erebus's smoky form shuddered. "No, there has been no sign of her. And, personally, I am glad. She aided Finch and his friends before because our father told her she had to, nothing more. Now that she has done that, she has no further stake in what happens, so she has no reason to reach out and help again. I, however, do have reason." His eyes glowed brighter —two embers in the semi-darkness. "Thanks to me, you now have aid and the executive order. One Child of Chaos should suffice for any mortal's plan."

I hated that we'd gotten to this point. It sickened me that Davin had everything he'd asked for. He had the executive order, and Melody and Jacob had already agreed to play their parts in pretending to serve him. We were all bending to his will, no matter the pretense. I wanted to be positive, but it stuck in my throat like a fishbone. We might have had a scheme to bring an end to these dire and troubling times, but what if it cost us more than we realized? What if it didn't work?

*Get your head out of your ass!* Finch had busted his butt to get everything in order, and I wasn't going to piss on his parade. Besides, I was forgetting one important aspect—what if it *did* work? My brother's mad schemes had been a roaring success before, so why should this be any different? He might act the court jester, but he was actually one of the smartest people I knew. I just had to have faith.

"What do we do about the SDC and the non-magical part of our problem?" Remington cut through the ensuing silence.

I sighed. "I imagine that will have to wait a little while longer, until after we deal with Davin."

Cal raised a tentative hand. "I can help buy you guys some time. I have sway with the military, and I can lay some diversions and distractions if it means putting this asshole—whoever he is—to bed."

I smiled despite myself. *You really are starting to get the bigger picture, aren't you?* It was a long road of self-discovery, one I remembered walking like it was yesterday. But—just as I'd said to Cal—once Chaos had a hold of you, it was very hard to get away. No matter how hard you tried, it pulled you back in. And I saw that it already had a firm grip on the lieutenant. One that might work to our advantage.

Finch's hands suddenly shot up to his face, his palms pressing into his temples while his features scrunched in pain. "Argh... what the... ow, ow, ow, *ow*! Get out of my head!"

Ryann leapt into action. "Finch? Finch, are you okay?"

"What's happened? What's wrong?" I joined in her concern, hurrying to my brother's side. He flopped down onto the stool that Saskia had vacated, his shoulders hunched as he continued to push against his temples. I put my hand on his back, rubbing small circles between his shoulder blades. "Finch, what's wrong? Is it the gremlins?"

He squeezed his eyes shut. "No gremlins."

"Then what is it?" Ryann crouched in front of him, the two of us mounting a two-pronged attack of love and worry.

"It's... Apollo," he wheezed. "He's in my head."

Melody dashed into the love attack, making it a trio. "Apollo? He's sending a telepathic message to you?" She paused. "Yes, I suppose that would be possible, considering his power."

Finch winced. "His voice is in my brain. It's more than just possible."

"What is he saying?" I kept rubbing those small circles, scared to death for my brother. It didn't matter how many crazy things we'd been through; I'd always panic when he was hurting or when weird things started happening to him.

"Kaya is… in her bedchamber. His word, not mine. I'd have said… 'bedroom.'" Finch sucked in a sharp breath. "Davin had… enough of her lovey-dovey business and sent her to bed with no supper. My words, not his. That means… she's alone. Davin is… bored of her for one night. And no one is… watching her, except… Apollo."

"He's trying to make up for what he did before." Melody jittered with excitement. "Oh goodness, if this is true, then this might be our best chance of getting Kaya out so we can break her love spell!"

Erebus piped up. "Then we must act now!"

"Hold your horses," Finch rasped. "At least wait until my head has stopped splitting."

A loud bang on one of the cell doors made me whip around. Ovid's face appeared at the porthole of his prison. Honestly, I'd forgotten he was even here. Unlike Rasmus pre-spell, he'd been silent as a mouse until now.

"Finch!" he shouted. "Finch, please, you must save my daughter."

Finch laughed bitterly through his headache. "You've changed your tune."

"Heed me, Finch. I know that I am responsible, at least in part, for what has befallen her, and I know that I have no right to ask anything of you. But she is my only child, and though I have acted foolishly and self- ishly and despicably, I wish to make amends," Ovid begged. "Please, save her, so that things may be made right again. Please. Do not let her suffer any longer."

Finch lifted his head, peering out of one eye. "Why does everyone assume I haven't got breaking her spell on my list of things to do?"

"Maybe because she put you through hell?" Melody replied, painfully honest. That was one of the things I admired most about her. She rarely had a filter on what came out of her mouth.

He chuckled through gritted teeth. "Yeah, there's that. But no one deserves to be forced under someone else's will." He cast a sly glance at Erebus, which the Child of Chaos duly ignored. "I always intended to help her."

"Then you must go now, while you have the opportunity!" Ovid urged. "Davin will not be distracted for long. She is too valuable to his endeavors."

Finch slumped, his shoulders sagging. "Well then, guys and gals, I guess we're going back to Atlantis." He lifted the executive order scroll limply. "At least we have a good excuse for being there."

I reached for his hand and held it tight. "And you'll have me."

It was time I saw this fabled city for myself.

## TWENTY-THREE

## Finch

A stampede of peeved elephants had decided to run a marathon inside my skull. Whatever Atlantean wizardry Apollo had used, I felt the effects even after his voice had gone away. Not that I'd let a headache stop me from striking one task off my hefty to-do list.

After informing O'Halloran of our plan, we gathered on the shoreline of South Georgia Island. I should've hated this place by now, but it hadn't lost any of its stark beauty. Even if, in about two seconds, I'd be plunging back into its hideous waters.

"Are we all set?" We'd separated into two parties. Harley, Melody, Jacob, and I were in team numero uno, while Luke, Nash, Wade, and the rest of the old Muppet Babies were deploying in team numero dos. Melody had found another crack in the city's weakened forcefield, which meant we had two ways in. Two ways, one big element of surprise. Hopefully. My team would go through the gap that Hector had showed us, while the others were going to use the new one. Melody had given a frankly beauteous map to Luke. Seriously, the detail was astonishing. And I was supposed to be the one with cartography skills.

"One moment." Ever the spotlight hog, Erebus brought proceedings to a halt. He scanned the shore until he spotted what he was looking for. "I will need you to carry me, Finch. Do not ask questions, just do as I ask."

*Ah, the Gimli to my Legolas.* I had some snark and sass ready for him, but he was a moment too quick. His wispy form slithered away toward a green glass bottle that lay on the rocks. *He's not going to... oh, yep, he is.* I watched as he squeezed into the narrow neck of the bottle and swirled into the chamber.

"Finch!" His voice echoed from inside.

"Right. Carry you. Got it." I picked my way across the slippery terrain and stooped to grab the bottle. Lifting it to eye level, I observed his contained form for a moment or two. If I only had a stopper...

"I wish the other djinn could see you now." Kadar appeared, his mouth curling into a smug grin. "Their former overlord squished into a bottle, the way our people have been forced to do for centuries."

A spark of red flashed inside the bottle. "You will not breathe a word of this!"

"Says who?" Kadar puffed out his chest. "You don't own us anymore."

"No, but *you* are still a creation of Chaos," Erebus retorted in a disembodied voice. "There is plenty I can do to you if I do not care for your impertinence."

Raffe quickly took over. "Pay no attention to him."

*Raffe Levi, is that a sly smirk I see?* I didn't call him on it, in case Erebus really did exact some retribution, but Raffe was definitely enjoying this just as much as his djinn counterpart. After all, it wasn't every day you saw your old boss stuffed into a bottle. I'd have been a liar if I said I wasn't amused by the irony. Still, it would've been rude to bite the hand that was currently feeding us. With Erebus back to full power, we stood a chance against Davin. He was our secret weapon, neatly tucked away and ready to unleash hell.

"Melody? Would you do the honors?" I gestured to the expansive ocean.

She nodded eagerly. "Two bubbles, coming right up."

The rest of us lined up in an orderly fashion while the formidable chipmunk set to work, letting out a shriek as she waded into the bitter water. I noticed Luke get agitated. He'd already complained about being separated from Melody for this particular mission. It'd taken her a good ten minutes to bring him around, by which time the rest of us had been ready to go.

I got it. If I'd been in his position, and it'd been Ryann heading off into Davin's servitude, I'd have thrown a tantrum that would've impressed a toddler. Fortunately, Ryann was staying behind this time, which I was selfishly pleased by. I'd suggested she stay and watch over Rasmus, and she hadn't argued. I supposed she knew that if she came along and things went south, we'd be back in leverage territory—a bargaining chip against backstabbing.

"You'll be careful, won't you?" Ryann tickled the back of my neck with her fingertips. She'd come to wave us off. A bittersweet goodbye. On the one hand, I'd always want one last kiss before I plunged headfirst into danger. On the other hand, it made it harder to actually leave for said danger.

I smiled and kissed her forehead. "Always."

"Promise you'll come back?" She rose on tiptoe to kiss me.

I kissed her back, drinking it in. "Undomesticated equines couldn't keep me away."

Harley cleared her throat. "Sorry to interrupt you lovebirds, but I think the bubbles are ready."

I kept an arm around Ryann's waist and glanced out to the shallows. Melody stood in the midst of the icy water, pointing to the location of the two bubbles. With them being transparent and all, if she hadn't given us a guiding hand, we'd have been scrambling for the bubbles for ages. Luke had his arms around her, mirroring Ryann and me. He placed a gentle kiss on the top of her head, and she turned to look up at him, forgetting the bubbles for a second. Rising up on tiptoe, she grabbed his face and kissed him properly, both oblivious to the rest of the world. Just for that sweet moment. Danger may have been on the horizon, but love was definitely in the air. And goodbyes tended to make us realize, more than ever, what we stood to lose.

"I know you're not supposed to say this, but I'll be back." I ducked in for one more kiss. "I love you."

She held on to my shirt a moment longer. "I love you, too."

With that, I forced myself to step away from her. I didn't stop until I'd entered the water, resisting the urge to scream at the unrelenting cold. Melody broke away from Luke with one last kiss and kept hold of his hand until he waded too far into the water to stay connected. Only then did she resume her instructions. Using her pointing finger as my compass, I mustered some balls. Ironic, considering the current state of my real ones. Heaving in a breath, I dove beneath the surface and found myself inside a bubble pod similar to the one that Hector had formed. There had to be a way to do this without getting wet, but I guessed it was better than swimming the whole way.

"Room for a small one?" Harley appeared beside me.

My teeth chattered as I flashed her a grin. "Sure. Where is she?"

"Hey." She gave me a gentle punch in the arm as Melody and Jacob entered the bubble.

I maneuvered into the pilot position and extended my hands. Immediately, the bubble shot forward, knocking everyone sideways. "Sorry!" I said, glancing over my shoulder. "I'm new at this, and Hector made it look so easy."

"Do you want me to drive?" Harley cast me one of her withering looks.

"Nope, I've got it. Just need to be gentler with it." I put my hands out again and gave a subtle push forward. The bubble responded, cutting through the water at a less hair-raising pace.

On our left, the second bubble skimmed along seamlessly. Wade sat in the driver's seat, showing me up with his natural skill. Still, at least we had some space. Their bubble was crammed, like clowns in a clown car.

Sticking close to each other, we pressed on through the dark ocean. Melody served as our GPS, guiding us toward Atlantis. Only when we'd approached the eerie underside of the city, where the previous crack still showed the hidden world above, did Wade's team split off. They had the map that Melody had given Luke to follow. And, if everything went smoothly, we'd rendezvous with them at the showdown.

I brought the bubble to a halt and scoured the murk.

"Why have you stopped?" Jacob asked, his tone anxious.

"I'm just checking to make sure the coast is clear." I pressed my face to the bubble's surface, looking for the glint of scales or the whip of a tail. But the ocean lay still. No beasts to be seen. Still, my gut told me this was too easy. There was no way Davin wouldn't have known that his Nessies had been vanquished. And there was no way he wouldn't have replaced them with something else, executive order notwithstanding.

Harley let out a startled gasp. "What's that?"

My head snapped around toward her. "What's what?"

"That!" She jabbed a finger at the bottom of the city, where the solitary crack glowed faintly.

"Oh dear, oh dear, oh dear." Melody sat up straighter, her eyes wide.

Strange black ink spread out from the base of the floating city, barely perceptible unless you were looking for it. The tendrils spiderwebbed in front of the pale glow of our entrance, becoming more visible for a moment.

"What is it?" Jacob squinted.

"I don't know, but you can bet your ass it isn't good." I tried to ignore the heavy weight of dread that formed in my stomach. The inky ooze continued to descend, touching the edge of a stray chunk of driftwood that glided along, minding its own business. Quick as a flash, the sizeable log dissolved to nothing.

Melody yelped. "It's acid! Oh goodness, it's acid, and it's coming straight for us!"

I hesitated, trying to kick my brain into action. Everywhere I looked, the inky mist descended. I could've retreated with the bubble, but I suspected the acid would only come out again when we dared to return.

And there wasn't a clear spot where I could drive the bubble to evade the oncoming darkness.

"Finch!" Jacob shouted. "Do something!"

"I… I don't know what to do." Stark realization struck me. I had no idea how to get us out of this.

The first tendrils of acid made contact with the bubble. At first, nothing happened. But then, water trickled in, spilling down the transparent walls. The acid had started eating away at the magical exterior. It was nowhere near as quick as what it had done to the driftwood, but it wouldn't be long before we were completely exposed to its devouring power. We'd be reduced to nothing before we even set foot in Atlantis.

"Finch, with me." Harley took over. "Your Air works down here for breathing, right?"

I nodded.

"Melody, can you transform our skin into metal?" I could practically see Harley's cogs whirring.

Melody bit her lower lip. "Y-yes… yes, I can do that." She shook her head in frustration. "But you'll sink. You'll be too heavy."

"We'll deal with that. Right now, I need you to cover every inch of our skin in metal and do the same for yourselves. This bubble should be able to bear the weight and keep you afloat long enough for us to get rid of the acid. If it doesn't, then we'll keep hold of you with Telekinesis." Harley grasped Melody's hand. "You're going to be okay. I'm not letting anything happen to either of you, do you hear?"

Jacob couldn't even speak. I couldn't blame him. Acid surrounded us, nibbling away at the only thing between us and the freezing ocean and the acid itself.

"Melody?" Harley urged.

The feisty Librarian snapped out of her fear. "I'm on it, just… don't let me drown, okay? It's one of the worst ways to go. It's suffocation and panic until you run out of breath. I came close before. I don't want to go through that again."

Harley gulped. "I won't let you drown. I swear."

Melody wasted no time weaving her transformative magic. Reaching out for each of us in turn, she sent out pulses of rainbow energy that coated our skin in a layer of pure metal.

"Whoa..." I struggled against the instant claustrophobia. The metal covered every inch of us, with thick goggles over our eyes. And, inside the bubble, the additional weight was painfully noticeable. But the bubble held, sinking a yard deeper but no farther.

"We'll have to feed our Air between the metal layer and our actual skin," Harley instructed, sounding way calmer than I felt. "It'll be tricky but not impossible. Now, come on, before this acid eats through the bubble."

She pushed through the tensile surface of the bubble and plopped out into the acid-filled water. I went after her, though every instinct told me to stay put and take my chances. Immediately, the ocean chilled the metal layer. As far as insulation went, a suit of armor wasn't high on the list. But at least I didn't feel as heavy as I thought I would, though I was definitely sinking.

Harley sent a lasso of Telekinesis upward, the strand connecting with the underside of Atlantis. She stopped sinking. *Ah, you clever thing!* So that was how she'd planned to counteract the weight of the metal. I copied her, my body coming to a standstill in the water.

In the gloom, she signaled to me—a few taps on her chest before retracting and extending her fingertips, pantomiming a pair of headlights flashing. We might not have had the kind of telepathy that Huntress and Nash had, but we were siblings. That came with a language all its own. I understood what she was trying to say—she was going to use her Light, which meant I had to use my Darkness. Everything in balance.

It was probably a good thing we couldn't speak to each other. It meant I didn't have to tell her that I could literally see the acid eating through the metal covering her skin. Its progress was slow, but it was definitely causing damage to her thin suit of armor. I could only imagine what it was doing to mine.

She gave me the sign for "okay," and I returned it. It was go-time. She held out her hands for mine, and I gripped her fingers. Fixing on her goggled eyes, I dipped into my Darkness reserve and brought it into my palms. Fight fire with fire. But it worked for water, too. And the only way to clear this acidic mess was to dilute it and sweep it the hell away from here.

Black-tinged magic poured out of me at the same time a blinding pulse shot out of Harley. Our combined forces spiraled upward from our joined hands, creating a spinning vortex of Air and Water that threatened to drag us into it. But through the fogged lenses of the goggles, I watched something else get dragged into the cyclone. The acid. It twisted around and around until the entire vortex had turned black, all the acid collecting like it'd been vacuumed up.

Harley gave my hands a squeeze. We might've collected the acid, but now we needed to get rid of it. I'd have been happy to just send it off somewhere and hope for the best, but I guessed that wasn't my sister's intention. No, this called for something bigger. An eruption of Chaos that would dissolve every last drop of the acid, the way it'd dissolved that driftwood.

Dipping back into my Darkness reservoir, I poured as much as I could into my palms. Opposite, Harley did the same with her Light. The moment our affinities collided, they twisted together, forming a sparking orb of raw energy. It grew larger by the moment, sucking the acid vortex inside until there was nothing left. Gingerly, I drew one last burst of Darkness out of myself and let it flow into my hands. Harley must have had the same idea, because glinting white sliver snaked out of her palm and met its shadowy twin. They wrapped around each other before shooting upward, right into the center of the swelling orb.

We might as well have lit a fuse. As those last, interwoven strands disappeared into the orb, it unleashed an explosion so fierce that it threw my sister and me away from each other. Everything turned white as my body spun away from the epicenter.

Flying blind, I lashed out with Telekinesis, frantically trying to get a grip on the underside of Atlantis before I hurtled out too far. The lasso connected and jolted me to a sudden, whiplash-inducing halt. I dangled there, feeding Air into my mouth and trying to blink the white light out of my eyes.

*Harley?* I peered desperately through the murk to find my sister dangling from the city's underside on a string of Telekinesis. And, though our suits of armor had taken a beating, we were alive.

I waited a while to be totally sure the acid was gone. Satisfied, I swam back to the bubble and pushed inside. Harley appeared shortly after, the two of us gasping for air as Melody undid her spell. Sure, the bubble was half full of water and getting fuller by the moment, but we didn't have far to go. And I'd take icy water over acid any day of the week.

"Did you see that?" Harley grinned.

"Did I *see* that?" I laughed at her odd enthusiasm. "My retinas will never be the same."

Jacob coughed awkwardly. "I don't want to embarrass you, but you should both take a look at your clothes."

I stared down. "Oh, crap." Where the acid had managed to sneak through the metal, it'd eaten great big patches of my jeans and T-shirt. I knew threadbare was fashionable these days, but this was obscene. To spare Jacob and Melody's poor young eyes, I let a simple sheen of Mimicry flow over the missing bits. Harley's clothes weren't as bad, but I still sent out a bit of Mimicry to her, to cover a few unfortunately placed holes.

"Thanks." Harley ruffled my hair, only to pause abruptly. "What about the others? They'd have gotten stuck in that, too!"

"No, no, they're okay," Melody interjected. "They just came through on comms. Wade managed to guide the bubble through the acid mist before it could disintegrate."

Harley sank back. "That's a relief. I don't know what I would've done if..." She trailed off.

I jumped in. "We won't be able to rely on comms once we get inside the city. If it's anything like the last time, they'll cut out the moment we cross the threshold."

Harley groaned. "Of course they would."

"But Nash and Luke know their way around, and they know where to meet us." I offered an olive branch of comfort. "It just means radio silence until we can meet up again. That's probably a good thing. The last thing we need is Davin listening in."

"Good point." Harley visibly rallied.

Jacob raised a hand. "I don't want to alarm anyone, but we should probably get a move on before this bubble fills completely."

"Another excellent point," I agreed. We were already about waist-high in icy water, and I didn't fancy drowning inside a bubble after narrowly escaping an acid mist. And I had no idea how to repair this thing without a whole lot of chewing gum.

"I can help with that. I just needed to check for the right spell, since it's slightly different once the bubble is actually in the water." Melody sent out a few threads of rainbow energy, to heal the rifts in the bubble walls. It wouldn't do anything about the water already inside, but at least it wouldn't get any higher. Resuming my seat, I got the bubble moving again.

Soon enough, the four of us had passed through the underground tunnel network and were standing beneath the sewer grate that led to the palace gardens. We were soggy and full of holes, but the sweltering heat of Atlantis's underbelly would soon dry us out. As for the holes in our clothes, I couldn't do much about Harley's. See, this was where our paths diverged. Harley had the potion to knock Kaya out and an Ephemera filled with souped-up Portal Opener energy to get the queen out of Atlantis. A last-minute addition to our plan back at the Antarctic Coven. Meanwhile, I had my genie in a bottle, and an executive order and two shiny new playthings to deliver to Davin.

"Are you sure you know where you're going?" I didn't want Harley getting lost in this place.

She smiled. "Relax. I've got it all written down." She flapped the map—another Melody special—at me. "I'm going straight to Kaya's bedroom. I'll give her the potion, then use the Ephemera to get us both out of there and back to the Antarctic Coven. Saskia and Ryann are cleaning out one of the cells as we speak, in case she gets feisty when she wakes up and discovers that she's been separated from her slimy love."

I heaved a sigh. "I hate that you're doing this alone."

"I'm not. I've got all of you in this city in case anything goes wrong. And I've been known to get myself out of a jam, from time to time." Harley pulled me into a bittersweet hug, and I squeezed her back twice as hard.

"You know what I mean."

She chuckled into my shoulder. "I know, but you're not allowed to worry about me. I've got the monopoly on worrying."

"Says who?"

"Says me." She pulled away and planted a kiss on my forehead. "So you stay safe, or I swear I'll hunt you down in the afterlife and give you a telling-off like you've never had before."

I managed a smile. "Same goes for you."

"Deal."

I swallowed the lump in my throat. "I love you, sis."

"I love you, too." She pulled me in for one more hug before steeling herself for the mission to come. "I guess this is goodbye, for now. Next time I see you, we'll hopefully have Kaya safe at the coven and Davin ruing the day he ever met us."

"Let's hope so."

With a final flash of a grin and a determined glint in her eyes, she climbed into the palace gardens. I watched her go, bracing myself for my own mission. Davin's defeat rested in our hands, now. And if I dropped the ball... Davin would have everything he'd ever dreamed of. And our best shot at stopping him would've slipped right through my fingers.

*Best not drop the ball then, eh? That goes for you, too, Erebus.*

## TWENTY-FOUR

## Finch

---

Flanked by Melody and Jacob, and carrying my explosive message in a bottle, we arrived at the throne room a short while later. No messing around with back passages and secret entrances. We took the straightest route, entering through the front door. The guards on duty let us pass, no doubt informed by their king that we were expected. And a familiar face happened to be waiting for us by the imposing double doors of the throne room.

"Thebian." I gave him a curt nod.

"Finch," he replied in a monotone.

I glanced around the hallway and leaned closer to him, giving an air of cloak and dagger. "Actually, it's good you're here. I was wondering if you could do me a favor."

"A favor? What sort of favor?" Thebian looked anxious.

"Could you just check my back for a second? I think there's a knife sticking out of it, the one you and Apollo put there." I flashed him a sarcastic grin and earned a sour grimace for my comedic efforts.

"It was necessary." Thebian shuffled awkwardly, revealing that he hadn't been comfortable about the situation. Still, it hadn't stopped him from letting Apollo do it.

I offered him one of my finest withering looks. "And was it necessary to arrest Hector? You could've kept him out of it. You could've warned us what you were going to do, but no. All you do is serve Kaya blindly, even though she's pretty much a zombie right now. Ironic, considering the dead are popping up everywhere thanks to your new king."

"Hector's involvement was unfortunate," Thebian admitted. "But had we spirited him away from the rest of you, Davin would have known that something was amiss. Our ploy was necessary. It was not personal."

"Really? Because it felt kinda personal." I had a bee in my bonnet that wouldn't stop buzzing.

"As a way of making some small restitution for what we did, you will be pleased to hear that Hector is unharmed. He is imprisoned but otherwise well. His family is safe, also," Thebian assured us.

Melody gave him the evil eye. "Well, that makes it all better then, doesn't it?"

Thebian sighed, visibly agitated. "I understand your indignation, and, though you have no cause to forgive me, I hope that you will eventually find some comfort in the compromise. Davin is not interested in any kind of vengeance at present. He is behaving like a benevolent and merciful ruler."

"And you're buying that?" Melody demanded. I had to say, I enjoyed it when Melody got fierce.

Thebian looked elsewhere. "I... have my doubts." He'd lowered his voice to a whisper, being so close to the king's throne room and all. "Davin may desire love and adoration, but deep within himself, he is as he has always been. A monster. Sooner or later, that side of him will rear its ugly head."

"And I'm here to add even more fuel to his fire." My words dripped bitterness. I had to make my resentment sound real, in case that son of a blobfish happened to be listening. "We got him exactly what he wanted: Librarian, Portal Opener, and—the pièce de résistance—the executive order, freshly inked. Maybe that'll keep his ugly head down a while longer."

Thebian's face fell. "You retrieved his requests…"

"Didn't have much choice, since you turned us in." I needed him to know that he definitely wasn't off the hook, even if Apollo had sent me that brain DM.

"I can see that the ice is not going to thaw anytime soon." Thebian's shoulders fell as he turned to open the fancy-ass doors. "And if you have what he has asked for, then I suppose we should not keep His Majesty waiting."

I smiled sweetly. "No, we wouldn't want to do that, would we?"

Thebian ushered us into the cavernous space, which had long since lost its novelty. I hated this room. It was like being dragged into the principal's office but a hundred times worse, since the principal here was a power-hungry Necromancer with a serious messiah complex. What Davin really needed was Freud and a leather couch, so they could figure out where this desperation for adoration had come from. Hadn't his parents loved him enough? Had boarding school starved him of affection and made him feel abandoned? There had to be a root cause for his particular brand of cuckoo.

I turned my attention directly to the dais. Davin lounged on his throne like a cat about to get the cream, while the other stood mercifully vacant. Apollo had told the truth. He was standing right next to Davin's throne, having evidently witnessed Kaya's dismissal first-hand. She was nowhere to be seen, sent to bed for being an annoying barnacle of a love interest. It surprised me that her lapdog hadn't gone with her, but I guessed Davin probably wanted to keep Apollo in sight, until he proved himself loyal to both rulers. Plus, having another man in her bedchamber might've raised eyebrows.

*Go get her, sis.* I thought of Harley with a flutter of worry. She'd be running a gauntlet of guards and hurdles right about now, and if she got in trouble, there'd be no one to help her. Not that she needed help. But she was my sister; worrying was part of the package. We needed to buy her as much time as possible.

"How very punctual of you." Davin maneuvered into an upright position. "I gave you twenty-four hours, and you come back in half the time. I must say, I'm surprised. I thought you'd run down the clock in some vague attempt to prove a point."

I shrugged. "Why would I bother to do that and risk missing the deadline altogether?"

Davin leaned forward in his seat. "The real question is, do you have everything I asked for? Did you persuade them by explaining that there'd be war if they didn't make the right choice?"

"It's a potent motivator," Melody answered for me. "When you threaten to let the entire world destroy themselves so you can take your pick of whom to resurrect, it does tend to light a fire under a person's backside. Unlike you, we're not okay with that happening. If I can stop one unnecessary death, then I'll do whatever I have to. Even if it means serving someone like you."

Davin chuckled. "As king, I decree that all death is unnecessary."

"Because you like playing God?" Jacob interjected. "You know that it'll never make you one, no matter how many people you bring back to life."

"I don't need to be a god. I just need to be the hero this world is sorely lacking." Davin adjusted his crown, though it didn't need adjusting. "Now, while it's rather endearing that you persuaded your friends to come here and serve me, Finch, I'm more concerned about my main request. Did you manage to achieve *all* of what I sent you out to do?"

*He thinks I've failed.* I saw the doubt in his eyes and felt the nervous energy bristling off him. He probably thought I'd brought Melody and Jacob as a buffer to lessen the blow of telling him that I hadn't managed to get the executive order. He clearly thought little of me. *Stupid man.* Hadn't he observed me from a distance while I'd gathered up all the goodies that Erebus had demanded to make his bodysnatching happen? He should've known by now that when I set out to do something, I made it happen.

"You mean… this?" I took out the tightly wound scroll. The red ribbon contrasted starkly with the creamy white paper, like a deep wound slashed into skin. Very fitting.

Davin's eyes widened comically slowly. "Why, that could be anything."

"It's not, though, and you know it." I strode up to the dais, unmolested by the guards on standby. "This is the executive order absolving you of your previous crimes, granting you immunity, and legitimizing the use of Necromancy. I don't think I missed anything, did I?"

"Give me that." A note of childish glee filled his voice as he snatched the order from my hand. His eyes flitted left to right as he read the words that the president had written, the decree that had been bound to Chaos. "'It shall hereby be sanctioned that Davin Doncaster has been absolved of all wrongdoing and all responsibility during the era of Eris...' yada yada... 'He shall be granted immunity from this day forward, preventing any retribution for acts, past, present, and future...' yada yada... 'The use of Necromancy will no longer be classed as prohibited and will no longer be punishable by a court of magical law. Instead, it will be looked upon as a free ability that is of benefit to the magical community...' yada yada... 'In the fabric of Chaos, let this be woven. Signed, Evelyn Gutierrez, President of the United Covens of America.'"

I huffed out a breath. "Satisfied? Or would you like me to go to Chaos itself for proof?"

"I feel the energy coming from it, connected directly to the heart of Chaos." His eyes peered over the top edge of the scroll. "I can't believe you actually got it. Now I understand why Erebus kept you around for so long. You are smarter than you look, which isn't saying a great deal. Still, I'm almost sorry that I doubted you. But you know how I feel about regrets—a total waste of time and energy."

*Let's see how you feel about that in a few minutes...* If everything went smoothly, Davin would be nothing *but* a great big ball of regrets. I had the bottle in my pocket, ready to go. And Erebus would be ready to unleash hell when that moment came.

"All of this, bound in Chaos." Davin's smirk bordered on maniacal. "This is everything I have ever wanted in one simple scroll. My carte blanche. I can do as I please, and no magical will be able to lay a finger upon me. No security team will be able to stop me. I am... invincible!"

Yep, definitely edging on manic territory here.

*Ah, but you're forgetting one little morsel of small print...* He wasn't as invincible as he thought. Omissions were important things. And he'd neglected to pick up on a big one.

I slipped my hand into my pocket, preparing for the grand reveal. No magical could lay a finger on him, but a Child of Chaos could. I took a shallow breath, gathering my courage. Gripping the neck of the bottle tight and bracing myself to hurl it at the vapid snake, I caught sight of Apollo shifting uncomfortably on the dais. He met my gaze, his eyes glinting with nerves.

Immediately, my stomach plummeted. Something felt... wrong. Very wrong. And Apollo's eyes said it all. Davin was onto us.

## TWENTY-FIVE

## Harley

I followed Melody's map by way of a service entrance around the eastern side, through the sun dappled gardens and into the awe-inspiring palace that towered over everything. As far as first impressions went, Atlantis was in a league of its own. The entire city—what I could see of it, anyway—seemed like it had been designed by the same mysterious architect, down to the last, minute details: a sea-glass orb embedded in the shining marble, a discreet carving of a sea creature, and a plaque depicting words that I didn't understand. Things only seen if you were paying attention. The palace was like a smorgasbord of delights, from the smallest carving to the imposing spires that twisted upward, emulating coral fronds.

But I didn't have time to admire the visual treats. Scouring the gardens for guards, I made quick work of checking for security hexes at the threshold of the service entrance. I sensed two, working in unison to keep out unwanted visitors, but they were child's play to undo. It was surprising that a place like this would rely on such simple hexing. Then again, I supposed they'd had to downsize the interior protective measures, with all the Atlantean Bestiary's energy being fed into the floundering forcefield. And Davin was hoarding the surface world's Bestiary energy for his grand resurrection plan.

After unpicking the hexes and watching the residual, inactive sparks flutter to the ground, I slipped into the palace.

*Okay, let's see what we have here.* I browsed Melody's map and followed the directions down the first corridor, hanging a right at the end of the passage. The halls were empty, since it was late evening, but that didn't mean there weren't patrols doing the rounds. And I certainly didn't want to get caught here. That would put Finch and his plan in danger.

I sank into doorways and ducked behind statues whenever footsteps echoed through the corridors, waiting for the nerve-shredding sound to pass before carrying on. All the while, as I hurried and stopped, sprinted and paused, crept and hid, my mind raced with a thousand wayward thoughts. One in particular persisted.

*What if we don't succeed?*

It was strange how Atlantis's appearance and Davin's pursuit of pseudo-heroism had stomped a great big boot of uncertainty onto my mind. The wedding I'd been looking forward to was now firmly on the backburner. And the stupidest part was, all my excited hopes and dreams seemed so futile and foolish now, when compared to global catastrophe.

But it didn't take away from the fact that I still wanted them, so badly. The pieces of the future that Wade and I had discussed, curled in bed until the early hours of the morning with the flash of some muted movie lighting his smiling face. The house we hoped to buy, and the color of the kitchen, or the type of shower we wanted in the bathroom, and how many dogs we'd have running around the garden of our dreams. Silly stuff that brought me so much joy. Kids came up sometimes, but I wasn't ready for that, especially with the whole Leviathan naming deal. Even without that, judging by the state of our world and the dangers that kept cropping up, I didn't know if I'd ever be ready to bring children into the world. Kids who'd been through the system like me could go one of two ways: they either never wanted to have children of their own, knowing how hard it could be if anything were to happen to them, or they wanted children more than anything, to make up for the crappy childhood that they'd had. I seemed to be an exception, falling somewhere in the middle.

Wade had a similar mindset, though he'd had an upbringing that a foster care kid like me could only dream about. He'd said he didn't mind either way; he only wanted to be with me, and we'd see how things played out after a few years of marriage. I mean, there was so much we still wanted to do and see. Though I guessed Davin's reign was likely to stop all that now, more than the arrival of a child would have.

*First, I've got to survive this disaster.* And I had to make sure everyone else survived too, with the sole exception being Davin freaking Doncaster. He'd relied on that amulet of his for too long. And if he couldn't die, then I sure as heck hoped Erebus had some kind of fitting, Tartarus-esque punishment ready for that weasel. Something like having his organs pecked out by eagles every morning, only to go through the same thing the next day, and the next day, and the next, until he'd come back from death so many times that he was nothing but a husk of who he'd been. Grim, but it was precisely the fate Davin deserved.

*Right... it should be this way.* I paused and looked down the gloomy hallway ahead. Atmospheric torchlight flickered from sconces that lined the elegant walls. A few figures eyed me from the confines of gold-framed paintings, putting me on edge. More than I was already.

A duo of armored guards turned the corner at the far end, leaving the hall to continue their night patrol. That meant I had a short window of opportunity to get in there, knock Kaya out, and get her out of there with Jacob's borrowed ability.

*Showtime.* Checking my pockets to make sure I still had the potion and the Ephemera, I slunk down the corridor. Melody had literally put an "X" over the door, which I thought was a nice touch. It made it simple, at least.

Turning the handle, I ducked into the bedroom and closed the door behind me. Inside, the room was dark except for one dim lamp that glowed from a table on the far side of the room. And beyond a window that ran across the far wall, the firefly glints of the city of Atlantis twinkled gently. It could've been any other city, looking at it like this. Only, there wasn't nearly enough neon, so the color scheme was a lot more... celestial. As though I were in an observatory, staring out at the constellations.

"Hello?" murmured a small voice from beside that solitary lamp. I noticed a faint shift of shadow, revealing a figure seated in an armchair. "Who is there?"

I fumbled for a light switch, hoping that some things transcended culture. "Queen Kaya?"

"Who calls for me?" The figure shifted again as the lights came on, dousing the bedroom in an unyielding glow. Her hand shot to her face and shaded her eyes, presumably so she could see me better. "I do not know you. Who are you? Why have you come here?" Panic exploded into her voice, and I knew I had only seconds before she sounded some form of alarm.

I raised my hands in a gesture of peace. "Please, don't be scared. I'm not here to hurt you. I'm just here to talk." Not completely true, but I needed to calm her down. Why couldn't she have been asleep?

"Who are you?" She rose from her chair, and sparks of pale blue light swirled around her. Weird, considering she hadn't so much as lifted a palm.

*These Atlanteans are powerful, remember?* I reminded myself. She could summon magic without using her hands, and that meant she really was a force to be reckoned with. Finch had mentioned something about this, calling them "Sentients," but I'd never seen it in action until now.

"An ally," I replied. "I'm here to help you, not hurt you." I took a step closer.

"Stay where you are, stranger!" Kaya snapped. "Do not try to fox me with vague speech. Tell me who you are, or you shall feel my wrath."

*Wow... and Finch was actually married to this woman.* I couldn't correlate my goofy, awkward brother and this queen in my head. She was... well, extraordinarily beautiful. Ethereal, in fact, with long silver hair and startling blue eyes, and the sort of bone structure that would've made a supermodel jealous. Plus, despite the spell she was under, I sensed her strength. It flowed off her in trembling waves, as did a cocktail of confused emotions: fear, sadness, anger, and a strange strand of what felt like love. But it didn't feel the same as real love. No, this seemed… artificial, hitting me in a weird way and sending pins and needles through my chest. There was definitely potent magic at play here, and it left a bitter taste in my mouth.

"My name is Harley Merlin. I'm a friend." I dared to take another step, but Kaya's sparks glowed brighter, and I backed off.

"Merlin?" Kaya spat. "Then you can be no friend of mine. I have heard of you, from the mouth of that traitor—your brother?"

I kept my hands up. "He's my brother, yes, but you're wrong about him. He wants to help you, too." I tried a different tactic. "Do you remember the last time you were under a love spell?"

She hesitated. "I do not like what you are suggesting."

I continued regardless. "When you and my brother were under a love spell, you both remembered things you weren't supposed to." I had to get her to listen. If I couldn't do that, then I at least had to keep her talking until I could get close enough to surprise her with the knockout potion and get her out of here. "That's because you can't give away a heart that's already taken. That's what he told me. His heart was taken by Ryann, and your heart was taken by Erebus. You remember Erebus, right?"

A flicker of pain flashed in her eyes. "Of course. He betrayed me, almost as vilely as your brother did, though at least he had the common sense to refrain from interfering in my love for Davin. My king, my paramour, my light."

*Oh, please...*

"You loved Erebus once. I've got a sneaking suspicion that you still love him, but you're finding it hard to remember things. Is that right?" I shuffled forward. To my relief, her sparks didn't get any brighter. "Is your head fuzzy? Do you keep trying to think of things, but they slip away?"

Kaya looked away. "I am fatigued, that is all. My love has urged me to rest in order to restore myself. I have been through a great deal of emotional turmoil, of late. It is only natural that it should take its toll on one's clarity of mind."

"That's not it, though. I'm not saying you aren't exhausted. If you're feeling anything like the rest of us, I'm guessing you wouldn't mind sleeping for a week." I mustered a hint of a smile. "But that fuzziness in your head has nothing to do with fatigue. *Davin* did that to you. He's using a love potion to control you. I know, deep down, you believe me. You just can't remember."

Kaya's Chaos sparks dimmed slightly. "I would know if I were under a spell." In truth, she didn't sound convinced.

"And how do you feel? Do you feel like yourself? Would the Kaya you know fawn and preen and cling to a man like this?" I switched gears to tough love. "I don't know you. I can only go by what I've been told, but Finch speaks very highly of you, even now. He called you strong, and smart, and fierce. But the woman I'm looking at doesn't fit that description. The woman I'm looking at is scared, and confused, and controlled."

Kaya's eyes glinted with annoyance. "How dare you speak to me like that!"

"I dare because I have to," I shot back. "I dare because you're not yourself, and you know it. I dare because your entire city, and the people you love so much, are endangered by the man you think you're in love with. They need you to snap out of this and take back control. We all do."

I edged even closer, until there were barely a few yards between us. She didn't attack; she just stared as though she were trying to figure me out. Honestly, I had no idea if my words had a chance of breaking through that magicked skull of hers, but I hoped that something I'd said would make a modicum of sense to her. All I had to do was trigger a memory and get the real Kaya back for a moment—long enough for me to pour the knockout potion down her throat. After that, the Antarctic Coven's cells would keep her safe until Erebus could free her from the love spell, the same way he'd unraveled the one on Finch.

"Davin is protecting this city at my side. He cares for my people as though they were his own." It didn't even sound like she was talking to me anymore. Instead, it sounded as though she was trying to convince herself.

"Is he?" I stepped toward her. "Or is he tricking them with fancy magic, using power he's stolen from the surface Bestiary, so they all bow down and adore him? It's subterfuge, not benevolence. All of it is designed to get Davin what he wants: ultimate power. He's chosen adoration as his means to get there, instead of violence and fear. But make no mistake, he'll use your people as pawns if he has to. He'll send them out to the battlefield without batting an eye. He'll use them, the same way he's used you."

Kaya flinched. "Used me? Davin would not use me. We are equals."

"Then tell me why he tried to plunge a knife into your heart. Tell me why he went behind your back to spring himself from prison, and joined forces with your father to dethrone you. Tell me why he let Faustus kill you, only to bring you back and pour that potion down your throat. Which, by the way, he didn't drink himself." I hit her with every tale that Finch had told me. "Does that sound like someone who really loves you, or does that sound like someone who's using you to get what he wants? Davin has always wanted to be the lord of the land, and you happened to be the quickest way to gain that status. He also sacrificed the strength of your Bestiary to perform the spell that infiltrated our own. I bet if you went down there now, you'd find it in a terrible state."

Her eyes widened, as if she was recalling something. "Iso... I have not spoken to her in some time."

"Iso?" I managed another step while she was distracted by thought.

"My dearest friend. I had forgotten her name, until you spoke of the Bestiary just now. I can see her, but... the image is hazy." Kaya's forehead furrowed in frustration. "Why?"

"It's the love spell. It altered your mind, and I'm guessing it made you forget about all the people who could knock some sense into you. We can go to your Bestiary right now and speak to Iso. She'll see the truth—that you're not yourself. If you don't believe me, then perhaps you'll believe her."

Kaya nodded slowly. "I want to see her."

"Then let's go." I stretched out my hand to her, praying she'd take the bait. I had no intention of going to the Atlantean Bestiary with her. If this went the way I wanted it to, she wouldn't get to see her friend, either. But this was the only way to save her.

Kaya reached out and took my hand, taking me by surprise. "Yes. Let us go."

I had my chance. Dipping into my Light, I prepared to launch an immobilizing spell through my hand and into hers. We needed as many layers of protection as magically possible. She was no ordinary person. Like tranquilizing a rhino, you never knew how much you'd need to take the beast down.

Kaya gripped my hand suddenly, her mouth twisting into a cold smile. "Unfortunately, you will not be going where I am going."

"What?" I tried to wrestle free, as a weird numbness spread through my fingertips. Her eyes flitted behind me. "A trap was set, Miss Merlin. And you walked directly into it."

I turned my head just in time to see a blinding flash erupt. Then... darkness.

## TWENTY-SIX

## Finch

N*o, no, no!* I wasn't letting this opportunity slip through my hands. No way, no how. Maybe I was misreading the situation. Maybe Apollo's face just had that expression as a default setting after being roped into Davin's service. Either way, no one was taking this shot from us.

I whipped out the bottle and lifted my arm to hurl it at the dais where Davin stood. The slippery toad grinned, palms up. I understood why a millisecond later. A blast of magic hit me square in the chest, freezing me in place like one of those fishy-tailed Ganymede statues that littered Atlantis. I urged my arm to move, to propel the bottle toward Davin. But it didn't budge. My fingers were immobilized around the neck of the bottle, my arm no longer listening to the neurons firing in my skull.

"Not today, you smarmy wretch!" Melody surged forward. She got all of five steps before a second blast struck her. She went down like a sack of potatoes, her legs swiped from under her.

"Aaaaaargh!" Jacob didn't bother with an insult, just a battle cry. He sprinted for the dais and managed to avoid Davin's first attack, only to run into the second. It struck him hard in the face, his body arching backward like a slow-motion Rocky. He crashed to the ground, groaning.

Davin smiled. "How charming."

I tried to open my mouth to howl a million choice words at Davin, but my lips wouldn't move, either. Frustration pounded through my veins. I had the bottle in my damn hand! All I had to do was throw it, let the glass smash, and Erebus would come hurtling out. I guessed there was a physiological reason he couldn't slither back out of the narrow neck by himself, or he'd have done it by now. To come so friggin' close... I wanted to tear my brain out of my head and trample it to sludge.

"Come now, you know me better than that." Davin flicked his wrist, and I dropped to my knees. Panic shivered through my useless body. This was no run-of-the-mill immobilization spell. No, he'd brought out the big guns: a puppet spell, so he could toy with me to his heart's content.

I shot a "help us" glare at Apollo. But the painfully loyal advisor gazed back with panic glinting in his own eyes. Right now, he seemed as frustrated as me.

"Your Majesty," he said nervously. "He brought you your executive order."

"Do you think I don't see that bottle in his hand?" Davin didn't even look at him. "I am aware of your deceit, Apollo, so he has you to thank for this. I knew you would give in to your weakness and attempt something foolish."

Apollo gulped. "Pardon?"

"I gave you a test, Apollo. Needless to say, you failed miserably." Davin smirked as he strolled around the dais, knowing he'd trumped us all again. "Why else would I have sent Kaya to her chambers? I wanted to see what you would do, and you went and squealed like a little piggy. Just as I suspected you would. You are all so ridiculously predictable."

I struggled to get past the puppet spell, but my body wouldn't listen. The spell had me firmly in its grip, pumped up by the stolen power of the Bestiary. I had zero control. And Melody and Jacob were still down, trying to recover from Davin's strike. Melody had managed to get to her knees, but Jacob rolled in pain, rubbing his jaw.

*Dammit, Apollo... why didn't you do some recon first?* But I couldn't place the blame solely at his feet. We should've sensed there was something a little too convenient about this. Davin had used Kaya and the effects of the love spell to trick us all. Man, every time I thought I couldn't despise him more, he pulled a stunt like this and my hatred levels amped up.

"Now, be a good boy and lower that bottle to the floor." Davin bent his index finger downward, and my arm imitated the movement. A slight *clink* announced the moment the bottle touched the ground. Only then did Davin step forward to retrieve it, ducking in and out in a nervous way that belied his confidence. Maybe he'd seen me get out of enough scrapes to think I could wriggle out of this puppet spell. Unfortunately for me, it held fast.

Davin observed the bottle, watching the black mist swirl inside. A pleased smile curved the corners of his lips. "I should thank you, Finch, for doing the hard work for me. It's not easy to coax a Child of Chaos into his own imprisonment. And now, he'll be the most prized artifact in my collection."

"He's a cosmic being. He can get out of there whenever he wants." Jacob dragged himself into a sitting position. His eyes squinted with obvious pain.

"No, I can't," Erebus whispered to me from inside the bottle. The black smoke glowed red. "My form is too densely packed. I cannot escape without having the bottle smashed."

"You'd think so, wouldn't you?" Davin laughed at Jacob, too distracted by his own peacocking to hear the stuck Prince of Darkness. "Fortunately, that isn't the case. Have you ever seen one of those ships in a bottle?"

Jacob frowned.

"It's the same problem." Davin put the bottle in his pocket. "Once the ship is inside, you can't get it out again. Not without smashing the bottle. The cells of his being are too tightly packed to slither out again. Stowing himself away in there comes at a price, and he simply doesn't have the toll to release himself. And I'm certainly not going to do it." He echoed Erebus's exact sentiments.

I eyed Davin in silence, furious and exasperated to the point that I thought my frozen body might explode. How could it be that he was always one step ahead?

"You have to find a way to smash it," Erebus urged.

Melody regained her feet. Staggering a little, she surged forward again with a palmful of rainbow magic and lashed out at Davin. I'd have shouted at her to stop, but my lips were still glued shut, awaiting the tug of the puppet master's permission.

He didn't even flinch, and he didn't have to raise his hands, either. Violet magic coursed out of him and swirled around his body, creating a personal forcefield. The rainbow magic bounced off harmlessly and drifted to the floor in a flurry of useless sparks. Melody sent out a fresh barrage that began to nibble away at his forcefield, readying another palmful for the man inside.

"You're just not getting it, are you?" Davin shook his head as more purple-tinged Chaos surged out of him and passed straight through the shield. It slithered toward Melody and twisted around her like a glowing snake. She tried to fend it off, and Jacob found the strength to jump back in to help. He grimaced with every step, a bruise blooming across the side of his face. But Davin's magic proved too strong. The purple tendrils constricted, bringing Melody to her knees, her face contorted in pain. If Luke had been here, he'd have rushed toward her, prepared to rip that Chaos off her with his bare hands if he had to. But Luke wasn't here. And the cavalry wasn't coming. Or, if they were, they were walking into a fight they wouldn't be able to win.

I stared at Jacob, trying to communicate with just my eyes. *Get out of here. Go regroup. We failed.*

He gave me a reluctant nod and raised his hands. Bronze flashes leapt from his fingertips. But he didn't get any further. A fresh set of purple tendrils branched away and wrapped around Jacob's legs, gliding silently up his body and working their way down his arms. The poor kid panicked, flailing wildly to try and get them off, but the tendrils carried on until they reached his hands. The bronze sparks died, rendered inert by whatever Davin had done.

Next thing I knew, Jacob was on his knees as well. He unleashed a howl as the violet Chaos gripped him in a vise. His hands balled into fists, and his body went rigid. But he could've bellowed until his lungs gave out, and it wouldn't have made the slightest difference. None of us were getting out of our respective immobilization spells. Not with the power of the surface Bestiary at Davin's fingertips. He didn't have to lift his hands, and he wasn't even breaking a sweat. The Bestiary was doing all the hard part for him, making spellcasting as easy as slicing through butter with a hot knife.

*He was prepared for us. He knew what we'd do.* He liked to claim we were predictable, but that was bull this time around. We'd been careful. Not as careful as we could've been, maybe, but I couldn't think of a single way he could've known about the bottle. I'd have understood if he'd caught us red-handed in Kaya's bedroom, but he hadn't. We were in the throne room, and I'd brought him everything he wanted. None of that should have made him suspicious. Yet, he'd countered our every move as if he'd seen us do it already. True to our Atlantean surroundings, I smelled something fishy.

"Are we done?" Davin asked, a note of sass to his words. "It really is fruitless of you to continue fighting me like this. I'm sure it makes you feel better, but it *is* futile. By now, hundreds of people will be on their way to these shores to beg entry into Atlantis. People who will do anything to defend me after what I have done for them."

"The novelty will fade," Melody replied ominously. Her voice registered strangely—much deeper and more detached than anything I'd heard come out of her mouth before. "With joy will come misery, and glee will turn to guilt, once the living understand what you have taken from the resurrected. Death is a part of life. The universe demands balance, and it will redress it."

Davin looked frightened for a moment, but it quickly passed. "Nonsense. If I wasn't put on this earth to use these powers, then I would not have been born at all." He started pacing again. "I've spent the past few hours performing miracles—Chaos-sanctioned miracles." He stopped to wave the executive order at us. "I've resurrected humans and magicals alike. Soon, my kingdom will expand with those who treasure me and what I can do. And their love will see me rise to lofty heights, the likes of which have never been seen."

He waxed lyrical to the point that I almost didn't notice a side door opening.

*Kaya?* The queen led a contingent of royal guards into the throne room. And my heart damn near vacated my chest. Between two of the soldiers hung a figure, her half-conscious body being dragged along the floor like a mop. My sister.

*No!* How could I not have realized this was coming? If Davin had set a trap for us, then of course it was bound to snare my sister. He'd just nabbed two Merlins for the price of one.

"My love, there you are," Davin purred. "As punctual as ever. I take it you aren't hurt?"

"No, my darling. I am unharmed." Kaya's hand delved into her robe pocket and removed a vial. "Although, I suspect this wretched girl intended to use this on me and would have succeeded, had you not fore-warned me. I believe it is some kind of spell that would have rendered me unconscious. I also found this about her person." She took out the Ephemera that we'd painstakingly filled with Jacob's ability. "I do not know what this is, but I do not care for it."

Davin went to her and placed a kiss on her cheek before taking the Ephemera out of her hand. "This is a device that can borrow the ability of another magical, my love. And it's ripe with Portal Opening power. They wanted to take you from me."

I noticed that he'd barely looked at the Ephemera, but he wasn't speculating about its contents. It was like he already knew what we'd attempted. Down to the last detail.

"I would never permit that," Kaya protested.

Davin chuckled and kissed her again. "No, my sweet, I know you wouldn't. I'm only sorry you had to go through such unpleasantness."

"I do not mind, given that the cause was righteous." She scowled at my sister, and my hackles rose. If I could've screamed the place down, I would've. Anything to get Kaya to see what she'd become and try to snap her out of this spell. Verity would turn in her grave if she saw what was happening to her daughter. Unless Davin had already brought her back to life, that is. *Yeah, as if he'd bring another queen into the equation.*

However, it seemed I wasn't the only one who'd had about enough of Davin and his machinations. Apollo hurried toward Kaya and sank to his knees. He grasped for her hands and held them tightly, gazing into her eyes with desperation.

"Kaya, you must come to your senses. You were in no danger. We were endeavoring to aid you, to free you of this love spell that Davin has placed upon you. Your love for him is not real!" Apollo said desperately. "He is using you for his own benefit. I would not have put you in such a situation, but I had no choice. You will not listen, and you cannot see the truth that lies before you—that this is not who you are! This is not right. Think of your mother. She is in the afterlife, awaiting you on the day of your death, many years from now. Think of how she would feel, seeing you now! She would be horrified!"

"I enjoy a rousing speech as much as the next person, but I think that's quite enough from you." Davin stepped in and smacked Apollo on the back of the head with another jolt of purple Chaos. Apollo fell immediately, lying unconscious on the floor. "I will allow him to live for your sake, my love. I know he is dear to you, even if he has made some missteps."

Kaya gazed at her friend, her expression unreadable. "Thank you, my dear. He has evidently had heretics whispering in his ear."

*The only whispering heretic here is your so-called darling!* I wanted to shout it in her face, but I still couldn't speak. An infuriating predicament for me when there were so many comebacks I'd have loved to launch at Davin.

"Speaking of individuals whispering in ears." Davin turned and fixed his cold eyes on me, a sickening grin on his lips. "You're probably wondering how you got caught, aren't you? I imagine you thought you'd been exceptionally clever. Blink twice if I'm right."

I couldn't help it. I blinked twice.

"Do you know what the best kind of spy is?" Davin's gaze glittered with mischief. "The kind that doesn't even know they're a spy."

"What… are you… talking about?" Melody wheezed, straining against the pain.

Davin toyed with the bottle in his pocket. "I might have expelled Ovid from Atlantis, but I did so with a purpose." He paused for dramatic effect as the room fell silent. "He has no idea that I've been watching and listening through him. A little addition that I made when I brought him back to life. That's the beauty of a resurrected mind—it's malleable, like an impressionable child. Thanks to him, I heard every word and saw everything you've been up to beyond these walls."

Fury boiled in my belly, as fierce as an inferno. I'd have given anything to lash out with magic, but the puppet spell held me immobilized. That bastard had done it again. He'd slithered his way ahead of us and called out checkmate before we'd even moved our first pawn.

In this game, the king was the most powerful piece on the board. And I didn't mean King Ovid.

## TWENTY-SEVEN

# Finch

The reach of Davin's scheming barreled into me with the force of an avalanche, turning everything on its head. I might have been stunned, but surprised? Nothing he did surprised me anymore.

And the finishing flourishes just kept coming. Harley had a souped-up Cuff around her neck, since she had a way of escaping the ordinary surface brand. Erebus couldn't get out of his "itty-bitty living space" without outside help. Apollo was out cold. And everyone else had joined the remake for NSYNC's "Bye Bye Bye" video. We were mere puppets, dancing on Davin's strings.

*There you are, strutting like an overstuffed peacock.* Davin had the world in the palm of his hand, having foiled all his foes in one fell swoop.

"Guards, put Cuffs on them. I abhor using manipulation spells, but these miscreants gave me no other option." Davin gave the instruction, and his followers hopped to it. We couldn't even pretend to fight back as they clapped the damn things on us. But on the upside, I could talk again. And man, did I have some things to say.

"We got what you wanted, and you're still not grateful. Look at you, all pouty because you *had* to use a manipulation spell. Not exactly kingly behavior, if you ask me. Who are you trying to kid, huh? We all know you get a kick out of puppeteering people and making them sink to their knees in front of you. It makes you feel like a big man, doesn't it?" I rattled out the words like I'd been mute for a year.

Davin lifted a finger to his lips. "Learn when it's prudent to be quiet, Finch. Unless you'd like a gag to go with that Cuff around your neck."

"Only if it matches," I shot back.

He laughed a little too loudly. "Fine, chatter all you like; it makes no difference to me. I learned how to block out the sound of your voice a long time ago. Although, I did enjoy listening to you spill out all your secrets when you thought no one was listening."

"You nasty, self-absorbed, snaky mother—"

"Ah, watch your language!" Davin interjected. "We wouldn't want to taint the pure ears of these Atlanteans with your vulgar tongue, now, would we? Guards, could you bring the Librarian and the Portal Opener to me, please?"

The Atlanteans glanced at each other in confusion.

I snorted. "I don't think they know what you mean, Your Royal Smugness."

"Those two!" Davin jabbed a finger toward Melody and Jacob, and the guards hurried into action like they'd been cattle prodded. I sensed I might've ruined the moment for Davin, but not enough to make me feel better about this catastrophic screw-up.

Melody and Jacob tried to resist as the guards dragged them toward Davin, but the painful spell he'd put on them had drained them of their energy. They both looked pale, their foreheads slick with sweat. And as they came to a halt in front of Davin, I noticed their knees knocking together, struggling to bear their weight.

"You are welcome here in Atlantis." Davin turned on the schmooze. "You will both serve me well in this kingdom, and I much prefer having the real deal to a meagre Ephemera that only works once." He cast me a knowing look that boiled my blood. A taunt about our failed mission.

Melody lifted her chin in defiance. "My knowledge is mine, to give to those who prove themselves worthy. You're not one of those people, so you can forget it. And if you think you can use some nasty little spell on me to crack my mind open, you can forget about that too. Librarians have defense mechanisms unlike anything you've ever seen."

*Don't encourage him...* Davin liked the easy life, but he'd never shied away from a challenge. Still, I had to admire her ferocity.

Jacob nodded weakly. "Same goes for me. I won't do anything to help you."

Davin sighed like the diva he was. "I don't exactly need your consent to get you to do what I want. I have the power of the Bestiary at my fingertips." He leered at Melody. "We could always test how strong those defense mechanisms are, for the sake of science. I remember what happened to your predecessor, Odette. She gave up the goods in the end. It nearly killed her, and it turned her into a drooling halfwit, but I know it's not impossible to crack open the mind of a Librarian. I imagine I will find it much easier than Katherine did, given my present strength."

Melody faltered. "That was different."

"Was it? I don't think so." He arched an eyebrow. "Here's the crux of all this, to make it very simple for you two. I have the means to bend you to my will, but I'd rather you did so freely. It's much better for my image."

"How about you take your image and shove it where the sun doesn't shine?" I retorted. Not my finest work, but it served its purpose. "The sooner everyone knows what sort of person you really are, the better."

Davin smiled tightly. "I wouldn't be so quick to lash out with the insults, Finch. Your sister can be charged with crimes against the crown at a moment's notice, and that comes with some fairly steep consequences." He gestured to Harley, who battled with consciousness between two guards. "I'd rather avoid any further unpleasantness. Besides, you ought to count yourselves lucky."

"*Lucky?*" I blurted out. "Did your brain get starved of oxygen while you were in that cell?"

He ignored my remark. "Your Light and Darkness will come in very handy for my future endeavors, so you are both potentially still of use to me. That makes you fortunate. You get to live and serve me, to become an integral part of what will become a utopia. You've already proven your-selves worthy of a place in paradise, so it's only right that I reward you." He smoothed his fingertips across the executive order, googly-eyed over the words that made him invincible. I'd never seen him so giddy.

"Do you want us to leave you two alone?" I snarked. I never should've handed that scroll over. I should have burned the thing before he touched it.

Davin continued to fondle the executive order, until even the guards looked awkward. "This is what I've longed for. The world will adore me. Those who don't understand what I'm trying to achieve won't be able to lay a hand on me."

"I don't think anyone understands what you're trying to achieve." I glowered at him. "People won't forget what you've done, and they won't forget who you used to be pals with."

Davin continued, proving that he had indeed learned to block out my dulcet tones. "It'll be for the best if I keep the Bestiary under my control, too. You never know when you might need some additional power." He chuckled to himself. "And it always pays to have a bit of leverage. Although, I'm not too worried about the covens coming after me now that I have *this*. I might even reveal all the covens and nip the problem in the bud—let the magical and non-magical issue solve itself, however they see fit. It doesn't affect me, either way."

He just had to poke the hornet's nest, didn't he?

"You gave your word that you wouldn't do that." I clenched my jaw until I thought my teeth might break. "You got what you asked for. I did my part, now you do yours. Keep the covens out of this!"

Davin stomped down from his stage and didn't stop until he was nose-to-nose with me. "I would've kept my word if you hadn't been stupid enough to think you could pull a fast one on me. You keep forget-ting that I'm the only person who's ever tricked their way out of Erebus's service. I wrote the rulebook on fooling people, you ingrate!" His hot breath puffed in my face. "So, no. The threat stands. If any magical tries to rise against my vision, the covens will pay for it."

Out of the corner of my eye, I spotted movement in the far corner of the throne room. Thebian crept slowly through a side door. Anxiety lodged in my throat. Davin had his back to that side door, and I knew I had to keep him on his path of self-aggrandizing if I wanted to stop him from seeing Thebian. Apollo's desperation and confusion had convinced me that they were actually on our side. Well... Kaya's side.

"And what if the magical world persuades the non-magical world that *you* are the threat?" I made sure I didn't look at Thebian. "People don't like things they can't explain. Then, there's all the crime to think about. If people don't fear a death sentence, you can bet your ass the murder rate is going to skyrocket. And they'll do it for fun, just to see what happens. You'll cause hell on earth, not paradise."

Davin's cheeks burned a furious shade of red. "All those who flout my generosity will understand that such heinous acts won't be tolerated. I will have paradise, and I will rule it all."

On the other side of the throne room, Thebian's Esprit blade brightened. He pointed the tip in Davin's direction and worked his unique magic—the kind that could forge a weapon out of nothing. An arrow of pure light shot away from him. It cut through the air, silent and deadly. At first, I wondered if Davin was the target. But, as the arrow hurtled onward, making barely a whisper, I understood its true trajectory. It pierced straight through Davin's pocket, ripping a nice hole in his sharp Atlantean suit. The glass inside it shattered.

Darkness erupted from Davin's pocket and swirled upward, red eyes glinting in a seething mass of wispy shadow. Erebus had entered the game, at last. In that split second of ingenuity from Thebian, everything had changed.

Davin whirled around in panic, his eyes widening as he looked upon Erebus. "Kaya! Kill Erebus!" he blurted out.

I didn't know if that was even possible. Nevertheless, Kaya's expression morphed into one of grim determination. Without raising her hands, blue tendrils snaked out of her and made their way toward Erebus. She couldn't tell Davin no, thanks to the love spell's influence, but the eyes were the windows to the soul. They didn't lie. And right now, they were telling me that she still loved Erebus, and she really didn't want to do this. The tendrils picked up speed and pummeled in Erebus's direction, forcing his smoky form to twist out of the way of their attack.

"Kaya!" he shouted in a disembodied voice. "You know me. I'm not the one you want to hurt. Attack Davin!"

But she was helpless to do anything but follow Davin's order.

I leapt forward to try and wrestle Davin to the ground, but he smacked me with a fresh burst of purple-tinged Chaos. It hit me in the gut, sending me skidding backward. And man, did it hurt. Still, I wouldn't let pain keep me down. Staggering to my feet, I scoured the throne room for that wormy bugger, ignoring the strange, cold sensation that branched out from the point of impact. He ran for a side door, with two guards right behind him, carrying Melody and Jacob over their shoulders. He had the three things he'd asked for, and he was getting away with them.

"Get back here!" I howled, taking off after the Necromancer. The side door slammed long before I reached it. I yanked at the handle and tried to get it open, but it stayed shut. And I couldn't use any magic, considering the Cuff around my neck.

"Finch." Thebian came running. "Here, let me deal with that. You will need your Chaos if we are to stop that wretched man." He fiddled with the mechanism at the back of the Cuff, feeding his magic into the lock. I waited impatiently, tapping a foot on the marble floor. Every second I spent here added to Davin's head start. And I didn't want him getting ahead of me ever again.

Across the room, the situation appeared to be getting worse. Erebus kept trying to solidify his form, but Kaya wouldn't stop launching powerful attacks at him. No matter where he whizzed away to, her Chaos followed. Her marksmanship was impressive, to say the least. She assaulted him from every angle… and looked thoroughly miserable about it. Her hands clutched at her chest, and tears streaked down her cheeks. The way her fingertips raked at her heart was painful to watch, as though she thought she could just tear out the cause of her suffering. But her Chaos had its orders, and she had to obey.

"Kaya! Stop this!" Erebus disappeared into the shadows beneath the upper balcony of the throne room. The tendrils skittered after him, seeking him out in the darkness. He couldn't hide from her.

"I... cannot," Kaya whimpered. "I must kill you."

Erebus shot back out and flew as high as he could, his red eyes staring down at her. "You can fight this. Davin is controlling you. You must take back control, or at least let me close enough to give it back to you."

Kaya shook her head, sobbing wretchedly. "I must do as my... love has asked."

"I'm your love. Or I was. Remember that and hold on to it. Just let me close to you, and I will take the spell away!" Erebus begged. Another army of tendrils chased him, forcing him to stay on the move.

"No. No. It is not possible." She dipped her chin to her chest and wept. She was as much a puppet as the rest of us. Only, she didn't know it. If she wouldn't let Erebus near her, then there was nothing anyone could do to snap her out of her magically enforced loyalty.

"Almost there." Thebian drew my attention back to him.

I tried to swallow my irritation. "Any time to—" The words died on my lips as the side door burst open again, right in front of us. The cuff clattered to the floor as Thebian and I stumbled backward, face-to-face with a horde of royal guards that had come to finish what Davin was too cowardly to do himself. After all, he had his image to consider.

Chaos erupted from them in a bevy of colored strands that tore across the room. And they were shooting to kill. A hex sailed past my shoulder, the sting of it searing my cheek. A very near miss, with more of the same about two seconds away from hitting their mark.

I turned to make a break for cover, only to pull up short. The hex missed me... but Thebian hadn't been so lucky. He'd been a few inches to the left of me, standing in the wrong place at the wrong time. His eyes widened in surprise as glowing red threads spread across his body, working their way up his neck. A spluttering sound rasped out of his throat. His eyes bulged, and his face turned a sickening shade of purple. "Thebian, no!" I yelled. But it was too late.

He fell backward, and I shot out a cushion of Air to break his fall. It deflated slowly, lowering his body to the ground in an almost graceful display. Not that there was anything graceful about this. I skidded to his side, creating a wall of Telekinesis behind me to divert the hexes that burst through the room in a frenzy.

"Thebian? Thebian?" I shook him by the shoulders, but he didn't move. His eyes stared vacantly at the ceiling, his mouth a shocked "O." I shook him again, more violently this time. Still, he didn't move. And I knew he wouldn't move again.

Thebian was dead. Another name to add to the long list of victims whose blood stained Davin Doncaster's hands.

## TWENTY-EIGHT

## Finch

T*hebian... I'm sorry. I'm so, so sorry.*

There was no time to mourn him or even deal with his body, lifeless on the ground. I had to catch Davin before he got too far ahead. If he reached safety, he could rally the entire city against us. He was the human equivalent of a hydra—cut off one of his heads, and he just grew another one. And I was getting sick of this snake slithering free of our grasp.

I looked to Harley, who'd been left unattended in the melee. The flurry of activity and magic seemed to have roused her slightly. She had picked herself up off the floor and was scanning the room with fear and focus.

"Sis!" I sprinted for her. I felt awful leaving Thebian behind, but I didn't have an alternative.

She blinked, shaking off whatever the guards had done to her. "What happened? I was in her bedroom, ready to give her the potion. Then there was a flash. And now I'm... where am I?"

"No time to explain. You need to get Kaya out of here before she actually manages to kill Erebus." I searched for the seething mass of black and found him darting behind the chandeliers overhead. "The potion is still in

Kaya's dress pocket. Get it down her throat and get her out of here. Though, you might need Erebus to portal her to the Antarctic Coven, since Davin took the Ephemera. He took Melody and Jacob too, and we can't let him slap some controlling spell on them."

She nodded, visibly strengthening in front of my eyes. I had no idea how she did that. "Go. I'll deal with this." She squinted at Kaya, who had some serious anti-Child of Chaos tricks up her sleeve. Crazed orbs of vivid aquamarine light shot out of her, but they weren't your average hexes. These things looked sentient, and they wanted to take a chunk out of Erebus. Like cruise missiles on target-lock, they trailed Erebus no matter where he went. He couldn't hide from them. One touched a shadowy frond, and the black particles dispersed, torn right off his being.

"Kaya! Desist!" Erebus roared, sounding as though he were in pain. Whatever those mad orbs were, they had power. Perhaps even the power to actually kill a Child of Chaos. I supposed it wasn't impossible, considering that Kaya and her father had been working on a spell that could eject a Child of Chaos from the submerged version of Atlantis. But this had taken it up a notch, making me wonder if Kaya's scientists had been working on something a little more permanent.

Kaya sobbed violently, her entire body shaking. "I cannot. I have already told you. I must defend the man I love."

"You don't love him! Remember! For the love of Chaos, you have to remember!" Erebus shouted back. Another fleet of orbs zoomed after him, getting closer. He twisted and turned and dove out of their path, but their numbers were increasing. It'd only be a matter of time before he had nowhere left to run.

"Go," Harley urged, drawing my eyes back from the fight. "I'll do what I can here, but you're right—you have to find Davin before he does something horrible to Melody and Jacob."

I felt time ticking away. "You need to start the reversal spell for the Bestiary when you can. It's on the back of that map that Melody made for you. Use it and fix this, for all our sakes."

Harley nodded. "I'll get it done. Davin isn't winning this. I can't wait to see his face when he loses."

I lurched forward and hugged my sister tight. "You better live through this, you hear me? I want to walk you down the aisle and whisper something threatening to Wade when I give you away. You're not taking that moment from me."

She gripped me. "I love you, too. And I'm having that wedding. Davin isn't stealing it."

I flashed her a nervous grin. "You give 'em hell, okay?"

"Bury that snake, Finch. Once and for all." She released me, and I turned on my tail and ran for the side door. We didn't have time to say anything else. That would all have to wait until I'd knocked that godforsaken crown off Davin's inflated head.

I launched a barrage of Air at the crowd of guards loitering by the side door. They tumbled like bowling pins, stunned by the power. I didn't even bother to look back as I sprinted into the passageway beyond, determined to reach Davin before he could wreak any more havoc on the people I cared for.

*You're not the only Primus Anglicus descendants in the building, lads and lasses. The blood in these veins goes back to the big man himself. King Arthur's right-hand guy: Merlin.* And that alone made their bloodlines pale in comparison. Even Erebus and Lux had commented on my prowess. If there was ever a time to get cocky, it was now.

I set my mouth in a grim line as I faced more of Davin's blindly loyal soldiers in the gloom of the passage. With no hesitation, I lashed out with Telekinesis and the whip of Earth-forged vines that surged from the ground to claim their victims.

A bellow of pure rage tore from my throat as they kept coming. Each one fell before me, their balance snatched out from under them by my various lassoes. A few groups came at me en masse and instantly regretted it. I bowled them over with a volatile torrent of Air and Fire. It ripped right through the passageway like bleach down a drain, clearing the path ahead. And I didn't even attempt to pick my way through their groaning, writhing bodies. I ran over the ones in my way.

Drawing steady breaths, I sprinted like never before. My blood sang with all the might of the Sanguines. It kept my wits about me, urging my legs to jump when there were too many stunned soldiers blocking the route. And, more strangely, it seemed to slow my concept of speed and time and space down to an almost dreamlike pace. I felt as though I were in slow-motion mode in a first-person shooter, able to fling away a guard before he'd even managed to muster a hex or a curse. No wonder Nash had been an asset to the magical military.

*That reminds me...*

"Luke? Nash? Wade? Come in!" I pushed my finger against the device lodged in my ear canal. Silence echoed back. I hadn't expected to hear anything from them, but I'd had to try. That was the truly infuriating part about Davin's secret spying: he'd known about everything and every*one*. If they weren't already captured and on their way to prison, it wouldn't be long before they were. Now I knew for certain that I was flying blind, totally on my own. A raging bull, crashing through attackers as if a matador had waved a red flag.

*So be it.*

I dipped my head and charged on, throwing a trio of soldiers to the ground and leaping over them into the next corridor. Whatever happened, I had to get to Melody and Jacob. They were the world's most valuable magicals: the Librarian and the last known Portal Opener. If Davin wrangled them under his influence, they could collectively cause more madness than everything that'd already happened. Davin would have the power to go where he wanted in a heartbeat and draw on the entire knowledge of Chaos for whatever plans he devised. I'd only witnessed a sample of the insane spells Melody had in that incredible mind palace of hers, but it was enough to know for damn sure that I wasn't about to let them fall into Davin's hands.

*Welcome to Last Chance Saloon, kids.* We'd failed to pull one over on Davin, but Thebian had tossed us back into the running. His last, brave act had lit a fire under Davin. And people under duress could make mistakes. So Thebian's courage had lit an inferno under me, too.

I might have been on my own, but I had hope. And I'd left my sister to set the ball rolling. She had the power to shift the balance here, by reversing the Bestiary spell and taking back that energy. Melody had told us both how to do it. I had a note in my pocket, and Harley had hers on the back of her map. We were about to show Atlantis what it truly meant to be a descendant of the very first Primus Anglicus.

*And, Davin, you're going to wish you'd drowned.* After I finished with him, that amulet of his would be no more than costume jewelry. He'd screwed with the Merlins for the last time.

## TWENTY-NINE

# Harley

C ome on, Merlin. Get your head back in the game. I shook off the fuzzy feeling that'd trailed me since the ambush in Kaya's bedroom. Finch had set the tone, and I needed to match him. He'd given me important tasks, and I couldn't let him down with so much at stake.

I assessed the situation. Finch had managed to take out a fair number of guards on his way out of the throne room, but they were slowly getting back to their feet. And there were plenty more who hadn't met the sharp end of Finch's fury. The only person who didn't stand was a man I didn't recognize. He wore the same armor as the other soldiers, but I'd seen him help Finch get that Cuff off his neck. That meant he was an ally. One who appeared to have fallen in the line of duty.

*Your death won't be in vain, whoever you are.* But it served as a stark reminder that I had one of those Cuffs around my own neck. There had to be a way to remove this thing. I'd made easy work of Atomic Cuffs before; how different could this one be? Dipping into my Light, I tried to get some Chaos to form in my palms, but nothing happened. That wasn't good. Especially not with a horde of guards spilling into the room, intent on wiping us all out.

"Apollo!" I ran for the other unfamiliar soldier. Having seen him get knocked out by Davin after trying to urge some sense into Kaya, I guessed he was probably the only person in this room who didn't necessarily want me dead. Aside from Erebus, although his whims changed as often as night turned to day. Plus, I knew Apollo's name. Finch had told me all about him—the good, the bad, and the ugly. I had to hope for more good.

I skidded to my knees at his side and gave him a sharp slap across the cheek. It was a two-for-one slap—some payback for turning my brother over to Davin, and the quickest way to wake an unconscious person.

His eyes shot open in alarm. "Did you just... hit me?"

"You were out cold," I said bluntly. "Can you get this Cuff off my neck?"

Apollo squinted at me. "Who are you?"

"Harley Merlin, sister of Finch. Pleasure to meet you." I gave a mock salute. "Now, can you get this thing off or not? You might not have noticed, but we're in the middle of a warzone, and that queen of yours is trying to kill a Child of Chaos. So help me, or we're all going to be dead, and you can bet your shiny chest plate that Davin won't be bringing us back."

His disoriented expression shifted to one of focus. "I can remove the Cuff. Turn around."

I did as he asked, watching the fracas while his fingertips worked deftly on the lock. Kaya's rabid puffs of light were giving Erebus the runaround, chasing him around pillars and behind chandeliers and into the cloistered walkways that lined the throne room. Each time he tried to slow down, they rocketed toward him, forcing him to wisp away again. I guessed it was supposed to keep Erebus in his loosest smoke form, so he couldn't gather his energy into a more concentrated shape.

Kaya was a wreck—there was no nice way to put it. Her body shivered as though she'd been dunked in the ocean beyond the walls of Atlantis, and her face had turned puffy with the salt of the tears streaming relentlessly down her cheeks. She kept clawing at her chest, until she'd all but pulled away the collar of her robe, and I saw livid red lines beneath, where her fingernails had raked across her blindingly pale skin.

*You've done wrong, but you don't deserve this. Nobody does.* I thought back to a time, in an eerie corridor beneath the New York Coven, when Wade had been under one of Katherine's curses. He'd tried to strangle the life out of me... and would've, if Finch and Garrett hadn't been there to stop him. I'd never forgotten the image of his twisted face bearing down on me. Nor could I forget how devastated he'd looked afterward, when he'd realized what he'd done. Kaya had to be going through something similar right now. And if she wasn't, she would when that love spell broke. *If* it broke.

"There." Apollo pulled away the Cuff and let it drop to the floor.

I turned back to face him. "Thanks. Now, I need to know if you're with me. I get that your loyalty is to Kaya, but she's in desperate need of our help. I have to know that I can rely on you, and you're not going to stab me in the back."

But Apollo wasn't looking at me anymore. His gaze fixed on something over my shoulder, his eyes wide in horror. "Thebian... no, it cannot be. What happened to him?"

I put a hand on Apollo's shoulder to reclaim his attention. "He's dead, Apollo. I'm sorry for your loss, I really am, but we'll both be following suit if we don't fight back. Are you with me?"

"I..." He shook his head, as though trying to get his thoughts in order. A moment later, he lifted his chin in angry defiance. "Yes. I will fight at your side. You can rely on me."

"Then let's floor these suckers." I gestured to Kaya. "Once we've done that, we need to get your queen out of here. I'm sure you'll agree that she needs to be as far from this place as possible until that love spell can be broken."

He furrowed his brow. "As long as I may go with her."

"Deal." There was a chance that Erebus would be able to break the love spell here, without Kaya having to set foot outside the city, but it required the same action—knocking Kaya out and subduing her long enough for him to work his magic.

With Apollo at my side, we began to retaliate. The majority of the guards had regrouped to turn their focus on us. Unfortunately for them, I planned to make a preemptive strike. So did Apollo, by the looks of it. One moment, he was at my side, and the next he'd spiraled into the air in a twist of black fog. He reappeared beside a cluster of guards and clanged two of their heads together with a sharp shove. The other guards didn't have time to react before he wrenched a spear from one of them, beating the rest on their heads and delivering non-fatal blows to their armored bodies.

*Showoff.* Closing my eyes for as long as I dared, I delved into the reservoirs of my twin affinities. It'd been a long time since I'd done this, and it'd more or less broken me the last time. But we needed to give everything we had to this fight. Dragging up a strand of each, I poured both into my palms and raised my arms. My eyes opened, burning with the fire of my Light and Dark combined. Between my hands, a powerful ball of raw energy churned, lacing the white tendril with the black. It fizzed and flickered, hissing with pure power. A few of the remaining guards stopped dead in their tracks, eyeing the seething ball with worry. I guessed they hadn't seen anything like this before.

*Too bad.*

With a firm push of my palms, I unleashed the mighty orb upon the throne room, guiding it with my thoughts and hands, twisting my fingertips this way and that to direct it. It thundered into the first group of guards and sent them flying, their armor-plated figures exploding outward. A few collided with the throne room walls and crumpled to the floor, all of the fight battered out of them. As for those who skidded across the ground, they had the common sense to stay down as thin veins of the white and black strands crisscrossed over their defeated forms, holding them in place.

I formed a circle with my right hand, sending the violent orb on a fresh trajectory. It careened into another set of guards, with Apollo teleporting out of the way at the last moment to avoid the same fate. The startled assailants sailed into the air, like plastic bags in a storm, only to tumble back to the ground with a series of hefty thuds. A satisfying percussion, if ever I'd heard one.

The balance of power had begun to shift. Davin wasn't here anymore. He'd run off, leaving these guards to do his dirty work. However, in his absence, they didn't have anything to prove to him. And, faced with something like this pummeling ball of raw Chaos, they were evidently weighing their options. The first few dropped their weapons and made a run for it, sprinting away from my magical wrecking ball and darting through the nearest exit. They served as a catalyst for the rest, all of them making a frantic exodus until there was no one left but me, Apollo, Erebus, and Kaya. I had no doubt that they'd be back. After all, they probably feared Davin more than me. But for now, we had a window of opportunity that we couldn't waste.

"Apollo! Get to Kaya! I need what's in her pocket!" I barked, trying to discern Apollo's black mist from Erebus's.

He appeared at my side a moment later. "I apologize, Miss Merlin, but I cannot aid you in this. I will go with her if she must leave Atlantis, but I will not help you to restrain her. It is against my duty of care to cause her any harm, even if it is ultimately for her benefit."

I shot him a look of irritated disbelief. "That's a joke, right?"

"It is not. I cannot lay an uncouth hand on her."

"Remind me to give you another slap when this is over," I muttered, realizing that I was going to have to take down Kaya on my own. A queen against a former street rat. Then again, I'd always been one to back the underdog.

Taking a moment to catch my breath, I took control of the massive ball of united affinities again and hurled it in Kaya's direction. With her entire focus still leveled against Erebus, and Davin's instruction still in control, she didn't make any move to defend herself until the crackling orb was almost on top of her. At the very last moment, she raised a wall of blue-tinged light, forced to release her persistent hex critters. The churning ball slammed into the last-moment forcefield with an explosion so loud that it shattered the glass of the throne room's domed ceiling. Shards twinkled in a crystalline downpour as I ducked, covering my head with my arms to avoid getting skewered by one of the daggers. I could've used a blast of Air to protect myself, but that would've sent the shards shooting out in all directions. And there were still folks here who I didn't want to get spiked.

A few splinters stung my flesh, but it was nothing I couldn't handle with the adrenaline pulsing in my veins, taking the edge off the pain. My head snapped up as the clatter dwindled to a tinkling. The forcefield hadn't quite protected Kaya from the powerful ball of blended Chaos. It had shattered on impact, and Kaya now lay on the ground, struggling to stand. I took my shot. Sprinting across the dais, I leapt at the queen and tackled her to the ground.

Maneuvering wildly, I managed to pin her face to the floor. My knee wedged into her back. I guessed I could understand why Apollo hadn't wanted to get involved, but that didn't mean I wouldn't make good on my promise to slap him again. Using a move from my foster kid days, I grappled for her hands to try and wrench them behind her back. But she wasn't done yet.

Blue sparks pulsed from her body. Before I knew what was happening, they swirled around me and gripped me in a vise. Pressure crushed my ribs. My lungs battled for air, my throat closing as the blue sparks continued to constrict.

*Oh no, you don't!* I dipped back into my dual affinities and forced them into my hands. With the last breath I had left, I lashed the interwoven tendrils into her back. She bucked underneath my knee, the blue sparks vanishing in a flurry of miniature blasts that sent cold air rushing past my face. Cat fights weren't really my thing, but I had to find that potion and get it down her throat if we stood any chance of winning this battle. If we could get Kaya back to normal, we might have an ally who would actually help fix the mess Davin had made. But Kaya had to be a willing participant, and right now, she was anything but.

As more sparks started to appear, I hit her with another burst of blended Chaos. She cried out in pain, and my heart wrenched. Hurting her wasn't the point of this exercise. I just needed her to back down for a minute so we could get her the help she needed.

"Unhand me!" Kaya wheezed. "I am the queen of Atlantis, and I will have you punished for this insolence!"

I dug my knee in harder and hit her with one last blast of combined Chaos. "I'm sorry, Kaya, but I think you'll thank me soon. I'm trying to help you."

She slumped forward, breathing heavily. "You... will not... get away with... this."

Praying that she was subdued enough not to hit me with that constriction spell again, I wasted no time. Reaching into her pocket, I plucked out the knockout potion and ripped the stopper out with my teeth. She started to stir again, and I knew time was fast running out. I lunged forward and slipped my arm under her neck, tilting her chin back at an awkward angle. With the bottle open, I pinched her cheeks with my free hand and poured the vivid orange liquid into her mouth. Immediately, I shifted the hand on her cheek to her mouth and clamped my palm over her nose and lips, to make sure she couldn't spit the stuff out. A moment later, beneath the crook of my other arm, I felt her swallow the liquid. She went slack immediately.

"Thank Chaos for that." Gently, I lay her on the floor and sat back, panting from exertion.

"I do not think Chaos is responsible for your brawling skills." Erebus appeared in front of me, his edges solidifying to a more human shape. "If I didn't know you were acting in her best interests, I would have hurled you across the room for causing her such pain."

I cast him a withering look. "I didn't see you coming to help."

"I had to ensure those irksome hexes were truly gone." He sank to his wispy knees at Kaya's side. He'd just put his hand out to touch her when things took a turn for the perilous. Her body convulsed violently, a gurgling cough spluttering from her mouth. The bright orange liquid pooled out onto the floor, regurgitated by an aggressive cough.

"What did you do?" I sniped at Erebus, my eyes wide.

Apollo skidded along, squaring up with the Child of Chaos. "What is the matter with her?"

Erebus's red eyes filled with panic. "I didn't do anything. I hadn't even touched her."

My heart sank like a stone. "Her body's rejecting the potion."

"Why would it do that?" Apollo muscled his way to the top spot beside Kaya, forcing Erebus to step back.

I shook my head. "I don't know. It's just a knockout spell. It shouldn't be doing this to her." I grabbed her and hauled her over into the recovery position, in case she choked on the orange mess her body was intent on expelling.

Erebus's eyes flared with anger. "This is Davin's doing. He must have put protocols in place to prevent anyone from interfering with his love spell, including the use of other magical potions. Her body is in defensive mode, rejecting anything that would seek to meddle with her mind."

A much more concerning realization dawned on me. "If she's reacting like this to a knockout potion, what would happen to her if you tried to break the love spell?"

Erebus's black mist twisted ferociously. "I can only imagine, and that is terrible enough for me."

"Does this mean the love spell cannot be broken?" Apollo's face fell, suggesting he already knew the answer.

"I'd say that's about the gist of it, yeah." I watched as Kaya's face morphed from pale to a deathly pallor. Her lips were tinged with blue, her eyes rolling back into her head. I reached forward to brush a strand of hair from her face when a sudden ripple of violet-tinged magic made me snatch my hand back. It rushed over the length and breadth of her body, with two glints of purple flashing in her eyes before her lids closed and her breathing steadied to a shallow, slumbering rhythm.

"Is she…" Apollo trailed off in unspoken horror.

Erebus shook his head. "No. She is not dead, but she is in a sort of... living death." He sounded relieved and scared in equal measure. The latter being a sentiment I'd never expected to hear from him. "A trance initiated by the defensive mechanisms."

"Which means she can't perform the Witness part of the reversal spell." Davin had screwed our plans again by leaving booby traps in Kaya's mind, rendering her useless if anyone tried to interfere with his scheme. That weaselly scumbag had literally thought of everything.

I reeled back in alarm as Erebus threw back his head and unleashed a roar so passionate and terrible that it probably would've shattered the glass dome all over again. A fierce, dark pulse of visceral shadow erupted from him. It cut through me and swept into the throne room, leaving me with a bitter chill that coursed through my veins, icy and unpleasant. Truthfully, it felt like all the misery and sadness I'd ever experienced, pressing down on me all at once. This was the might of Erebus's grief. I glanced over at Apollo to find him in a similar state, though I couldn't tell if it was from Erebus's blast or his own grief over Kaya's circumstances.

In the corner of my eye, I noticed shadows slipping across the throne room like a sea of snakes. They circled the space, while several loud bangs splintered my eardrums. My head whipped around in time to watch the last few doors slam shut. Strange, smoky chains slithered across them.

"No one will enter this room, and no one will leave," Erebus rasped. Slowly, he brushed his fingertips across Kaya's arm, though he was careful not to actually make contact with her skin. His misty shoulders sagged, his body hunching over as he looked upon his love. We didn't know if the potion had done the damage, or if it had been Erebus's touch. He'd said he hadn't touched her, but I'd seen it with my own eyes. He *had*, and a moment later, she'd succumbed to this.

"I can't look at her like this." Erebus held his head in his hands. "This is not her. She is powerful and beautiful and formidable, and he has stolen all of that away from her. He has corrupted her in the foulest way. He has seized her mind—the one thing she values above all else, and he has turned her into… this. A sleeping damsel who can't be awoken. I will never forgive him for it."

My heart burned with exasperation, the cogs in my mind slowing to a dumbstruck tick. We should've known Davin would play dirty, leaving nothing off limits. I should've been feeling pure, unadulterated hatred right about now, but I didn't. I just felt… lost. We thought we'd failed, only to have hope shoved back under our noses, thanks to the dead soldier still lying on the ground. But now, Davin had stolen that hope away again, blindsiding us in the process.

Without Kaya, we had no way to perform the reversal spell to seize back control of the Bestiary. Without Kaya, Davin remained the most powerful person in Atlantis. Without Kaya, Davin had free rein to do whatever he liked with the world beyond. So much rested on her, but she was out cold, powerless to help us. Which meant we were all back at square one, with no hope, no way out, and no fight left to carry on.

I wasn't sure if even Finch could make a difference.

## THIRTY

# Finch

*Where are you, you slimeball?* I pounded through the unrelenting maze of corridors, following the faint sound of Davin's echoing footsteps. I had to be close. I could feel his sleazy energy radiating through the hallways, like a Chernobyl of arrogance and assholery. I didn't know how long I'd been running for—a few minutes, an hour, a lifetime? But it didn't matter. I'd keep running until my lungs gave out or I had Davin Doncaster getting measured for a casket. Whichever came first.

"I thought you weren't a coward!" I yelled into the gloom. "What are you running away from, huh? Little old me? I thought I wasn't a threat! How about you face me like the king you think you are!"

I rounded a corner into another hallway and spotted three shadows vanishing into a corridor at the far end. All the despair and anger pumped up a notch, driving me down the hallway at full pelt.

I veered into the left-hand corridor, and my heart jumped a mile at the sight before me. Davin lumbered along ahead, dragging Melody and Jacob behind him by way of that nasty little puppet spell. Apparently, even stolen energy from the Bestiary couldn't substitute for athletic prowess. I realized he must've dumped the guards who'd been carrying my friends, so they could try and hold me back. Well, that hadn't worked out too well for them, or Davin.

"Hey!" I barked. "Turn around and face me, you ass!" Not my cleverest, but it felt right. Now that I had him in my sights, he wasn't slipping away again. No more weaseling. He'd slithered out of his last close shave, but now he was going to get what was coming to him. I had to succeed, not only for me, but for the world that he wanted to charm to its knees. This was the tipping point. If I failed, that'd be it... game over.

Davin ignored me and carried on down the corridor, yanking his two human balloon animals behind him.

"I know you can hear me!" I shouted breathlessly. Raising my palms, I threw a lasso of Telekinesis. The edge of it touched him, only to recoil like it'd been electrocuted. I tried again with a barrage of Air, aiming carefully so it wouldn't inadvertently hurt Melody or Jacob. The wall of Air powered through the hallway and skimmed right over Davin as though he wasn't even there.

*What the—?* A choice expletive threatened to leap off my tongue. That friggin' executive order had clearly come into play, meaning I couldn't touch a hair on Davin's miserable little head. Chaos rules were in full effect.

I heard Davin's laughter pinballing between the corridor walls, and something flipped inside my head. He thought he was invincible. He thought he was untouchable. He thought he'd already won. But I had news for him. Even if I had to strangle him with my bare hands and face the consequences of disobeying a Chaos-forged rule, I would. As far as I was concerned, the term "unbreakable" was more of a suggestion. No one was *supposed* to break it, but that didn't mean there wasn't a way. All I had to do was wrangle Davin into submission, and then Erebus could finish the rest. If the Child of Chaos hadn't already been offed by Kaya's spells, that was.

"Give it up, Finch. You can't hurt me. You might as well submit now!" Davin called back.

"You'd like that, wouldn't you?" I retorted, urging my burning thighs to keep sprinting. "You're the one who's going to be begging for mercy!"

Davin shot a glance back over his shoulder, his lips curling into a lopsided smirk. "No, I don't think so."

As though summoned, royal guards burst from the doorways that lined the hallway. With spears raised and Esprits glowing, they marched across the corridor with a clank of armor and blocked my path. Temporarily. I'd had enough of these shiny punks getting in my way, and nothing—nothing—was going to stop me from getting to Davin and saving my friends. It was all related, after all. Save my friends, save the world.

"You should've stayed where you were, polishing those chest plates or whatever it is you do when you're not trying to skewer me." I erupted like a veritable Vesuvius. And I didn't give them a chance to get organized. I rarely dipped into both my affinities at once, but this seemed like the time for a party trick. Grasping threads of both, I tugged them into my palms and unleashed hell—a wall of simmering, volatile wrath made physical. I shoved it forward and watched it race down the hallway. It knocked the guards aside like they were made of paper, all of them collapsing to the ground.

I barely missed a step in my pursuit of the Necromancer. I sprinted on, bounding over bodies like they were lines of chalk and I was in a mad game of hopscotch. The guards weren't important to me at the moment. They'd recover from this. But the same couldn't be said for my friends, or myself, or anyone who didn't fit under Davin's umbrella of loyalty.

"It's over, Davin! Stop!"

Davin was still running as fast as his inferior legs could carry him. And I bet he wished he hadn't worn his fancy robes today, since they threatened to trip him with every stride he took.

As I barreled along, more guards streamed into the corridor. Davin had clearly called for them with some kind of telepathy, granted by his stolen Bestiary power. That stuff was making him harder and harder to beat. And he'd already been immortal to begin with.

I raised my palms and released another barrage of blended Chaos, scattering the guards again. But for every cluster I kicked to the curb, another miniature army pooled in to take their place. Every door stood open, with more and more guards flooding in. And it was beginning to get a little crowded. I skidded to a halt to stop myself from running head-first into a porcupine of spears. There were too many, and they were too close.

I lifted my hands, only to have a spear slice my wrist. I retracted my hand and hissed against the pain that shot up my arm. It was only a small pause, but it gave the guards enough time to rally together. They marched toward me in a shield wall, moving in perfect unison. Frustrated, I retreated a few paces and tried to spot Davin, but I couldn't even see him anymore through the throng of guards.

"For Chaos's sake!" I snapped. My palms rose again, only to get smacked by a spear. That was the beauty of a long, pointy stick—it could slap my hands away without its wielder having to get too close.

*I need to get through!* But all my avenues had closed. And my desperation only climbed each time I tried to raise my hands and had them swept to the side again.

A white blur sailed over the top of the phalanx, coming from behind, and landed on the shoulders of a soldier on the front line. Jaws gnashed, and a growl tore through the air. Huntress had entered the fight. Her target flailed in a vain attempt to get the beast off him. But that only made her more determined, her jaws clamping down on his shoulder.

Another cry went up as a clash of steel added its melody to Huntress's fierce growl. I squinted to try and see what was going on. Nash crashed through the shield wall, guns blazing. Well, *sword* blazing. He wielded a huge blade and used it to formidable effect, spinning it deftly, like he'd gotten too invested in Medieval Times and accidentally discovered some latent talents.

"You better be glad you're wearing armor!" Nash hit one of the guards in the face with the hilt of his sword before driving the blade forward to jab the pointy end into the chest plate of another. It didn't pierce the metal, but it was enough to knock the dude back and give him something to think about.

Luke suddenly bounded up beside me. He raised his hands and clenched them into tight fists. The Atlanteans' armor responded instantly, a whole slew of them getting tugged forward against their will. He made the motion again, targeting the middle line of soldiers. As they fell forward, they sent all the rows in front of them toppling like dominoes until I faced a mountain of downed guards. And three grinning faces.

"You know, this eleventh hour crap isn't cool," I muttered.

Nash sheathed his sword. "Would you rather we'd left you to get impaled?"

"Good point." I nodded up the hallway. "Talk and run, guys. Talk and run. Davin's trying to get away, and he's got Melody and Jacob."

With Luke, Nash, and Huntress flanking me, I sprinted down the corridor after Davin. He'd gotten a head start, but now I had backup. And I had Huntress to sniff out his stink if he'd gotten too far ahead.

"What happened to you guys?" I asked mid-stride. "And where did you get that sword, Nash? Kind of an upgrade from those knives you love so much."

"Davin's cronies caught up with us," Luke interjected, his eyes fixed dead ahead. With Melody in danger, I was surprised he even had the capacity to talk. "They threw us in prison, but they made the mistake of putting us in the same cell as Hector."

Nash nodded, panting a little. "That guy has more tricks up his sleeve than Penn and Teller."

"Did you just make a joke? A *Penn and Teller* joke?" I aimed for some levity, since it sounded like we'd all been through the wringer. Plus, it calmed me down, something I needed now more than ever. I'd obviously noticed that there were several members missing from their party, my future brother-in-law among them.

Nash shrugged. "I've been known to crack one from time to time. Anyway, we helped each other. A mutual effort."

"Tell me Wonderboy is still alive." I couldn't let the question linger a moment longer. "Wade—is he okay?"

Luke nodded. "We split up after escaping the prison, but he was alive the last time we saw him."

Enjoying some temporary relief, I settled into determined silence and pounded the plush carpet like a damned treadmill. Huntress ran on ahead of us, sniffing Davin out. Where she went, we followed.

Huntress veered off down a particularly narrow corridor, forcing us to run in single file. By now, my heart was pretty much in my throat. I couldn't suppress the notion that I might have been delayed too long. Maybe Davin would get away after all, since that seemed to be his MO.

And maybe he'd take Melody and Jacob with him.

At the end of the corridor stood an archway, leading out onto a quaint terrace that overlooked the city. Davin stood in the center, with purple tendrils slithering from his palms and constricting around Melody. It looked like we'd walked in on a torture scene. Clearly, this was Davin's great escape plan—to inflict pain on Melody, in the hopes of forcing Jacob to open a portal for him to run away until the dust had settled. Jacob had been through enough death in his short life. He wouldn't risk anyone dying because of him. Davin knew that, and his favorite pastime was manipulating a person's weaknesses.

"What's the matter, hallways too cramped to get a decent portal going?" I finally stopped and let my searing lungs catch up. As Davin's constriction briefly let up, prompting a pitiful whimper from Melody, Luke went almost white hot with rage.

Davin smirked. "It's fortunate for me that the palace is full of these charming terraces."

"Pack it in, Davin. This is over. We've got—" My tongue seized in shock. Behind Davin, a figure clambered over the sheer edge of the terrace and paused to dust herself off. A figure I knew intimately well.

"Ryann?!" My heart stopped. "What the hell are you doing here?" I'd left her behind for a reason—her presence here gave Davin leverage. And too many members of our team were hostages already.

*Not Ryann, too.*

She merely smiled, weirdly calm and serene. And she didn't look winded at all after shimmying up a whole damn *building*. But as soon as she spoke, it all made sense. "Not Ryann, dear Finch."

Davin's eyes bugged out of his head, his tendrils evaporating. "W-what?!"

*Oh, you beauty... you absolute beauty!* Turns out, Lux hadn't abandoned us at all.

## THIRTY-ONE

# Finch

"Lux? As in—" Davin faltered, gawking at Ryann. He wasn't the only one. How had she even managed to get here? And when had Lux come back? But I was too grateful to look a gift horse in the mouth.

"As in the Child of Light, daughter to Chaos itself, yes. Do not pretend you do not know me," Lux interjected. "Although, I suppose you and I were only briefly introduced the last time we met. You *have* been a busy boy since then, haven't you? I hear of your endeavors, Davin, and I have seen much through Ryann's eyes, but I tend to avoid conversing with wastrels when possible. This is something of an exception."

Davin squared his shoulders and straightened like a soldier on parade. He clearly didn't want Lux to see that she'd rattled him with her sudden appearance.

"You don't impress me, Lux." He narrowed his eyes at her. "Perhaps you would have, in your natural form. But you decided to turn up to the soiree in a mortal body, and that means your powers are limited. So, if this is supposed to frighten me, you've missed the mark."

He had a point. Why had Lux come in Ryann's body? Erebus hadn't had much difficulty getting inside the city in his natural form, now that it was on the surface.

"I fear it is you who has missed the mark, Davin. You see, Ryann and I have been working around the limits of a mortal body." Lux smiled coolly. "In fact, we have discovered a way for me to be more powerful than ever, by channeling my energies through a human conduit. We have communed on an entirely new and remarkable level, aided by the cosmic instruction of my dear sister, Gaia. With her guidance, we have attained an unprecedented symbiosis."

Understanding crashed into my skull like a brick through a window. If Ryann had been communing with Lux on this new level, that explained the blackouts. Fatigue had seemed like the obvious explanation, but perhaps that was what Ryann had wanted us to believe. She'd been keeping a secret. A pretty big one, at that! Then again, with Davin spying on us through Ovid, she'd been right to keep it to herself. Otherwise, none of us would've witnessed this glorious vision of him being totally and utterly gobsmacked.

"That's… not possible." Davin stumbled over his words, clearly not knowing which way was up anymore. Ryann and Lux had conspired to achieve what we couldn't.

Lux didn't reply. She didn't have to. She simply gave a casual snap of her fingers—well, Ryann's fingers. A pulse of white light burst out of her in a series of powerful ripples that cut across the terrace. The puppet spell on Melody and Jacob broke, along with the Cuffs around their necks. Davin wheeled around and stared, dumbfounded, as the Cuffs hit the ground and his intricate spell work unraveled before his eyes. Lux had delivered the first major blow to Davin's plan. And he knew it. His eyes said it all.

"A very clever trick, but that doesn't impress me, either." Davin rallied, a fresh smirk pulling at his lips.

"What are you, Shania Twain?" I probably should've kept that one in my head, but hey.

He ignored me and whipped out the executive order. "You can use trickery and involve as many of your cosmic siblings as you want, but it won't make a difference." He grinned, pleased with himself. "I've got *this*. I'm untouchable."

Lux chuckled. "And what is that?"

"This is an executive order signed by the president herself. It's Chaos binding—your father made this possible, so I should really send him a thank you card." Davin waved the paper with almost childish glee. "But it's so much more than a piece of paper. This order means no magical can touch me. Not Finch. Not Kaya. Not you. Not anyone!"

Lux's chuckle evolved into a full-blown bout of hysterics. Davin looked at her with visible fear. Clearly, he'd thought she would bow down to this scrap of paper. "No *magical*, Davin." Her laughter snapped to a jarring halt. "Do I look like a magical to you?"

*Oh, Lux, you terrible beauty.*

Davin blinked as though he didn't quite understand the question or the inference.

"I am no mere magical," Lux continued. "I am a Child of Chaos. Which is why you should always, *always* check the small print." Her head bent backward, and a wave of pure, fierce light detonated from deep within her chest. My heart lodged in my throat, terrified of what this kind of power might do to Ryann's body. But I couldn't focus on it for long. As in, I literally couldn't focus on her. The light built to an intensity as retina-scalding as the sun itself, seconds before it shot out of her in a corkscrew of fizzing energy. It pummeled into Davin before he had the chance to react. He howled as the torrent thundered into him, filling him with that terrifying light from head to toe.

The hostages scrambled to safety, ducking behind a statue of Ganymede. Naturally, Luke ran straight for Melody, pulling her into his arms. She clung to him in relief while Nash and Huntress went to take care of Jacob, who kept trying to look at the inferno ahead of him, only for the light to make him flinch away.

As for me... I stood with my hands across my eyes, peeping through my fingers as the scene unfolded. I didn't care if it *did* burn out my retinas.

I had to watch this. All of it. Every moment, so I could imprint it on my memory for the rest of my days. After all our near misses and failures, this felt incredible in a grim way. Davin's cockiness had led him to believe he couldn't be beaten. He'd escaped Erebus and foiled our plans, but he hadn't banked on the wife coming back to finish what her husband had started.

"I had planned to lock my husband somewhere far away as punishment for his transgressions." Lux's voice boomed across the terrace from Ryann's small frame. A crack splintered some of the terracotta flagstones, which were unable to bear the pressure of her deafening words. My eardrums weren't faring too well, either. Another sacrifice I was willing to make to witness every detail of Davin's comeuppance. "However, when we were bound together, forgiveness was part of the bargain. It might take me a long time to make peace with him, but you—*you* are a far greater threat than he has ever been. And I can only lock one entity in that terrible place—the center of the earth."

"NO!" Davin screamed. He couldn't move. I watched him struggle to free himself, but the violent force of the light made it impossible.

Lux's eyes shone, her whole body aglow. "Due to your immortality, all the work I have put into creating a prison in the center of the earth will not go to waste. You have proven that you deserve such a sentence, with your complete lack of respect for the natural order of this world and the balance therein. Not to mention the way you have flouted the gift my father gave you and disdained his name. You cannot buy adoration, Davin. You should have realized that during your time at Katherine's side. Now, you will spend an eternity locked inside the earth's core. There will be no escape."

Time slowed to a weird sluggishness, as though the fabric of the universe were being dragged into the ferocity of Lux's light. And Davin was the dead star at the center, his power sputtered out. He opened his mouth in a horrified, soundless scream at the exact moment he finally realized that he had well and truly lost. I watched it all, my heart swelling with satisfaction and relief and elation. After more than a year of dealing with this pest, the exterminator had finally been called. Sure, he couldn't die, but an eternity locked in the center of the earth was a fitting fate. And to someone like Davin, it was a fate worse than death. He'd have nobody to monologue to except himself, and nobody around to adore him and fan his ego.

*"Rydych wedi halogi tir hwn. Rydych chi wedi datgelu eich hunanoldeb a'ch drygioni. Rydych chi wedi profi'ch hun yn elyn i'r byd hwn. Byddwch yn cael eich cosbi. Gadewch i Chaos eich llusgo i lawr lle na fyddwch chi byth yn dod i'r amlwg eto. Gadewch i unigedd fod yn unig ffrind i chi. O fewn y ddaear fe welwch eich carchar. Dyma'ch tynged. Byddwch wedi mynd. Gyda fy nerth rwy'n eich condemnio i dragwyddoldeb o garchar. Cyn belled fy mod i'n byw byddwch chi'n aros yno. Gadewch i Chaos fynd â chi. Dyma'ch tynged."*

The spell poured from Lux's mouth, making the ground beneath us tremble and her whorls of light slow to a crawl. She was speaking Welsh —the first language of magic. And it felt powerful. Anciently powerful. The kind of powerful that could destroy planets and align stars.

"You… can't! I only wanted… to be… adored!" Davin cried out. "I wanted… to be… loved!" His words fell on deaf ears. Nobody cared. He'd given that up by allying himself with my mother, trailing me from mission to mission to get in Erebus's way, backstabbing everyone he could, stealing the Bestiary, threatening to expose the covens, snatching my pals, and upsetting the balance of the natural world. He'd had a second chance to live out his life when he'd vamoosed from the Battle of Elysium. He could've stayed under his rock, and none of this would've happened. But that wasn't his style, and now his warped pursuit of heroism and total control had come back to bite him in the ass.

Lux repeated the spell six more times. At the end of lucky number seven, a detonation of raw energy expelled from her with such fury that I was thrown to the ground. It slammed into Davin's chest and lit him up like a Christmas tree, until I could see every organ, every bone, every vein. Then, slowly and horribly, he started to disintegrate. The fragments of his being came loose from his solid form. Each particle drifted into the air and vanished, until nothing remained but a bodiless head. Davin's scream pierced the atmosphere for a lingering moment, only to be silenced again when his throat disappeared. His mouth stayed open, giving Edvard Munch's *The Scream* a run for its money.

And then the light imploded in on itself, and… he was gone. Not a bit of him left. An open space where he'd once stood. My eyes lifted hesitantly toward Lux as her glow ebbed. She'd made good on her promise. Wherever Davin was now, he couldn't bother us anymore. He'd finally gotten what was coming to him. From here to eternity, he'd be the king of nothing and no one, and he only had himself to blame.

## THIRTY-TWO

# Finch

"Is it... over?" Melody peered around the statue of Ganymede. Hers was the first voice to break the heavy silence that followed Lux's spell.

I stared at the spot where he'd been. "I... uh... I think so." Until she'd asked that, the magnitude of what Lux had done hadn't quite hit home. Davin had been a perpetual Weeble in my life, always springing back up even when I'd been certain he'd stay down. That would take a lot of unlearning. In the months and years to come, I knew I'd still be watching over my shoulder, expecting him to reappear. But it would be a wasted effort. Lux had sent him to the one place from which there was no escape, not even for him.

Lux bowed her head, panting hard. "It is over. Davin now resides in the center of the earth, in a prison of my own construction, where he will never be a menace to any world—magical or otherwise—ever again."

With her words, a huge weight lifted off my shoulders. It was as though I'd been stooping for years and I'd finally straightened up. Davin was gone. He was really, really, really gone, and he wasn't coming back! Lux had saved our world from his imminent mayhem, and I regretted every bad word I'd ever said about her. She hadn't jumped ship at all; she'd just been rowing alongside without us knowing.

"You planned this all along?" I couldn't hide the awe and confusion in my voice. As schemes went, this was a tricky one. There was a lot that could've gone wrong. And we hadn't known any of it.

Lux exhaled, and the glow vanished from her eyes. Ryann had taken the proverbial wheel. "She and I both planned it, with Gaia's help." She looked to me with an apologetic expression. "I know you're probably upset that I didn't tell you, but Lux made me swear to keep it secret from everyone. She worried that Davin might have a way of finding out. She was right. And if I'd breathed a word, none of this would've been possible."

I got to my feet and dusted off the debris of Lux's spell. "You don't need to explain." I started walking toward her. "I'm just glad that you're okay and Davin is gone. I don't care how it happened. You pulled the stunt to end all stunts. Both of you... you're incredible. You stopped him!"

I was about to yank her into the tightest squeeze she'd ever felt when my legs suddenly gave out and I tumbled to the hard ground. My knees crashed into the splintered terracotta flagstones and my body sagged, feeling like a dead weight. *What the hell?* Beads of sweat formed on my brow, and a cold shudder tingled up my spine, everything feeling strange and surreal.

"Finch? Finch, what's the matter?" Ryann lunged forward to help me, only for Lux to take over and lurch backward.

The Child of Chaos moved to a safe distance. "You are going into a Purge, Finch. A mighty one."

"What?" I wheezed. My lungs were on fire, and my stomach churned like I'd eaten a platter of week-old shrimp.

"You are going into a Purge," she repeated. "Everyone, stay back."

"Stay back? Why do we have to stay back? How bad can his Purge be?" Nash frowned, glancing from me to Lux. Huntress gave a sharp bark, and his eyes lit with understanding. "Oh... I see."

Luke wrapped his arms around Melody like a human shield. "What is it?"

Nash hesitated. "Huntress can sense danger in the air, and it's coming from Finch."

"He has never Purged before, due to his Suppressor. Be assured that it will be volatile." Lux edged closer to the rest of the party.

I shook my head as pain shot through me like an electric shock. "I... can't. I'd have... known it was... coming. They don't... just come out of nowhere. There are... warning signs! I can't be... Purging."

"Sometimes they can be more spontaneous, and you have built up a great deal of Chaos in the last year alone. A powder keg, if you will. Tell me, have you delved into both your affinities of late?" Lux's tone held an odd, soothing quality that alarmed me even more than the weirdness pulsing through my veins. I didn't know if I could handle maternal Lux. Normal Lux was bad enough.

My eyes widened. "Yes, but... that wouldn't... be enough, would it?"

"It might have been the spark to ignite it," Lux replied. "You have performed many a powerful spell since your Suppressor broke, as I have said, and yet you have not Purged. That is peculiar, no matter how powerful you may be. Everybody Purges. Yours has evidently been delayed, and now the time has come for it to be unleashed."

"Now?!" She wasn't lying when she'd said I'd used a formidable spell or two in my time and that it'd never led to a Purge. But it seemed ridiculous that something as small as dipping into both affinities half an hour ago could've been enough to trigger this. This was the magical equivalent of Al Capone getting arrested for tax evasion.

Lux nodded. "I am afraid so, Finch. I can sense it. It will not be long."

I opened my mouth to make a sassy retort, but this Purge had other ideas. Pain gripped my innards, and my body curled forward, my fingernails raking the ground to try and take the edge off. All I could do was pray that this thing wouldn't rip me apart. Right now, it didn't seem unlikely.

Agony pulsed through me, and I arched my back like I'd fallen into the pivotal scene of *An American Werewolf in London*. It felt as though my spine was about to burst through my fragile skin and my bones were going to shatter to pieces.

"It looks like it's tearing him up! Can't you throw a buffer on him or something, to calm it down?" Nash asked, looking to Melody.

"He has to endure it as it is," she murmured sadly. "It's a Purge—it can't be stopped, and no sedative in the world can take away the pain. Considering his heritage and how powerful he is, it's not supposed to be easy, but he needs to push through it. A Purge isn't fatal... well, not usually. There are some exceptions, of course."

I gritted my teeth. "Not... helping!"

Another burst of pain cut through me. A nauseating retch climbed my throat, but nothing came out. My stomach didn't get the memo. I dry heaved again and again, bracing my hands against the ground and praying for this to end. Everything was agony. I could almost feel my cells expanding, threatening to burst and end me.

My body lurched forward, and a blinding pain exploded in my chest. For a moment, I thought my lungs had vaporized. Black smoke oozed from my torso, wisps rising into the air like a pale imitation of Erebus. It triggered another dry heave that expelled a cascade of dense black mist onto the floor. It pooled and swirled there for a few seconds, rolling like ghoulish dry ice. Then it rose into the air and began to take on a form.

Through blurry eyes which half bulged out of my strained face, I watched the mist stretch. Limbs began to appear, and a definite head. A glittering sheen drifted across the smoke monster, solidifying the beast into the spitting image of my father: Hiram Merlin.

*Is this some kind of twisted joke?* I stared at my Purge beast. It smirked back at me before shifting into my sister, and then Nash, and then my first childhood girlfriend who'd dumped me for Richmond McCreary in fourth grade. Finally it shrank into a tiny, fluffy creature that looked halfway between a cotton ball and a really furry Pomeranian.

*Puffball? No... is that you?* I hadn't seen that terrifying ball of fluff since the Mapmakers' Monastery, when I'd been tripping the proverbial light fantastic after eating those insane oranges.

"Hello, Finch. Did you miss me?" It giggled and transformed into an exact copy of me. The only difference was the eyes, which glinted at me, jet black.

"Stop… doing that," I rasped. "What are… you? You're not supposed to be… able to Shapeshift."

"Actually, we've never found the limits of a Purge beast's range of abilities," Melody interjected with her endless fountain of knowledge. "I suppose it's not so strange that your Purge beast happens to have some of your qualities and is a bit… *unusual*. It's not as though you'd Purge something feeble. The furry thing was cute, though. Perhaps you could ask it to stay in that form?"

The Purge beast smiled coldly. "Did you miss me?" it repeated.

"What are you?" I struggled to my feet.

"I am you, and you are me." It folded its arms across its chest, imitating one of my stances perfectly. The jaunty tilt of the shoulder, one leg behind the other.

I cast a pained look at my friends. "Please tell me one of you has a Mason jar?"

"I don't think so, Finch." With a disapproving *tut*, it leapt into the air and vanished with a thundercrack.

I blinked rapidly, as though my eyes were playing tricks on me. "Where did it go?"

The others rushed forward to help me to my feet. Huntress sniffed the air, trying to figure out where the Purge beast had gone. Even Lux seemed baffled as she glanced around. And no one had any answers. Not even Melody.

"It… vanished," she said.

"Well, I can see that! Or, rather, I can't." I huffed in exasperation. How the hell was I supposed to catch a Shapeshifting Purge beast who could disappear at will? And I definitely had to catch it. I couldn't leave that thing out in the world, not without knowing what it was. Harley might have Purged a shiny new version of an old Child of Chaos, but that didn't mean my Purge beast would be benevolent. I had more Darkness in me than she did, after all. I mean, what if my Purge beast turned out to be the antithesis of Gaia? That would've been just my luck.

"Can Purge beasts do that?" Luke waved his hand through the air, as though the beast were merely hiding in plain sight. "Can they just run away from their Purgers?"

Melody shrugged. "I've never seen it before, but I don't see why not. It is a creature of Chaos, after all. It can go wherever the Chaos takes it, if it wants to. And it's not your average Purge beast, considering who Purged it."

"All right, the word 'Purge' no longer has any meaning." I raised my hands in mock surrender. "And we don't have time to worry about this now. We need to get back to the throne room. Harley's still there, trying to wrangle the Atlantean queen. She's going to need backup."

Lux nodded. "That would be advisable. While Davin may no longer have control over the Bestiary, thanks to what I did to him, no one else does, either. The reversal spell must be completed."

I pushed away all the residual aches and pains that pulsated inside me. "Well then, get your running shoes on."

Davin might have been thwarted, but this wasn't over yet.

## THIRTY-THREE

# Harley

I didn't know if I should be watching a Child of Chaos so emotionally laid bare. It felt like I'd encroached on something secret and terrible.

After locking the throne room with his smoky chains, he hadn't moved from the dais where Kaya lay, dead to the world. He'd been afraid to touch her before, but I guessed her catatonic state had changed things. What harm could he do, when the damage had already been done? Now, he held her in his arms as though she were the most precious being in the universe, and the merest breath could make her dissipate into the ether and never return. His shoulders shook faintly, though no tears fell from his eyes. In this natural form of his, I supposed he wasn't able to cry.

"I am sorry, Kaya... sorrier than you can know." He smoothed the hair from her face. "I am sorry I could not do more to save you. I am sorry I wasn't better, thinking only of myself and my desires and my losses. I am sorry I wasn't the person you deserved, able to love you with honesty and integrity instead of lies and deceit."

*He really does love her.* These were the words of someone who'd given their whole heart to another, and that heart was breaking. Davin had managed to get in one last jab in case anyone tried to unravel what he'd done, an awful defense mechanism that'd robbed Kaya of more than her mind.

*Did Finch catch up to you, you sly rat?* I hoped so, though nothing had changed here to suggest that Davin had met a well-deserved end. And the reversal spell continued to hover just out of our reach. Kaya was the key, and she couldn't even open her eyes. Another blow in the long game that Davin had been playing this entire time.

"We are in dire straits, are we not?" Apollo came to stand beside me at the edge of the dais, away from Erebus's heartbreaking misery.

I nodded. "And then some. He's locked us in here, the love spell is fighting back, and we can't start the reversal spell without Kaya, so yeah. I'd say this is where our journey ends."

Suddenly, the smoky chains shattered, and the doors burst open. As I spun and raised my palms to fight, a new voice sliced through the tense atmosphere. "It is not like you to be so quick to surrender."

Ryann walked at the head of the pack, though a strange glow shimmered across her skin and burned in her eyes, which suggested that it wasn't Ryann at all. Plus, I knew that voice. I'd heard it in Elysium, and it wasn't something I would forget in a hurry.

"Lux?" My jaw hit the floor. As far as I had known, Ryann was safe and sound back at the Antarctic Coven. But now she strode across the throne room toward us, leading Wade and the rest of the Rag Team, plus Finch and his new team.

Ryann-Lux chuckled. "You remember me. I'm flattered."

"But... how can you be here?" I floundered a little. "We left you back on the shore."

"I am a Child of Chaos, Harley. I can leap galaxies in a single bound. A meager expanse of ocean is hardly a challenge." She flashed me a smug grin.

Wade came running up to me, pushing past Ryann-Lux. "We've been trying to get in for the last half hour. Nash, Luke, and Huntress went after Finch and we came here, but the doors were locked and we couldn't get in. Chaos, I was so worried about you!" He pulled me into his arms, and I sank into them as though he were a lifeboat in a deadly storm.

"It's been… interesting." I held on to him, nuzzling his neck, grateful to have him safe in my embrace again. "As for the locked doors—that was Erebus. He's not doing too well. Neither are we, to be honest."

"What do you mean?" He tilted his head back to look me in the eyes.

I sighed, glancing from him to the others. "Davin had a contingency plan. I gave Kaya the knockout potion, and she went into some kind of fit. She's been unconscious ever since, and I don't think she'll come out of it anytime soon."

"What?" Finch raced up the steps to Kaya, his mouth twisting into a grimace. "That colossal pile of steaming cow crap!"

"I take it you didn't find him, then?" I couldn't hide the disappointment in my voice.

His hands balled into angry fists. "We caught up to him, and Lux shoved him into the center of the earth. But without Kaya, we can't reverse the Bestiary spell, and that means we're all in trouble. If it has no channel for its energy, I bet my left ass cheek it's going to start glitching, same as Atlantis's Bestiary."

Any hope of a tearful, joyful reunion went up in smoke as understanding drifted around the room. Any joy I felt after hearing about Davin was extinguished by the knowledge that the Bestiary was still in danger.

"But Davin's gone?" I tried to focus on the glimmer of hope.

Finch nodded. "Lux appeared out of nowhere and basically pulled the rug out from under him, but I should've guessed his stench would linger."

In my periphery, I noticed Lux approaching Erebus and his lover. The Rag Team kept their distance, no doubt sensing the gravity of the situation. Even I wasn't sure what was going to happen. I'd heard the lengthy tale of Lux and Erebus's marital turbulence from Finch, and the sight of her husband clutching another woman probably wasn't what a wife wanted to witness. Frankly, I was still struggling to get past the fact that it wasn't Ryann. She looked like Ryann and walked like Ryann, but when she opened her mouth… she spoke with the voice of someone who'd lived for millennia.

"Erebus?" she said softly, taking me by surprise.

He lifted his red eyes. "Have you come to gloat?"

"No. I am taking the path of forgiveness. That was what we promised when we were bound together, and I must keep that vow, even if I dislike your choices." She sank down beside Kaya and let her fingertips hover just above the queen's limp body. "Davin added an element of Light to this spell. I can feel the faint pulse of it within her."

"Why would he do that?" Erebus tilted his head, no doubt wary of his wife's sudden calm. After all, tempests usually came right after. "I take it Davin wasn't part of your path of forgiveness? I am in complete agreement where that's concerned, but… what did you do to him?"

Lux smiled. "I put him in a place where he can never disturb this world again. I will explain in greater detail later, when you are not so emotionally charged." She gave him a knowing look, though he didn't react. He sat there with a blank expression. "As for his reasoning in adding Light… I will not call it a love spell, as it is no such thing. This is a control spell, pure and simple. And I imagine Davin utilized an element of Light because he assumed I would never undo anything that might keep you and Kaya apart."

"Was he right?" Erebus's voice was thick with emotion, his hands protectively grasping Kaya to him.

Lux sighed and sank back on her haunches. "He underestimated my capacity to forgive, just as he underestimated my ability to defeat him."

"You really defeated him?" I fought not to burst into unexpected tears. Everything had seemed hopeless a minute ago, and now this Child of Chaos was telling me our greatest enemy had been vanquished. It was a lot to take in, added to the unsettling fact that she'd possessed my adoptive sister. And then there was the sight of everyone else, alive and well, and back where they belonged… together.

"Ryann and I both did, with Gaia's input." Lux glanced over her shoulder at me. "Your adoptive sister is surprisingly wily when the people she loves are under duress. She is as responsible for Davin's demise as I am, in case you were about to snipe at me for possessing her mortal body. She allowed me in. I'd say it worked out rather well."

*He's gone... He's actually gone.* It didn't feel real. Davin had been a thorn in our sides for so long that I supposed it would take some time for us to realize said thorn was no longer lodged in our skin. I urged my tired mind to comprehend it, but it crashed against a wall of disbelief. Besides, until the Bestiary spell had been reversed, I wouldn't be able to take any pleasure in the fact that Davin had been dealt with. Until that moment came, his evil deeds would continue in his stead, even if he wasn't here to drink in the glory.

Erebus drew Lux's attention back. "Why would you lift a finger to help her, after everything I put you through?"

Lux reached out for Erebus's smoky hand. "Because I need to, in order to complete what I set out to do. But also because... I don't want to be bitter for the rest of eternity. If I wanted that, I would have put myself where Davin is." She lowered her head, and I swore I saw tears glinting in Ryann's eyes. "I have been sad for much too long, and it is time to let go of pain so that I may find peace in my own existence. Granted, Father might have helped me reach this conclusion, but the decision to choose a gentler path is my own. I was brought into being to be kind and merciful and benevolent, not cruel and sour and vengeful. I forgot my duty because I let pain blind me. I will not do so again."

"The Child of Light. Here you are," Erebus murmured.

"Yes, here I am." Lux retracted her hand and folded both in her lap. "I cannot stop you from falling in love with another. And if I truly wish to find happiness of my own, then I must let you go. I have to let you be happy with whoever has your heart, because I don't have it anymore. Nor do you have mine. We have been together for so long, you and I. Perhaps too long."

*Well, that might be the most mature and heartbreaking thing I've ever heard.* I leaned against Wade, grateful that we had each other without bitterness or resentment or hurt. I'd often wondered what it would be like to live forever with the person I loved, but perhaps it was best not to find out. Instead, Wade and I would live out our mortal lives together, and then we'd find one another in the afterlife, where the peace and harmony of that realm would ensure that we never ended up like these two.

"I love you," Wade whispered.

I peered up at him. "I love you, too."

Meanwhile, I spared a thought for Finch. If I found it hard to deal with Ryann being possessed, then he had to be going out of his mind. No doubt he wanted to wrap her in his arms and feel the relief of having her close and safe and alive. But he couldn't even touch her, as long as she had Lux camping out inside her. If he did, he'd likely get a slap on the wrist, if not hurled across the room. Even with Davin gone, he couldn't catch a break.

*Soon, Finch... soon.* I hoped that with all my heart.

"Does this mean you can help Kaya?" Melody raised an anxious hand, her other arm around her boyfriend's waist. They made a sweet pair. In fact, looking around the throne room, we all made pretty fine pairs, right down to Nash and Huntress. Which meant that the only people who had no one to call their own were Lux and Apollo. One suffering from unrequited love, and one giving up her husband because his heart had wandered elsewhere.

Lux stretched out her hands and cracked her knuckles. "I would not be here if I couldn't. Indeed, I believe I can dispense with the love spell *and* implement the reversal spell at the same time, with a little additional energy."

"Additional energy? I thought you were a Child of Chaos." Santana sprinkled some sass into the conversation.

Lux chuckled. "A reversal spell of this magnitude requires a more readily available power source—one connected directly to the magical and mortal world." She turned and eyed Finch and me with pointed stares. "You two. Come and sit with me. Considering the gifts my father has given you, you might as well make yourselves useful."

Hesitantly, I stepped away from Wade and went to kneel beside Lux.

Finch followed, though he was being unusually quiet. I guessed he still had Ryann on his mind, worrying about how all this spell-breaking would affect her. But he also looked very pale, and there was a waxy sheen to his forehead, as though he'd just run a marathon or been hit with a bout of food poisoning.

Lux reached out and took our hands—mine in her left, Finch's in her right. She dipped her head and closed her eyes before beginning to chant in a language I'd never heard before.

"*Iawn y camweddau erchyll hyn. Dadwneud yr hyn sydd wedi'i wneud. Dadwneud yr edafedd sydd wedi clymu at ei gilydd i ryddhau'r hyn a gymerwyd. Dychwelwch bŵer i'r man lle cafodd ei ddwyn. Gwrthdroi'r hyn sydd wedi'i wneud. Torri'r cadwyni hyn ac ildio rheolaeth. Gyda chryfder golau a thywyll a'r undod o fewn y sillafu hwn. Gadewch i bopeth gael ei adfer.*"

I gasped as my Light responded to the strange, lilting words that danced poetically off her tongue. It was as though my Chaos was hypnotized by her enchantment. A tendril pulled away from the reservoir within me and snaked into my arm, sliding down until it reached my hand and channeled into Lux. I glanced at Finch and saw the same thing happen to him, though the magic that jumped from Finch into Lux's palm was tinged with black. Darkness and Light, in perfect harmony.

Lux repeated the chant over and over until I'd lost count. With each repetition, she drew more power from Finch and me while delving into her own. Soon enough, the throne room thrummed with the potency of our triple threat. The doors rattled on their hinges, and the scattered shards of glass bounced in time to the vibrations. All the while, Lux's voice grew louder and louder, compelling and ancient in its strength. I would've clamped my hands over my ears to block out the roar if Lux hadn't been clutching my fingers tight.

Suddenly, a high-pitched sound splintered the atmosphere. At first, I thought the sheer volume had given me tinnitus, but then Finch's ears pricked up, and I realized I wasn't the only one hearing that noise. It was subtle, like a dog whistle or the kind of high note a half-full champagne flute sang with the right touch. But it was definitely there, emitting from

Lux and pulsing out into the wider world. A real pulse followed shortly, more like a gust of wind than a grand display of light and magic. Nevertheless, it careened through the throne room's wall and disappeared beyond.

A moment later, everything stopped. The noise, the pulse, the chanting. Lux let go of our hands and fixed her gaze on Kaya, waiting for something to happen. We all watched. Time ticked by agonizingly slowly as Kaya remained motionless. But then, a faint flicker of life moved beneath Kaya's eyelids, followed by a soft groan. Erebus lurched forward in desperation.

"Kaya? Kaya, can you hear me?" He clutched her shoulders and shook them gently.

Her eyes opened, blinking up at the four weirdos staring down at her. "I... was in darkness. A cage that I could not escape." She sat bolt upright and flung herself into Erebus's waiting arms. "I was so afraid, Erebus. I did not know where I was, but I could see all that happened, as though it was a life that belonged to someone else. I tried to scream, but no one heard. I was forced to watch everything unravel before me, helpless to prevent it!"

"You are safe now." Erebus cupped the back of Kaya's head as sobs wracked her chest. I felt her pain to some extent, knowing what it was like to be locked outside your own body. Nomura had projected me into an astral plane after Katherine had threatened the life of his son, Shinsuke. He'd detached me from my physical body and trapped me outside of it. Had it not been for Gaia, I might never have escaped.

"We must capture Davin and see him punished for this!" Kaya pulled away from Erebus, a vein of strength returning to her voice. "Whatever love spell he placed upon me, it was not the sanctioned potion. It was horrific. Utterly horrific. A nightmare brought to life."

Lux cleared her throat. "There is no need. He has already been dealt with. Now he is the one in a cage, and there will be no salvation for him."

Kaya frowned in confusion. "He has been dealt with?"

"He has, and now all that he did has been undone." Lux bowed her head gracefully. Even faced with the woman her husband loved, she showed an integrity that left me in awe. Perhaps she really had decided to be a better version of herself. I hoped she would find happiness of her own out there, somewhere. I mean, Apollo was available, and he was quite a catch. But that was probably a little too convenient. In the real world, not everyone got a neat, happy ending. Not even cosmic beings.

"Do you feel that?" Melody ran to the throne room window and looked out. "Tell me you can all feel that."

Curious, I put out my Empath feelers and almost jumped at the energy that bristled back. Somewhere in the far distance, a message was being relayed, written in the pure emotion of raw Chaos: the Bestiary was in a state of euphoric glory, roaring back to life.

## THIRTY-FOUR

## Harley

"The Bestiary." Lux's eyes shone. "It is singing."

Melody jittered excitedly. "It's so beautiful! I can feel it washing over me. Look—all the little hairs on my arm are sticking up! Who needs an opera when you can hear the Bestiary itself singing out into the world, restored to its rightful place?"

It felt as though someone were singing a familiar lullaby, a tune everyone could recognize, but nobody knew where they'd heard it before. It made my heart swell and my body ease, all the tension in my muscles releasing. Lux had saved us, not only from Davin's plans, but from potentially losing the Bestiary altogether. She'd finally acted like the Child of Light she was born to be, bringing hope and prosperity instead of envy and anger.

With the music still ringing in our ears, Kaya surprised everyone by pulling away from Erebus and shuffling forward to kneel before Lux. With her head dipped and her hands clasped in her lap, she looked as though she were about to go into confessional—or expected an axe to fall on her neck.

"I have no words to express my gratitude, Lux." Her voice came out as a shy murmur. "You have rescued my nation from a tyrant and ensured that his diseased reign will not spread to the surface. However, though it might sound selfish in light of all that everyone has endured, I must know what you intend for Atlantis. For, if you ask us to submerge again, you must know that we cannot survive much longer with our limited resources."

Lux lifted Kaya's chin, the two women looking straight into each other's eyes. "You were promised an independent nation, and that is what you shall receive. You are all children of my father. You will not be forced to hide any longer." She gave a small smile. "I will bind Atlantis to the surface Bestiary so that this forcefield can remain, keeping your city separate and protected, yet connected. Those who wish to see the wider world will be permitted to do so. This should not be a prison, but a liberated independent state: the Atlantean Coven—the largest in known history."

Kaya hiccupped, tears trickling down her cheeks. "How can I ever thank you enough?"

"Ensure that Atlantis exists in dignity and harmony, and claim no stake on the rest of the magical world. That is what I ask in return." Lux sounded as though she were struggling to hold back tears. She was doing all this for Kaya, and for the rest of magical society, without expecting any personal gain. If anything, she stood to lose more than she'd begun with. Her husband would certainly stay with Kaya, now. So where would Lux go? What would she do, without a wayward husband to wrangle? Perhaps it would give her the chance to do everything she'd ever wanted, without worrying about the transgressions of another. I hoped so. Ignorance might've been bliss, but the truth could set you free.

Lux put her hands to the sides of Kaya's face and began to chant once more. "*Ffurfio bondiau newydd rhwng yr endidau hyn. Gadewch i'r ddinas hon fod ynghlwm wrth bŵer y byd. Gadewch i hud lifo trwy'r waliau hyn a'i gysylltu â chanol popeth. Rhowch y cryfder y mae wedi'i ddiffygio. Ei gysylltu â'r byd. A gadewch i'r ddinas hon godi i fawredd yn ei hannibyniaeth. Dyma fy ewyllys. Gadewch iddo gael ei wneud.*"

"What language is that?" I whispered to Melody, as vivid white light jumped from Lux's palms and into Kaya. It percolated into Kaya's chest, causing a sudden glow to shine where her heart lay. The same glow reflected in Lux, both of their hearts burning with pure light.

"Welsh—the first language of magic. Your ancestors would've spoken it." Melody smiled, still giddy from the Bestiary song echoing through the world.

Two strands of Chaos reached from Lux and Kaya's hearts and met in the center. Lux repeated the chant twice more, hitting the fabled power of three. The moment she'd spoken the last word, their connected Chaos rose in a pillar of twisting light. It shot straight through the now-shattered dome of the throne room. The two women were left breathing hard as the last of the energy dispersed.

"That was a hell of a light show, but what *was* that?" Finch entered the chat, still looking like he was suffering through the worst hangover of his life. Worse than the SDC's last Christmas party, where he'd accidentally mistaken the soft punch for the hard punch. Wade had found him in the Bestiary, dancing with the satyrs in his birthday suit, using breadsticks as makeshift panpipes. Tobe had had to carry him like a baby—a very drunk, naked baby—back to his room. Wade and Tobe had been sworn to secrecy, but naturally, Wade had told me everything.

"You will see." Lux lifted her head skyward. On cue, a faint pulse rippled across the forcefield, which could be seen through the broken dome.

Lux, of all people, had just saved Atlantis.

"Hey, here's a thought." Finch folded his arms across his chest, swaying a little. "What if neither I nor Davin were the hero in the legend of the Luminary? What if all this time, it was Lux? It makes sense. A stranger would arrive from the outside world to save Atlantis. It never said the hero had to be human."

"Legend of the what now?" Santana put up a hand. I had to admit, I had no idea what was going on, either.

Lux chuckled, ignoring her. "Legends are stories, designed to thrill and mystify, but they are still only stories. Besides, I am not sure I fit the marriage part, unless Kaya would prefer to have two queens rule over Atlantis?"

Erebus looked horrified. That would've been a heck of a twist, if Kaya and Lux had walked off into the sunset together.

Kaya laughed, taking hold of Lux's hand to add to Erebus's discomfort. "I think you are divine, Lux. However, I might have embellished the part about marriage. The legend actually states that the broken queen will find love, and that the hero will be married, and that marriage is what will aid Atlantis in its direst hour. I assumed the three things were related, but now I am... unconvinced."

Finch waggled a finger. "You know what they say about assuming, Kaya."

She frowned. "What do they say?"

"It makes an ass out of you and me. And I'd say that's pretty spot on, considering what we've been through." He flashed a weary grin. There was definitely something off with him, even if he was cracking his usual jokes.

"Ah." Kaya nodded in understanding. "Now, I imagine the broken queen falling in love referred to... well..." She cast her eyes down, unable to say aloud that she loved Erebus. But we all knew. She soldiered on. "And the marriage part is likely a nod to you and Erebus, working together to rescue Atlantis."

"Hello? What's this legend you're talking about? You're going to have to give us a bit more info here," Santana interjected.

Lux sighed softly. "It does not matter what the legend is, or if it held some truth. We have prevailed of our own accord, and we did not need a story to guide us."

"*You* prevailed," Kaya corrected. "Thanks to you, the city of Atlantis has been given new life, and we can now exist in peace, independent and yet united with the rest of the magical world."

Finch cleared his throat. "I'm all for the peace and love vibes here, but you're in for a long chat with the magical authorities about this Atlantis plan."

I nodded. "He's right. The authorities will want to make sure this will fit with their rules and regulations. Considering who you are and the level of power inside this city... I'm sure it'll be fine, but there'll be a few hills to climb."

"Hills..." Kaya whispered in a faraway tone. "I have never seen hills."

"Look out the window." I gestured to where South Georgia Island lay and suddenly remembered that we still had Kaya's father locked in a cell in the Antarctic Coven. I guessed we could deal with that later, along with trying to figure out what to do with all the dead people who weren't dead anymore.

*Thanks again, Davin.*

Kaya rose to her feet and walked to the window for her first look at the surface world with eyes that weren't controlled by Davin. She gripped the sill, and her shoulders slumped. Not exactly the reaction I would've expected from her, seeing so many beautiful things for the first time: a true-blue sky, mountains, snow, the rocky shoreline, and birds wheeling overhead.

"I cannot be the queen of Atlantis any longer, can I?" She didn't turn, but her body language gave away her sadness. It was the weary stance of someone who knew that they had to relinquish what they held dearest.

"No, you cannot." Lux went to her, but there was no smug satisfaction in her voice. "You have committed crimes against humanity and the magical world, even before Davin put you under his influence. As part of a royal dynasty, you know that such things cannot go unpunished."

Was it weird that I felt a bit sorry for Kaya? She'd put my brother through the wringer and had wanted to conquer the surface world. She'd only changed her mind because of her father's betrayal. Even if she was remorseful now, that didn't take away from the harm she'd done, or the torment she'd put Finch and Ryann through with her *first* false marriage. If I'd been in Atlantis then, I'd have slapped her stupid. But watching her come to terms with the stark reality, the urge to see her get her comeuppance faded away.

"Apollo?" Kaya called. He duly hurried to her.

"Yes, Your Majesty?"

Kaya brushed tears from her eyes and straightened. "I renounce that title. Lux is correct—I have behaved abhorrently." She took Apollo's hand in hers. "As such, I ask you to take my place as ruler of our nation. It has been a very long while since there has been a new bloodline upon the throne, but now is the time. With so much change in the air, Atlantis must follow. You will lead us to harmony and excellence, for you are one of the people, and you have an exemplary mind for leadership. You always sought to dissuade me whenever I wandered down the wrong path, though I did not always listen."

"Kaya… I…" Apollo fumbled for the right words. He clearly didn't want this. He'd shown his loyalty to Kaya time and time again, and now she was asking him to usurp her. The final act of a queen who might've been great, had she not given in to the temptations of power.

"Do not refuse, Apollo. I would see Atlantis in kindly, intelligent hands. And I know of no hands safer than yours." She lifted his hand to her lips and kissed it. "Take my crown and wear it as your own. I am unworthy of it. Let this be my penance."

Apollo didn't move. The poor guy probably didn't know what to do with himself. And I didn't know if it was my place to step in, but I did. Going to Kaya, I gently removed the crown from her silver hair and turned to place it on Apollo. He flinched, but after a moment he bowed slightly to allow me to place the crown atop his head. It was strange how such a simple act could alter an entire line of succession.

"I… will see that Atlantis flourishes in this new world." Apollo found his voice again. "I will make sure that it follows the coven rules as an independent state. And I will ensure that this city and our people can find comfort, nestled here above the ocean."

Erebus took a few steps closer to Kaya, but she raised a hand to keep him at bay. "There is more to my atonement, Erebus. I must pay for my foolishness. Which is why I cannot love you or be loved by you, and I cannot take what belongs to Lux—the savior of our city." Blue sparks emerged from her body and hurtled toward him, spiraling around his smoky edges. "I am sorry, Erebus. I did love you. I do love you. But we are never to be together."

Lux looked surprised as the blue sparks spun faster around Erebus. A moment later, he disappeared in a blast of blue-tinged energy, expelled from Atlantis. Evidently, Lux had expected Kaya and Erebus to get their happy ending. She hadn't expected Kaya to refuse the love that had come between her and her cosmic partner.

"Kaya?" Lux said, stunned. "Why did you do that?"

"I should not gain when I am undeserving. Now, it is time for us all to leave, for there is much for us to remedy in the surface world, and I must begin my exile and face whatever may come." Kaya turned her blue sparks on herself and the rest of us. A fierce white tear ripped through the air above us.

"Don't you dare chuck us in the—!" I heard Finch call out, a moment too late, as we were expelled from Atlantis.

## THIRTY-FIVE

# Finch

Kaya managed to miss the freezing cold ocean this time. A damn good thing, for once. Sure, I'd Purged a mischievous, possibly malevolent monster into the world, but at least we weren't soggy. Plus, Davin was gone, Kaya had done the right thing, Apollo had a crown on his head, and Lux had proved that she could be pretty decent when she wanted to be. Silver linings all around.

We were spat out on the shore of South Georgia Island, where a baffled but slightly relieved-looking Mage Council awaited us. O'Halloran and Levi stood with them, their conversation coming to a halt as we fell from the sky. The traditional phrase might have been "raining cats and dogs," but right now, it was raining magicals.

"When did you get back?" Harley wasted no time pointing out the obvious as she stumbled to her feet after our rough landing. "I thought you all had scurried off at the first sign of trouble."

Their golden boy, Jasper, looked shifty. "We returned not long ago, under the instruction of the president. A power surge was detected here, and, as you are technically under our jurisdiction, she sent us to investigate."

Tobe prowled from the Antarctic Coven at that exact moment. "And, as I informed them, that power surge was the reunification of the Bestiary with all the world's covens. They attempted to gain entry to the Bestiary, but I would not permit it. It is still settling back into its old roots. It is not to be disturbed."

"Is everything… functioning?" I asked anxiously.

Tobe gave a regal nod. "Indeed. The atrium is thrumming away at its leisure, and the beasts are calming. However, it is prudent to watch over the Bestiary for a while to ensure there are no residual problems. It is unused to being moved around so frequently and having its energy stolen by miscreants. Recovery time will be necessary."

"I guess it'll have to stay here a while, huh?" Santana crouched to the ground as another creature emerged from the Antarctic Coven and wrapped itself around her like a scaly scarf. Slinky peered over Santana's shoulder at me and lashed out his tongue, his reptilian eyes glinting.

*Ah, my old nemesis. We meet again.* After all, what would my life be without an enemy or two?

Tobe gestured to our wintry surroundings. "This is an ideal location for the Bestiary's recuperation. Few know of the Antarctic Coven's existence, and it is a troublesome place to reach." His wings ruffled in the bitter breeze. "And, as the SDC is no more, and there has been no news as to its potential restoration, I think it wise that the Bestiary remain here until I am otherwise instructed."

"You look like her." Kaya stepped out of the congregation and gaped at Tobe. "My Iso, my sweet, sweet Iso—you are so very similar."

"Iso? Pardon?" Tobe's amber eyes shone with confusion.

I interjected. "She's you, but… well, a she." I paused. "Actually, no, she looks more like a white tiger instead of a lion. But the rest is pretty much the same. Wings, claws, fangs, et cetera. Oh, and she's in charge of the Atlantean Bestiary. A Beast Mistress, if you will."

"There is another like me?" Tobe's talons tapped the ground anxiously.

"Yes, Purged by the mighty Ganymede herself," Kaya said. "Though I do not suppose I will ever see her again." My heart lurched slightly at the sadness in her voice. She'd been a huge pain in my ass recently, but she was taking her self-imposed punishment to the extreme.

"Might I speak to you about this Iso?" Tobe held out his hand, and Kaya took it. The two of them wandered a short distance to talk in private. Perhaps Tobe was interested in Iso for personal reasons.

With Kaya otherwise engaged, the Mage Council filled the silence.

"The president and the rest of the world leaders were relieved to hear that the Bestiary has been restored." The Irishwoman spoke first. It almost sounded like a thank you, but without the actual gratitude.

"So were we." Dylan grinned triumphantly, but none of the Mage Council mustered a smile in return.

I couldn't help myself. Uncomfortable situations were my playground. I decided to lay on the charm, to see if I could eke a real thank you out of them. "We're grateful you went along with Harley and me on this one, even if you didn't make it easy. Who knows where we'd be if we were still sitting around, talking about next steps and whatnot."

Lux chuckled, still in Ryann's body. "Typical of the upper echelons of magical society. They rely upon rules. Without rules, there would be mayhem. However, they are inclined to forget that, on occasion, a little chaos is precisely what the situation calls for."

I hesitated with my next question, not wanting to seem unapprecia-tive. "Lux, do you think you might release my girlfriend at some point? I'm glad the two of you have turned into pals and everything, but I… miss her." More than that, I needed to see for myself that their newfound alliance hadn't done any damage to Ryann. Lux had knocked out some mighty powerful spells back there. Not the kind that fragile mortal bodies were known for enduring too well.

"All in good time," Lux replied. "When all is resolved, I will give you your paramour back, unharmed and as good as new. Fear not."

A Mage Council woman with a Spanish accent grasped at her colleagues' sleeves. "Did he just call her 'Lux'?"

"Oh, right. I guess we've got a lot to fill you in on, huh?" I dove right in, telling them everything that had gone on since we'd left the Antarctic Coven.

When I was done, Harley gave me a subtle nod and finished the story. "And Apollo is the Atlantean king now. But… yeah, I think that's about it." She gestured to the new monarch, who stood awkwardly on the shore.

"Then we owe our lives to you, Lux." The same woman gave an awkward curtsey. "You are truly gracious, to have taken the time to aid us in our moment of need. Erebus, too."

*Aww...* Erebus would hate that he was missing out on all this ego-stroking. Though it was probably for the best that Kaya had booted him from Atlantis. The last thing this scene needed was the melodrama of two lost souls who loved each other but couldn't be together. That sort of sadness would only dull the euphoria of having stopped a global catastrophe.

Jasper, the golden boy, nodded until I thought his head might fall off. "We will erect monuments to you both, to honor your deeds."

"There is no need for that," Lux replied coolly. "You should focus on the mess in the wider world, instead of building unnecessary statues that are inevitably unflattering. Focus on a plan for the Fleet Science Center, and to reduce the collateral damage that has been created because of the SDC's expulsion. My assistance ends here. Children of Chaos are not a panacea for your mortal problems. You cannot, and should not, rely on us for everything. No, this is something that you must all figure out together, because you have entered a new era. Non-magicals now know about magical existence. What you will do now—well, that is up to you."

O'Halloran raised his hand like a schoolboy in class. "Levi and I have agreed to work together on a containment of the SDC, the Fleet Science Center, and its surrounding areas. It will involve a mass mind-wiping, which includes the resurrected so they don't remember that they were previously dead. That will be followed by a smaller, selective mind-wiping operation beyond the containment zone."

Levi shot a sour look at the Mage Council. "Indeed, we were just waiting on the agreement of the Mage Council and the upper echelons."

"I suggest you speed things along." Lux delivered a stern stare to the fawning Mage Council.

Mairead clasped her hands and did a few weird dips that I guessed were meant to be bows. "We'll speak te the president now and have permission granted before ye can say 'Chaos and all his Children.'"

"Good." Lux seemed pleased. I wondered how she actually felt about the magical world potentially being exposed. After so many centuries, maybe she wouldn't have minded something new. But she'd left the ball in our court, and we were too set in our ways to take that kind of step.

Just then, a cloud of black smoke spiraled from the heavens and landed on the slick rocks of the shoreline. My heart skipped a beat, thinking my pesky Purge beast had returned to try on a few more skins. But the edges solidified to reveal a pesky beast of a different kind. One who refused to be sent away by the woman he loved.

"Erebus?!" Lux and Kaya cried in unison, the latter breaking away from her matchmaking session with Tobe.

"Why have you returned?" Kaya turned paler than usual. "I sent you away. You should not have come back."

Erebus's body churned like the ocean beyond. "I came back because I can't do this anymore. I can't keep existing in this manner. Like Moros before me, I no longer want the duties that come with being a Child of Chaos. I do not want the darkness. I do not want to be Darkness any longer. I am exhausted by the loneliness and constrictions and painful eternity of it all, and I am tired of looking upon the mortal world and seeing only what I cannot have. They touch, taste, feel, love, and bring new life into this world. It is ordinary to them. But to me, it is a dream I have chased hopelessly for centuries. I cannot be... *this*, anymore." He pressed a wispy palm to his chest. "I know I should not say so, but the time I spent in my mortal body was the happiest of my life, despite everything. I felt more in that brief period than I have experienced in centuries of existence. *That* is what I want, not this."

Lux's face fell. "No... you do not know what you are saying. Do not speak of Moros." Her breath caught in her throat. "Do not tell me that you wish to return to the Chaos stream. I could not bear it. It almost broke me when he went away. I would... not recover, if you were to do the same. We might have our differences, but I still need you to exist. Even if you were a universe away or locked in the center of the earth, I would still want you to exist."

"As would I." Kaya trembled beside Lux, her eyes filling with tears.

I'd lived under Erebus's thumb for so long that the thought of his nonexistence was too strange to contemplate. Don't get me wrong, I didn't want to be in his servitude anymore. But, like Lux had said, I still wanted to know that he was around. A Child of Chaos 911 line to call when things got tough.

Erebus walked to his wife and touched a hand to her face. "You misunderstand me, Lux. I do not want to disappear. I want to *live*. Really live, instead of this strained existence." He drew a deep breath, though I was pretty sure he didn't have lungs. "I am ready to surrender my power to someone else. I would rather possess a body and live out the rest of my natural days with Kaya than spend eternity in the isolation of an other-world that doesn't even belong to me. You might as well have locked me in the center of the earth, after all."

Kaya gasped. "With me? In a mortal body?" She shook her head. "I have already explained to you that I am undeserving. To have your love, and live with you in this world, would be a joy I should not be permitted."

"Losing Atlantis was your punishment, Kaya." The words tumbled out before I could stop them. "You're not a bad person; you just made some colossal errors in judgment. But you've paid for those, and you'll keep paying by being exiled from the city that you've given everything to. You don't need to keep whipping yourself."

"She should be arrested, Finch." Harley gave me a stern look.

"No, she shouldn't." I held my ground. "She thought she was doing the right thing. While that might not sound like a good excuse, you have to think of it from her perspective. Her people were persecuted and sent into hiding at the bottom of the friggin' ocean. She didn't know what our world was like, and that it didn't need saving. She thought it was the same as when Ganymede ran from it. So, call it even for the ancient crimes that her people suffered through."

Harley's features softened a touch. "That's up to the authorities, Finch. Councilors?"

"Lux? What do you think?" Jasper waited for the Child of Light's opinion.

Lux shrugged. "I happen to agree with Finch. Besides, if Erebus is set on relinquishing his power, then he will prove to be an excellent guardian to Kaya, to ensure she does not step off the straight and narrow again."

"A little naïve, don't you think?" I retorted.

"Love nourishes protection. And now that he has her love, he will not risk losing it, in any capacity. He will not risk her freedom or their future together." Sadness punctuated her words, and my sympathy for her grew.

Selena jittered excitedly. "Then it will be done, Lux. As long as Erebus and Kaya are both compliant with the rules and stay out of the covens' way, I don't see why Kaya can't be free." She paused, her forehead crinkling. "Although, I'll add that you shouldn't interfere with non-magicals, either. Exile is exile. You should both keep away from as many people as possible, for the sake of peace. And Kaya will, of course, have to have a Dempsey Suppressor fitted, so we can rest assured that her superior power will not be misused."

*Holy crap...* Could this really mean what I thought it did?

I glanced at Erebus. "Are you really going to do this?"

He smiled through his smoky face. "Why? Will you miss me?"

"*Pfft*, don't flatter yourself." I turned away, uncertain what my eyes might say. "My sanity will be restored. I just want to check that you've properly thought this through."

He nodded solemnly. "I have."

Melody bounded in, her intrigue visibly piqued. "But how would that even work? I thought you were either a Child of Chaos or you weren't."

Lux took Erebus's hand in hers. "There are nuances, Melody. You should know by now that there are always nuances. In order for Erebus to surrender his power, someone else must take his place."

"Ah, like Nash giving his Sanguine abilities to Finch?" Melody nodded in understanding, while the Mage Council looked suitably horrified. I wouldn't have mentioned that little tidbit, since it was none of their damn business, but c'est la vie.

"Precisely," Lux confirmed. "Though, as you can imagine, it involves a much larger personal sacrifice. Anyone taking Erebus's place would have to accept all the trappings of being a Child of Chaos: an existence outside of the mortal world, restrained by endless rules and regulations, without a mortal body."

I nudged Lux in the ribs. "You're not exactly selling it."

"There are also benefits, of course." Lux laughed. "A universe of knowledge, the ability to traverse galaxies in a millisecond and design an otherworld in whatever image you please. And there is the ability to help others, within Chaos's limits, and to view the mortal world whenever you like. As well as creating beasts and creatures to keep you company and give you eyes in the mortal realm. Then there is the eternal life to consider."

Remington raised a hand. To be honest, I hadn't even noticed his presence until now. "I'd like to be considered."

Dylan yelped as though he'd been prodded in the butt cheek. "What?! Are you insane?!"

Remington came to the front of the group. "Not at all."

"Remington, I don't think you've thought about this," Jasper managed to say, equally shocked. "You're a sensible man. I know it sounds enticing, but it comes with a lot of conditions."

Remington gave a sad smile. "I haven't wanted to stay in this world since Odette got taken from it, but I knew I had to persevere. It's what she would've wanted. But what if I could bring her spirit into an otherworld? Would that be possible?"

"She was a Librarian. Her soul still resides in an active tributary of the Chaos stream, in a place reserved for those chosen by my father." Lux lowered her gaze. "As such, it would indeed be possible for her spirit to be redirected to an otherworld. You would have that power, if you chose to take Erebus's place."

"And I've always wanted to help people, but that hasn't been easy here. There are too many hoops to jump through. If I were a Child of Chaos, I'd be able to do more for individual people. I can take a leaf out of Lux's book and have priests and priestesses who can do good on my behalf, or aid those who might summon me. Within the limits of Chaos rules, of course." Remington's thoughts rattled out into words as he turned to Dylan. "I think this is something I have to do. I know it might not make sense to you, but it makes perfect sense to me."

Melody smiled. "She is waiting for you."

Dylan's eyes glistened with tears. "This is for Odette?"

"If I can spend eternity with her, then I have to seize that opportunity," Remington replied. "What couple wouldn't do that for each other?"

I coughed. "Lux and Erebus?"

"We are different," Lux interjected, giving me a cold look. "We were created and bound together without a say. Remington *chose* Odette. Now he desires to find her again, so they can begin again where they left off. That is the sort of love that lasts forever. Indeed, it is the sort of love that lures Children of Chaos into giving up their power."

Erebus sighed sadly. "Lux..."

"Do not offer me pity." She turned her face away. "I do not need it."

*How far that little candle throws her beams. So shines a good deed in a weary world...* Never had Shakespeare rung truer, and I usually had no idea what the guy was getting at with all those iambs and pentameters. But it hit deep this time. Lux had already done so much, at the expense of everything she'd ever known.

"Uncle, are you sure?" Dylan hovered at Remington's side.

"If it means I get her back, then yes." Remington tugged his nephew into a tight hug. "And I'll only be a word away. Send for me and I'll come running. Whatever you need, whenever you need it, I'll be there."

Dylan clung to him. "I'll miss you."

"You won't have to," he assured him. I personally knew he was right.

"Does this mean you will trade places with me?" Erebus interrupted the touching moment.

Remington released his nephew. "Yes. I'll trade places with you."

"Thank Chaos you didn't put your hand up, Levi." Nervous laughter bubbled up my throat. "Poor Kaya would have wished she *had* been arrested if she had to spend the rest of her life with you trailing after her. Of all the volunteers Erebus could've had, at least he got a good-looking one."

An awkward silence stretched across the shoreline… until Dylan burst into a fit of hysterics. His laughter seemed to give everyone else permission, and a ripple of relieved chuckles rolled around the congregation. The only one unamused was Levi.

Raffe patted his old pa on the back. "Oh, come on, you've got to admit that's funny!"

"No, I don't." Levi pursed his lips. I had to be grateful he wasn't my director anymore.

"Should we begin?" Erebus brought a sense of solemnity back to the icy shore.

Remington gave Dylan's shoulder a manly squeeze. "I don't see any reason to delay."

"Kaya?" Evidently, Erebus had realized the one minor hiccup in his transformative plan. She hadn't actually agreed to the idea yet. "If I do this, will you allow me to stay with you until our days are done?"

A mixture of emotions drifted across her features. Hope, confusion, doubt, and… yep, there it was, clear as day: love. "I have lost a great deal already, through my own faults. I thought I was strong enough to send you away, but… I cannot. If you are willing to sacrifice eternity for me, then I am willing to set aside my guilt."

"I think that's our cue." Remington moved toward Erebus.

"I will ask you one last time—are you willing to give up your mortal form and switch places with me?" Erebus's voice carried a note of nerves. "Once this begins, it cannot be reversed."

Remington took a steadying breath. "I'm willing."

"Very well." Erebus grasped Remington's arms. We all took a step back as the exchange began. The Child of Chaos's darkness swirled inside the confines of his natural form, while his red eyes shone brightly. Gradually, the black mist that was being held together by the sheer force of Erebus's mind started to unravel. And the ensuing strands threaded into Remington's body, turning his veins black beneath his skin.

Remington's eyes widened as the smoke pooled into them, blackening to two glinting coals. His hands balled into fists as Erebus's smoke continued to sink into him, his body shaking violently against the sudden invasion. We all watched in nervous awe as the last wisps of Erebus's being disappeared inside Remington. There were two entities inside that body now, and they would soon split again. If everything went according to plan, that was. Things had been a lot shinier, and a lot less panic inducing, when Gaia had been the one changing things up. But that was her way, to make everything as beautiful as possible. As for Erebus, he was a little rougher around the edges.

A moment later, Remington's head flew back and his mouth wrenched open. Dense black mist poured from between his lips and surged upward in a tornado, prompting the rest of us to retreat farther. The pillar of darkness twisted up and up until no more mist escaped Remington's mouth. As his body snapped back, his eyes blinking in confusion, the torrent of blackness cascaded back to the ground and began to take shape. Faint edges appeared. And two shining, silver eyes peered out of the vague facial features. Not red anymore. The cosmic lease had changed hands.

"This feels… bizarre." Erebus's deep, commanding voice boomed from Remington's former mouth.

"I agree," the silver-eyed mass replied in Remington's voice. "I can hear… everything. The entire universe, calling to me."

Erebus attempted a smile in his new face. "And I don't hear anything."

Remington must've taken all of Erebus's Chaos, as well as his smoky form. After all, you couldn't have one without the other. And that meant

Erebus was now mortal in the most basic sense of the word. No magic, no Chaos, no power; just a fleshy meatsuit and the woman who loved him.

"Are you hurt?" Kaya approached Erebus hesitantly.

He shook his head. "I feel better than I have in centuries."

I cast him a knowing look. "You won't be saying that when you're in your sixties and even getting out of a chair makes you ache."

"I look forward to the sensation." Erebus laughed and scooped Kaya into his arms, swinging her around. I stole a glance at Lux, who'd turned to watch the ocean instead. She was stronger than I would've been. In fact, I was in awe of her.

Jasper cleared his throat to draw attention away from the happy couple. "Now that this exchange has been made, perhaps we should take Miss Kaya to see Dr. Krieger, so she can have her Suppressor fitted?"

"I suppose it is just." Kaya relented, a joyful grin still on her face. She might have lost Atlantis, but she'd gained Erebus. Now, they'd be able to live out their lives together as ordinary humans. As happy endings went, I guessed that was a pretty good one, even if it meant Lux wouldn't get hers.

*Or perhaps she will.* Maybe freedom from her cosmic marriage was precisely what the proverbial doctor had ordered.

As for the real doctor, Erebus led Kaya away to the Antarctic Coven, with Santana and Tatyana acting as their guard. The former queen had an appointment with Mediocrity. And their departure signaled more farewells.

"I must go." Remington wrapped his smoky arms around Dylan. "Odette is waiting for me, and I need to bring her to my otherworld, wherever it might be." He let go of Dylan and addressed the rest of us. "It has been the pleasure of my life to work alongside all of you, and I hope you won't be strangers. Call for me if ever you have need. I'll be there."

"We will," Harley replied, with sad eyes.

Remington's edges blurred slightly. "Well, then... let's see what this Child of Chaos business is about."

"I will come to check on you in due course." Lux managed to turn back to face the group, now that Erebus had gone. "You will need guidance in this new existence, and I will ensure that you get the right start."

"Thank you, Lux. And... I'm sorry for your loss."

She fidgeted with the edge of Ryann's shirt. "You need not be. I will flourish and persevere. I always do."

With a nod, Remington disappeared in a puff of black mist, to begin his new life in whichever otherworld Chaos picked for him. I prayed he'd find Odette there, so the two of them could finally have the happiness my mother had ripped away from them.

Another awkward silence blanketed the gathering, with everyone side-eyeing each other. Nobody knew what to say. So, I guessed I'd have to be the ten-ton polar bear once more—breaking the ice.

"So, what's the plan for Atlantis then, King Apollo?" I flashed him a tight grin, hoping he'd take the hint.

He flinched. "Please, do not refer to me as such. I might wear the crown, but I am no king. Indeed, though I have not had long to contemplate it, I believe that I might implement a republic upon my return. I simply cannot imagine a throne without Kaya upon it, and I certainly do not want to be treated as a monarch."

*Okay, let's try this again...*

"Sounds good to me. Give the power to the people." I punched the air and felt like a total goof. "But what about the future of Atlantis? You've got the California Mage Council right here if you, you know, wanted to strike a deal. They're not the government, or global leaders, but they can pass a message on."

His eyebrows shot up. He'd finally caught on. "Ah, yes, of course." He turned regally to face the officials. "As the current ruler of Atlantis, I would like to state our intentions. Atlantis will become an independent republic, but it will fulfill the responsibilities of a coven, since we are now bound to the surface Bestiary. We will adhere to your magical laws, as long as we are left in peace. However, we will forge a border through which Atlanteans and other magicals may pass, in the spirit of trade and unity and progression."

The Mage Council exchanged thoughtful glances.

"I do not see a problem with that." Jasper answered first. "Paperwork will need to be drawn up, but I believe the global leaders will agree to those terms. They seem very reasonable."

"And the magical world will be more than happy to welcome the descendants of the Primus Anglicus back to the surface," Levi interjected, likely to get himself a foothold in what would soon be the world's biggest and most powerful coven—a political move that would go down in history as one of the most monumental moments in magical existence. Try saying that ten times fast.

Nash folded his arms across his plaid chest. "What about everyone who's been resurrected? Atlantis is full of them, but so is the surface world. What are you all going to do about that?"

"Those in Atlantis will remain living." Apollo's voice gathered in strength. Maybe he had an air of kingliness about him, after all. "It would be cruel to kill them all over again, and as there has already been an agreement to wipe the minds of non-magicals, I believe that is the fairest solution."

Selena nodded. "We concur."

"Necromancy will have to remain legitimized, unfortunately, but you can ensure that the government goes back to the old rules." Harley added her two cents, gesturing at the Mage Council. "You know, making sure people know that Necromancy is frowned upon."

"Though there are only two Necromancers left in existence." Melody sprinkled her knowledge onto the situation. "And I doubt either of them has the same delusions of grandeur that Davin had, so it's unlikely we'll ever see anything on this scale again."

I gave a halfhearted snort. "I guess something had to survive Davin's brief reign. It wouldn't be him if he didn't leave some kind of lasting mark."

Honestly, I still couldn't quite believe he was gone. But he was. And the world would be restored, and all the mess Davin had made would be cleaned up, slowly but surely. And, you know what, though I was hesitant to admit it... that felt really friggin' good.

Maybe I'd get my happy ending, too.

## THIRTY-SIX

## Finch

Rainclouds rolled in over the dilapidated landscape of South Georgia Island's old whaling post. The Antarctic wind picked up, howling through the derelict houses and making the rusty winches and hooks clank against their metal fixtures. None of us were dressed for this weather, and teeth had started to chatter. Now that Remington had left and Erebus and Kaya were on their way to their ever after, it felt like something was coming to an end—a tangible conclusion to a long road.

Lux wandered away from the group and went to stand on a narrow ledge that jutted out over the crashing water below. The spray burst upward at regular intervals, misting her face with freezing water. But she didn't seem to mind. In fact, she closed her eyes and raised her chin, as though enjoying the sensation.

I decided to hang back and leave her to whatever moment she was having. After everything that had happened today, she deserved some peace and quiet.

Not everyone was on the same page, though. Melody took Luke's hand and led him toward that rocky outcrop, approaching with furtive caution. They were close enough that I heard what she said. And I remembered that there was at least one more complicated relationship that needed smoothing over.

"Lux?" Melody tapped her on the shoulder.

She didn't turn. "Mm-hmm?"

"Can I ask you a question?"

"I don't know, can you?" Lux replied, with a half-smile. *I guess even Children of Chaos aren't above that old joke.*

"It's just… you know Chaos and its rules better than anyone." Melody peered up at Luke, the anxiety obvious in her saucer-like eyes. "What do you think will happen to Luke and me if we carry on as we are? I love him, and he loves me, and we want to be together. I know being a Librarian doesn't allow for love, but I don't want to give up on it. But is there going to be some kind of cosmic retribution if we stay together?"

Lux's shoulders sagged. "Chaos itself rarely interferes with the love lives of Librarians. The rule is there to protect those with the gift from weakness that can be manipulated by mortals, not cosmic beings. If you are careful and sensible, which I know you are, then you can have all the happiness you desire. As we have seen, some rules are meant to be bent or broken. And you deserve happiness, Melody. It is the least the world can give you, when you bear such responsibility. So take this as my blessing. I cannot protect you from those who might try to use you, but I can ensure that Chaos looks upon your union with ambivalent—if not fond—eyes."

"Thank you." Luke put his arm around Melody and squeezed her to his side.

Melody nestled her head into his chest. "Yes, thank you. I'm not going to give up out of fear. You have to hold on to love, right?" Melody looked stricken when she realized what she'd just said.

Lux blinked, and a tear rolled down her cheek. "Until you have to let it go, yes." She hurriedly brushed the tear away. "But that is my story, not yours. You have something remarkable, and you should enjoy it as long as possible. And now, I must be on my way. I have a new life to figure out, and… I do not know where to begin. If only Children of Chaos could get drunk." She laughed, and her eyes brightened. And I got the feeling she'd be okay.

Lux put a tentative hand on Melody's shoulder—the closest thing to a hug that she was capable of. Then, sighing wearily, she walked away from the wild ocean and its icy sea spray and sought me out. But to my surprise, she did hug me. And I had no idea what to do, holding my hands like rigid planks at my sides.

"Goodbye, Finch," she whispered in my ear. "Be good, won't you?"

"I'll try." I patted her awkwardly on the back. Weird, considering she was in the body of my girlfriend, who I was more than eager to scoop into an embrace. "Thank you again for everything you've done. We wouldn't be standing here if it wasn't for you."

She grinned as she let me go. "No, you would not, and don't forget it. I expect you to shower Ryann with gifts for her part in saving the world. A non-magical, unraveling Davin's plans—who would have thought it?"

"I would." I meant it. "Nothing that woman does surprises me. She's… incredible, magical or not. And it helped that she had a pesky Child of Chaos camping out inside her."

"Touché." Lux took a step back. "This is the last you will see of me for a while. Perhaps, if you are very lucky, you will never see me again. Then again, I might pop in from time to time, just to frighten the life out of you."

"And here I was, thinking you'd turned over a new leaf." I smiled, feeling a strange tug of sadness in my chest. She'd been a royal pain in my ass, but I'd miss the old harpy.

"Goodbye, Finch." She didn't wait for me to reply. In the blink of an eye, she erupted from Ryann. Her glowing, gossamer form rose up and drifted away on the Antarctic breeze, carried into the sky and out of our lives. Perhaps forever. And while that was sad in a way, it meant one amazing thing… I had my Ryann back.

She leapt at me like a spider monkey and wrapped her arms around me, gripping me so tight that I thought an eyeball might pop. I laughed and hugged her right back, no longer awkward. With her, my hands knew exactly what to do.

I ran my fingers through her sea-salted hair and tilted her face up to meet mine. My lips had been starved of her for so long, but I didn't have to go hungry anymore. I kissed her softly, tasting the sea on her mouth. And she responded in kind, our lips moving in a familiar, delicious rhythm. I felt eyes watching us, but I didn't care. Nothing could ruin this moment.

"Your sister is here, in case you'd forgotten!" Harley chirped, sounding amused. I might or might not have flipped her the bird. A kindly gesture between siblings.

"Were we like this when we got together?" Wade added his commentary.

Raffe laughed. "You were way worse! We had to knock on every door in the SDC, just in case."

"That's a blatant lie!" Harley protested.

"It's really not." Dylan chuckled. "You were awful."

"I'm a teenager, and even I thought you guys were too much." Jacob could never resist an opportunity to make his elders feel like they were the ones in need of chiding.

O'Halloran cleared his throat. "We even thought about staging an intervention. There was a very real hygiene risk."

"That's not true!" I could feel Harley's embarrassment from here. I wished they'd all shut up, too. They were really killing the vibe here.

"I love you so much," Ryann whispered, pausing for a moment. It brought me right back into our little bubble.

I cupped her face and gazed into her beautiful eyes. "I love you so much, too. I've missed—hang on, what's that in your eyes?" My neck craned to get a better view. Flecks of gold glinted in the sky blue of her irises, and two faint dots of light glinted in her pupils. "Please, for the love of Chaos, tell me you're not Lux playing a really friggin' mean trick on me."

"It's me, Finch. I swear." She looked startled. "Why, what's wrong?"

"You've got all these glittery bits in your eyes." I scrutinized them more closely.

"I do?" She patted herself frantically for a mirror. Instead, Melody pulled her over to a nearby rockpool, where tide-trapped water lay flat, and touched the surface. The water hardened and turned reflective, and Ryann kneeled to peer into it like she expected to see Mufasa staring back. "Holy crap! When did that happen?"

Jacob walked over. "I thought I sensed something weird."

"Weird? What kind of weird?" Ryann got back up and descended into panic mode.

"I don't think it's anything you should be worried about, but there's like a... residue of Chaos in you. With Lux piggybacking for so long, some was bound to rub off." Jacob shrugged, apparently unfazed.

Ryann flipped from panicked to excited in a heartbeat. "I've got Chaos?"

"A bit, yeah," Jacob replied. "It's not an ability, though. It's just... there, hanging around."

"Do you think it might manifest into some type of ability? A teensy-weensy bit of one?" Ryann grabbed me, her speckly eyes shining.

Jacob thought for a moment. "I don't know. I'd have to ask Krieger."

"What if Lux sensed my desire for magic?" Ryann jittered animatedly. "What if she gifted me a touch of Chaos in return for my 'service' as her vessel? Do you think that could be possible?"

I tucked a strand of hair behind Ryann's ear and kissed her. "I think Lux is capable of anything, these days. Maybe she got her sister to pull a few strings."

"We *did* meet Gaia!" She shrieked, hopping about like she'd woken up on Christmas morning to find a shiny new bike under the tree. "Oh, Finch, can you imagine? I'd explode with happiness!"

"Let's see how things play out, huh? We can have Krieger monitor you, and if Jacob senses an ability forming, you'll be the first to know." I liked her enthusiasm. It made her even more beautiful, if that was possible. I wanted this for her. But I kept a lid on my excitement, in case it didn't work out.

"I love you!" She jumped up into my arms and kissed me passionately, her whole body alive with nervous energy.

"I love you more." I laughed through our kiss and struggled to keep hold of her. These arms had taken a beating with the whole Purging episode. And they weren't quite equipped for holding up beauteous, over-excited women. But I held on, determined to be the heroic romantic protagonist. Just this once.

Fortunately, O'Halloran gave me a reason to set her down.

"I hate to break up all this good feeling, but we've got work to do." He ran an anxious hand through his hair. "First and foremost, what are we going to do about the SDC? It obviously can't go back to hiding in the Fleet Science Center, since it's not there anymore. And I don't want the SDC to have to relinquish the Bestiary before it's time for us to give it to another coven. Keeping the Bestiary here is fine temporarily, but we need to put our heads together and think long-term."

Tobe ruffled his wings. "Another location will have to be chosen for the SDC, where it can be rebuilt. Once that is done, I see no reason why the Bestiary cannot be reattached. That is my preference. I am fonder of the SDC and its inhabitants than I have been of any prior coven." He flashed a shy, fanged smile that gave me the warm and fuzzies. Everyone needed a Tobe.

"What about somewhere around the Cabrillo Monument? I took Tatyana up there a few times," Dylan suggested. "It's beautiful, it's out of the way, and there aren't any buildings around it. Plus, it's way smaller than Fleet, so there'd be less to get wrecked if anything like this happened again."

Harley nodded eagerly. "That's perfect! There aren't as many people coming and going as at the Science Center. And it's in the national park, so we can pretend to be rangers or guides while we're out and about."

"I can help divert the military, so you can do whatever you need to move your coven." A tall woman I didn't recognize patted her radio. "I'm still not entirely sure how that works—moving an entire building—but I'm guessing you guys know, and... I'd like to be a part of it."

*Ah, Harley reeled in another fish.* She had a knack for that. The sole exception being Kenzie—Harley's Everest in terms of recruitment. I knew my sister was still peeved about not being able to persuade my old pal, but that was Kenzie. She did her own thing, and no one could change that.

"Thank you, Lieutenant." O'Halloran gave her a military nod. "We'll need all hands on deck for Operation Amnesia."

"Operation Amnesia?" I raised an amused eyebrow at him.

He shrugged. "Well, it's better than calling it Operation Mind-Wipe." He clapped his hands together. "We'll dispatch to the Fleet Science Center and do a full cleanup of the rubble first, then start with the on-site mind-wiping. I'll speak to Astrid and ask her to work her technical wizardry on the media—see if she can manipulate the news reports, social media feeds, et cetera, to explain everything with the party line: the disaster occurred because of a devastating gas pipe explosion that tore the building apart."

I noticed that Garrett and Astrid weren't present on the shore, and neither was Saskia. I presumed they were watching over our two prisoners in the Antarctic Coven or helping Krieger out with Erebus and Kaya.

The lieutenant pushed her hands into the armholes of her flak jacket. "I'll assist your people with tracking all the military officers and soldiers who were present so they can have their minds wiped, too. It might take a while to track everyone down, but that's the beauty of the army—there's always a paper trail."

O'Halloran looked marginally less stressed, despite the enormity of the situation. "We'll have to find all the resurrected non-magicals, too. They can be mind-wiped so they don't remember dying and just consider themselves lucky survivors."

"Harley and I will get the agents together and work on making all traces of the SDC disappear. Artifacts, spell books, that sort of thing."

Wade gestured toward the new woman. "And we can use Cal's intel to locate any items that already got shipped off and get ahead of any investigations that have been started."

"Took the words right out of my mouth." Cal glanced around the group. And I could've sworn I saw her smile. A real smile, as though she saw something she liked in this motley crew. Who knew, maybe it'd be enough to persuade her to join us. Although I wasn't sure which category she'd fit into. She wasn't an old Muppet Baby, and she wasn't a new Muppet Baby. I guessed I'd have to come up with a third band. Miscellaneous Muppet Babies, maybe?

I wrapped my arm around Ryann's waist and kissed her hair, inhaling that familiar scent of strawberry and vanilla with a new touch of saltwater and ozone. Or perhaps that was the scent of Chaos.

"Anyone else thinking this is going to be very long and very boring?" I muttered.

Ryann nudged me in the ribs. "Finch!"

"What? It is." I chuckled, just happy to have her back in my arms. "But I'm not saying we won't succeed. We've been through a lot worse. We just don't usually have to trudge through the tedium afterward."

"You must take into account the possibility that some people might slip through your nets." Tobe added a note of solemnity to the proceedings. "You will have to be careful and leave no stone unturned. Even then, there might still be non-magical people in this world who will henceforth know of magic."

*Well... no one said it would be easy.* But we were ready to protect our world, again. After all, wasn't that why we were all here?

## THIRTY-SEVEN

## Harley

A clear morning graced San Diego, the sky cloudless and the sun giving me a warm wake-up kiss, even though I'd been up since dawn. I swirled my second coffee in its paper cup.

"I doubt I'll ever get the dust out of my lungs," I lamented to Wade. We sat on a grassy knoll a short distance from the wreckage of the Fleet Science Center. Although, these days, it looked more like a demolition site than a disaster zone. Scaffolds, builders, cranes, diggers... the whole nine yards. They were in that morning lull of procrastination, but soon the skull-splitting sound of a pneumatic drill and the clank of machinery would fill the silence.

Wade chuckled as I leaned into his side. "It's taking shape, huh?"

"I guess so, though it'll be ages before it starts looking like a building again. Non-magical construction takes way too long." It had been a month since we'd landed back on the South Georgia Island shoreline and put our cleanup plan into action. So far, it'd been fairly smooth. Well, as smooth as a mass mind-wiping and general collateral damage limitation could be.

He sipped his coffee. Only his first of the day. "The plans look good, though, and the agents are doing a decent job of keeping things contained." We had an entire team pretending to be laborers and over-seers, covertly making sure nothing magical cropped up. Quite a lot had been discovered in the rubble so far, but it'd been spirited away before any non-magicals could get their hands on it.

"Did Cal check in?" I wanted to lie back in the grass and bask like a lizard. I honestly couldn't remember the last time we'd had a day off, and with things winding down, it felt like one was long overdue.

He took out his phone and flashed the screen at me. "She's got a short list to get through today, but we're almost under a hundred mind-wipees to go."

"Mind-*wipees*?" I laughed, peering up at his freaking beautiful face.

"We can't decide what else to call them." He grinned down at me, and I felt the sun get a little brighter. Cheesy, sure, but a fiancée had a right to get a bit cheddar about the man she loved.

"What about the online conspiracy theorists?" I took out my phone and waved it at him. We'd been doing a lot of work on our phones lately, checking in with this person and that person, and making sure everyone was on the same page. "We can't deal with all of them, and if we take every single site down, it's going to look like a major FBI sting. It'll only confirm what they think they already know."

Wade leaned down and planted a kiss on my shoulder. "I wouldn't worry about the conspiracy theories, pickle. No one's any closer to the truth, and Astrid is monitoring it like a demon. At the moment, the favorite theory is aliens. So I'd say it's SETI's problem."

"ET phone home." I put my index finger up and pressed it to his cheek, using the voice and everything. I blamed Finch. He'd been forcing us all to spend quality time together before the wedding, and that meant sitting in a room, going through what he called the "absolute classics of modern cinema."

He laughed and put his finger to mine. "Be gooood, Elliott."

"We've turned into dorks, haven't we?" I smiled, loving the idea.

"I think we were always dorks, in our own way." He cuddled me to him and sipped from his cup. "Do you think Kaya and Erebus are doing this, right now?"

"Pfft. I think they got a way better deal than we did. They're probably sipping Italian coffee on their fancy balcony in Capri, gazing at a picturesque sea." I wasn't bitter... *much.* Erebus and Kaya had chosen the exile of champions, running off together to enjoy the delights of the surface world before settling on a snazzy villa overlooking the coast. I guessed Kaya couldn't let go of the sea.

Wade kissed my forehead, chuckling against my skin. "I think they're doing more than just sipping coffee."

"Wade!" I playfully grimaced at him, pretending to be disgusted. Erebus and Kaya had sought their tranquil haven for another reason. Last we'd heard, they were trying to have a child together—what Erebus had always dreamed about. And he'd spared no details to poor Finch, who'd become something of an expert in human behavior to the former Child of Darkness. My brother might have been free of Erebus's servitude, but he'd fallen straight into servitude of a different kind. Constant calls about human anatomy, how to be romantic, how you knew when you had food poisoning, and what a pear was supposed to taste like.

"Right. On that note, we should get going." Wade stood and held out his hand to me. I took it and got to my feet, dusting grass off the seat of my pants. We'd come here to check on the progress of the Fleet Science Center, but that wasn't the only job we had to tick off our list this morning. First, we had to swing by Colonel Morris's office to get him to hand over all his evidence. And second... we had a wedding to get to. Ours.

Heading up the street, we dipped into an alleyway and sketched out a chalk door that'd take us straight to military HQ. Cal had made the arrangements and said she'd ping us when it was good to go, which must've been why Wade had checked his phone. Either that, or he'd received his millionth text from Mrs. Smith about the ceremony. Who knew floral arrangements, limos, tasting menus, and wedding paraphernalia could turn a logical, calm woman into a mother-in-lawzilla? I'd figured it was best to put our phones on silent and enjoy this last calm moment together before the big event. Most people would've been at a nice hotel making sure they were all primped and preened for their nuptials. But that wasn't us.

We stepped through the chalk door into a storage closet. *Ah, memories.* Poking our heads through the door, we emerged into the stern gray corridors of the military base. Wade had a map on his phone, courtesy of Cal, and we followed it through the hallways until we came to the spot marked "Colonel Morris's Office." There, we spotted Cal. She casually walked toward us and gave a subtle wink.

"Will we see you later?" I whispered.

She flashed me a grin. "Wouldn't miss it for the world. Jacob's coming to get me. I think he's doing a few portaling jobs today, under Mrs. Smith's orders. You know, she really should've considered a career in the military." She frowned, eyeing me from head to toe. "I hope that's not what you're wearing to your own wedding. Mrs. Smith will hang you out to dry!"

"I've got everything packed, don't worry." I couldn't imagine the drama if I walked up to my own wedding in a pair of black jeans, a T-shirt, and my favorite leather jacket. I had a feeling it'd quickly turn into a funeral. Mine.

"Okay, well, I'll leave you to it." Cal hurried down the hallway so we could get on with our last pre-wedding task. I watched her go, grateful that she'd stuck around and become a heck of an ally. After all this cleanup business was over, she'd mentioned that she might try her hand at the magical special forces, and I couldn't think of anyone better suited.

"Ready?" Wade asked, hand raised to knock.

"Oh, yes."

He rapped on the door, and we went in without waiting for permission. Colonel Morris sat behind his desk, his head raising sharply as we entered. A flicker of recognition passed across his eyes.

"Captain... uh... Captain?" He sounded dubious, like he couldn't quite remember my name. Then again, I'd never told him my real name, so that wasn't exactly a shocker. "What are you doing here? I didn't have any appointments scheduled for this morning."

"No, we don't have an appointment." I strode up to the desk, hoping I looked intimidating.

Wade played the bad cop to my mildly aggressive cop. "We're here to ask you to hand over all the evidence you collected from the Fleet Science Center site. It's a matter of national importance."

The colonel barked out a laugh. "You're not serious."

"Oh, we're very serious." I planted my hands on his desk and gave him my best interrogation lean.

"Forget it." The colonel sat back in his seat, still laughing in our faces. "I'm about to submit all my findings to the National Security Council. The Department of Defense will be moving ahead with our investigation. Even if we *have* had trouble getting some of the witnesses to testify. They claim not to have seen anything, but we all know that's not true."

I unleashed a sharp sigh. "Listen, I've got a wedding to get to, so I'm not going to beat around the bush. You're completely out of your element here, and you need to hand over all that evidence immediately. Here's why." I leapt into a brief explanation of the magical world and what had really happened to the Fleet Science Center. I gave him my best, "And you'd do better to forget everything about it, because it'll start mass panic and a potential war if you don't" speech. He gaped at me in disbelief, blinking slowly.

Before he could utter a single world, a loud beep went off and Wade swiped his phone from his pocket. "Ah, crap. We need to get a move on, or we're going to be late. People are arriving, and Mrs. Smith is freaking out. Santana may or may not be freaking out too, and there might or might not be a video of her ranting about feeding me to Slinky for jilting you."

"But we're not done here." I tried not to laugh at the idea of my friend in full protector mode.

"I think we are." Wade waved a hand at the colonel. "There's no point telling the colonel all this, since he won't remember anyway." We'd come here to give the colonel a chance to give up the goods willingly, but we had a backup plan. It was the one piece of good advice that Katherine Shipton had ever given, and I'd never forgotten it.

I huffed. "I hate mind-wiping."

"Sometimes it needs to happen." Wade walked around the desk, while I kept my gaze fixed on the baffled colonel.

"I'm sorry, Colonel." I pushed off the desk.

"Sorry?" The colonel looked alarmed, but it'd all be okay soon. Wade put his hands on either side of the colonel's head and threaded a spell into his skull. The colonel's eyes turned blank and his jaw went slack as he sank under the influence of Wade's magic.

"Give us the evidence you've collected," Wade instructed.

The colonel stood and went to a heavy-duty safe in the corner. Zombified, he turned the combination until the safe clicked open. He reached inside and removed a large metal box with several folders piled on top before handing the materials over to Wade. My husband-to-be passed them off to me while he worked his magic. He'd become a pro at the art of amnesia during his years at the SDC, and the whole thing took less than five minutes.

Of course, being the lovely man he was, he made sure to put the colonel back in his chair before he finished the procedure. The colonel's eyes stayed blank as we scampered away with the evidence. It'd be a few minutes before he came around, and we couldn't be there when he did. Not if we wanted to avoid some tough questions that might make us even later to our own wedding.

Cal hurried up to us as we left.

"I thought you were signing off," I said, closing the door in case the colonel came to while we were chatting.

"I wanted to make sure everything went well in there. I wouldn't be able to enjoy myself, otherwise." She paused, looking sheepish. "And Jacob messaged me, saying that Mrs. Smith told him to tell *me* to get your asses in gear."

I raised the box of goodies. "All good."

"Phew." She still looked sheepish. We found out why a moment later, when she slipped another name into Wade's hand. "Not too many more to go."

Wade groaned. "Today? Really? Is this your idea of a wedding present?"

Cal shrugged. "Sorry. I tracked down a few more, and I figured you'd be too busy for me to hand the name over later."

"We're too busy now!" Wade protested, shoving the name into his pocket.

"Right! Yes. Asses. In gear. Now." Cal gave us both a firm shove, and we had no choice but to obey. Finding the closet again, we wasted no time sketching a chalk door back to San Diego. Now, a normal magical might've wondered why we weren't getting a portal with Cal and Jacob, but I'd already decided to arrive at my wedding in style. And no amount of tardiness or threats from Mrs. Smith would take that dream from me.

"I can't believe she gave us a name as a wedding present," Wade muttered, as the edges fizzed and cracked, forming the doorway to our future.

I laughed, too excited to care. "Relax. Santana and Raffe can handle it tomorrow. Right now, I don't want any doom and gloom, or Mrs. Smith will have your guts for garters." I launched myself at him for one last kiss. "We've got a freaking wedding to get to!"

## THIRTY-EIGHT

# Finch

*C all me the White Rabbit, because I am LATE!* I tore down the street at full pelt, my polyester suit doing nothing to prevent the torrents of sweat pouring everywhere. I'd foolishly visited the new SDC site to go through the CCTV videos that Astrid had sent over the night before. And by the time I finished, the cars had friggin' left without me! True, I probably should've dealt with the video footage later, but there was something about my Purge monster that had me on constant watch. I'd confided in our resident nerd about my worries, and she'd set up an entire surveillance system to find the sneaky, smoky bastard like it was no more effort than putting together a Lego set. Although, I guessed that depended which Lego set you were putting together. The Millennium Falcon? Forget it. That called for a PhD in engineering.

I bulldozed my way down the sidewalk, determined to get to my sister's wedding on time if it killed me. And I didn't mind if a few slow-walking casualties were necessary to achieve that goal. Seriously, why did people just stop in the middle of the street? And why, oh *why* did some of them trail along like a bunch of snails? In fact, a snail would've been faster!

As I ran, I thought about what I'd seen on the tapes. We didn't know what that Shapeshifting critter could do, or how dangerous it really was, yet. And I wasn't about to let something I'd Purged cause havoc in the world. But my sly monster was keeping its head down. There'd been a few possible sightings on the tapes, including one smudgy shadow coming up on a Paris Metro camera and another streak of darkness appearing on CCTV in Rio de Janeiro, of all places. But none of those were rock-solid evidence of his activities. The only recent sighting that gave me any sort of hope was the terrifying Puffball sighting. That ball of fluff and bad advice had shown up on camera in Florence, sitting on the roof of the Duomo. He'd been spotted again on the steps outside Marie Laveau's old haunt in New Orleans, and then a third time perched on the apex of the Sydney Opera House. Choosing landmarks, almost like it wanted to be found.

*I'm going to have to hop around the world again, aren't I?* I powered forward, squeezing around a couple. I wasn't going to let this ruin my day, or my sister's. It just sucked that I was going to have to do another world trip to find that smoky wretch.

I skirted the corner and saw the church up ahead. Dispensing with any other thought aside from seeing my sister get hitched, I ploughed on until I reached the doors. Giving it my best Aragorn, I burst through.

"Don't start yet! I'm here!" I shouted, only to find the congregation still milling around in the foyer. Heads swiveled like a parliament of owls to stare at me.

Garrett laughed at my grand entrance. "I might be wrong, but you don't look like the bride."

Puzzled, I scoured the group for any sign of Harley and Wade. "Huh? I thought I was going to be late. Where are the bride and groom?"

"Beats me!" Santana strode over, with Slinky lashing his tongue in sympathetic irritation. "The cars arrived to pick Harley up from Ryann's and Wade up from Garrett's. But neither of them were where they were supposed to be!"

Ryann ran up at that moment, breathless. And, man, she had gone and stolen my breath away, too. She was dressed in a silky purple gown, and her hair was done up in some kind of messy bun, with Arwen curls framing her face. She looked incredible.

"Sorry! Have they arrived yet?" She snuggled into my side like a magnet, and I had to resist playing with those elfin curls.

"No, and Santana's about to go nuclear." Raffe put his arm around Santana's shoulder, which Slinky took as an invitation to give him a nauseating lick. *Ugh.* Why had she even brought that thing with her? The guests may all have been magicals, but there were non-magicals outside. I guessed he'd play dead or something and look like a grisly scarf, if anyone passed by and noticed.

"Oh, right." Ryann steadied her breaths. "There was a slight change of plans this morning. I forgot to tell you, with my mom calling me every ten seconds, but they went out to deal with that colonel first."

Santana's cheeks turned red. "They went on a mission, *now?*"

"What's happening?" Tatyana poked her head into the conversation, flanked by her sister and Dylan. I didn't want to be all prim and proper about it, but Saskia didn't look dressed for a wedding. More like for a night in the club, or like she was preparing a sting to rob rich men blind. I pitied any of the singletons who'd get cornered at the reception.

"The bride and groom aren't here. They took a detour, apparently," Raffe replied.

A portal tore open inside the foyer, and six figures tumbled out: Melody, Luke, Nash, Huntress, Cal, and Jacob. The latter looked flustered when he saw us standing there.

"Sorry we're late. I had some trouble finding Nash in Manitoba." Jacob wiped sweat from his brow. "Has it started? I guess not, since you're all standing around." He caught sight of Saskia, and I swear the poor boy's eyes nearly bulged out of his skull.

"Don't worry, no one's as late as the bride and groom." Garrett waved to Astrid, who had her nose buried in Smartie—the third wheel in their relationship. Or maybe that was Garrett. It changed on the daily.

"They're not here?" Melody slipped her hand into Luke's. Both of them looked snazzy, with Luke in a dark green suit that Melody had definitely picked out, and her in a matching, satiny jumpsuit. A surprisingly muted color palette for Melody, but it suited her. It made her look more... mature. Then again, perhaps that was just her demeanor. Atlantis had definitely forced her to grow up a bit, away from the sheltered existence of the Winchester House. But her lollipop earrings suggested that she hadn't lost all her quirks. I was glad.

Astrid pushed her glasses up the bridge of her nose. "They're on their way. According to Smartie, they should be about—"

A loud screech split the air, making all of our heads whip around. Daisy, the old hunk of junk, skidded around the corner in the most impressive handbrake turn I'd ever seen and sped down the street toward the church. Harley was at the wheel, her veil flying back behind her, as she pulled the car to an emergency stop right in front of us.

*Man... why'd I have to have such a cool sister?* I thought I'd made a dramatic entrance, but it was frankly pedestrian compared to this.

Harley jumped out in all her bridal finery, and I noticed that she'd worn her heavy-duty military boots underneath. Typical sis. Ryann rushed to try and fix her hair and wrangle the veil into submission, but Harley just grinned at her.

"Apologies for the fashionably late arrival." She held her hand out for Wade as he jumped out the other side, still buttoning up his shirt. "We had duties to attend to, but we're good to go now. Let's get this wedding on the road!"

I eyed her. "I thought it was bad luck for the groom to see the bride before the wedding."

"Come on, after all the bad luck we've had this year, I think we're probably all right." She opened her arms. "How do I look, brother?"

I looked at her, all dressed up for her wedding day. She was wearing a simple white dress that Mrs. Smith had spent a month painstakingly crafting out of her own nuptial gown and the fabric from Hester's wedding dress. Ryann had insisted on it, though she'd asked Mrs. Smith to save some fabric for her. A good sign, I hoped. Around her neck, she wore the Merlin pendant that Isadora used to wear. The real one, tracked down by a spell that Melody had conjured, not the Katherine replica that had turned Wade gaga. Although, he'd probably go gaga again just looking at his wife-to-be. And in her hair, she wore three feathers given to her by Tobe, and the wildflowers I'd picked for her from the reserve near the SDC's new location. As for the bouquet, that had been diligently constructed by the Muppet Babies, old and new. Sprigs of heather and plump cream roses, interwoven with little trinkets and keepsakes that were dear to every one of them.

Tears welled suddenly. "You look... perfect." Our dad, her mom, our aunt, and everyone she cared about were here to celebrate, in some way. She wore emblems of them all. And I'd never seen anything so bittersweet in all my days. It really was perfect, down to the heavy-duty boots.

"You really think so?" Harley smoothed a hand down the front of her dress and smiled sadly at the lace and silk beneath her fingertips. No doubt she was wondering how her mom had felt on her own wedding day. She hadn't been running around wiping minds ten minutes *after* the wedding was supposed to start, that was for sure.

I nodded. "You brought everyone with you. That makes it perfect."

Her face fell and her eyes brimmed with tears, making her look like a lost child. "I wanted them to be here."

"They are, Harley. They are." I stepped forward and looped my arm through hers. "Now, are you ready for this? It's not too late to change your mind." I grinned.

She sucked in a deep breath. "So very ready." She cast a look back at Wade that said, *I'll see you at the altar.* He gave her a nod and headed into the church, with everyone else following him inside. Which left the three of us—Harley, Ryann, and me—in the foyer awaiting our cue.

"Do I have to give you away? That seems so anti-feminist." I managed to chuckle through the emotion in my throat.

"Hush, you, or I'll get someone else to walk me down the aisle. Tobe, maybe. That'd make for some interesting pictures." She squeezed my arm, and I felt her excitement bubble into me.

I smiled at her. "Don't you dare."

Just then, Ryann's bridesmaid bouquet went up in flames. She dropped it sharply, swearing under her breath. "Dammit! I'm sorry, Harley." She pushed the ensuing ashes around with the tip of her shoe. "I think I might have to go bouquet-less." That had been happening more and more lately —a reaction to the Chaos residue inside her. Although, Jacob still claimed he couldn't sense any abilities on the rise.

Harley laughed and scooped us both in for a hug. "Now you finally get to feel how I did as a kid, accidentally blowing things up all the time."

I grasped them both—my whole world—tight, though my eyes turned skyward. *You'll give her back, good as new, Lux? Good as new?* It looked like the Child of Light had granted my love a gift, after all. And it wasn't even our wedding.

Not yet…

## THIRTY-NINE

## Harley

Two years had gone by in the blink of an eye since the battle against Atlantis. Or, rather, the last fight against Davin Doncaster. But that didn't roll off the tongue quite as nicely. You'd have thought the magical world would've settled in that time, but the aftershocks still rippled through our society, all across the globe. Mainly due to the unexpected influx of Atlanteans wanting to integrate into the surface world. That required a whole new government division, to prevent any animosities between clashing cultures: the Atlantean Cultural Integration Services. ACIS for short.

And who'd gotten themselves the top spot? That's right. Little old me, Harley Merlin-Crowley, Head ACIS Officer extraordinaire. I'd double-barreled our names to keep the Merlin line going, in case Finch decided not to have kids. Every time someone mentioned children, he turned pale, so I guessed it'd be a while before he could even contemplate the idea, and Ryann wasn't in any hurry. Though there'd been a lot of talk about kids lately, with Astrid and Garrett married and expecting, and their own wedding coming up in a couple of weeks. Usually, Finch's panic was something I'd joke about, but he'd confided in me why it made him so uncomfortable. He was worried that he'd pass his gremlins on to any children he might have. While it saddened me that he had such a weight on his shoulders, I understood his aversion. And, to add to those fears, he'd had an upbringing that would put anyone off parenthood. So it paid to have all bases covered where the Merlin name was concerned.

I mean, Wade and I weren't sure about the idea yet, either. My childhood should've been idyllic, but I'd had it yanked out from under me by a vengeful aunt. Who was to say that couldn't happen to any future children of ours? There were no vengeful aunts, as far as I knew, but we lived in a perilous world, with terrible news filling the TV channels and internet every single day. And I didn't know if I wanted to bring small ones into that.

"So, this is where you'll stay for the first few months of your integration." I led my latest clients through the new hallways of the relocated SDC. I'd been a bit stunned when Hector had arrived with his daughter, Iphigenia—otherwise known as Genie. She was a sweet creature, with the usual Atlantean silver hair and a pair of huge sea-green eyes. But I supposed after Hector's various imprisonments and the death of his wife, they had more reason than most to leave Atlantis.

O'Halloran and a vast team of magical builders had rebuilt the SDC to the exact specifications of the old one, so not much had changed aside from the view outside the windows. I had to say, even though I missed Balboa Park, I loved looking out and seeing nature everywhere. And it made me get out of the SDC more often to hike around the nature reserve, which was definitely a good thing. All that fresh air had left me glowing. Even Finch had commented on it. Plus, the Bestiary was back, which brought me comfort. I liked having Tobe nearby, even if he'd been acting weirdly around me lately, always offering me treats and sniffing me whenever I paid a visit. I guessed he was going through something, since he'd started having little beastie dates with Iso. Or maybe he was trying to show his gratitude, considering that I'd been the one to suggest they meet up to talk shop. They made a cute couple, that was for sure.

"All this, just for us?" Hector peered into the apartment. We'd added a new wing to the SDC to house the Atlantean expats. They had to go through rigorous lessons before they could actually step out into the outside world—learning all about the surface world's culture, history, politics, et cetera. And they needed to have visas and documents drawn up so they could move freely between covens and around the non-magical world.

"Yep, all for you." I crouched in front of Genie. "Now, how would you like to go and see the swimming pool?"

Her eyes brightened. "Do you mean the ocean?"

I chuckled. "No, it's not as big, but you'll be able to go and swim in the ocean once you're all settled here."

"I'd like to see it!" she chirped, putting out her hand to take mine. I looked at Hector to make sure it was okay. He nodded, a proud smile on his face, and I led her down the hallway toward the SDC's pool.

At midday, the pool was pretty full of swimmers and idlers, with lots of folks taking advantage of the beautiful terrace. It overlooked the reserve and was a hotspot for people looking to relax. We followed Genie to the pool's edge, where she crouched low and swept her hand through the water.

"Will Genie be taught here for a while, then?" Hector stood beside me, watching his daughter with a soft expression of pure love. "I presume we both have to go through the 'integration' process."

I nodded absently, a clamminess creeping up the back of my neck. Geez, it was hot in here. "We've got excellent teachers who make it fun for the kids. Even though some Atlantean children are older than the teachers are." I gave a stifled laugh. The heat was really getting to me. I started fanning my face to stave off the humidity.

"Are you okay?" Hector eyed me with concern.

"I'm fine, I just need to—" *Oh, no.*

I bent over and threw up into the water. I couldn't help it. Believe me, I wouldn't have chosen the pool as my first option for barf receptacle. Genie looked up at me in alarm before putting her little hand on my back and patting me gently.

"Are you sick, Miss Harley?" She peered at me.

"I think so, Genie." My head was spinning, and I didn't fancy falling face first into my own vomit, so I knelt and braced my hands against the pool tiles.

"Can I fetch you some medicine?"

"I'll be okay in a moment. It's just the heat. But thank you." I smiled at her to reassure her. She was older than me, even though she was still a kid and looked like a kid, and a glimmer of maturity showed through. A gentle spirit, if ever I'd met one.

Lifting my throbbing head, I spotted Jacob bobbing in the pool a short distance away. And he did not look happy to be swimming in my vomit water. The embarrassment factor amped up as a flood of worried colleagues and acquaintances swarmed around me, trying to help me up and asking a million questions.

"Harley? What the heck?" Santana appeared through the crowd and shooed everyone else away. "Raffe just darted out and said, 'Harley hurled in the pool.' I didn't believe him, so I'm going to owe him an apology. Crap, *mi chinguita*, are you okay?"

I brushed off her concern. "I'm fine. I must've eaten something off at breakfast, that's all. And this heat isn't helping."

"Come on, let's get you out of here." Santana grasped my hand and started to lead me away from the pool. We'd only taken a few steps when my Water abilities went haywire. The pool churned, and great waves whipped up into a frenzy, making the unsuspecting swimmers hurry for the edges before they were engulfed.

*What the—?* Spiraling columns of Water burst from the pool and slithered toward me like gigantic sea serpents. They spun around me, and I lost Santana in the currents, her hand wrenched away from my arm. I stood, petrified, in the center of a turbulent column of water, isolated from everyone who rushed to my aid.

"What's going on?" I demanded, my heart pounding.

A deep, familiar voice drifted from the water. *"It is time. The child must be named."*

The column of water collapsed, and I was left feeling even shakier, wondering if I'd just imagined what I'd heard. But I knew I hadn't. Santana swept forward to keep me standing as I threatened to topple over.

Leviathan had summoned me. There could be no mistaking it. Which meant one thing—I had a child he wanted to name. With his supernatural powers, he'd confirmed, before I'd even suspected, that I was… pregnant.

*I can't be… can I?*

I'd almost forgotten the promise I'd made, to allow that monster to name my firstborn. But he hadn't. And soon, he would come to collect.

I pressed a hand to my stomach, trying to feel the flicker of life inside. It was too early, of course, but now I knew there was something in there. Leviathan had revealed it. My unborn child, growing within me. A child fated to be named by Leviathan. What would that mean? I had no idea. Right now, I couldn't even get past one boggling fact…

I was going to be a mother.

# HARLEY MERLIN 18: Leviathan's Gift

Dear Reader,

Thank you for reading *Finch Merlin and the Legend of the Luminary*. I truly hope you enjoyed this one!

I am now thrilled to announce Harley Merlin 18: **Persie Merlin and Leviathan's Gift** - releasing **May 7th, 2020**...

*"The child must be named."*

A name can contain enormous power. But for Persie Merlin-Crowley, the powerless daughter of famed magicals Harley Merlin and Wade Crowley, her name hasn't given her much in terms of abilities. That is, until her eighteenth birthday comes around and she Purges a gigantic Hydra that terrorizes the coven.

How could that be possible, if she's never cast a spell in her life?

Then her mother reveals the deal she made with Leviathan almost twenty years before—a deal that let the monster name her firstborn Persie. Or rather, *Persephone*, as is her true name. He has given her the "gift" of Purging all manner of beasts... so that she may become the Queen of the Underworld like her namesake.

Persie is left reeling. She's spent her life doodling monsters in the margins of notebooks and dreaming of far-off adventures. Now, she'll have to stay under her mother's supervision so her rogue Purges don't wreak havoc. Unless she can find another way to control her powers…

When she learns about The Basani Institute, a monster-hunting program in Ireland, she knows this is her one chance. Alongside her Atlantean best friend and Uncle Finch's annoying kid, she sneaks out to audition to become a monster hunter.

**But Leviathan's gift is one that never stops giving…**

I've included the first 3 chapters as a bonus sneak peek at the end of this book!

Order your copy of *Persie Merlin and Leviathan's Gift.*

Visit **www.bellaforrest.net** for details.

And I'll see you very soon, in this next exciting chapter…

Love,

Bella x

P.S. Sign up to my VIP email list and you'll be the first to know when my books release:

**www.morebellaforrest.com**

(Your email will be kept private and you can unsubscribe at any time.)

P.P.S. You can also follow me on **Twitter** @ashadeofvampire;

**Facebook** BellaForrestAuthor;

or **Instagram** @ashadeofvampire

# BONUS Chapters

## Chapter 1

PERSIE

*There is nothing I would not do for those who are really my friends. I have no notion of loving people by halves, it is not in my nature.* Jane Austen's poetic gem resonated with me. Which was why I was letting my friend, Genie Vertis, drag me into trouble, once again. Although, she was doing it for me, so maybe we were both guilty.

I say "friend," but she was more of a sister, really. And siblings had a way of getting each other into a whole lot of trouble. At least, that's what I'd gathered from my mom and Uncle Finch's epic gab sessions. They were the stuff of SDC legend, and both could wax nostalgic for hours. As for me, I didn't have siblings to test the theory on. Only Genie. But she was all the sibling—and all the trouble—I'd ever need.

"I'm sweating bullets, here!" I hissed to Genie. She waltzed beside me, not a care in the world, having picked up the smaller pile of books to "carry back to the library"—the shaky story we'd decided to go with. In comparison, I looked like a juggler with a severe hand cramp, trying to keep the tomes from toppling. I didn't want to drop them. For one, they'd clatter and make everyone stare. For two, I hated books getting damaged, which was why I always glared at page-folders and spine-benders. *Book-mark, anyone?*

Genie smirked. "I'd say you've got more of a glossy sheen. It suits you. Like I keep saying, you should come running with me. Cardio is good for the soul."

"Running is for psychopaths." I swerved to keep my tower of books steady. "Seriously, why aren't you nervous right now? I've never seen anyone so calm about sneaking into the Bestia—"

"Shh!" She put a finger to her lips. "First rule of sneak club, you don't talk about sneak club. Besides, I have a naturally innocent face." Her slate-gray eyes twinkled. Wherever there was mischief, my friend was never far behind. And neither was I, since I was never far from her. Wrong place, wrong time, all the time. Though she rarely got as much heat as me, even with an Atlantean dad. That was what happened when your parents were the Merlin-Crowleys—I *always* took the rap.

"Like one of those Russian hamsters that look super cute but won't hesitate to take a chunk out of your finger?" I peeked at her over my books, though my sardonic smile went to waste behind the leathery, musty blockade.

She stuck her head out to the side and puffed out her cheeks. "Hamster? I'm more like a duck."

"Everything rolls off your back?" I teased.

"Nope, though I like the way your mind works." She paused to shuffle her feet wildly, making me snort into the spine of *Rare Purge Beasts of the Northern Seas.* "Serene on the surface, paddling like heck underneath!"

With laughter in my belly, the nerves ebbed, and we slunk farther up the main hallway of the SDC toward the Isadora Merlin Library. It had been renamed after a great-aunt I'd never met, though I felt as though I knew her from the stories I'd heard. Tales told by firelight lingered in the mind, conjuring unforgettable memories that seemed as real as my own. That branch of my family name had been a double-edged sword throughout my almost eighteen years on this earth. On the one hand, I absorbed the old stories like a sponge, desperate to learn everything and anything about the characters whose lives had enriched my ancestry. On the other, you really couldn't look anywhere in this coven without seeing the Merlin name somewhere, an ever-evolving fanfare of triumph and magical success—and a sharp contrast to my own shortcomings.

It was a cosmic joke with me as the punchline: a Merlin with no magic.

"Incoming!" Genie shoved me into the shadow of one of the imposing bronze dragons, the ever-dutiful sentinels of the SDC, standing guard with watchful gemstone eyes. I hoped they wouldn't snitch on us.

"Who is it? I'm flying blind here." I nodded to the stack of books, the dust of them itching my nostrils. One sneeze, and the whole thing would tumble floorward. *You poor babies... I'm going to take good care of you until we put you all back in alphabetical order.* I tended to immerse myself in the vivid worlds of fiction and the escapism within their creamy pages, but non-fiction served its purpose. Yes, I might have associated non-fiction books with endless study sessions and weighted eyelids, and I might have cursed their names when the words wouldn't stay in my skull, but that didn't mean they deserved rough treatment. It wasn't their fault that I associated them with a bad time.

"The Levi-Catemaco clan." Genie ducked around a metal trunk of a dragon leg and peered into the corridor, putting on her best espionage performance. *Genie Bond, license to cause mischief.*

I wished I'd gotten a look. Marius Levi-Catemaco, the eldest of Raffe and Santana's four adopted kids at nineteen, had the sort of heaven-sent face that could've been torn out of *GQ*. Ruggedly Spanish, all dark and tan and good enough to nibble on, he set many hearts aflutter. And neither Genie nor I—otherwise sensible young women—were immune.

"It's like everything slows down when he walks," Genie whispered dreamily. "He must have a personal fan with him. Nobody's hair moves like that without outside help."

"I'm about to need some outside help myself," I huffed. The books were getting heavier by the moment.

She winked back at me, her Atlantean face tattoos shining slightly.

"We can't go anywhere until the Osmonds have passed. Might as well enjoy the view." When she went outside, the tattoos were hidden by an embedded magic, but she preferred to go au naturel inside the safe confines of the SDC.

"How do you even know who the Osmonds are?" As far as I knew, Atlantean integration hadn't covered the history of popular music.

"Blame your uncle. He blasts that stuff from his car when he thinks no one's around." She grinned from ear to ear. "But I'm *always* around. You should enlighten him about new music, to save his dignity. And get him to update his technology, too. He still uses CDs."

I smiled, thinking of my favorite uncle. My only uncle, but still my favorite. "I think that'd be like trying to close the stable door after the horse has bolted." Fortunately, I hadn't developed my musical tastes from him, but I owed him for my love of literature. He'd given me a pile of classics at age eleven or twelve, and I'd never looked back, devouring every novel the library held and beyond, like a regular Matilda. Only, I couldn't move things with Telekinesis.

"Okay, the coast is clear. Tip some of those books onto mine." Genie shuffled up to me and let me tip the top tome onto her stack, in a precarious exchange. Not much of a relief, but enough to keep me going. With the load a bit more even, she stepped out of the dragon shadows, dusting off her ripped band tee. I doubted she'd ever heard a single song by Prince and the Revolution. She just wore it to annoy her dad, who'd have preferred to see her in the adapted traditional attire that most integrated Atlanteans wore.

"You know, it's funny that he's called *Marius*." She flashed me the look that let me know a punchline was coming.

I humored her, the constant comedy enabler. "Why's that?"

"Because I wish he would." She cackled, flipping her long silver braid over her shoulder. The white-gold feather barrette at the top of the braid glinted in the coven's warm, atmospheric lighting. Her Esprit.

I rolled my eyes. "How did I not see that one coming?"

"You had to have known. You know me too well." She gave me one of those looks that existed solely between lifelong friends—an expression of love that encompassed almost eighteen years. She'd been alive way longer than that, given the formerly extended lives of Atlanteans, but I'd known her all my life, from day one. Before that, actually, as my mom liked to tell us. Genie had been there when my mom had found out about me, and our friendship had been sealed by the fates from that day forward. But her papers said she was nineteen, so that's what she went with.

We pressed on up the hallway, weaving in and out of dragon statues, and took a left, avoiding as many people as possible. Not easy in a packed coven, but Genie had surprising stealth and a good nose for suspicious glances. Everyone knew us here, and everyone knew our past endeavors: practical jokes and harmless tricks, mostly.

"Are you playing a game, or something?" A voice brought us to a sudden halt. A boyish face appeared shortly afterward, poking around the side of a reptilian limb. Kestrel Merlin—my cousin. My uncle swore he'd named him purely after a bird, like he himself had been. But I knew better. *A Kestrel for a Knave* was one of Uncle Finch's favorite books— mine, too—and he'd traumatized me with the film when I was probably too young to see it. I still hadn't gotten over that ending.

"Kes! You scared the life out of us!" Genie sank against the wall with a dramatic sigh.

He looked slightly abashed. "I'm sorry. I didn't mean to. I just wanted to know what you were up to."

"Who says we're up to anything?" I blurted out. Rookie mistake. I sounded as guilty as I felt.

He swept auburn curls out of his blue eyes. "I meant, I was just curious about what you were doing. It looked like you were playing a game." He observed the dual stack of books that Genie and I had split between us. "Or doing some light reading?"

I tried to shift the weight of the books and almost upended the entire stack. "Sorry, Kes. We've got to get these back to the library before we get a fine."

"Oh, well, let me help you. I don't mind heading that way." He reached out for my books, but Genie wedged herself between us like a human barricade. He was a sweet kid, not a bad bone in his body. A relief for Uncle Finch and Auntie Ryann, considering the rotten eggs that had cropped up in the Shipton line, but we couldn't have any witnesses to what we were actually doing. Especially when I'd been forbidden from doing exactly what we were about to do.

"We appreciate the offer, but we wouldn't want to dent our strong, independent woman image." Genie cut in.

He stepped back and raised his hands in understanding. "Of course, my bad. I keep forgetting when it's appropriate to be chivalrous. Dad says I shouldn't bother, but then Mom smacks him and tells me to ignore him, so it's hard to know."

"I love chivalry, but we're working on our biceps." Genie offered him one of her most dazzling smiles. The shine reflected in his eyes, and a flush reddened his cheeks, bringing out his freckles. She had that effect on most of the opposite sex, even kids like Kes, without intending to.

He chuckled awkwardly. "Well, you... uh... do that, then. I'll just... uh... be on my way." He gave a peculiar half-bow. "I hope you don't get fined."

"Same here. I could do without another lecture from my dad on how to be a responsible adult." Genie laughed like she was joking, but I heard the truth in her words. These days, she always seemed to be at odds with her dad. I supposed that was part of growing up, but I knew it bothered her. She loved her dad. She didn't want to fight with him, but she also felt like they were from different worlds. And she wasn't entirely wrong.

Kes waved before heading back down the hallway. He turned back once or twice, his expression bemused, but he didn't try and investigate further. Where our family was concerned, sometimes it was better not to.

We carried on, my arms about ready to give out. With the strain tingling through my veins, rendering my hands numb, I began to doubt our cover story. We could've gone with something easier to carry. Essays, perhaps? Or a few folders that needed to be returned? It was too late for that now.

"How are your arms?" Genie picked up on my ongoing struggles.

"Arms? What arms? I can't even feel them anymore."

"Then give me another book, and let's hurry." We made another wobbly exchange, and she pushed forward with renewed energy. I struggled to match her, lagging behind on the last stretch. But at least we were almost there.

After a few more minutes, we finally reached the library entrance—an elegant feat of architecture, with two pillars to either side, carved vines twisting up them to form a triangular archway. A frieze within the archway depicted stone intellectuals in elegant poses: reading books, strumming lyres, and scribbling on curved scrolls. And, at the triangle's apex, a large version of the Merlin pendant stood in pride of place, gemstones glittering. An homage to the woman who'd once worn it: Isadora Merlin.

"We need to be seen, right?" I checked in with my accomplice. We could've dumped the books on the side table by the entrance, but I wanted to make sure these books went back to their proper homes.

Genie nodded. "We should head in, make sure we get seen by Mrs. Tibbs, and slip out again *without* her seeing."

"Okay." I sounded more confident than I felt. I knew I'd have to rally strength from somewhere. This was only phase one—the ruse. Phase two had yet to be put into motion.

Genie led the way into the library—one of my favorite places in the whole coven. Wall-to-wall worlds, each one brimming with adventure, romance, characters waiting to be fallen in love with, and villains a person could love to hate. I adored the smell more than anything, the musty, inexplicable scent of escapism.

"Hi, Mrs. Tibbs." Genie waved a hand at the sourpuss who sat at the reception desk a short distance ahead. She didn't wave back. She never did. "Ah, ever the chatterbox."

I stifled a giggle. "You'll get us kicked out!"

"That'd mean her having to get out of her chair. I think we're good." Genie hustled toward the returns cart and toppled the books onto it with an overly loud thud. I winced, certain it would draw attention to us. I waited for the cry of, "Girls! What are you doing?" but it didn't come.

Hurrying in case it was only a delayed reaction, I performed an awkward squat so the books wouldn't get hurt. I set the whole pile down with as much care as possible before flexing my aching arms.

"That feels good."

Genie stepped forward to give my forearms a squeeze, massaging some life back into them. "You ready for phase two?"

"I hope so," I replied uncertainly.

"You've got this, Persie. You've been waiting to speak to that monster for years. And I'm not going anywhere. I'm with you, all the way." She smiled, and I felt a bit of courage stir inside me. Her pep talks never failed to make me feel braver.

I drew in a sigh. "Okay. Let's do this."

"That's my girl!" She dove in to give me a quick, necessary hug before dragging me into one of the stacks. "Now, I need you to hold very still. This is one of my grandpa's tricks. I've been practicing like crazy so it'd be perfect for today, but my skills are still a bit glitchy."

"Glitchy how?" It always made me nervous when she said things like that.

"Let's just say, fifty percent of the time I've phased in and out."

My heart pounded harder, like a runaway horse. "Phased in and out of what?"

"Visibility. Relax, I've got backup tricks, and if we get caught, I'll say it was all my idea." She held my shoulders. "Now, remember to stay still. We're going to have to be up close and personal until we reach the creature's box."

"He has a name, you know." A stiff chuckle puffed out of my nose.

Genie raised a finger. "Ah, but when you name something, you give it power. If you keep thinking of it as just a creature, you won't be so afraid."

"Huh. That actually makes a lot of sense."

She tapped the side of her head. "Not just a hat rack, my friend. Now, shush, I need to concentrate."

Neon-green Chaos sparked out of her body as she gripped me tight. It flowed from her chest to her arms, and into me, without so much as a twitch of her fingers, since she was a Sentient. The telltale sign of an Atlantean. I had no idea what sort of spell she was using, but her grandfather had been an infamous thief who'd never been caught. That called for a trick or two, and she'd certainly picked up a few family secrets.

Suddenly, the pain hit. A fierce heat that began at the point of contact and pulsed through the rest of me at lightning speed, as though someone had doused me in fire ants. Judging by the strained expression on her face, she felt it too.

"Is it supposed to... feel like this?" I gasped, my throat burning.

"I... think so," she gasped back. "A few minutes... of pain, to get... answers. That's got to be... worth it, right?"

It hurt too much to reply.

"I think we're good... to go. Stay... close," she instructed, after a few more agonizing seconds.

*Remind me never to get on your bad side.* Genie never failed to amaze me with her brilliance, but it could also be a little frightening at times. She literally had no fear whatsoever, and a whole box of tricks at her disposal, courtesy of her grandpa. A trait I envied and admired.

Pulling me with both hands, she headed for the library door. Mrs. Tibbs would be our alibi, if anyone asked where we were. She'd seen us come in, but she wouldn't see us go out. At least, that was the plan, providing nothing... glitched.

At the door, my entire body tensed up against the pain and the fear of discovery. I glanced back at Mrs. Tibbs, but her head stayed down, as she was evidently transfixed by something on her desk. If rumor was to be believed, she frequently enjoyed a bodice-ripper while wiling away the hours in the library. And the smirk on her face suggested she'd delved into the kind of book that would've had my beloved Austen turning in her grave.

Still holding on to each other, we bolted out the door after someone else entered. If we'd opened it ourselves, it would've sounded alarm bells. Not literally, of course, but Mrs. Tibbs had a renowned eagle eye. Our window of opportunity had opened. Sucking in a deep breath, I hurtled alongside my friend, grateful that the shield around us stopped anyone from seeing. My version of running wasn't graceful. Give me a set of pencils and a fresh page in a sketchbook, and I could toil away for hours without breaking a sweat. Give me a novel and I would demolish it, front to back, without pausing. But give me a sprint... and I looked like a frazzled crab trying to figure out how all its legs worked at once.

Fortunately, our destination lay a short distance down the hallway, but that didn't stop the nerves pounding in my chest, like a marching band had taken up residence between my ribs. I realized, with some disappointment, that I'd have made a terrible spy. I didn't have the calm for it. Even familiar faces proved unsettling. I spotted two men wandering up the corridor toward us and grabbed Genie, pulling her back into a recess, the two of us pressing as flat as possible, even though we were hopefully still invisible. *Dylan and Garrett!* Two guys who might as well have been uncles! The sight of them had almost given me a coronary.

"Don't... worry. They can't... see us," Genie wheezed through the pain. Both of us poked our heads out like meerkats, still connected. "If we wait a few... more seconds, they'll... be gone."

"I'm starting to think this... was a bad idea," I admitted. Genie tended to be the guts of our operations, while I provided the anxious hair-pulling. In fact, she'd been the one to suggest we do this. I'd spoken about a certain creature so many times, I'd finally broken the camel's back. She'd all but insisted we take matters into our own hands and actually act on my curiosities instead of just speculating.

"We're so close, Persie. Leviathan... is within shouting... distance."

At the sound of his name, a fresh wave of anxiety washed over me. "I think I'm going to... be sick. But that might... be the pain." It simply wouldn't let up. "Anyway, I thought... we weren't using... his name?"

"Argh... sorry, I forgot. This pain... is messing with my head." Genie chuckled and gave me a nudge in the ribs. "It's okay, I... promise. I know a thing or two about... sea beasts from my mom's old journals. There's nothing in there... that you can't handle. And Leviathan... is frozen in a box. He can't hurt... you. This is your shot at getting answers, Persie. Or do you want to carry on, never... knowing what the deal with him is? If that's the case, we can turn around."

Genie stared at me expectantly, the green-tinged forcefield swimming around us.

She was right. I needed answers. But... *What if he says something I don't want to hear?* I didn't say it out loud.

See, when I was a kid, I'd wandered away from my parents while they were speaking to Tobe in the Bestiary. I remembered feeling a weird pull, magnetic and intense, toward a certain door, and I'd beelined to it. I managed to push the door open and take a few steps into a strange, huge hall with a large box at one end. If I closed my eyes, I could still see every detail, down to the elaborate patterns of frost on the panes of the box, like breath in winter. Anyway, my mom and dad had caught up to me before I could get any farther, and that was when they'd laid down the ban. From that day forward, I was forbidden from entering that hall, and Tobe had made sure to keep watch and see that the embargo prevailed.

*What don't they want to tell me?* I'd tried to pry answers out of them, but they refused to discuss it. Actually, no, that's not specifically true. They'd given me a tantalizing nugget that I couldn't forget. They'd said, "Leviathan is dangerous and presents an unknown threat to you." And that was all they'd say. So, here I was, edging closer to potential answers. Despite the potential for danger.

"Keep going or... give up. Your choice." Genie delivered an ultimatum. One I needed to hear. If I left now, I'd lose my nerve and have to stay silent on the subject forevermore. But if I steeled myself, then I wouldn't have to wonder anymore. I could know, one way or another, if Leviathan had answers for me. That was worth being brave for.

I flexed my hands a few times to dispel the nerves that had gotten bunched up in my fingers. "Let's keep... going."

She gave my shoulders a squeeze. "You're doing... the right thing." She peered around to make sure Garrett and Dylan were gone. "So, we should probably... hurry up before I... can't hold this anymore."

*I've come too far to turn back now.* I repeated the mantra, trying to stave off any more doubts that might send me back the way I'd come. After all, I didn't carry those books and endure this forcefield for nothing.

Genie pushed me forward on the home stretch. She stayed beside me with her hands on my arms, acting as my cheerleader, until we reached the Bestiary doors just up the corridor: two enormous black monstrosities with golden lion heads roaring out in place of handles. This time, we had no choice but to open the door ourselves. I only hoped Tobe's security system wouldn't pick up on the anomaly.

Opening it just enough, the two of us crept into the vast expanse of glass boxes and Purge beasts beyond. My eyes darted toward the formidable atrium at the center of the space, fueling the magical world one Purge beast at a time. It never failed to amaze me. All these beings, swirling inside their boxes, had come from magicals, hurled into existence when the time was right.

*Another thing I'll never get to experience.* I didn't mind that one so much. The creatures might have been wild and wonderful, morphing out of black mist into beasts that littered mythologies and legends the world over, but it sounded like a painful feat for all involved. And I doubted I could ever have lived up to my mom's benchmark of birthing a freaking Child of Chaos. Yeah, my mom was cooler than most. A gift and a curse.

"This is... it," Genie whispered excitedly. With my friend tucked behind me, we stalked toward the far door, where Leviathan's secrets awaited me. And, since Tobe hadn't come screeching between the boxes to catch us in the act, I guessed her trick was working, and we hadn't been spotted coming in.

*Just keep going. Just keep going. Just keep going.* My nerves were alight. I looked around for signs of Tobe, knowing he could appear at any moment and blast this attempt out of the water. But the avenues between the glass boxes stayed empty, and we continued walking. It was almost more than my nervous heart could bear.

A sharp clatter sounded to my left, and I clamped my hand over my mouth before a proper scream could unleash itself, echoing out into the Bestiary and ruining everything. A gargoyle slobbered on the glass pane beside me, bumping its ugly head against the box as though it wanted to make dinner out of me.

"Easy there, jitterbug. They can't hurt you. Those boxes are designed to keep them in," Genie reassured me, her voice more even. I guessed she'd gotten used to the burning sensation.

"What if it cracks the glass?" I hissed, my eyes glued to the monstrous face only inches from my own.

She laughed softly. "It won't be a gargoyle that cracks one open, that's for sure."

"That's... not comforting." I curled my hands into fists and tried to pull myself together, as Genie continued her advance toward Leviathan's hall.

I tried to focus on the glass boxes instead of my imminent breakdown. Whorls of black smoke twirled inside, like ink dropped in a glass of water. When I painted, there was nothing more satisfying than that first dip of a paintbrush into the water... I loved it. Plumes of pastel, twirling in the liquid, creating beautiful shapes that invited the eye to interpret. I saw whole worlds in one cup of water. Worlds I could never emulate on paper. They belonged to the transient medium of that solitary glass—a temporary glimpse of beauty that wasn't made to last.

"Here we go!" Genie said excitedly, breaking me out of my reverie. At least I felt calmer. Or I had, until she'd spoken.

She pushed through the door into Leviathan's hall, keeping the shield up to avoid any watchful security. "I can't keep this going for very long," she explained. "You've got about five minutes until I have to admit defeat. This is killing me, and I don't imagine it's a walk in the park for you, either, but it was the only thing I could think of to fox Tobe's security system."

*Five minutes... will that be long enough?* At the far end of the cavernous hall, which echoed emptily, there stood a huge glass enclosure. It was just as I'd remembered it, down to the frost patterns that dusted the surface. Behind the frost, however, I saw something that hadn't been there before. Subtle movement, shadowed and furtive, making it seem as though the box were full of beings that drifted in and out of view.

"I can't do this." I stopped abruptly, my heart beating out an entire carnival in my chest. The idea had been easier to deal with than the reality. Now, faced with what I wanted, I didn't know if I wanted it anymore. There was something... *off* about this room. The space thrummed with menace, cold and biting, sending up the hairs on the back of my neck. And that glass enclosure stood at the center of it all, the core of the danger.

Genie whirled around. "You're kidding, right? But he's right there!"

"I know, but..." I trailed off, my mind sparking in a thousand directions. I wanted to find out more about him, direct from the source. I wanted to understand this strange connection between us—the one that had driven me to this very door, twelve years ago. I wanted to understand why I wasn't allowed in here and what my parents weren't telling me. Leviathan had the answers. I just needed to keep going and get them.

Genie pressed on. "Look, I know you're freaking out. It's only natural. You're about to speak to an ancient monster about some weird bond between the two of you. *I'd* be having a bit of a freak-out as well, if I were in your shoes."

I sighed. "No, you wouldn't. You'd stride up to that box and... demand answers. You wouldn't hesitate."

"It's all about faking it until you make it, Persie. I act brave when I don't feel brave. I act confident when I'm not. I trick my mind into believing it." She smiled at me. "Your mom and dad don't have the answers you're after. Only *he* does. And the truth can set you free. But if you really don't want to do this, we can go back. I mean it. I'm not going to make you do anything you don't feel ready for. Just know that I'm going to support you through this if you do decide to go for it. It's totally up to you."

*Why does this feel all wrong?* I wondered if the dutiful daughter side of me was getting in the way. I rarely set a foot out of line, and when I did, I was always quick with an apology, ready to face the consequences. But this had something to do with who I was. Leviathan held the key to a door that had been locked all my life. A door I would never have known existed, had I not stumbled on this place when I was little. And that magnetic pull would only continue to grate on me if I turned back now. Besides, wasn't it better to ask forgiveness than permission?

"You're right." I made my choice.

Genie offered me an encouraging look. "I'm here, no matter what. I'm not going to let anything happen to you. I know this is what you need to do. But I've got you, okay?"

"Thank you." It didn't seem like enough, but it was all I had. I only wished I didn't have to rely on her to stop anything from happening to me. If I'd had magic of my own, I'd have been able to protect myself. Truthfully, I'd never felt the absence of Chaos more keenly than I did at that moment. Nobody really wanted to be the damsel of their own story. Still, if I had to have a white knight, I was glad it was her.

With the shield still up, we approached Leviathan's enclosure. Our footsteps ricocheted faintly between the vast walls, sounding small and insignificant. I fixed my eyes forward, not wanting to look away from the glass box. Fear, anticipation, dread, hope, and a million other emotions swarmed inside me like the black mist in that box.

"He's... coming." I gulped. A core of black throbbed in the center of his frozen block, and a sudden vibration cut right through the heart of me. It shot out from the middle of the box and didn't stop, a steady thud, like war drums approaching. And I didn't know if it was just my imagination, but I swore I heard the sound of ice cracking. I might not have been able to see the monster yet, but I could feel him. His presence shivered up my spine, prickling the hairs and making my hands shake violently.

Suddenly, a voice boomed through the yawning hall, and the force-field vanished. The sound had startled Genie so hard that she'd let it go.

"Iphigenia Vertis and Persephone Merlin-Crowley!"

I whipped around, lightning fast, to find myself face-to-furry-chest with a very grumpy, very disapproving Tobe. I tilted my head up to look him in his feline eyes—a beautiful shade of layered gold and chartreuse and bronze, with flecks of brown and green and silver that made the color impossible to replicate. Believe me, I'd tried.

"We... uh... I just wanted to... uh..." I gave up. It was obvious what we'd been doing.

"You both know that this place is prohibited." Tobe strode ahead of us and waved a chunky paw across the front of the enclosure. A sheen of bronzed light shot up, concealing the box from view. He'd raised a barrier to prohibit sight and sound, and now I couldn't see or hear anything. I couldn't even feel the unnerving coldness that whispered of menace. In a split second, that barrier had blocked it all.

*And we've just been caught breaking a major rule... for nothing.* Genie and I exchanged a glance of dread. Tobe was levelheaded, and though he might have been disappointed, he hadn't yelled or gotten angry with us. But it wasn't the Beast Master I was afraid of.

# Chapter 2

HARLEY

I stood out on my office balcony, mug of coffee in hand, and let the perfect San Diegan afternoon wash over me. Gulls wheeled overhead and the trees whispered their secrets, egged on by the balmy breeze that swept over the national park. I took a sip and nestled farther into my light sweatshirt. I didn't get peaceful moments to myself like this very often. Still, life as a whole was quieter than it used to be. Nearly twenty years had gone by since Atlantis rose, and no shiny new tyrants had reared their ugly heads since. Apparently, they'd gotten the message.

*The world, magical and non-magical, is for no one's taking.* I took a longer sip and winced as it scalded my tongue.

These days, I viewed the past and present as pre-Persie and post-Persie. I saw the passage of time in her growth and in the mirror every morning. Pesky new lines around my eyes, my skin a little less elastic, regardless of what pricey creams I piled on. But Wade still loved me, no matter how time changed me. And I loved him. Differently, I guessed, from those heady days when we were young, but oddly the same. We were just a bit softer, maybe.

"Eighteen..." I said the number aloud against the bronzed landscape.

"How can she be turning eighteen already?" It seemed like the more years went by, the faster they came.

I vowed not to cry into my coffee. My emotions were all over the place, and seeing my baby grow up wasn't the only thing I had to worry about.

I closed my eyes and recalled the fateful day that Persie had come into the world. I had barely been able to enjoy my pregnancy due to fear, and I'd even had Melody delve into her Librarian back catalogue to surround me with as many protective hexes as possible, in the hopes it'd keep Leviathan away. But there had been no escaping him.

Exhausted from the birth, and sore in places no woman deserved to be, I'd drifted off to try and claw back some energy. I don't know how long I was out, but something woke me sharply. Like bursting out of a nightmare, sweaty and breathless. I blinked awake to find a swirling mass of water leering over the cot beside me. My nameless newborn's cot, with her inside it, pink and new and beautiful. Leviathan had come to seal the deal that I'd made with Echidna, Mother of Monsters. And, somehow, he'd managed to send out his mind and manipulate the water in the Infirmary from the safety of his Bestiary box to make it happen.

"You put in a sterling effort," he said.

"Go to hell," I replied, trying to will strength into my weakened form.

He ignored me. A faceless churning of water. If only he'd been voiceless, too. "I have come to name the child."

"I didn't think you were here to bring balloons."

He laughed. "So beautiful. So fresh." He reached forward with a tendril of water to touch her hand, and I lashed out with a jolt of Air to push his tendril away. A warning.

"Don't touch her!" I snarled. I felt an overwhelming instinct to protect my child from him, spurred on by rage and panic. He'd caught me at my most vulnerable, but I still had some fight left when it came to my baby. I'd always have some fight left for her.

"Temper, temper." But he retreated. "I do not want unpleasantness."

I flipped back the covers, making to get out of bed but hoping he wouldn't call my bluff. "Then go away!"

"Stay at your bed. Rest." He bobbed around to the far side of my little girl's cot. "She will need you to be strong."

"I'll show you how freaking strong I am." I swung my legs over the edge of the bed and prayed for Wade to come back from grabbing coffee. Undoubtedly, Leviathan had waited until I was alone.

"There is no need." Leviathan reached forward again. This time, his watery touch brushed her cheek, leaving a glistening streak. "She is Persephone. She has been named. And when she reaches maturity, I will bestow a second gift." A glowing green bead of light floated out of his watery form and sank into my baby's chest. She didn't stir, as though nothing had happened. I tried to lunge for him, to stop it, but he'd already gone. Leaving a puddle on the floor where he'd been.

The deed had been done. My daughter had been named, and I'd had no say in it whatsoever. And if I went against him... well, it wasn't worth facing the consequences of breaking a deal like that. The only thing we'd been able to do was shorten her name to Persie, so we didn't have to be constantly reminded of the creature who'd tied her fate to his in some unknown way.

*Some unknown way...* That was the worst part. He hadn't left us any instructions or details. He'd swooped in, named her, told me about a gift, and left again. The gift concerned me the most, especially as Persie edged closer to eighteen. I'd tried to get more out of him several times, but his lips had been sealed. Which proceeded to worry me even more, over the years. Deliberate silence represented a greater threat than frank honesty.

Feeling the familiar anxiety grow, I watched a plump brown bird flutter to its nest. Chicks chirped, open-mouthed, for juicy worms. If only human parenting were that simple. Keep them fed, keep them alive, then kick them out when they were ready to fly. I'd tried to be a normal mom, I really had. But with Leviathan's shadow over our lives, I'd turned into more of a helicopter parent than I cared to admit. Always hovering over Persie, trying to protect her from just about everything. I'd shot a fireball at a bumblebee once, and even pushed a nasty older kid who'd been bullying her into a pond with a sneaky push of Telekinesis. Not my proudest moment. Maybe it was partially the foster kid coming through, too. I'd never known safety or consistency as a kid. I might have gone overboard with Persie, to make up for what I'd only found with the Smiths, years too late to make much difference.

"Go easy on her, sis. Squeeze too tight and she'll try to wriggle free," Finch had advised, a long time ago. He'd been a bit more cavalier in his approach to parenting. The "let them eat mud and fall out of trees so they'll learn their lesson" kind of dad. Typical Finch. Then again, he had two of the politest, most levelheaded kids in the known universe: Diana and Kestrel. Kes couldn't do enough for people. Kind and sweet and earnest at thirteen years old, I occasionally doubted he belonged to Finch at all. Diana, on the other hand, had more of an edge to her. Six months younger than Persie, she was whip smart, like her mom, with the same dry humor as her dad. A potent mix of genes that made for one formidable young woman. They had Ryann to thank for that, for sure. She had this natural maternal instinct about her that I envied. It had never come intuitively to me. I'd just muddled through as best I could, hoping love would be enough to not screw Persie up.

*Have I squeezed too tight?* I loved her more than anything. From the moment I knew she existed, my heart had been hers. Everything I'd done, I'd done out of fear for her safety. When she'd asked me about Leviathan, I'd been as honest as I could: it was an unknown threat, but he was dangerous. The only thing I'd omitted was the depth of their bond—that he'd named her. But that was only to stop her from thinking about herself, and her name, in a different way. A bad way. At least, that's what I'd convinced myself.

*Oh, and the ominous gift he intends to give her.* I'd left that part out, too. It would only have cast a shadow over her life, the way it had cast a shadow over mine and Wade's. She'd have constantly looked forward, instead of living in the moment. I hadn't wanted that for her. I'd wanted to bear that weight for her. And, deep down, I still hoped I could stop it. I'd stopped evils before. If I threw enough firepower at the problem, why couldn't I save my daughter, too? Then, she'd never have to know she'd been in peril.

"We thought the dangers were over, didn't we? We thought we'd have a normal life when all those old troubles were over with." I dwelled on the distant memories we all shared, the old Rag Team. Now, we were moms and dads, complaining about wayward kids and stressing out over exams and homework and lunch prep instead of global catastrophes. And there must've been something in the water, almost two decades ago, because kids had come left, right, and center. Finch and Ryann had a wedding and Diana soon after, followed by Kes, five years later. Astrid and Garrett had Merrick the same year that Diana and Persie came into our lives. Then Santana and Raffe had trumped us all by adopting four kids! Marius was nineteen. Azar, their only daughter, had just turned seventeen. Both of them so beautiful they literally stopped traffic. Then they'd adopted Cy, a feisty ten-year-old with a love for all bugs, which had led to a few unpleasant discoveries—scorpions running loose in the coven, beetles in his hair, that sort of thing. And Angelo, who was six going on sixty. He cracked me up, sometimes saying things that sounded like Nash.

*I should give him a call.* The new Muppet Babies, as Finch called them, stopped by from time to time, but it had been a while since we'd made proper plans to see each other. Too long. I supposed adult life did that.

*I should call Tatyana, too.* She was the one person from the old squad who wasn't around anymore. After a messy breakup with Dylan about ten years ago, she'd packed up and headed back to Russia with Saskia. I hadn't checked in with her as much as I should've. Though I guessed it worked both ways.

"Our work is never done, it seems," I told the bird, though it wasn't listening to my human problems. In addition to the Leviathan issue, magicals had been disappearing recently, and we didn't know why. We'd been tracing the incidents and trying to locate the missing people, to no avail. Another reason I had to keep close watch over Persie. Her name

and her vulnerability could well make her a target, and I wouldn't have
been able to live with myself if anything bad happened to her.

Suddenly, the door opened, and in walked Tobe, Persie, and Genie—
the latter two looking guilty as sin. I hurried in from the balcony.

"Harley." Tobe bowed, his wings ruffling. "Apologies for the interruption. I am afraid I have rather disheartening news."

"Is that so?" I put my mom voice on, as Persie refused to meet my gaze.
I knew it couldn't have anything to do with her lessons, since Tobe had
brought her here. And she was a model student. My mind whirred to try
and figure it out—something harmless, probably. A prank or joke that
Tobe hadn't found funny. Other than the occasional slap on the wrist for
that kind of thing, Persie had a clean record. A fact I couldn't have been
prouder of.

"I thought I would leave your daughter with you while I take Miss
Vertis to her father," Tobe continued.

Genie huffed a sigh. "And what a treat that'll be."

"I'm sure it won't be so bad," Persie reassured her, her voice tight with
anxiety. I liked Genie, even if I occasionally had concerns about the
Atlantean's impish influence. The two of them were like cream cheese
and jelly—a pairing that shouldn't have fit, yet somehow did. She always
brought Persie out of her shell, coaxing her out of her room when she
otherwise would have buried herself in sketching and books.

"He'll throw the book at me. And you know how heavy those things
are." She flashed Persie a resigned smile. "In fact, if you listen really
closely, I'm pretty sure you can hear the vein in his temple popping from
here."

My daughter laughed, but not much. The pair of them clearly knew
they were in deep crap. I just didn't know what sort of crap... yet.

"What did they do?" I asked.

"I discovered your daughter and Miss Vertis attempting to approach
Leviathan's enclosure," Tobe replied. "Indeed, they might have achieved it,
had the gargoyles not warned me of their presence."

*What?! After everything I've said?* The peaceful afternoon turned sour in a heartbeat. I gripped my mug to try and stop the world from spinning. She knew better than that! I'd told her of the danger. I'd warned her so many times. What was she thinking, trying to sneak in behind my back to see that slimy creature? This proved it. That girl needed a helicopter parent, nearly eighteen or not. I'd never let the "if you live under my roof, you live under my rules" cliché slip out of my mouth, but I felt dangerously close.

"We shall be going, now." Tobe gave Genie a stern look.

"Lead the way, Beast Maestro."

He grumbled in the back of his throat, bordering on a reluctant chuckle. "Maestro?"

"I think it suits you." She looped her arm through his, and he was too gentlemanly to pull away. Instead, he escorted her out of the room like they were heading to a swanky ball. I even caught sight of a half-amused, half-bemused grin on his face as they exited. That girl had a way of winning over just about anyone, even in a situation like this. The only person immune to her charms was her father, which was probably for the best.

Persie stayed by the door. Head down, shuffling awkwardly, she emanated remorse. The question was—did she feel sorry because of what she'd done, or because she'd been caught?

"Go easy on her." Finch's words came back into my head. I paced a little, tapping the side of my mug frenetically. I had to keep calm. If I blew a fuse at her, she'd run in the opposite direction. Yes, she needed reining in, but there were ways to go about it. I had to keep reminding myself of that.

Silence stretched between us. Then, all at once, our voices rose in a clash.

"What were you—" I jumped in.

"Before you start yelling, I just want to—"

"—thinking! I *told* you about Leviathan. I've warned you about—"

"—make it clear that I didn't have a choice. We don't know what his deal is. I don't know what his—"

"—going there, so many times. I thought you understood! Do you think I make these rules up for a laugh?" I had no idea if she was even listening.

She held my gaze, wide-eyed. "Mom, will you listen to me? I'm trying to explain!"

I fidgeted with the pendant around my neck, the same one Isadora had worn. The Merlin heirloom made me feel closer to those I'd lost along the way. I clutched it tight in my palm and tried to draw strength from it. My parents had never had the chance to deal with a teenager. I often wondered what sort of teenager I'd have been, if things had been different. I had a feeling I would've been just as headstrong. They might've wanted to kick me out of the nest, by the end of it. So perhaps I owed Persie a chance to remedy this.

I took a steadying breath. "Then explain."

"I know you didn't want me going near him, but I had to! You don't know why he's a threat to me. Isn't it better to find out, instead of wondering?" She shoved her hands into her jeans pockets. *My* jeans, but I wasn't about to bring that up now. "He won't speak to you. I thought... I thought he might speak to me."

"You shouldn't have done that," I said flatly. Without magic, she was vulnerable in most magical situations, which I supposed added to my overprotectiveness. But this was on another level. Leviathan spelled pure, unadulterated danger. And she had nothing to defend herself with, even if she'd taken Genie with her. Even an Atlantean was no match for someone like him.

"Why not? He's behind magic glass, and I had Genie with me. Plus, I knew Tobe was around if we needed help." Her eyes hardened. I hated seeing her like this, set against me. "I need answers, Mom. I can't keep pretending everything's fine, when there's this secret about me that nobody knows. Why shouldn't I know what the deal is between us? It's better than not knowing and waiting for some... *whatever* to take me by surprise!"

She had a point. A very good one. And, with her eighteenth birthday fast approaching, I didn't know how much longer we had before Leviathan finally gave up his secrets and revealed the true extent of his threat. But…

"It's my job to keep you safe." I didn't know what else to say.

She looked away. "How do you plan to do that, when you don't even know what kind of danger I'm in?"

I heaved a sigh, speechless. I didn't have an answer. Only a silence that spoke volumes and a gathering dread in the pit of my stomach.

## Chapter 3

PERSIE

"See, you can't give me an answer!" My voice took on a pathetic note. A high-pitched, unnatural sound, as though I'd sucked in a whole balloon of helium. What was it about being in front of your mom, knowing you'd done wrong, that regressed you back to childhood? I summoned what I hoped sounded more like maturity. "No one can... aside from Leviathan."

"It doesn't matter if I don't know the specifics. I know he's dangerous, and that's all that matters." My mom tapped the side of her mug, a jarring sound that pecked at my skull with woodpecker precision. "And I know how to protect you. I've been doing it your entire life, and I was protecting people long before then, too. Do I need to remind you that—"

My eyes threatened to roll back into my sockets. "That you saved the world... twice. But this is different! I don't want to fight anyone. I don't want to save the world. I just want the truth." I bit the inside of my fleshy cheek. Anything to stop my voice from rising again. In the famous words of Michel de Montaigne, fabled philosopher of the French Renaissance: *He who establishes his argument by noise and command shows that his reason is weak.* Or, more simply, once you shouted, you lost the argument.

"We don't know the truth. We only know what we know." My mom kept tapping. An endless percussion that made me want to stick wax balls in my ears, Odysseus-style. "And I've faced Leviathan before. He's as nasty as they come, and twice as tricky. It's not a matter of walking up to his glass box and asking for answers. That's not how he works."

"Does it matter? You have no answers, but Leviathan *does* have answers. You don't want me speaking to him, but he's the only one who knows the truth. Catch-22 doesn't even cover it!" I looked at anything and everything other than my mom, from the sea glass paperweights she kept on her desk—a gift from the Atlanteans, in vivid shades of blue and green—to the pieces I'd painted that adorned her walls. Abstract splashes of color and light with flavors of Kandinsky, poured from my mind into my paintbrush and onto canvas. They'd made sense when I'd painted them. Now, not so much.

"It's for your safety, Persie." The party line, stuck on repeat.

"I'm eighteen in less than a week, Mom. I'll legally be an adult. If that's not the point when you stop babying me, then when will it be?" Desperation crept into my tone, constricting my throat. "How long are you going to stuff me in bubble-wrap?"

My mom froze. "I'm not! I'm helping you, even if you don't see it now."

I dug my thumbs hard against the denim belt loops. "But wouldn't it be better if we got ahead of anything Leviathan might have planned?" After all, knowledge provided the best form of defense. Know your enemy, and that sort of thing. Although, I didn't even know *why* Leviathan was the enemy, only that he was dangerous. More than that, I longed to be able to protect myself, instead of feeling as though my mom had to do all that for me. How could I ever be independent, living my own life, if we carried on like this? I'd be in perpetual child limbo.

"It's all taken care of. You just have to stay away. That's all I ask. That's all I've ever asked." Her eyes hardened—my eyes. The color of the sea on a summer day. My gift from her, like the dark curls from my dad.

I stood my ground. "What do you mean, it's 'taken care of?' Since when?"

"Since the moment I found out you were coming into our lives, I've been putting defenses in place. He's not going to get you. I won't let him." She peered down into her coffee. I wondered what she saw in there. Enough hope to convince herself it was true?

"He's broken through before, though, right?" I knew all about his eerie message to her by the SDC's pool, when she first found out about me.

"Yes, but almost two decades is plenty of time to shore up the defenses. Melody and I never stopped working on solutions." Her body language gave more away than she thought. An Empath should've been better at hiding her emotions, but doubt and guilt radiated from her in waves. And she wasn't finding any answers in that mug. Ironically, it was a chipped, ancient mug with "#1 Mom" half-scratched off the ceramic. A Mother's Day gift from about a million years ago.

I gulped down a lump of tension in my throat. "Maybe I've got a solution that suits all of us."

"Oh?" She lifted her head, wary. A red strand of hair narrowly avoided a caffeine dip.

"Actually, it's something I've been thinking about for a while, same as most people my age." I gulped again, to try and shift the pesky lump. "The SDC is my home, but..."

*Ah, how do I phrase this?* I didn't want to come off as ungrateful or spiteful, or like I was childishly trying to win this argument with underhanded tactics. But if I didn't say this now, chances were, I never would.

"I think I'd like to move to another coven." I wiggled my tongue inside my mouth, wondering if those words had actually come out of my mouth. "It's hard enough here, with the Merlin dynasty hovering over me—Little Miss Magicless. But it's even harder under Leviathan's shadow, with you and Dad treating me like I'm made of glass."

Mom walked forward, compelled by maternal instinct to come closer. And I had a childish instinct to step back. "Persie..."

"You don't want me to go near Leviathan, and I get that you know more about him than I do. But you have to see it from my perspective. It's a huge temptation, having him nearby and knowing there's this big gap in who I am that only he can reveal. So maybe I take myself out of the equation. Maybe I put some distance between us, so I don't keep wondering all the time." I kept talking, determined not to clam up. "The SDC is your territory. It belongs to you and Dad. I see your names, and I hear all those stories about everything you did before you had me, and I'm so proud that you're my parents. But... I want something that's mine. A place to start fresh."

Mom fell silent, pausing halfway across the room as though someone had flipped her off-switch. "I... didn't know you felt that way."

I took a deep breath. "I'm nearly done being taught here. Plenty of people move on when they're my age." Her eyes burned into me, but not in a harsh or angry way. The heat of sadness, more than anything else. Confusion, maybe. "Genie and I were looking through some prospectuses for other covens. There's one in Austin that sounds like it was made for me. They've got this Mediocre development program, where Mediocres get specialized training to boost their abilities. And it's pretty there, so I can keep up with my painting, and there are programs that Genie's interested in, too."

Mom stepped closer, weirdly cautious. As if I were a fawn she didn't want to spook. "Persie..."

"I realize this is all a bit of a shock, but I know you'll come around once you've looked at the prospectuses. And it'll get me away from the SDC, and from Leviathan, and I can start building a life of my own, and—"

"It's not that," she interrupted, closing the gap between us. Her hand grazed my upper arm, her expression gentle and sympathetic. "A Mediocre development program wouldn't do you any good, Persie. You aren't a Mediocre. You don't have any magic at all. I hate to put it so bluntly, but it's the truth."

*Ouch.* That never got easier to swallow.

"That's why it's better if you stay here," my mom went on. "We can protect you here. You might not have magic, but you're still a Merlin, and we have one of the best non-magical relations departments in the US.

This coven doesn't belong to your dad and me—it belongs to all of us. You belong here."

"What if I want something else?"

Mom relaxed her hold on me and stepped back, turning her eyes downward. "We can revisit it in a few years, once we understand the threat from Leviathan."

*A few years?!* Speech evaded me. Literature liked to keep its madwomen in attics—take the wife in Jane Eyre, for example—but I'd wind up as a basement dweller, hiding out until I hit forty. The magicless girl who vanished into the darkness and never emerged, driven insane by her overbearing parents.

"Besides, the magical world might look like it's at peace, but it's not safe out there for someone like you. Your name and your... uniqueness make you vulnerable." Mom softened her voice. A sure sign that I wasn't going to like what she had to say.

"What does Dad think about this?" I shuffled away from her touch. It felt too much like a shackle around my arm.

"He... agrees with me." Her hesitation said everything.

"Does he, or are you just saying that?" I bit my tongue so I wouldn't spew out something I wouldn't be able to take back. "He's always saying he wants me to be happy. If he knew I wasn't happy staying here, he'd let me leave."

My mom lifted her chin. A mannerism I hadn't inherited. "Your dad wants what's best for you, and he knows that means staying here. I'm not the bad guy here. I'm trying to keep you alive."

"Not everything is life and death!" I exploded a little—at least, enough to make her eyes widen in surprise. "Saving the world twice is great and everything, but it's messed with your head. You think everything is a catastrophe waiting to happen, when all I'm asking for is the same thing a million other eighteen-year-olds ask for! Freedom."

"You aren't the same as a million other eighteen-year-olds," she reminded me. As if I needed reminding.

"Aren't I?" My eyes turned steely. "I don't have magic. That makes me the same as most of the population."

Mom clenched her jaw, her cheeks sucking in. "Persie, you asked me to see things from your perspective, and I *do* understand your frustration. But see things from mine. You're my only child, and there's a monster who wants something from you. I can only fight him if you're near me."

*Because I'm so useless and defenseless that I need you to stand up for me?* It saddened me, looking at my mother, to wonder how much this stemmed from my lack of magic. I was constantly second-guessing my relationships with everyone around me, and it sapped so much of my energy, making it harder to think and breathe clearly.

I loved her more than anyone else in the world. But I wondered if she'd ever see me as an equal, with my own ideas and capabilities and contributions. Eighteen was a milestone for a reason—the ascent into adulthood. But she didn't seem to realize that. Instead, the older I got, the harder she appeared to cling, refusing the inevitable truth. One day, I would leave. One day, I'd be my own person.

I found some grit at the back of my mind. "And we're right back where we started. You haven't listened to a word I've said."

"I have, Persie, but I'm asking you to listen to me in return."

I straightened, pulling my hands out of my pockets. "We're never going to agree on this. So, as long as you won't let me speak to Leviathan, and I don't get answers, I'm going to start looking for other covens to call home—somewhere to put as much distance as possible between me and this secret that's followed me my whole life. If you won't help me, then I have to help myself. I won't wait for the axe to fall."

I turned, even though I knew we weren't finished. Unspoken words lingered heavy in the atmosphere, like clouds gathering, chasing me out of the room. The lightning would strike later, after simmering awhile. Holding my head high and putting one foot in front of the other, I resisted the urge to storm out of there. And I refused to let the clouds break now, with silly tears stinging my eyes. For once, I might have won an argument with my mother. At least temporarily.

Brushing away the hot tears that had fallen regardless, a quote from

Voltaire popped into my head: *A long dispute means that both parties are wrong.* It seemed he'd missed an important exception in the case of Merlin women—what if we were both right, in a way? In either case, arguing with my mom left me feeling like a salted slug, all dried up and fizzing. The brief victory meant nothing, not when we'd both pay for it in future tension.

Between Genie and me, seeing eye-to-eye with our parents verged on the impossible.

Ready for more?

**Harley Merlin 18: Persie Merlin and Leviathan's Gift** releases May 7th, 2020. Order your copy to continue reading. Visit www.bellaforrest.net.

See you there!

Love,

Bella x

P.S. Sign up to my VIP email list and you'll be the first to know when my next book releases: **www.morebellaforrest.com** (Your email will be kept private and you can unsubscribe at any time.)

# Read more by Bella Forrest

Darkblood (Book 4)

Darktide (Book 5)

Darkbirth (Book 6)

Darkfall (Book 7)

## THE GENDER GAME

(Action-adventure/romance. Completed series.)

The Gender Game (Book 1)

The Gender Secret (Book 2)

The Gender Lie (Book 3)

The Gender War (Book 4)

The Gender Fall (Book 5)

The Gender Plan (Book 6)

The Gender End (Book 7)

## THE GIRL WHO DARED TO THINK

(Action-adventure/romance. Completed series.)

The Girl Who Dared to Think (Book 1)

The Girl Who Dared to Stand (Book 2)

The Girl Who Dared to Descend (Book 3)

The Girl Who Dared to Rise (Book 4)

The Girl Who Dared to Lead (Book 5)

The Girl Who Dared to Endure (Book 6)

The Girl Who Dared to Fight (Book 7)

## THE CHILD THIEF

(Action-adventure/romance. Completed series.)

The Child Thief (Book 1)

Deep Shadows (Book 2)

A Bond of Blood (Book 9)

A Spell of Time (Book 10)

A Chase of Prey (Book 11)

A Shade of Doubt (Book 12)

A Turn of Tides (Book 13)

A Dawn of Strength (Book 14)

A Fall of Secrets (Book 15)

An End of Night (Book 16)

**Series 3: The Shade continues with a new hero...**

A Wind of Change (Book 17)

A Trail of Echoes (Book 18)

A Soldier of Shadows (Book 19)

A Hero of Realms (Book 20)

A Vial of Life (Book 21)

A Fork of Paths (Book 22)

A Flight of Souls (Book 23)

A Bridge of Stars (Book 24)

**Series 4: A Clan of Novaks**

A Clan of Novaks (Book 25)

A World of New (Book 26)

A Web of Lies (Book 27)

A Touch of Truth (Book 28)

An Hour of Need (Book 29)

A Game of Risk (Book 30)

A Twist of Fates (Book 31)

A Day of Glory (Book 32)

**Series 5: A Dawn of Guardians**

The Chain (Book 3)

The Keep (Book 4)

The Test (Book 5)

The Spell (Book 6)

BEAUTIFUL MONSTER DUOLOGY

(Supernatural romance)

Beautiful Monster 1

Beautiful Monster 2

DETECTIVE ERIN BOND

(Adult thriller/mystery)

Lights, Camera, GONE

Write, Edit, KILL

For an updated list of Bella's books, please visit her website: www.bellaforrest.net

Join Bella's VIP email list and you'll be the first to know when new books release. Visit to sign up: www.morebellaforrest.com

CPSIA information can be obtained
at www.ICGtesting.com
Printed in the USA
LVHW030311200521
687961LV00001B/9